Mary Balogh is a *New York Times* bestselling author. A former teacher, she grew up in Wales and now lives in Canada.

Visit her website at www.marybalogh.com

Seducing an Angel

A Huxtable Family Novel

Mary Balogh

piatkus

PIATKUS

First published in the US in 2009 by Bantam Dell,
A division of Random House, Inc., New York, USA
First published in Great Britain in 2010 as a paperback original by Piatkus
Published by arrangement with the Bantam Dell Publishing Group

A CIP catalogue record for this book
is available from the British Library.

ISBN 978-0-7499-4296-0

Typeset in ACaslon Regular by Palimpsest Book Production Limited,
Grangemouth, Stirlingshire
Printed and bound in Great Britain by CPI Mackays, Chatham ME5 8TD

Papers used by Piatkus Books are natural, renewable and recyclable
products sourced from well-managed forests and certified
in accordance with the rules of the Forest Stewardship Council.

 **Mixed Sources**
Product group from well-managed
forests and other controlled sources
www.fsc.org Cert no. SGS-COC-004081
© 1996 Forest Stewardship Council

Piatkus
An imprint of
Little, Brown Book Group
100 Victoria Embankment
London EC4Y 0DY

An Hachette UK Company
www.hachette.co.uk

www.piatkus.co.uk

1

'What I am going to do is find a man.'

The speaker was Cassandra Belmont, the widowed Lady Paget. She was standing at the sitting room window of the house she had rented on Portman Street in London. The house had come fully furnished, but the furnishings as well as the curtains and carpets had seen better days. They had probably seen better days even ten years ago. It was a shabby genteel place, well suited to Lady Paget's circumstances.

'To *marry*?' Alice Haytor, her lady's companion, asked, startled.

Cassandra watched with world-weary eyes and scornfully curved lips as a woman walked past in the street below, holding the hand of a little boy who clearly did not want either to have his hand held or to be proceeding along the street at such a trot. Everything in the lines of the woman's body spoke of irritation and impatience. Was she the child's mother or his nurse? Either way, it did not matter. The child's rebellion and misery were none of Cassandra's concern. She had enough concerns of her own.

'Absolutely not,' she said in answer to the question. 'Besides, I would have to find a fool.'

'A fool?'

Cassandra smiled, though it was not a happy expression, and she did not turn to direct it at Alice. The woman and child had passed out of sight. A gentleman was hurrying along the street in the opposite direction, frowning down at the ground in front of his feet. He was late for some appointment, at a guess, and doubtless thought his life depended upon getting where he was going on time. Perhaps he was right. Probably he was wrong.

'Only a fool would marry me,' she explained. 'No, it is definitely not for *marriage* that I need a man, Alice.'

'Oh, Cassie,' her companion said, clearly troubled, 'you surely cannot mean—' She did not complete the thought, or need to. There was only one thing Cassandra *could* mean.

'Oh, but I do, Alice,' Cassandra said, turning and regarding her with amused, hard, mocking eyes. Alice was gripping the arms of the chair on which she sat and leaning slightly forward as if she were about to stand up, though she did not do so. 'Are you shocked?'

'Your purpose when we decided to come to London,' Alice said, 'was to look for employment, Cassie. We were *both* going to look. And Mary too.'

'It was not a realistic plan, though, was it?' Cassandra said, laughing without amusement. 'Nobody wants to hire a housemaid-turned-cook who has a young daughter but is not and never has been married. And a letter of recommendation from me would do poor Mary no good at all, would it? And – ah, forgive me, Alice – not many people will want to employ a governess who is more than forty years old when there are plenty of young women available. I am sorry to put that brutal truth into words, but youth is the modern god. You were an excellent governess to me when I was a child, and you have been an excellent companion and friend since I grew up. But your age is against you now, you know. As for me, well, unless I somehow disguise my identity, which would not work when it came time to offer letters of recommendation, I am doomed in the employment market, and in any other, for that matter. No one is going to want to hire an axe murderer in any capacity at all, I suppose.'

'Cassie!' her former governess said, her hands flying up to cover her cheeks. 'You must *not* describe yourself in such a way. Not even in fun.'

Cassandra was unaware that they had been having fun. She laughed anyway.

'People *are* prone to exaggerate, are they not?' she said. 'Even to fabricate? It is what half the known world believes of me, Alice – because it is *fun* to believe such a prepos-terous thing. People will run screaming from me, I daresay, every time I step out of doors. It will have to be an *intrepid* man that I find.'

'Oh, Cassie,' Alice said, tears swimming in her eyes. 'I wish you would not—'

'I have tried making my fortune at the tables,' Cassandra said, checking off the point on one finger as though there were more to follow. 'I would have come away more desti-tute than I already was if I had not had a stroke of very modest luck with the final hand. I took my winnings and ran, having discovered that I do not have anything like the nerve to be a gambler, not to mention the skill. Besides, I was growing very hot indeed under my widow's veil, and several people were quite openly trying to guess who I was.'

She tapped a second finger, but there was nothing further to add. She had not tried anything else, simply because there was nothing else to try. Except one thing.

'If I cannot pay the rent next week,' she said, 'we will all be out in the street, Alice, and I would hate that.'

She laughed again.

'Perhaps,' Alice said, 'you ought to appeal to your brother again, Cassie. He surely—'

'I have already appealed to Wesley,' Cassandra said, her voice hard again. 'I asked for shelter for a short while until I could find a way to be independent. And what was his answer? He was very sorry. He would love to help me, but he was about to leave on an extended walking tour of Scotland with a group of his friends – who would be seriously inconvenienced if he let them down at the last moment. Where exactly in Scotland would I send this new appeal, Alice? And would I beg more abjectly this time? And for you and Mary and Belinda as well as for myself? Oh, yes, and for you too, Roger. Did you think I had forgotten you?'

A large, shaggy dog of indeterminate breed had got up from his place before the hearth and limped over to her to have his one ear scratched – the other was all but missing. He limped because he was also missing one leg from the knee joint down. He looked up at her with his one good eye and panted happily. His coat never looked anything but unkempt, even though it was clean and had a daily brushing. Cassandra ruffled it with both hands.

'I would not go to Wesley even if he were still in London,'

she said, after the dog had lain down at her feet and set his chin down between his paws with a huff of contentment. She turned back to the window and drummed her fingertips slowly on the sill. 'No, I am going to find a man. A *rich* man. Very rich. And he will support us all royally. It will not be charity, Alice. It will be employment, and I shall give excellent value for money.'

There was a hard edge of contempt to her voice, though it was unclear whether her scorn was directed at the unknown gentleman who would become her protector or at herself. She had been a wife for nine years, but she had never before been a mistress.

Now she would be.

'Oh,' Alice said, her voice filled with distress, 'has it really come to this? I will not allow it. There has to be another answer. I will *not* allow it. Not when one of your reasons is that you feel obliged to support me.'

Cassandra's eyes followed an ancient carriage as it lumbered its way along the street below the window, its coachman looking as aged as it.

'You will not allow it?' she said. 'But you cannot stop me, Alice. The days when I was *Cassandra* and you were *Miss Haytor* are long gone. I may have very little left. I have almost no money and absolutely no reputation. I have no friends beyond these doors and no relatives who will inconvenience themselves in order to help me. But I do have one thing, one asset that will assure me gainful employment and restore comfort and security to our lives. I am beautiful. And desirable.'

Under other circumstances the boast might have sounded unpardonably conceited. But it was made with hard mockery. For, of course, though it was perfectly true, it was nothing to be conceited about. Rather, it was something to be cursed. It had secured her a wealthy husband at the age of eighteen. It had brought her countless admirers during the nine years of her marriage. And it had brought her, within a ten-year period, a deeper misery than she had ever dreamed a lifetime could hold. It was time to use it for her own gain – to acquire rent for this shabby house and food for the table and clothes for their backs and a little extra to set aside for a rainy day.

No, not a *little* extra. A great deal extra. Never mind bare subsistence and rainy days, when they would be so dearly bought. She and her friends would live in luxury. They *would*. The man who was going to pay for her services would pay very dearly indeed – or watch someone else claim her instead.

It did not matter that she was twenty-eight years old. She was better than she had been when she was eighteen. She had put on weight – in all the right places. Her face, which had been pretty then, had acquired a more classic beauty since. Her hair, which was a rich copper red, had not darkened over the years or lost any of its luster. And she was less innocent. A great deal less. She knew what pleased men now. There was one gentleman out there somewhere in London right now, at this very minute, who was soon going to be willing to squander a fortune on possessing her and buying exclusive rights to her services. There was more than one gentleman, in fact, but only one whom she would choose. There was that one gentleman who was aching for the sensual delight of possessing her, though he did not even know it yet.

He was going to want her more than he had wanted anyone or anything else in his life.

She *hated* men.

'Cassie,' Alice said, and Cassandra turned her head to look inquiringly at her, 'we have no acquaintances here. How can you expect to meet any gentlemen?'

She sounded triumphant, as if she wanted the task to be hopeless – as no doubt she did.

Cassandra smiled at her.

'I am still *Lady Paget*, am I not?' she said. 'A baron's widow? And I still have all the fine clothes and accessories Nigel kept buying me, even if they *are* somewhat outdated. It is the Season, Alice. Everyone of any importance is here in town, and every day there are parties and balls and concerts and soirees and picnics and a whole host of other entertainments. It will not be at all difficult to discover what some of them are. And it will not be difficult to find a way of attending some of the grandest of them.'

'Without an invitation?' Alice asked, frowning.

'You have forgotten,' Cassandra said, 'just how much every hostess wants her entertainment remembered as a great squeeze. I do not expect to be turned away from any door I choose to enter. And I shall walk boldly through the front doors. Once will be enough – more than enough to serve my purpose. You and I will go walking in Hyde Park this afternoon, Alice – at the fashionable hour, of course. The weather is fine, and all the beau monde is bound to turn up there to see and be seen. I will wear my black dress and my black bonnet with the heavy veil. I daresay I am known more by reputation than by looks – it is a number of years since I was last here. But I would rather not risk being recognized just yet.'

Alice sighed and sat back in her chair. She was shaking her head.

'Let me write a calm, conciliatory letter to Lord Paget on your behalf,' she suggested. 'He had no right to banish you from Carmel House as he did, Cassie, when he finally decided to move there almost a year after his father's passing. The terms of your marriage contract were quite clear. You were to have the dower house as your own residence in the event of your husband's predeceasing you. And a sizable money settlement. *And* a generous widow's pension from the estate. None of which you ever got from him during that year, even though you wrote a number of times, asking when you might expect all the legalities to be settled. Perhaps he did not clearly understand.'

'It will do no good to appeal to him,' Cassandra said. 'Bruce made it quite clear that he considered my freedom a generous exchange for everything else. No charges were ever brought against me in his father's death because there was no proof that I had killed him. But a judge or a jury might well find me guilty regardless of the lack of conclusive evidence. I could hang, Alice, if it happened. Bruce agreed that no charges would be pressed provided I left Carmel House and never returned – and provided I left all my jewels behind and forfeited all financial claim upon the estate.'

Alice had nothing to say. She knew all this. She knew the risks involved in fighting. Cassandra had chosen not to fight. There had been too much violence in the past nine years – ten now. She had chosen simply to leave, with her friends and with her freedom.

'I will not starve, Allie,' she said. 'Neither will you or Mary or Belinda. I will provide for you all. Oh, and you too, Roger,' she added, tickling the dog's stomach with the toe of her slipper while his tail thumped lazily on the floor and his three and a half paws waved in the air.

Her smile was tinged with bitterness – and then with something more tender.

'Oh, Alice,' she said, hurrying across the room and sinking to her knees before her former governess's chair, 'don't cry. *Please* do not. I will not be able to bear it.'

'I never thought,' Alice said between sobs into her hand-kerchief, 'to see you becoming a *courtesan*, Cassie. And that is what you will be. A high-class pr— A high-class pros—' But she could not complete the word.

Cassandra patted one of her knees.

'It will be a thousand times better than marriage,' she said. 'Cannot you *see* that, Alice? I will have all the power this time. I can grant or withhold my favors at will. I can dismiss the man if I do not like him or if he displeases me in any way at all. I will be free to come and go as I choose and to do whatever I will except when I am . . . well, working. It will be a *million* times better than marriage.'

'All I ever wanted of life was to see you happy,' Alice said, sniffing and drying her eyes. 'It is what governesses and companions do, Cassie. Life has passed them by, but they learn to live vicariously through their charges. I wanted you to know what it is like to be loved. And to love.'

'I know what both are like, silly goose,' Cassandra said, sitting back on her heels. '*You* love me, Alice. Belinda loves me – so does Mary, I think. And Roger loves me.' The dog had padded over to her and was prodding one of her hands with his wet nose so that she would pet him again. 'And I love you all. I *do*.'

A few stray tears were still trickling down her former governess's cheeks.

'I know that, Cassie,' she said. 'But you know what I mean.

9

Don't deliberately misunderstand. I want to see you in love with a good man who will love you in return. And don't look at me like that. It is the expression you wear so often these days that it would be easy to mistake it for your real character showing through. I know it well enough, that curl of the lip and that hard amusement of the eye that is not amusement at all. There *are* good men. My papa was one of them, and he certainly was not the only one the dear good Lord created.'

'Well.' Cassandra patted her knee again. 'Perhaps I will quite inadvertently choose a good man to be my protector, and he will fall violently in love with me – no, not *violently*. He will fall *deeply* in love with me and I will fall deeply in love with him and we will marry and live happily ever after with our dozen children. You may fuss over them all and teach them to your heart's content. I will not refuse to employ you just because you are over forty and in your dotage. Will this make you happy, Alice?'

Alice was half laughing, half weeping.

'Maybe not the twelve-children part,' she said. 'Poor Cassie, you would be worn out.'

They both laughed as Cassandra got to her feet.

'Besides, Alice,' she said, 'there is no reason that all your life and happiness should be lived through me. *Vicariously* is a horrid word. Perhaps it is time you began to live on your own account. And love. Perhaps *you* will meet a gentleman and he will realize what a perfect gem he has found and will fall in love with you and you with him. Perhaps *you* will live happily ever after.'

'But not with a dozen children, I hope,' Alice said with a look of mock horror, and they both laughed again.

Ah, there was so little opportunity for laughter these days.

It seemed to Cassandra that she could probably count on the fingers of one hand the number of times she had felt sheer amusement during the past ten years.

'I had better go and dust off my black bonnet,' she said.

Stephen Huxtable, Earl of Merton, was riding in Hyde Park with Constantine Huxtable, his second cousin. It was the fashionable hour of the afternoon, and the main carriageway was packed with vehicles of all descriptions, most of them open so that the occupants could more readily take the air and look about at all the activity around them and converse with the occupants of other carriages and with pedestrians. There were crowds of the latter too on the footpath. And there were many riders on horseback. Stephen and Constantine were two of them as they wove their way skillfully among the carriages.

It was a lovely early summer day with just enough fluffy white clouds to offer the occasional welcome shade and prevent the sun from being too scorching.

Stephen did not mind the crowds. One did not come here in order to get anywhere in a hurry. One came to socialize, and he always enjoyed doing that. He was a gregarious, good-natured young man.

'Are you going to Meg's ball tomorrow night?' he asked Constantine.

Meg was his eldest sister, Margaret Pennethorne, Countess of Sheringford. She and Sherry had come to town this spring after missing the past two, despite the fact that they had had newborn Alexander to bring with them this year as well as two-year-old Sarah and seven-year-old Toby. They had decided at last to face down the old scandal dating from the time when Sherry had eloped

11

with a married lady and lived with her until her death. There were still those who thought Toby was his son and Mrs. Turner's – and both Sherry and Meg were content to let that sleeping dog lie.

Meg had backbone – Stephen had always admired that about her. She would never choose to cower indefinitely in the relative safety of the country rather than confront her demons. Sherry himself had never had much difficulty engaging demons in a staring contest and being the last to blink. And now, because all the fashionable world had been unable to resist attending the curiosity of their wedding three years ago, that same fashionable world was effectively obliged to attend their ball tomorrow evening.

Not that many would have missed it anyway, curiosity being a somewhat stronger motivating factor than disapproval. The *ton* would be curious to discover how the marriage was prospering, or *not* prospering, after three years.

'But of course. I would not miss it for worlds,' Constantine said, touching his whip to the brim of his hat as they passed a barouche containing four ladies.

Stephen did the same thing, and all four smiled and nodded in return.

'There is no *of course* about it,' he said. 'You did not attend Nessie's ball the week before last.'

Nessie – Vanessa Wallace, Duchess of Moreland – was the middle of Stephen's three sisters. The duke also happened to be Constantine's first cousin. Their mothers had been sisters and had passed on their dark Greek good looks to their sons, who looked more like brothers than cousins. Almost like twins, in fact.

Constantine had not attended Vanessa and Elliott's ball, even though he had been in town.

'I was not invited,' he said, looking across at Stephen with lazy, somewhat amused eyes. 'And I would not have gone if I had been.'

Stephen looked apologetic. He *had* just been on something of a fishing expedition, as Con seemed to realize. Stephen knew that Elliott and Constantine scarcely talked to each other – even though they had grown up only a few miles apart and had been close friends as boys and young men. And because Elliott did not talk to his cousin, neither did Vanessa. Stephen had always wondered about it, but he had never asked. Perhaps it was time he did. Family feuds were almost always foolish things and went on long after everyone ought to have kissed and made up.

'What *is* it—' he began.

But Cecil Avery had stopped his curricle beside them, and Lady Christobel Foley, his passenger, was risking life and limb by leaning slightly forward in her flimsy seat in order to smile brightly at them while she twirled a lacy confection of a parasol above her head.

'Mr. Huxtable, Lord Merton,' she said, her eyes passing over Con before coming fully to rest upon Stephen, 'is it not a *lovely* day?'

They spent a few minutes agreeing that indeed it was and soliciting her hand for a set apiece at tomorrow evening's ball, since her mama had only just decided that they would go there rather than dine with the Dexters as originally planned, but she had already told simply *everyone* that she was not going and consequently was positively *terrified* she would have no dancing partners except dear Cecil, of course, who had been her neighbor in the country *forever* and therefore had little choice, poor man, but to be gallant and dance with her so that she would not be an *utter* wallflower.

Lady Christobel rarely divided her verbal communications into sentences. One had to concentrate hard if one wished to follow everything she said. Usually it was not necessary to do so but merely to listen to a word here and a phrase there. But she was an eager, pretty little thing and Stephen liked her.

He had to be careful about showing his liking too openly, however. She was the eldest daughter of the very wealthy and influential Marquess and Marchioness of Blythesdale, and she was eighteen years old and had just this year made her come-out. She was very marriageable indeed and very eager to achieve marital success during her first Season, preferably before any of her peers. She was likely to succeed too. If ever one wished to find her at any large entertainment, one had merely to find the densest throng of gentlemen, and she was sure to be in their midst.

But she had her sights set upon Stephen, as did her mama. He was well aware of it. Indeed, he was well aware that he was one of the most eligible bachelors in England and that the females of the race had decided this year more than in any previous one that the time had come for him to settle down and take a bride and set up his nursery and otherwise face his responsibilities as a peer of the realm. He was twenty-five years old and was, apparently, expected to have crossed some invisible threshold at his last birthday from irresponsible, wild-oat-sowing youth to steady, dutiful manhood.

Lady Christobel was not the only young lady who was courting him, and her mother was not the only mother who was determinedly attempting to reel him in.

Stephen liked most ladies of his acquaintance. He liked talking with them and dancing with them and escorting them to the theater and taking them for drives or walks in the park. He did not avoid them, as many of his peers did, for fear of stepping all unawares into a matrimonial trap. But he was not ready to marry.

Not nearly.

He believed in love – in romantic love as well as every other kind. He doubted he would ever marry unless he could feel a deep affection for his prospective bride and could be assured that she felt the like for him. But his title and wealth stood firmly in the way of such a seemingly modest dream. So – though it seemed conceited to think so – did his looks. He was aware that women found him both handsome and attractive. How could any woman see past all those barriers to know and understand *him*? To *love* him?

But love *was* possible, even perhaps for a wealthy earl. His sisters – all three of them – had found it, though all three marriages had admittedly made shaky beginnings.

Perhaps somewhere, somehow, sometime, there would be love for him too.

In the meanwhile, he was enjoying life – and avoiding the matrimonial traps that were becoming all too numerous and familiar to him.

'I believe,' Constantine said as they rode onward, 'the lady would have been happy to tumble right out of that seat, Stephen, if she could have been quite sure you were close enough to catch her.'

Stephen chuckled.

'I was about to ask you,' he said, 'what it is between you and Elliott – and Nessie. Your quarrel has been going on for as long as I have known you. What caused it?'

He had known Con for eight years. It was Elliott, as executor of the recently deceased Earl of Merton's will, who had come to inform Stephen that the title, along with everything that went with it, was now his. Stephen had been living with his sisters in a small cottage in the village of Throckbridge in Shropshire at the time. Elliott, Viscount Lyngate then, though he was Duke of Moreland now, had been Stephen's official guardian for four years until he reached his majority. Elliott had spent time with them at Warren Hall, Stephen's principal seat in Hampshire. Con had been there too for a while – it was his home. He was the elder brother of the earl who had just died at the age of sixteen. He was the eldest son of the earl who had preceded his brother, though he could not succeed to the title himself because he had been born two days before his parents married and was therefore legally illegitimate.

It had been clear from the start that Elliott and Con did not like each other. More than that, it had been clear that there was a real enmity there. *Something* had happened between them.

'You would have to ask Moreland that,' Constantine said in answer to his question. 'I believe it had something to do with his being a pompous ass.'

Elliott was *not* pompous – or asinine. He did, however, poker up quite noticeably whenever he was forced to be in company with Constantine.

Stephen did not pursue the matter. Obviously Con was not going to tell him what had happened, and he had every right to guard his secrets.

Con was something of a puzzle, actually. Although he had always been amiable with both Stephen and his sisters, there was an edge of darkness to him, a certain brooding air despite his charm and ready smile. He had bought a home of his own somewhere in Gloucestershire after his brother's death, but none of them had ever been invited there – or anyone else of Stephen's acquaintance, for that matter. And no one knew how he could have afforded it. His father had doubtless made decent provision for him, but to such a degree that he could go off and buy himself a home and estate?

It was none of Stephen's business, of course.

But he did sometimes wonder *why* Constantine had always been friendly. Stephen and his sisters had been strangers when they suddenly invaded his home and claimed it as their own. Stephen had the title Earl of Merton, one that Con's brother had borne just a few months previously, and his father before that. It was a title that would have been Con's if he had been born three days later or if his parents had married three days sooner.

Ought he not to have been bitter? Even to the point of hatred? Should he not *still* be bitter?

Stephen often wondered how much went on inside Con's mind that was never expressed in either words or actions.

'It must be as hot as Hades under there,' Constantine said just after they had stopped to exchange pleasantries with a group of male acquaintances. He nodded in the direction of the footpath to their left.

There was a crowd of people walking there, but it was not difficult to see to whom Con referred.

There was a cluster of five ladies, all of them brightly and fashionably dressed in colors that complemented the summer. Just ahead of them were two other ladies, one of them decently clad in russet brown, a color more suited perhaps to autumn than summer, the other dressed in widow's weeds of the deepest mourning period. She was black from head to toe. Even the black veil was so heavy that it was impossible to see her face, though she was no more than twenty feet away.

'Poor lady,' Stephen said. 'She must have recently lost a husband.'

'At a pretty young age too, by the look of it,' Constantine said. 'I wonder if her face lives up to the promise of her figure.'

Stephen was most attracted to very young ladies, whose figures tended to be lithe and slender. When he did finally turn his thoughts to matrimony, he had always assumed he would look among the newest crop of young hopefuls to arrive on the marriage mart and try to find among such crass commercialism a beauty whom he could like as well as admire and whom he could grow to love. A lady who would be willing to look beyond his title and wealth to know him and love him for who he was.

The lady in mourning was nothing like his ideal. She did not appear to be in the first blush of youth. Her figure was a little too mature for that. It was certainly an excellent figure, even though her widow's weeds had not been designed to show it to full advantage.

He felt an unexpected rush of pure lust and was thoroughly ashamed of himself. Even if she had not been in deepest mourning he would have felt ashamed. He was not in the habit of gazing lustfully upon strangers, as so many young blades of his acquaintance were.

'I hope she does not boil in the heat,' he said. 'Ah, here come Kate and Monty.'

Katherine Finley, Baroness Montford, was Stephen's youngest sister. She had perfected the skill of riding only since her marriage five years ago, and was on horseback now. She was smiling at both of them. So was Monty.

'I came here to give my horse a good gallop,' Lord Montford said by way of greeting, 'but it does not seem possible, does it?'

'Oh, Jasper,' Katherine said, 'you did not! You came to show off the new riding hat you bought me this morning. Is it not dashing, Stephen? Do I not outshine every other lady in the park, Constantine?'

She was laughing.

'I would say that plume would be a deadly weapon,' Con said, 'if it did not curl around under your chin. It is very fetching instead. And you would outshine every other lady if you wore a bucket on your head.'

'Dash it all, Con,' Monty said. 'A bucket would have cost me a lot less than the hat. It is too late now, though.'

'It is very splendid indeed, Kate,' Stephen said, grinning.

'But I did not come here to show off the riding hat,' Monty protested. 'I came to show off the lady beneath it.'

'Well,' Katherine said, still laughing, 'that was clever of me. I have squeezed a compliment out of all three of you. Are you going to Meg's ball tomorrow, Constantine? If you are, I insist that you dance with me.'

Stephen forgot all about the curvaceous widow in black.

2

It took very little effort on Cassandra's part to learn of Lady Sheringford's ball. She simply looked about the fashionable area of Hyde Park until she saw a largish group of ladies – there were five of them in all – strolling along the footpath together and talking quite animatedly among themselves as they went. Cassandra led Alice toward them and then strolled along ahead of them and listened.

She learned a great deal she did not wish to know about what was most fashionable in bonnets this year and about who looked well in such hats and who looked so dreadful that it would really be a kindness to tell them if only one could summon up the courage. She learned about the endearing antics of their children – each one trying to outdo the others. The antics were endearing, Cassandra suspected, only because their victims were nurses or governesses rather than the mothers themselves. It sounded to her as if every single one of the children described was a spoiled brat of the first order.

But finally the tedious conversation yielded a harvest. Three of the ladies were planning to attend Lady Sheringford's ball tomorrow evening at the home of the Marquess of Claverbrook on Grosvenor Square. A surprising venue, that, one of them observed, since the elderly marquess had been a recluse for years and years before he had finally left his home again to attend the wedding of his grandson three years ago. He had not been seen since. Yet now there was to be a ball at his house.

Rumor had it, though, apparently, Cassandra learned without being at all interested, that he spent a great deal of his time in the country with his grandson and his great-grandchildren. And that his granddaughter-in-law, the countess, had learned how to coax him out of the sullens.

Lady Sheringford's ball at the Claverbrook mansion on Grosvenor Square, Cassandra recited mentally, committing the relevant details of the conversation to memory as she tried to ignore the myriad irrelevant ones.

Three of the ladies were going, though none of them *wanted* to, of course. It was really quite incomprehensible that a lady as respectable as Lady Sheringford had been willing to marry the earl when he had behaved so shockingly just a few years before that he ought never again to have been received by decent folk.

Gracious heaven, he had even had a *child* with that dreadful woman, who had left her lawful husband in order to run away with him – on the very day he had been pledged to marry her husband's sister. It really had been a scandal to end all scandals.

The three were going to the ball anyway, though, because everyone else was going. And really one was interested to discover how the marriage was progressing. It would be surprising indeed if it were not under severe strain after three whole years. Though no doubt the earl and his lady would put on a show of amity for the duration of the ball.

Two of the ladies were *not* going. One had a previous engagement, she was relieved to report. The other would not step over the doorstep of a house that contained the *Earl of Sheringford* even if everyone else was willing to forgive and forget. Even if someone were to offer her a *fortune* she would not go. It was most provoking that her husband positively refused to attend any balls when he knew that she loved to dance.

Better and better, Cassandra thought. The Countess of Sheringford lived under a cloud cast by the earl's reputation as a rake and a rogue. It was unlikely they would turn anyone away from their doors, even without an invitation. Though clearly the earl's reputation was going to bring more guests to the ball than it would drive away, curiosity being the besetting sin of the *ton* – and probably of humanity in general.

The Sheringford ball would be it, then. It was tomorrow night. Time was of the essence. She had enough money left for next week's rent and for food for another couple of weeks. Beyond that there was a frighteningly empty void in which money would need to go out but none would be coming in.

And she had dependents as well as herself to house and clothe and feed. Dependents who could not, for various reasons, provide for themselves.

Alice walked silently and disapprovingly at her side. Cassandra had shushed her as soon as they had started strolling ahead of the five ladies. It was a loud, accusing silence that she held, though. Alice did not like this at all, and that was perfectly understandable. Cassandra would not like it if *she* had to stand helplessly by while either Alice or Mary plotted to prostitute herself so that she could eat.

Unfortunately, there was no alternative. Or if there was, Cassandra could not see it, even though she had lain awake for several nights looking for one.

She glanced around as they walked, feeling a little as though she were at a masquerade, her identity effectively hidden behind a mask and domino. Her black veil was her mask, her heavy widow's weeds her domino. She could see out – dimly – but no one could see in.

It was surely as hot as hell beneath the black clothes and the veil. She waited hopefully for clouds to cover the sun, but they were few and far between.

The whole of the beau monde must be squashed into this really quite small segment of Hyde Park. She had forgotten what the fashionable hour was like. Not that she had ever been a part of it. She had married young, and she had never had a come-out or an accompanying Season. Her eyes moved over all the ladies in the crowd and noted their bright, fashionable, costly attire. But it was not upon them that she focused her attention. They meant nothing to her.

It was at the gentlemen that she looked closely and consideringly. There were many of them, all ages and sizes and conditions. A few of them looked back at her despite her disguise, which must be singularly unappealing. She saw none she particularly fancied. Not that she had to *fancy* the man who was going to put money into her empty coffers.

Her attention caught and held upon two particular

gentlemen, not just because they were both young and handsome, though they *were*, but because there was such a startling contrast between them that she felt she was looking at the devil and an angel.

The devil was the older of the two. She would put him in his middle thirties if she had to guess. He was very dark of both hair and complexion, with a handsome, rather harsh face and eyes that looked black. It seemed to her that he might be a dangerous man, and she shivered slightly despite the terrible heat in which she was enclosed.

The angel was younger – probably younger than she. He was golden blond and classically handsome, with regular features and an open, good-humored face. His mouth and eyes – she was sure they were blue – looked as though they smiled frequently.

Her eyes lingered on him. He looked tall and graceful in the saddle, well-muscled legs showing to advantage in tight buff riding breeches and black leather boots as they hugged the sides of his mount. He looked slender but well formed in his dark green close-fitting riding coat. It molded itself to his frame, and she knew that it must have taken all of his valet's strength to get him into it.

Angel and devil had both noticed her and were looking – the devil boldly and appreciatively, the angel with what looked like sympathy for her widowhood.

But then they were distracted by the sight of someone they knew – two people actually, a very fashionable lady on horseback and her companion, a man who was mockingly handsome.

The angel smiled.

And perhaps sealed his doom.

Something about him suggested an innocence to match

his angelic looks. He was no doubt a very wealthy man indeed – Cassandra had just realized that the women behind her were talking about him.

'Oh,' one of them said with a sigh, 'there is the Earl of Merton with Mr. Huxtable. Have you ever seen a more gorgeous man than he? And all that wealth and property to go with the looks. As well as the title. And golden hair and blue eyes and good teeth and a charming smile. It does not seem fair that one man should have so much. If I were just ten years younger – and single again.'

They all laughed.

'I think I would prefer Mr. Huxtable,' one of the others said. 'In fact, I know I would. All that brooding darkness, and those Greek looks. I would not mind if he set his boots beneath my bed one of these days when Rufus was gone.'

There were shrieks of shocked glee from her companions, and Cassandra noticed when she glanced at Alice that her lips had thinned almost to the point of disappearing altogether and that there were two spots of color high in her cheeks.

Angel and innocence and wealth and aristocracy, Cassandra thought. Could there be a more potent mix?

'I am either about to melt in a puddle on the path,' she said, 'or explode into a million pieces. Neither of which is something I would enjoy. Shall we leave the crowd and walk home, Alice?'

'Some people,' her former governess said as they set off across an almost deserted lawn, 'ought to have their mouths smacked and then washed out with soap. It is no wonder their children are so badly behaved, Cassie. And then they expect their *governesses* to exert discipline without scolding or slapping the little darlings.'

'It must be very provoking to you,' Cassandra said.

They walked for a while in silence.

'You are going to go to that ball, are you not?' Alice said as they stepped out onto the street. 'Lady Sheringford's.'

'Yes,' Cassandra said. 'I shall be able to get in, don't worry.'

'It is not about your *not* getting in that I worry,' Alice said tartly.

Cassandra lapsed into silence again. There was no point in discussing the matter further. Alice must have come to the same conclusion, for she said no more either.

The Earl of Merton.

Mr. Huxtable.

Angel and devil.

Would they be at the ball tomorrow evening?

But even if they were not, plenty of other gentlemen would be.

Cassandra was forced to spend some of her precious diminishing hoard of money on a hackney coach to take her to Grosvenor Square the following evening. It really would not do to walk the distance at night, dressed in evening finery, especially when she had no male servant to accompany her. Even so, she did not ride the whole way. She had the driver set her down in the street outside the square and then walked in.

She had timed her arrival to be on the late side. Despite that fact, there was a line of grand carriages drawn up outside one of the mansions there. The windows of the house blazed with light. A red carpet had been rolled out down the steps and across the pavement so that guests would not have to get their dancing shoes dusty.

Cassandra crossed the square and stepped onto the carpet, up the steps, and inside the house in company with a loudly chattering group. She handed her cloak to a footman, who bowed respectfully when she murmured her name and made no move to toss her out into the night. She moved to the staircase and climbed it slowly along with a number of other people. Presumably there was still a receiving line at the ballroom doors and that was what was causing the delay. She had hoped to avoid that by coming late.

She had forgotten – if she had ever known – that in order to be late at a *ton* entertainment one really had to be very late indeed.

Everyone about her was greeting everyone else. Everyone was in a festive mood. No one spoke to the lone woman in their midst. No one gasped in sudden outrage, either, or pointed an accusing finger or demanded that the impostor be removed. As far as she knew, no one even looked at her, but then she looked directly at no one and therefore could not be sure.

Perhaps no one would remember her after all. She had come to London two or three times with Nigel, and they had attended a few entertainments together. But it was altogether probable no one would recognize her now.

That hope soon became quite irrelevant. She gave her name to the smartly uniformed manservant outside the ballroom doors with cool, languid voice and, though he consulted a list in his hand and clearly did not find her name there, he hesitated only a moment. She raised her eyebrows and leveled her haughtiest look on him when he glanced up at her, and he gave her name to the majordomo inside the doors, and *he* announced it in a loud, clear voice.

No one could have missed hearing it, she thought, even if they had been humming with fingers pressed into both ears.

'Lady Paget,' he announced.

And with those two words went any hope of anonymity.

Cassandra proceeded to shake the hands of the dark-haired lady she presumed to be the Countess of Sheringford and of the handsome man beside her, who must be the notorious earl. But this was no time to study the two of them with any sort of curiosity. She curtsied to the elderly gentleman who was seated beside them. She assumed he was the reclusive Marquess of Claverbrook.

'Lady Paget,' the countess said, smiling. 'We are so happy you could come.'

'Enjoy the dancing, ma'am,' the earl said, smiling too.

'Lady Paget,' the marquess said gruffly, inclining his head to her.

And she was in.

As easily as that.

Except that her name had preceded her inside.

Her heart thumped in her bosom, and she opened her fan and plied it languidly before her face as she moved farther into the ballroom and began a slow promenade about its perimeter. It was not an easy thing to do. The room was crowded. Yesterday's five ladies had been proved quite correct in their prediction that large numbers would come, even if only out of the spiteful hope that the marriage whose nuptials they had all attended three years ago was visibly crumbling.

Cassandra had felt an instinctive liking for the earl and countess. Perhaps it was because she could identify with their notoriety and sympathize with the pain it must have caused them – and probably still did.

Being alone was not a comfortable feeling. Every other lady appeared to have an escort or a companion or chaperone. Every gentleman seemed to be part of a group.

But it was not just her lone state that was causing her discomfort. It was the atmosphere in the ballroom. As a chill feeling of dread crawled up her spine, she knew that her name had indeed been heard by more people than just the Earl and Countess of Sheringford and the Marquess of Claverbrook.

And those who had *not* heard were now hearing it as fast as whispers could circle the ballroom. As fast as wildfire could spread in a gale, in other words.

She stopped walking, unfurled her fan, and plied it slowly in front of her face as she looked about her, her chin high, her lips curved into a slight smile.

No one was looking directly at her. And yet everyone was seeing her. It was a curious contradiction in terms, but it was perfectly true. No one had stepped out of her path as she walked, and no one stepped back from her now that she was standing still, but she felt isolated in a pool of emptiness, as though she were wearing an invisible aura that was two feet thick.

Except that she also felt naked.

But all this was no more than she had expected. She had decided not to use a false name, or even her maiden name. And she had come with an uncovered face tonight. There was no black veil to hide behind. It was inevitable that someone would recognize her.

She did not believe she would be tossed out even so.

Indeed, all this recognition might well work to her advantage. If the *ton* had come here tonight in large numbers to see a man who had once eloped with a married lady, how much more might they be fascinated by the sight of an axe murderer? Rumor and gossip loved that description of her, she understood, far more than it would have loved anything more approximating to the truth.

She looked deliberately about her, secure in the knowledge that no one was going to meet her eyes and catch her staring. She did not recognize anyone. She concentrated upon the gentlemen, realizing as she did so the difficulty of the task she had set herself. There were young and old and everything in between, and all were immaculately dressed. But there was no way of knowing which among them were married and which single, which were wealthy and which poor, which had strong moral scruples and which were debauched – and which were somewhere between those two extremes. She had no time to find out what she needed to know before making her choice and her move.

And then her eyes alit upon a familiar face – three of them, actually. There was yesterday's devil, looking just as satanic tonight in black evening clothes. The lady who had been on horseback yesterday was standing beside him, her hand on his sleeve, and she was talking and laughing. The gentleman Cassandra had thought of as mockingly handsome looked on, an amused smile playing about his lips.

The devil looked across the room from beneath his brows, and his eyes locked on Cassandra's. She fanned her cheeks slowly and gazed back. He raised one eyebrow and then lowered his head to say something to the lady. She laughed again. They were not, Cassandra guessed, talking about her.

The devil was Mr. Huxtable. Cassandra continued to look at him for a few moments. He had given her an opening, which she might use later if no better prospect presented itself.

'I saw you looking at me earlier, sir,' she might say, 'and I have been puzzling ever since over where we have met before. Do please enlighten me.'

They would both know that they had *not* met before, and he would know that she knew. But the door would have been opened and she would make sure that he stepped through it with her.

Except that she could not help feeling that he was a dangerous man. And when all was said and done, she was not an experienced courtesan. She was only a desperate woman who knew that men found her attractive. For years she had considered that fact to be a liability. Tonight she would turn it into an asset.

Her eyes moved onward. And then, directly opposite her across the ballroom, she saw her angel.

He looked even more handsome than he had yesterday in the park. He was dressed in a black evening coat with silver knee breeches, embroidered waistcoat, and crisp white shirt and neckcloth and stockings. He was tall and perfectly built – slender and yet well muscled in all the right places. And his golden blond hair, though short and well styled, was wavy and looked as if it might be unruly in its natural state. It looked like a halo of light about his head.

He was standing with a lady and a gentleman who resembled Mr. Huxtable to such a close degree that Cassandra looked quickly back at the latter to make sure he had not flown around one quarter of the ballroom ahead of her eyes. But this man was not dressed in unrelieved black, and his face was more good-humored. The two men must be brothers, though. Perhaps even twins.

Cassandra looked back at the angel – the Earl of Merton.

He was the only gentleman in the room about whom she knew anything at all. If the five ladies in the park were to be believed – and they had been right about this ball being a grand squeeze – he was a very wealthy gentleman indeed. And single.

And there was that air of innocence about him. Was that a good thing, though, or a bad?

And then, as had happened with Mr. Huxtable, his eyes met hers across the room and held her gaze.

He did not smile. Neither did he raise one mocking eyebrow. He merely gazed steadily at her as she slowly fanned her cheeks and then half smiled at him and raised her own eyebrows. He inclined his head slightly in return – then someone stepped in front of him and he was blocked from her view.

Cassandra's heart was fluttering. The game had begun. She had made her choice.

The dancing was about to begin at last – though she guessed she had been in the ballroom for no longer than five or ten minutes. The Earl and Countess of Sheringford had stepped onto the floor, and others followed them. The Earl of Merton, she could see, was in the line of gentlemen, smiling across at his partner, a very young and very pretty young lady. The orchestra, at a given signal, played a chord, and the ladies curtsied while the gentlemen bowed. The music of a lively country dance began.

Cassandra resumed her leisurely perusal of all the gentlemen in the room while the pool of emptiness about her appeared to expand.

Stephen had dined at Claverbrook House with his sisters and brothers-in-law, and with the Marquess of Claverbrook and Sir Graham and Lady Carling, Sherry's mother and her husband.

Meg had been quite nervous about the ball. She had been convinced no one would come, despite the fact that everyone else had agreed with Monty's prediction that the walls of the ballroom would have to be pressed outward before the evening was over in order to accommodate everyone who would wish to stand inside it.

And despite the fact that almost everyone who had been sent an invitation had replied in the affirmative.

The ball had been Meg's idea in the first place. There was no point in their coming back to town this year, she had said, if she and Duncan were going to creep in and hope that no one noticed. They might as well be quite brazen about it and throw a grand ball while the Season was in full swing. Her grandfather-in-law, who had been a total recluse for years before Meg's marriage to Sherry and not much better since then – apart from his rather frequent and lengthy visits to the country – had surprised them all by offering Claverbrook House for the event before either Elliott or Stephen could speak up to offer their own London homes.

And now Meg was a bag of nerves. At least, she was until the guests began to arrive – and continued to arrive and continued and continued until the early comers must have been wondering if the dancing would *ever* begin.

Of course, there was the major distraction that took all their minds off the lengthy wait. There was a gate-crasher. A woman, who had, rather shockingly, come alone. She *was* a lady – she was Lady Paget, in fact. She was also notorious, if that was a strong enough word. She had killed her husband just a year or so ago. At least, that was the story when it reached Stephen's ear.

With an axe.

'Which I very much doubt,' Vanessa, the Duchess of Moreland, said to both Stephen and Elliott as she stood between them, waiting for Meg and Sherry to leave the receiving line and begin the opening set. 'How could she take an axe, after all, without the gardeners stopping her and wanting to know where she was going with it so that they could do the job for her? She could hardly have told them she was taking it to chop Lord Paget to bits, could she, and would they be kind enough to do the job for her? Besides, unless she is a very strong woman, she would not be able to lift it high enough to do damage to any part of him higher than his ankles.'

'You have a point,' Elliott said, sounding amused.

'And if she really killed him,' Vanessa continued, 'and if there was proof that she did – that is, if someone *saw* her swing the axe – would she not have been arrested?'

'On the spot,' Elliott said. 'And she would probably have been swinging in a different way soon afterward. She certainly would not be gracing Claverbrook's ballroom right now looking for dancing partners.'

She looked up at him suspiciously.

'You are laughing at me,' she said.

'Not at all, my love.' He took her hand and raised it to his lips, winking at Stephen as he did so.

'But I do agree with you, Nessie,' Stephen said. 'I think we may discount the axe part of the story. Perhaps the rest of it too. One can only hope that her coming here uninvited is not going to ruin Meg's ball.'

'It will be talked about for weeks,' Elliott said. 'What hostess could ask more of her entertainment? I would wager everyone has already forgotten about what they all

34

think poor Sherry was guilty of. His perceived crimes pale in comparison with a female axe murderer. Indeed, I do believe we ought to thank the lady in person.'

Vanessa eyed him suspiciously, and Stephen looked across the room again to where Lady Paget was standing, a small empty space all about her as if those in close proximity expected her to draw an axe from beneath her gown and commence swinging with it.

He had glanced at her only once before, when the story had first reached his ears and she had been pointed out to him. He did not want the poor woman to feel that everyone was staring at her.

Why had she been foolish enough to come? And to come *alone*. And without an invitation. Of course, she would probably sit at home for the rest of her life if she waited for one of those.

She was a tall, voluptuously formed woman. And the gown she wore did nothing to hide her curves. It was of a bold emerald green and fell in soft folds from beneath her bosom. On a lesser figure, those folds might have hung loosely. On hers, they followed the curve of waist and hips and long, lusciously shaped legs. Its sleeves were short, its neckline leaving little of her bosom to the imagination. Apart from her elbow-length white gloves and a fan and dancing slippers, there were no other adornments on her person. She wore no jewelry at all and no plumes in her hair. It was a stunningly clever idea. For her hair was her crowning glory – and it surpassed all cliché. It was a glowing red and was piled in loose curls on her head, with wavy tendrils to draw attention to the creamy white, swanlike perfection of her neck. Her face was pure beauty despite its bored, haughty, slightly contemptuous expression – a mask if ever Stephen had seen one. He doubted she was feeing as poised as she looked. It was impossible to see the color of her eyes, but there seemed to be a slight, alluring slant to them.

All this he had seen the first time he glanced at her. This time he saw immediately that she was looking directly back at him. He resisted his first instinct, which was to look hastily away. It was probably what everyone else was doing as soon as she glanced their way. He looked steadily back at her. And *she* did not look away from *him,* as he had expected she would do. Her hand slowly plied her fan. Her eyebrows arched arrogantly upward, and her lips curved into an expression that was half smile, half not.

He inclined his head to her just as Carling and his lady joined them to inform them that the dancing was about to begin.

Stephen went to claim the hand of Lady Christobel Foley, who had just happened to stroll past him with her mama when they entered the ballroom earlier and had stopped to bid him a good evening. Before they strolled away again, it had been arranged that the set he had reserved with her yesterday in the park would be the opening set, and that he would dance another with her later in the evening.

He glanced toward Lady Paget again when he and his partner were standing in the lines waiting for the orchestra to begin playing. She was standing in the same place, though she was no longer looking at him.

And he felt a sudden jolt of recognition. Not that he knew beyond all doubt that he was correct. Nevertheless, he was as sure as he could be that Lady Paget was that widow all in black he and Con had seen yesterday when they were out riding.

Yes, it was surely she, though she looked quite startlingly different.

Yesterday she had worn a heavy disguise.

Tonight she stood exposed to the shock and censure of the *ton*.

Tonight she wore only the disguise of her cool indifference, even contempt for everyone's opinion.

3

The second set would have to be the one, Cassandra decided. She could not stand here all night without looking ridiculous – and without making this whole painful exercise pointless.

But when the opening set ended, the Earl and Countess of Sheringford came to speak with her. She saw them coming and raised her fan again. She half smiled and half raised her eyebrows. If they were going to ask her to leave, she was not going to give anyone the satisfaction of seeing her embarrassed.

'Lady Paget,' the earl said, 'despite all our efforts to keep the ballroom cool by having all the windows opened, it is overwarm in here after all. May I have the pleasure of fetching you a drink? Wine, perhaps, or sherry or ratafia? Or lemonade?'

'A glass of wine would be very welcome,' she said. 'Thank you.'

'Maggie?' he asked his wife.

'The same, please, Duncan,' she said, and watched him walk away.

'Your ball is very well attended,' Cassandra said. 'You must be gratified.'

'It is a great relief,' the countess admitted. 'I hosted a number of events for my brother before I married and felt no more than a twinge of anxiety each time. It never occurred to me in those days that some massive disaster might occur to spoil the event. This is the first entertainment I have hosted in London since my marriage three years ago, and everything feels different, most notably the level of my confidence. Perhaps we ought to have returned sooner, but we have both been so happy in the country with our children.'

She was the massive disaster that was threatening to ruin this particular evening, Cassandra understood. She pursed her lips and said nothing.

'I have been terrified,' Lady Sheringford continued, 'that no one would come to the ball except my brother and sisters and mother-in-law, though it was a comfort to know that they would all at least bring their spouses – except my brother, of course. He is not married yet.'

'You need not have feared,' Cassandra said. 'The notorious always draw attention to themselves. People are incurably inquisitive.'

The countess raised her eyebrows and would have spoken, but the earl had returned with their drinks.

'Perhaps, Lady Paget,' he said as Cassandra sipped her wine, 'you would do me the honor of dancing the next set with me.'

She smiled at him and at his lady, then back at him.

'Are you sure,' she asked, 'you would rather dance with

me, Lord Sheringford, than beg me to leave Claverbrook House?'

'Perfectly sure, ma'am,' he said, smiling and exchanging a glance with his wife.

'We are sufficiently acquainted with . . . notoriety, Lady Paget,' the countess said, 'to be happy to ignore it in others. Especially when the other person is our guest.'

'Your *uninvited* guest,' Cassandra said, drinking more wine.

'Yes, even then,' the countess agreed. She laughed unexpectedly. 'I met my husband at a ball to which he had not been invited. I have always been thankful that we were both there anyway. I might not have met him otherwise. Please enjoy yourself.'

Someone had touched the countess on the shoulder and she turned to see who it was. It was the devil, Cassandra could see – Mr. Huxtable.

'Oh, Constantine,' the countess said, smiling warmly, '*here* you are. I was afraid you had forgotten that you were to dance this next set with me, and I would be left a forlorn wallflower on the sidelines.'

'Forgotten?' he said, slapping a hand to his heart. 'When I have lived all day in eager anticipation of just this moment, Margaret?'

'Oh, foolish!' She laughed. 'Have you met Lady Paget? Constantine Huxtable, Lady Paget, my second cousin.'

He fixed her with a steady look from very dark eyes, and bowed.

'Lady Paget,' he said. 'My pleasure.'

Cassandra inclined her head and fanned her face.

'Mr. Huxtable.'

She read speculation in the polite stare of his eyes.

But he would definitely not be the one, she decided. For those eyes also looked somewhat hard and dangerous, as if he were warning her without the medium of words that if she had come with the intention of casting some cloud over this ball of his second cousin's, she might find herself answering to him. He would be too much of a challenge. She might have been intrigued by him if this were merely a game she was playing. But it most certainly was not.

'Your ball is a grand success, Margaret,' he said. 'As I predicted it would be.'

He continued to look at Cassandra as he spoke.

Cassandra drank the rest of her wine.

'I believe the dancing is about to resume,' Lord Sheringford said, taking her empty glass from her hand and setting it down on a table close to the wall. 'Shall we, ma'am?' He offered his arm.

'Thank you.' She set her hand on his sleeve and let her fan fall on its string from her other wrist.

She wondered if the earl and countess were merely trying to control the potential damage her presence at their ball was likely to cause or if they were simply being kind. She rather suspected the latter but was thankful to them either way.

Cassandra looked at the earl curiously as they took their places in the set. How could he have abandoned his poor bride on her wedding day? But her lips twitched with something like amusement when she thought that perhaps *he* was looking just as curiously at *her*, wondering how she could possibly have killed her own husband. With an axe, no less.

The orchestra began to play and they danced while Cassandra looked about. They were the focus of much

41

attention, she and the earl. The two notorious ones. But why watch them? What did people expect to happen? What did they *hope* would happen? That she and the Earl of Sheringford would suddenly clasp hands and make a dash for the ballroom doors and freedom and a reckless elopement?

The mental image caused her to smile openly, though with a contemptuous curl of the lips. And she met the glance of the Earl of Merton at the same moment. He was dancing with the lady with whom he had been talking before the first set began.

He smiled back at her.

It was definitely at her he smiled. He looked at no one else before returning his attention to his partner and bending his head to listen to something she was saying.

Stephen danced the second set with Vanessa. He would have danced it with Lady Paget if he had not already reserved it with his sister. He was very glad to see that Meg and Sherry had gone to speak with her at the end of the opening set and that Sherry had led her out for the second.

Stephen felt sorry for her.

That was doubtless a foolish waste of sympathy. Where there was smoke, there was usually *some* fire, even if just a tiny spark. He really did not believe the axe murder story – though it was more description than story, as it came without supporting details. He was not sure he believed the murder story at all, in fact. She would be in custody if it were true. And since a year or more had passed since her husband's death, she would probably be long dead herself by now. Hanged.

Since she was very much alive and here tonight at Meg's ball, either she was not her husband's murderer at all or there was sufficient lack of evidence that no arrest had yet been made.

She looked bold enough to fit the part of murderess, however. And that startlingly glorious hair of hers suggested a passionate nature and a hot temper. Despite what Nessie had said about a woman's ability to heft an axe, Lady Paget looked strong enough to him.

All of which were thoughts and speculations that were unworthy of him. He knew nothing about either her or the circumstances of her husband's death. And none of it was any of his business.

He did feel sorry for her, nevertheless, knowing that almost everyone else in the ballroom was having similar thoughts to his own but that many would not even try to rein them in or allow her the benefit of any doubt.

He would dance the next set with her, he decided, before remembering that it was to be a waltz and that he liked to choose one of the very young ladies for the waltz – one who was more his ideal of feminine beauty than Lady Paget was. He especially wanted to do so this evening, as the third set was also the supper dance and he would be able to sit beside his partner during the meal. He had several candidates in mind, though all were much in demand as partners and all might already be engaged for the waltz. A few, of course, could not dance it anyway because they had not yet been granted the nod of approval by one of the patronesses of Almack's Club. The waltz was still considered rather too risqué a dance for the very young and innocent.

He would dance the set after supper with Lady Paget,

then. Maybe some other gentleman would have the courtesy to dance with her or at least converse with her during the waltz. Perhaps she would not even still be here after supper. Perhaps she would slip quietly away now that she had discovered that her reputation had preceded her to London. It would be something of a relief if she *did* leave. He did not particularly want to dance with her.

Miss Susanna Blaylock had already promised the waltz to Freddie Davidson, Stephen discovered when he approached her after the second set. She looked quite openly disappointed and told him that she was free for the *next* set. Stephen reserved it with her. It was, of course, the dance after supper.

And then, before he could continue with his quest for a waltzing partner, a few of his male acquaintances drew him into their group to ask his opinion upon whether one of them ought to purchase a set of matched bays or matched grays to pull his new curricle. Which would look more sporting? Which would be more manageable? More fashionable? Faster? More suited to the colors of the curricle? Which would the *ladies* prefer? Stephen joined in the discussion and the bellows of amused laughter it occasioned.

If he did not draw away soon, he thought after a couple of minutes, there would be no lady left to dance with him – and he hated not to waltz.

'Why not one gray and one bay?' he suggested with a grin. 'Now, *that* would draw you all the attention you could possibly desire, Curtiss. But if you fellows will excuse—'

He was turning as he spoke and did not finish his sentence because he almost collided with someone who was passing close behind him. Sheer instinct caused him to grasp her by the upper arms so that she would not be bowled entirely over.

'I do beg your pardon,' he said, and found himself almost toe-to-toe and eye-to-eye with Lady Paget. 'I ought to have been looking where I was going.'

She was in no hurry to step back. Her fan was in her hand – it looked ivory with a fine filigree design across its surface – and she wafted it slowly before her face.

Oh, Lord, her eyes almost matched her gown. He had never seen such green eyes, and they did indeed slant upward ever so slightly at the outer corners. Viewed against the background of her red hair, they were simply stunning. Her eyelashes were thick and darker than her hair – as were her eyebrows. She was wearing some unidentifiable perfume, which was floral but neither overstrong nor oversweet.

'You are pardoned,' she said in such a low-pitched velvet voice that Stephen felt a shiver along his spine.

He had noticed earlier that the ballroom was warm despite the fact that all the windows had been thrown wide. He had not noticed until now that the room was also airless.

Her lips curled into a faint suggestion of a smile, and her eyes remained on his.

He expected her to continue on her way to wherever she had been going. She did not do so. Perhaps because – oh. Perhaps because he was still clutching her arms. He released them with another apology.

'I saw you looking at me earlier,' she said. 'I was looking at you, of course, or I would not have noticed. Have we met somewhere before?'

She must know they had not. Unless—

'I saw you in Hyde Park yesterday afternoon,' he said. 'Perhaps I look familiar because you saw me there too but do not quite recall doing so. You were dressed in widow's weeds.'

'How clever of you,' she said. 'I thought they made me quite unidentifiable.'

There was amusement in her eyes. He was not sure if it was occasioned by real humor or by a certain inexplicable sort of scorn.

'I do recall,' she said. 'I did as soon as I saw you again tonight. How could I have forgotten you? I thought you looked like an angel then, and I think it again tonight.'

'Oh, I say.' Stephen laughed with a mingling of embarrassment and amusement. He seemed particularly inarticulate this evening. 'Looks can deceive, I am afraid, ma'am.'

'Yes,' she said, 'they can. Perhaps on further acquaintance I will change my mind about you – or would if there *were* any further acquaintance.'

He wished her bosom were not quite so exposed or that she were not standing quite so close. But he would feel foolish taking a step back now when he ought to have thought to do it as soon as he let go of her arms. He felt it imperative to keep his eyes on her face.

Her lips were full, her mouth on the wide side. It was probably one of the most kissable mouths his eyes had ever dwelled upon. No, it was definitely *the* most kissable. It was one more feature to add to a beauty that was already perfect.

'I beg your pardon,' he said, stepping back at last so that he could make her a slight bow. 'I am Merton, at your service, ma'am.'

'I knew that,' she said. 'When one sees an angel, one

must waste no time in discovering his identity. I do not need to tell you mine.'

'You are Lady Paget,' he said. 'I am pleased to make your acquaintance, ma'am.'

'Are you?' Her eyelids had drooped half over her eyes, and she was regarding him from beneath them. Her eyes were still amused.

Over her shoulder he could see couples taking their places on the dance floor. The musicians were tuning their instruments.

'Lady Paget,' he said, 'would you care to waltz?'

'I would indeed care to,' she said, 'if I had a partner.'

And she smiled fully and with such dazzling force that Stephen almost took another step back.

'Shall I try that again?' he said. 'Lady Paget, would you care to waltz *with me*?'

'I would indeed, Lord Merton,' she said. 'Why do you think I collided with you?'

Good Lord.

Well, *good Lord*!

He held out his arm for her hand.

It was a long-fingered hand encased in a white glove. It might never have wielded an axe, Stephen thought. It might never have wielded any weapon with deadly force. But it was very dangerous nonetheless.

She was very dangerous.

The trouble was, he really did not know what his mind meant by telling him that.

He was going to waltz with the notorious Lady Paget – and lead her in to supper afterward.

He would swear his wrist was tingling where her hand rested on his sleeve.

He felt stupidly young and gauche and naive − none of which he was to any marked degree.

The Earl of Merton was taller than Cassandra had thought − half a head or more taller than she. He was broad shouldered, and his chest and arms were well muscled. There was no need of any padding with his figure. His waist and hips were slender, his legs long and shapely. His eyes were intensely blue and seemed to smile even when his face was in repose. His mouth was wide and good-humored. She had always thought that dark-haired men had a strong advantage when it came to male attractiveness. But this man was golden blond and physically perfect.

He smelled of maleness and something subtle and musky.

He was surely younger than she. He was also − and not at all surprisingly − very popular with the ladies. She had seen how those who were not dancing had followed him wistfully with their eyes during the last two sets − and even a few of those who *were* dancing. She had seen a few glance his way with growing agitation as the time to take partners for the waltz grew close. Several, she suspected, had waited until the last possible moment before accepting other, less desirable partners.

There was an air of openness about him, almost of innocence.

Cassandra set one hand on his shoulder and the other in his as his right arm came about her waist and the music began.

She was not responsible for guarding his innocence. She had been quite open with him. She had told him she remembered seeing him yesterday. She had told him she had deliberately discovered his identity and just as deliberately collided with him a short while ago so that he would dance with her. That was warning enough. If he was fool enough after the waltz was over to continue to consort with the notorious Lady Paget – axe murderer, husband killer – then on his own head be the consequences.

She closed her eyes briefly as he spun her into the first twirl of the dance. She gave in to a moment of wistfulness. How lovely it would be simply to relax for half an hour and enjoy herself. It seemed to her that her life had been devoid of enjoyment for a long, long time.

But relaxation and enjoyment were luxuries she could not afford.

She looked into Lord Merton's eyes. They were smiling back at her.

'You waltz well,' he said.

Did she? She had danced it once in London a number of years ago and a few times at country assemblies. She did not consider herself accomplished in the steps.

'Of course I do,' she said, 'when I have a partner who waltzes even better.'

'The youngest of my sisters would be delighted to take the credit,' he said. 'She taught me years ago, when I was a boy with two left feet who thought dancing was for girls and wished to be out climbing trees and swimming in streams instead.'

'Your sister was wise,' she said. 'She realized that boys grow up into men who understand that waltzing is a necessary prelude to courtship.'

He raised his eyebrows.

'Or,' she added, 'to seduction.'

His blue eyes met hers, but he said nothing for a moment.

49

'I am not trying to seduce you, Lady Paget,' he said. 'I do beg your pardon if—'

'I do believe,' she said, interrupting him, 'you are the perfect gentleman, Lord Merton. I know you are not trying to seduce me. It is the other way around. *I* am trying to seduce *you*. And determined to succeed, I may add.'

They danced in silence. It was a lovely, lilting tune that the orchestra played. They twirled about the perimeter of the ballroom with all the other dancers. The gowns of the other ladies were a kaleidoscope of color, the candles in the wall sconces a swirl of light. Behind the sound of the music there were voices raised in conversation and laughter.

She could feel his heat, flowing into her hands from his shoulder and palm, radiating into her bosom and stomach and thighs from his body.

'Why?' he asked quietly after some time had elapsed.

She tipped back her head and smiled fully at him.

'Because you are beautiful, Lord Merton,' she said, 'and because I have no interest in enticing you into a courtship, as most of the very young ladies here tonight do. I have been married once, and that was quite enough for this lifetime.'

He had not responded to her smile. He gazed at her with intense eyes while they danced. And then his eyes softened and smiled again, and his lips curved attractively upward at the corners.

'I believe, Lady Paget,' he said, 'you enjoy being outrageous.'

She lifted her shoulders and held the shrug, knowing that by doing so she was revealing even more of her bosom. He really had been the perfect gentleman so far. His eyes had not strayed below the level of her chin. But he glanced down now and a slight flush reddened his cheeks.

'Are *you* ready for marriage?' she asked him. 'Are you actively seeking a bride? Are you looking forward to settling down and setting up your nursery?'

The music had stopped, and they stood facing each other, waiting for another waltz tune to begin the second dance of the set.

'I am not, ma'am,' he said gravely. 'The answer to all your questions is no. Not yet. I am sorry, but—'

'It is as I thought, then,' she said. 'How old are you, Lord Merton?'

The music began again, a slightly faster tune this time. He looked suddenly amused again.

'I am twenty-five,' he told her.

'I am twenty-eight,' she said. 'And for the first time in my life I am free. There is a marvelous freedom in being a widow, Lord Merton. At last I owe no allegiance to any man, whether father or husband. At last I can do what I want with my life, unrestrained by the rules of the very male-dominated society in which we live.'

Perhaps her words would be truer if she were not so utterly destitute. And if three other persons, through no fault of their own, were not so totally dependent upon her. Her boast sounded good anyway. Freedom and independence always sounded good.

He was smiling again.

'I am no threat to you, you see, Lord Merton,' she said. 'I would not marry you if you were to approach me on bended knee every day for a year and send me a daily bouquet of two dozen red roses.'

'But you *would* seduce me,' he said.

'Only if it were necessary,' she said, smiling back at him. 'If you were unwilling or hesitant, that is. You are so very beautiful, you see, and if I am to exercise my freedom from all restraints, I would rather share my bed with someone who is perfect than with someone who is not.'

'Then you are doomed, ma'am,' he said, his eyes dancing with merriment. 'No man is perfect.'

'And he would be insufferably dull if he were,' she said. 'But there *are* men who are perfectly handsome and perfectly attractive. At least, I suppose their number is plural. I have seen only one such for myself. And perhaps there really are no more than you. Perhaps you are unique.'

He laughed out loud, and for the first time Cassandra was aware that they were the focus of much attention, just as she and the Earl of Sheringford had been during the last set.

She had thought of the Earl of Merton and Mr. Huxtable yesterday as angel and devil. Probably the *ton* gathered here this evening were seeing him and her in the same way.

'You *are* outrageous, Lady Paget,' he said. 'I believe you must be enjoying yourself enormously. I also believe we ought to concentrate upon the steps of the dance for a while now.'

'Ah,' she said, lowering her voice, 'I perceive that you are afraid. You are afraid that I am serious. Or that I am not. Or perhaps you are simply afraid that I will cleave your skull with an axe one night while it rests asleep upon the pillow beside mine.'

'None of the three, Lady Paget,' he said. 'But I *am* afraid that I will lose my step and crush your toes and utterly disgrace myself if we continue such a conversation. My sister taught me to count my steps as I dance, but I find it impossible to count while at the same time conducting a risqué discussion with a beautiful temptress.'

'Ah,' she said. 'Count away, then, Lord Merton.'

He really did not know if she was serious or if she joked, she thought as they danced in silence – as she had intended.

But he was attracted – intrigued and attracted. *As she had intended.*

Now all she needed to do was persuade him to reserve the final set of the evening with her, and *then* he would discover which it was – serious or not.

But good fortune was on her side and offered something even better than having to wait. They danced for a long while without talking to each other. She looked at him as the music drew to a close and drew breath to speak, but he spoke first.

'This was the supper dance, Lady Paget,' he said, 'which gives me the privilege of taking you into the dining room and seating you beside me – if you will grant it to me, that is. Will you?'

'But of course,' she said, looking at him through her eyelashes. 'How else am I to complete my plan to seduce you?'

He smiled and then chuckled softly.

4

Stephen was feeling dazzled and uncomfortable, amused and bemused.

What the devil had he run into tonight – quite literally?

Had she really noticed him yesterday from beneath that dark veil of hers while he and Con had been noticing *her*, and then singled him out this evening and quite deliberately collided with him so that he would have little choice but to waltz with her?

I know you are not trying to seduce me. It is the other way around. I am trying to seduce you. And determined to succeed, I may add.

Because you are beautiful, Lord Merton.

I would rather share my bed with someone who is perfect than with someone who is not.

Her words echoed in his mind, though he could hardly believe he had not dreamed them.

He offered his arm when the music ended, and she linked her hand through it rather than setting it along his sleeve in a more formal manner. The ballroom was emptying fast. Everyone was heading toward the dining room and the salons to either side of it. Everyone was ready to eat and rest from the exertions of dancing.

And everyone was looking at the two of them. Or at least, since most people were too polite to stare openly, everyone was *aware* of them, focused upon them. It was not something he was imagining, Stephen knew. And it was understandable. Lady Paget's arrival at Meg's ball, uninvited, had caused a considerable stir.

He was not embarrassed by the fact that he was with her. Indeed, he was glad of it, since his escort would save her from any open insult or the cut direct, at which so many members of the beau monde excelled. He did not know any of the facts of Lady Paget's case, but Meg and Sherry had not turned her out. Indeed, they had gone out of their way to make her feel welcome. It behooved all their guests, then, to show her courtesy at the very least.

He spotted a small unoccupied table with two chairs squashed into one side of the salon to the left of the dining room and led Lady Paget toward it.

'Shall we sit here?' he suggested.

Perhaps it would be more comfortable for her here than at one of the long tables in the dining room, where she would be very much on public view.

'Tête-à-tête?' she said. 'How clever of you, Lord Merton.'

He seated her at the table and went into the dining room to fill a plate for each of them.

Had she really been offering herself to him as a *mistress*? Or did her intentions extend only to tonight? Or had he misunderstood altogether? Had she simply been joking with him? But no, he had not misunderstood. She had openly talked about seducing him. Lord, she had asked him if he was afraid she would kill him with an axe *while his head was upon the pillow beside hers.*

Someone caught hold of his arm and squeezed it tightly. Meg was beaming up at him.

'Stephen,' she said, 'I am *so* proud of you. And of myself for having raised my only brother to be a gentleman. Thank you.'

'For . . . ?' He raised his eyebrows.

'For dancing with Lady Paget,' she said. 'I *know* what it is like to be a pariah, Stephen, though no one has ever quite ostracized *me*. We all owe one another good manners, especially when we are making judgments upon one another based solely upon gossip and rumor. Will you sit with us for supper?'

'Lady Paget is in the next room, waiting for me to bring her a plate of food,' he said.

'Oh, good,' she said. 'Nessie and Elliott have gone to look for her. They intended inviting her to join them. I am proud of *all* of you. Though I suppose you are all doing it as much for my sake as for Lady Paget's.'

'Where is the Marquess of Claverbrook?' he asked.

'Oh, he has gone to bed,' she said. 'The foolish man insisted upon being in the receiving line and sitting and watching the first two sets, even though he was desperately tired and hates social occasions even when he is not. And then he started grumbling about the fact that we were going to allow the waltz. No one ever allowed anything so improper in *his* day. Et cetera, et cetera.' Her eyes twinkled. 'That was it. I banished him to his bed. Duncan swears that I am the only person who can manage his grandfather, but so could everyone else if they were not so *afraid* of him. He is a veritable lamb beneath all the ferocity.'

Stephen joined the line at the food table and filled two plates with a variety of savories and sweets in the hope that Lady Paget would like at least some of them.

When he returned to the salon, she was fanning her face, a haughty, contemptuous smile playing about her lips. All the tables around her were occupied. No one was talking to her or even about her – not audibly, at least, but it was obvious to Stephen that everyone was very aware of her. He guessed that some of the people there had chosen the salon deliberately *because* she was there, so that they could report on her behavior in drawing rooms across London for the next week or so and complain of the outrage of having had to share a supper room with her.

Such was human nature.

He set one plate in front of her and seated himself opposite with the other. Someone had already poured two cups of tea.

'I hope,' he said, 'I have brought you *something* that you like.'

She glanced down at her plate.

'You have,' she said in that low, seductive voice of hers. 'You have brought yourself.'

He wondered if she always talked so outrageously.

She was probably – no, she was *undoubtedly* the most sexually attractive woman he had ever set eyes upon. Her heat had seemed to envelop him all the time they waltzed, though she had danced quite properly and had not once tried to close the distance between their bodies.

'Were you afraid I would not return?' he asked her. 'Have you been feeling very conspicuous and self-conscious?'

'Because everyone here is expecting me to draw an axe from beneath my skirts and twirl it about my head while letting out a bloodcurdling shriek?' she asked him, her eyebrows raised. 'No, I take no notice of such nonsense.'

She was very forthright. But perhaps she had discovered that the best defense was often offense.

'Gossip usually *is* nonsense,' he said.

That scornful smile still hovered about her lips as she selected a lobster patty from her plate and lifted it to her mouth.

'Usually,' she agreed, raising her eyes to his as she bit into the patty. She chewed the mouthful and swallowed. 'But sometimes not, Lord Merton. You must wonder.'

He could only follow her lead.

'If you killed your husband?' he said. 'It is none of my business, ma'am.'

She laughed – and several heads turned openly their way.

'Then you are a fool,' she said. 'If you are going to allow me to seduce you, you ought perhaps to have a healthy fear of what I might do to you when your guard is down and you are naked in my bed.'

She was becoming more outrageous. He hoped he was not flushing.

'But perhaps,' he said, 'I am not *going* to allow it, ma'am. Indeed, I do not believe I would ever *allow* myself to be seduced. If I were to take a mistress or a casual lover, it would be something I *chose* to do because I wished it and because *she* wished it. It would not happen because I had fallen a mindless prey to a seductress.'

He really did not have any appetite, he realized as he looked down at his own plate. Why had he piled so much food onto it?

And why was he having this conversation? Had he really just spoken those words aloud to a lady – *if I were to take a mistress or a casual lover . . . ?*

Had he completely lost all sense of propriety? Outspoken and notorious as she was, she was still a lady. And he was still a gentleman.

'And I do not fear you,' he added.

Perhaps he ought to. Perhaps what he had just said to her was so much hot air. He had never kept a long-term mistress, though he was by no means a virgin. He had often slightly envied Con, who always seemed to find a respectable widow with whom to conduct a discreet affair when he was in town. A few years ago it had been Mrs. Hunter, last year Mrs. Johnson. Stephen was not sure if there was anyone this year.

If he himself was now considering taking a mistress or a lover – and, Lord help him, he *was* considering it – was it because he had suddenly chosen to do so quite deliberately and rationally in the middle of a ball or because he had been *seduced* into doing so by a woman who was quite blatant about her intentions?

She was not at all his type, he reminded himself. Not the type of woman he would ever consider for a *bride*, anyway. But he was not considering her for a bride.

Unbidden, an image of what she would look like naked on a bed flashed into his mind, and he felt an alarming tightening in the area of his groin.

Enough of this!

'Lady Paget,' he said firmly, 'it is high time we changed the subject. Tell me something about yourself. Something about your girlhood, if you will. Where did you grow up?'

She selected a small cake from her plate and lifted her head to smile at him.

'Mostly here, in London,' she said, 'or at one of the spas. My father frequented the gaming tables and went wherever the gambling crowds went and the stakes were highest. We lived in rented rooms and hotels. But lest you think this a pathetic story, Lord Merton, and one designed to draw your pity, may I add that he was as bountiful with his affections toward my brother and me as he was in wagering at the tables. And he had the devil's own luck, to quote him. By that he meant that he always won marginally more than he lost. I cannot even remember my mother, but I had a governess from an early age, and she was as dear to me as any mother could be. We saw a great deal of the world together, Miss Haytor and I – both in reality and through books. Your own upbringing would have been far more privileged than mine, but it cannot have been happier or more entertaining.'

For the first time he sensed that she was lying, though it was impossible to know about which details of her story. She just sounded too defensive to be telling the truth. Such a life, if the bare facts of what she had said were the truth, must surely have left a child with anxieties and insecurities. And every child, he believed, needed a fixed home.

'More privileged?' he said. 'Perhaps. I grew up at first in a vicarage in a Shropshire village – my father was the vicar – and then in a smaller cottage in the same village after his death. I lived with my sisters. Meg, now the Countess of Sheringford, was the eldest and, like your Miss Haytor, she was a splendid substitute mother. Nessie, now the Duchess of Moreland, is my middle sister, and Kate, now Baroness Montford, is next above me in age. I was the youngest. I had a happy boyhood until I inherited my title at the age of seventeen. It was a considerable shock since none of us had even known that I was next in line for it. I do not regret that I did not know, though. It can be character-building to grow up expecting to have to work for one's living and the support of one's sisters. At least, I hope it built my character. I understand privilege and all its advantages and disadvantages better perhaps than I would had I grown up with expectations.'

'Lady Sheringford is your *sister*?' she said, her eyebrows raised.

'Yes,' he said.

'And she married the notorious Earl of Sheringford,' she said, 'who ran off with another man's wife on his own wedding day not so many years ago and had a child with her.'

It always bothered Stephen that he could not tell the truth of what had happened both before and after Sherry took Mrs. Turner away from London the night before he was to marry Turner's sister. But he had promised Sherry that he never would.

'Toby,' he said. 'He is a cherished member of our family. Meg loves him as dearly as she loves her own two children. So does Sherry – the Earl of Sheringford. He is their son. My nephew.'

'I have touched upon a raw nerve,' she said, setting an elbow on the table and cupping her chin and one cheek in her hand. 'Why did your sister marry him?'

'I suppose,' he said, 'because he asked. And because she wished to say yes.'

She pursed her lips, and her eyes smiled their slightly scornful smile.

'You are annoyed,' she said. 'Am I being impertinent and intrusive, Lord Merton?'

'Not at all,' he said. 'I am the one who began the personal questions. Have you just recently arrived in town?'

'Yes,' she said.

'You are staying with relatives?' he asked her. 'You mentioned a brother.'

'I am not the sort of person relatives would wish to claim,' she said. 'I live alone.'

His eyes met hers.

'So very alone,' she said. But her lips were smiling too now, as though she mocked herself, and one gloved finger of the hand that had been cupping her face a moment ago was now tracing the low neckline of her gown, as if absently. The top joint of the finger was beneath the emerald green fabric. Her elbow still rested on the table.

It was very deliberate, he realized as he felt the heat of the room more acutely.

'You came alone in your carriage this evening, then?' he asked. 'Or did you bring a m—'

'I do not own a carriage,' she said. 'I came alone in a hackney carriage, Lord Merton, but I had the coachman set me down outside the square. It would have been lowering to arrive at the red carpet in a hired carriage, especially since I was uninvited. And yes, thank you, I will.'

'Will . . . ?' He looked inquiringly at her.

'Accept your offer to escort me home in your own carriage,' she said, and her eyes were laughing now. 'You *were* about to offer, were you not? You must not embarrass me now by telling me you were not.'

'I would be happy to escort you home, ma'am,' he said. 'Meg will lend one of her maids to accompany us.'

She laughed softly, a low, seductive sound.

'How very inconvenient that would be,' she said. 'How would I be able to seduce you, Lord Merton, with a maid looking on, or take you inside with me when I arrive home with her trailing along behind?'

He was being drawn deeper and deeper into this scheme, he realized. She really did mean to take him as a lover.

It was perhaps understandable.

She had arrived alone in London recently to the discovery that her reputation had preceded her. She was a pariah. Even her brother – if he was himself in London – had abandoned her. If she was to see any company, attend any entertainments, she must do so alone and uninvited as she had tonight. She was indeed very alone.

And doubtless lonely.

She was an extraordinarily beautiful woman. She was a widow and only twenty-eight years old. Under normal circumstances she might now be looking forward to a brighter future, her mourning period at an end. But Lady Paget stood accused in public opinion of having murdered her husband. It seemed clear that she did not stand accused by the law – she was free. But public opinion was a powerful force.

Yes, she must be dreadfully lonely.

And she had decided to try to alleviate that aloneness and that loneliness by taking a lover.

It was perfectly understandable.

But she had chosen him.

'You are not going to be tiresome, are you,' she asked him, 'and insist upon being the perfect gentleman? You are not going to hand me out of your carriage outside my door

and escort me to the doorsill and kiss the back of my hand as you bid me good night?'

He looked into her eyes and realized that sexual attraction and pity were a lethal mix.

'No,' he said, 'I am not going to do that, Lady Paget.'

She removed her elbow from the table and looked down at her plate. But nothing took her fancy there. She looked back at him. There was a pulse beating quite noticeably at the side of her neck.

'I really have no interest in staying at this ball any longer, Lord Merton,' she said. 'I have danced and I have eaten and I have met you. Take me home now.'

He felt that tightening of the groin again and fought the onset of lust.

'I am afraid I cannot leave yet,' he said. 'I have solicited the hands of two young ladies for the next two sets.'

'And you must honor such solicitation?' she said, her eyebrows arched upward.

'I must,' he said. 'I will.'

'You *are* a gentleman,' she said. 'How very provoking.'

The salon was emptying fast, Stephen realized. From the ballroom, he could hear the sounds of the orchestra tuning their instruments. He stood and offered Lady Paget his hand.

'Allow me to escort you back to the ballroom and introduce you to—' he began.

But Elliott was making his way toward them, and it was obvious to Stephen why he was coming. The family was rallying round – though whether for Meg's sake or his own was not clear.

' – the Duke of Moreland,' he said, completing his sentence. 'My brother-in-law. Lady Paget, Elliott.'

'It is a pleasure, ma'am,' Elliott said, bowing and looking as if it were anything but.

'Your grace.' Lady Paget inclined her head and grasped her fan as she stood. She looked instantly aloof and haughty.

'May I have the honor of dancing the next set with you, Lady Paget?' Elliott asked.

'You may,' she said, and set her hand on his proffered sleeve.

She did not look back at Stephen.

There was a grayish film on the surface of the untouched tea in their cups, he saw. Only two items had gone from her plate, none from his. Just a few years ago it would have seemed an unpardonable waste.

He had better go and claim his next partner before the dancing started again, he decided. It really would not do to be late.

Was he really going to sleep with Lady Paget tonight?

And perhaps begin a longer-term liaison with her?

Ought he not to know more about her first? More about the death of her husband and the facts behind the very nasty rumors that had preceded her to London and made an outcast of her?

Had he been seduced after all?

He feared he had.

Was it too late to change his mind?

He feared it was.

Did he *want* to?

He feared he did not.

He strode off in the direction of the ballroom.

The Duke of Moreland was the man who had been standing with the Earl of Merton when Cassandra had arrived at the ball. He was the man who looked very like yesterday's devil – Mr. Huxtable.

But the duke's eyes were blue and he looked somewhat less devilish than Mr. Huxtable and considerably more austere. He looked as if he might be a formidable adversary if one did something to cross his will.

She had done nothing. It was *he* who had asked *her* to dance. But he was, of course, a brother-in-law to Lady Sheringford and was doing what he could to contain the potential disaster of her appearance at his sister-in-law's ball. Perhaps he had also thought to rescue the Earl of Merton from her clutches.

Cassandra set her slightly scornful smile firmly in place.

The set was a lively one and offered very little opportunity for conversation. What little there was they spent in an exchange of meaningless pleasantries about the beauty of the floral decorations and the excellence of the orchestra and the superiority of the Marquess of Claverbrook's cook.

'May I return you to your . . . companion, ma'am?' the duke asked her when the set was at an end, though he surely knew that she had none.

'I came alone,' she said, 'but you may safely leave me here, your grace.'

They were close to a set of open French windows. Perhaps she would slip outside and stroll awhile. She could see that there was a wide balcony out there and not too many people. She suddenly longed to escape.

'Then allow me,' he said, taking her by the elbow, 'to introduce you to a few people.'

Before she could excuse herself, a brightly smiling older lady with a sober-looking gentleman approached them unbidden, and the Duke of Moreland introduced them to Cassandra as Sir Graham and Lady Carling.

'Lady Paget,' Lady Carling said after they had exchanged bows and nods, 'I am positively green with envy, if you will excuse the pun, over your gown. Why can I *never* find any fabric half so gorgeous whenever I look? Not that I would look good in that particular shade of green. I do believe I would fade into invisibility behind it. But even so . . . Oh, dear, Graham's eyes are glazing over, and Moreland is wondering when he can decently escape.'

She laughed and linked an arm through Cassandra's.

'Come, Lady Paget,' she said. 'You and I will stroll together and discuss dress and bonnet fashions to our hearts' content.'

And, true to her word, she led Cassandra off on a slow promenade of the perimeter of the ballroom floor as couples gathered on it for the next set.

'I am Lord Sheringford's mama,' Lady Carling explained, 'and I love him to distraction – though if you ever quote me on that, Lady Paget, I shall stoutly deny it. He has led me a merry dance over the years, but he will not have the satisfaction of knowing he has made me suffer, the wretch. However, he has, despite himself, I believe, made an extremely good match with Margaret. She is a treasure beyond compare. I dote upon her and upon my two grandsons and one granddaughter even if the first son *was* born out of wedlock, a fact that was not in any way his fault, was it?'

'Lady Carling,' Cassandra said quietly, 'I did not come here tonight to cause trouble.'

'Well, of course you did not,' that lady said, smiling warmly at her. 'But you *have* caused something of a sensation, have you not? And you had the nerve to wear that bright dress into the bargain. I suppose you had no choice but to bring that glorious red hair too, but of course the gown *does* draw even more attention to it than would otherwise be the case. I applaud your courage.'

Cassandra looked for irony in the words or in Lady Carling's manner but was not sure she could find any.

'I scolded Duncan a few years ago,' Lady Carling continued, 'when he attended a ball uninvited after returning to London with all the baggage of a horrifying scandal weighing him down. It was all *very* reminiscent of what you have done tonight. And do you know what was the very first thing he did after arriving at that ball, Lady Paget?'

Cassandra looked back at her, her eyebrows raised, though she thought she knew the answer.

'He collided with Margaret in the ballroom doorway,' Lady Carling said, 'and he asked her to dance with him and then marry him − all in one sentence, if he is to be believed. I *do* believe him because Margaret tells the same story and she is not prone to exaggeration. Yet they had never set eyes upon each other before that moment. Sometimes being daring and defying the *ton* can be a worthwhile venture, Lady Paget. I can only hope that you will be as fortunate as Duncan has been. For of course I do not believe there is any truth to that axe business. You would not be free or even alive, I suppose, if there were. Unless the problem is simply lack of proof, of course. But I do not believe it, and I am *not* going to ask. You must come to my at-home tomorrow afternoon. My other guests will be astonished and outraged − and will talk of nothing else for the next month. I will be famous. Everyone will come to all my other at-homes for the rest of the Season lest they miss something equally sensational. Do say you will come. Say you will have the *courage* to come.'

There was perhaps goodness left in the world after all, Cassandra thought as she smiled her half-scornful smile and looked about the ballroom. There were people who would treat her with courtesy even if their main motive *was* to avoid further embarrassment at the ball. And there were people who would reach out the hand of friendship even if they *were* perhaps partly motivated by selfish concerns.

It was far more than she had expected.

If she were not so desperately poor . . .

'I will think about it,' she said.

'I am sure you will,' Lady Carling said, and told Cassandra where her house might be found on Curzon Street. 'I have been delighted to take this break from dancing, Lady Paget. I never like to admit my age, but when I dance more than two consecutive sets or when I spend more than an hour playing with my grandchildren – the two who are not still nicely settled in a cradle – then I *feel* my age, alas.'

The Earl of Merton was dancing with a very young and pretty lady, who was blushing and gazing up at him with worshipful, sparkling eyes. He was smiling at her and talking to her and giving her the whole of his attention.

He was going to sleep with *her* tonight, Cassandra thought, and afterward she was going to do business with him. She believed she had done well. She knew she had attracted him physically. She had also very subtly engaged his pity. He thought her alone and lonely. It did not matter that it was at least partly true. *She would have it no other way.*

But she would draw him into her web, whether he really wished to be there or not. She needed him.

No, not *him*.

She needed his money.

Alice needed it. So did Mary and Belinda. And even dear Roger.

She had to remind herself of them. Only so could she bear the burden of self-loathing that suddenly descended like a real physical weight across her shoulders.

He was an amiable, courteous gentleman.

He was also a *man*. And men had needs. She would service those needs for the Earl of Merton. She would not be stealing his money. She would give good value in return.

She need not feel guilty.

'I have enjoyed the break from dancing too,' she told Lady Carling.

5

'Lady Paget,' the Duchess of Moreland said when the ball was over and crowds of people milled about, looking for spouses and offspring and shawls and fans, bidding friends and acquaintances good night, heading for the staircase and the hall below so that they would be there when it was the turn for their particular carriage to draw up in front of the steps. The duchess had just introduced herself. 'Did you come in your carriage?'

'I did not,' Cassandra said, 'but Lord Merton has been kind enough to offer me a ride home in his.'

'Ah, good.' The duchess smiled. 'Elliott and I would have been delighted to take you to your door, but you will be safe in Stephen's hands.'

Stephen. His name was Stephen. It somehow suited him.

The duchess linked an arm through hers.

'Let us go and find him,' she said. 'This end-of-evening crush is always the worst part of balls, but I am delighted there *is* a crush tonight. Meg was terrified that no one would come.'

Cassandra saw the Earl of Merton striding toward them before they had taken more than a few steps.

'Nessie,' he said, smiling at them both, 'you have found Lady Paget, have you?'

'I do not believe she was lost, Stephen,' she said. 'But she is waiting for you to take her home.'

It seemed to Cassandra that it took an age for them to leave the ballroom, descend the stairs, and make their way across the hall toward the front doors. But she soon realized why they were in no hurry. The duchess and Lord Merton were the Countess of Sheringford's sister and brother, and no doubt their carriages would be at the very back of the line.

Eventually there was no one left but the duke and duchess, Lord and Lady Montford, to whom the duchess introduced Cassandra, the Earl of Merton, Sir Graham and Lady Carling, and the Earl and Countess of Sheringford, who had just finished bidding their guests good night.

And Cassandra.

The irony of now being so very conspicuous when she had come uninvited to the ball did not escape her. Neither did the discomfort of being the only nonfamily guest still present. *Especially under the circumstances.*

Both Lady Carling and Baron Montford had offered to take her home in their carriages. She had assured both of them that Lord Merton had been kind enough to offer first.

'Well, Meg,' Lord Montford said, 'it is a good thing no one came to your ball. I dread to think how pushed and pulled and crushed we would all be feeling now if anyone *had.*'

The countess laughed.

'It did go rather well,' she said. And then, with a sudden look of anxiety, 'It *did,* did it not?'

'It was the grandest squeeze of the Season so far, Margaret,' Lady Carling assured her. 'Every other hostess for what remains of the spring will be desperately trying to match it and failing miserably. I overheard Mrs. Bessmer tell Lady Spearing that she must discover who your cook is and lure her away with the offer of a higher salary.'

The countess protested with a mock shriek.

'You have nothing to fear, Margaret,' the duke said. 'Mrs. Bessmer's main claim to fame is that she is a notorious pinch-penny. Her idea of more pay is doubtless to offer your cook one-fifth of what you are paying her.'

'I could challenge Ferdie Bessmer to pistols at dawn if you wish, Maggie,' the Earl of Sheringford offered.

The countess shook her head, smiling.

'Actually,' she said, 'it would be one-fifth of what *Grandpapa* is paying her, and if I were Mrs. Bessmer, I would not wish to annoy him.'

She looked apologetically at Cassandra.

'Lady Paget,' she said, 'we are keeping you from your bed. Do forgive us. Stephen is going to take you home, I understand. Please allow me to send for a maid to accompany you.'

'That will be quite unnecessary,' Cassandra said. 'I trust Lord Merton to be the perfect gentleman.'

The countess smiled again.

'I am delighted that you came this evening,' she said. 'Will I see you at my mother-in-law's at-home tomorrow? I do hope so. I hear she has invited you.'

'I will try,' Cassandra said.

And perhaps she would. She had come here tonight to find a wealthy protector, not to force her way back into society. She had assumed that that was impossible, that she would always be an outcast. But perhaps she need not be after all. If the Earl of Sheringford could do it, then perhaps so could she.

It was a long, long time since she had had friends – except for Alice, of course. And Mary.

And then, at last, Lord Merton's carriage drew up to the steps outside and he led her out and handed her inside before climbing in to sit beside her. He turned after a footman had folded up the steps and shut the door, to wave a hand to his family.

'The perfect gentleman,' he said quietly without turning his head back into the carriage as it pulled out of the square. 'It is what I have always striven to be. Allow me to be a gentleman tonight, Lady Paget. Allow me to see you safely home and then continue on my way to my own house.'

Her stomach lurched with alarm. Had she wasted this whole ghastly evening? Had it all been for nothing? Was she going to have to start all over again tomorrow? She hated him suddenly, this *perfect gentleman*.

'Alas,' she said, speaking low and injecting humor into her voice, 'I am being rejected. Spurned. I am unwanted, unattractive, ugly. I shall go home and cry hot tears into my cold, unfeeling pillow.'

She stretched out one hand as she spoke and set it on his leg, her fingers spread. It was warm through the silk of his breeches. She could feel the solidity of his thigh muscles.

He turned to her, and even in the darkness she could see that he was smiling.

'You know very well,' he said, 'that not a single one of those things has even a grain of truth in it.'

'Except, alas,' she said, 'for the hot tears. And the unfeeling pillow.'

She slid her hand farther to the inside of his thigh, and his smile faded. His eyes held hers.

'You are probably,' he said, 'the most beautiful woman I have ever seen.'

'Beauty can be a cold, undesirable thing, Lord Merton,' she said.

'And you are without any doubt,' he said, 'the most attractive.'

'Attractive.' She half smiled at him. 'In what way, pray?'

'*Sexually* attractive,' he said, 'if you will forgive me for such explicit speaking.'

'When you are about to bed me, Lord Merton,' she said, 'you may be as explicit as you wish. *Are* you about to bed me?'

'Yes.' He slid his fingers beneath her hand, lifted it away from his thigh, and carried it to his lips. 'But when we are in your bedchamber, the door closed behind us. Not in my carriage.'

She was content, though her next move was to have been to lean forward and kiss him.

He set their clasped hands on the seat between them as the carriage rocked through the darkened streets of London, and kept his head turned toward her.

'Do you live quite alone?' he asked.

'I have a housekeeper,' she said, 'who is also my cook.'

'And the lady with whom you walked in the park yesterday?' he asked.

'Alice Haytor?' she said. 'Yes, she lives with me too as my companion.'

'Your former governess?' he asked.

'Yes.'

'Will she not be shocked when you arrive home with a – a *lover*?' he asked her.

'She has been warned,' she told him, 'not to come out of her room when I arrive home, Lord Merton, and she will not.'

'You knew, then,' he asked her, looking very directly into her eyes despite the darkness, 'that you would be bringing a lover home with you?'

He was a tiresome man. He did not know how to play the game. Did he imagine that like a lightning bolt out of a blue sky she had been smitten with love as soon as her eyes alit upon him in his sister's ballroom? That everything had been spontaneous, unplanned? She had *told* him it had all been very much planned.

'I am twenty-eight years old, Lord Merton,' she said. 'My husband has been dead for more than a year. Women have needs, appetites, just as surely as men do. I am not in search of another husband – not now, not ever. But it is time for a lover. I knew it when I came to London. And when I saw you in Hyde Park, looking like an angel – but a very human and very virile angel – I knew it with even greater certainty.'

'You came to Meg's ball, then,' he asked her, 'specifically to meet *me*?'

'*And* to seduce you,' she said.

'But how did you know I would *be* there?' he asked her.

He sat back in his seat. But almost at the same moment, the carriage rocked to a halt outside her shabby-genteel house, and he moved his head closer to the window and looked out at it. She did not answer his question.

'Tell me, Lord Merton,' she said, her voice almost a whisper, 'that you are here not only because I set out to seduce you. Tell me that you looked across the ballroom at me earlier this evening and wanted me.'

He turned back to face her, and she could just make out his eyes in the prevailing darkness. There was an intensity in their gaze.

'Oh, I wanted you, Lady Paget,' he said, his voice as low as hers. 'And that is not just past tense. I *want* you. I told you earlier that when I go to bed with a lady it is because I choose to do so, not because I am unable to resist seduction.'

Yet he would not have spared a thought to bedding her tonight if she had not deliberately collided with him – or *almost* collided, just before the waltz began. He might not have even spoken with her or danced with her, unless he had done so for his sister's sake.

No, Lord Merton, she told him without speaking aloud, *you have been seduced.*

His coachman opened the door and set down the steps. The Earl of Merton descended, handed her down, and dismissed the carriage.

There was a certain feeling of unease, Stephen found, mingled with the pleasant anticipation of sensual pleasures. He could not quite understand the discomfort, except perhaps that they were in her home, where her servant and her companion were sleeping. It did not feel quite right.

Sometimes he despised his conscience. While he had lived an active, even adventurous life since he was a boy, he never had sown very wild oats, though everyone – including himself – had expected that he would.

To his relief, they encountered no one inside her house. One candle had been left burning in a wall sconce in the downstairs hall, and one on the upstairs landing. In the dimness of the light they shed, he could see that the house was respectable, if somewhat shabby. He guessed that she was renting it, and that it had come furnished.

She led him inside a square bedchamber at the top of the stairs and lit a single candle on the heavy dressing table. She angled the side mirrors so that suddenly it seemed as though there were many lights.

He shut the door.

There was a large chest of drawers in the room beside a door leading, presumably, into a dressing room. There were small tables on either side of the bed, each with three drawers. The bed itself was large, with heavy spiraling bedposts and an ornate canopy covered with a faded dark blue fabric that matched the bedcover.

It was neither an elegant nor a pretty room.

But it smelled of her, of that subtle floral scent she wore. And the candlelight was soft and flickering. It was an *enticing* room.

He wanted her.

Ah, yes, he wanted her very badly indeed. And he could find no rational fault with what was about to happen here. He was unmarried and unattached. She was a widow and was more than willing – indeed, she was the one who had initiated all of this. They would be harming no one by becoming lovers tonight – and perhaps remaining lovers through the rest of the Season. They would simply be giving pleasure to each other and to themselves.

There was nothing wrong with pleasure. There was everything *right* with it.

And there were no expectations on either side, no sensibilities to be hurt. She had been quite firm about the fact that she was not in search of a husband and never would be. He believed her. He was not in search of a wife. Not yet, anyway, and probably not for another five or six years.

But he felt uneasy.

Was it because of the rumors circulating about her?

Had she killed her husband?

Was he about to sleep with a murderer?

Was he afraid of her? *Ought* he to be?

He was not afraid.

Only uneasy.

He did not know her. But that was no cause for unease. He had not known any of the women with whom he had had sexual relations over the years. He had always treated them with courtesy and consideration and generosity, but he had never known any of them or wanted to.

Did he want to know Lady Paget, then?

She was standing beside the dressing table, looking at him in the candlelight, that strange smile on her face that seemed both inviting and scornful. He had been standing overlong close to the door, he realized, probably looking like a frightened schoolboy about to bolt for freedom.

He moved toward her and did not stop until he had his hands on either side of her surprisingly small waist and lowered his head to set his lips against the pulse at the base of her throat.

She was warm and soft and fragrant. And her body molded itself to his, her generous breasts pressed to his chest, her hips moving slightly to fit more comfortably against him, her thighs warm against his own. He could feel the blood pounding through his body, hammering in his ears, tightening his groin, and pulsing through his stiffening erection.

He lifted his head and kissed her lips, his own parted, his tongue seeking the warm, moist cavity of her mouth. She sucked it deep and pressed it against the roof of her mouth with her own tongue. Her hands slid up his back, beneath his coat and his waistcoat, and then down to spread over his buttocks while her hips moved suggestively and he stiffened further into arousal.

His own hands began the laborious task of opening the small buttons down the back of her gown. He lifted his head and stepped back when the task was completed to nudge the gown off her shoulders and down her arms and then down her body, taking her shift with it, exposing first her magnificent bosom, then her small waist and the alluring curve of her hips, and then her legs, which were long and shapely.

Her garments slithered down to form an emerald green and white heap at her feet, leaving her standing in white gloves and silk stockings and silver dancing slippers.

He could not take his eyes from her. There was something, he realized, even more alluring than nakedness, and this was it. He drew a deep, slow, steadying breath.

She stood looking back at him, her eyelids half drooped over her eyes, her arms at her sides until she extended one toward him and he slowly peeled back the glove and dropped it to the pile. She reached out the other hand and smiled that siren's smile.

When he was finished with the gloves, he went down on one knee before her and slid her stockings down her legs one at a time after first removing the garters. She set each foot in turn on his bent leg as he maneuvered stocking and slipper off the foot and tossed them behind him.

He kissed each instep, each ankle, the inside of each knee, and each warm inner thigh before standing again.

She was quite as lovely as he had anticipated. More so. She was not a small woman in any way, but she was perfectly proportioned, beautifully formed. She was magnificent.

What had ever made him believe that he found youthful slenderness desirable?

He expected that she would now proceed to undress him. Instead, she lifted both bare arms and kept her eyes on his as she drew the pins from her hair. She did it slowly, leisurely, as though there were no rush to get to the bed, as though she were unaware of the bulge of his erection or the barely suppressed quickening of his breathing.

Though her smile indicated that she was very aware indeed.

And her heavy eyelids suggested that she anticipated the main feast with as much desire as he.

He watched as her hair began to come down, and then swallowed as it all cascaded about her face, over her shoulders, and down her back. One heavy lock fell across a breast, and then settled in the valley between.

It was heavy, shining hair of a vibrant red. It was her crowning glory. For once that tired old cliché had real meaning.

He swallowed again.

'Let us go to bed,' she said.

He caught hold of the edges of his coat, just below the lapels, but her hands came up to cover his.

'No,' she said. 'Only your shoes, Lord Merton.'

Her hands left his and moved to the waist of his breeches. Her fingers worked deftly at the buttons while they gazed into each other's eyes. The flap dropped open.

'Now,' she said, moving her head forward and setting her lips softly to his as she spoke, 'you are ready. Now we are both ready. Let's go to bed.'

He thought for a moment that it was because she could not wait for him to undress. But he knew that was not it. He knew she was cleverer than he. His blood pounded, his desire was almost pain. And it had something to do with the fact that he was fully clothed in his ball finery while she was naked.

She led him toward the bed and threw back the covers before lying down on her back and raising her arms to him as he came down on top of her.

She wrapped her arms about him and moved her breasts and hips against him, murmuring to him with soft, unintelligible words as he settled between her thighs. One of her feet caressed his leg through his breeches and his stocking. With his hands and his mouth he explored her, caressing, teasing, kneading.

He felt her fingers free him from the fabric of his breeches and drawers and feather lightly over his erection. He drew a sharp breath.

She laughed softly and drew him toward the wet heat between her thighs. But no. This was *not* seduction. He was *not* a virgin schoolboy to be played with by a practiced courtesan. He slid his arm beneath hers so that she had to release him, and set his hand where his erection had been a moment ago. He explored her with light, teasing fingers, rubbing, scratching lightly, pressing a little way inside, describing small circles as he did so. With his thumb he found and lightly massaged that small spot that had her drawing a ragged, audible breath.

If he was to be the seduced and she the seductress, then she would also be the seduced and he the seducer.

There was to be equality in this encounter.

Pleasure for both, to be administered and to receive.

He took a firm grasp of her buttocks, positioned himself, waited for her to lift slightly toward him in wordless invitation, and pressed hard into her.

He heard her laugh softly as her inner muscles clenched tightly about him and her legs lifted from the bed to twine about his. He raised himself on his forearms and looked down at her. Candlelight whispered across her face and made flickering flames of her hair, tumbled across the pillow.

'Stephen,' she said, setting her palms against the lapels of his coat, sliding them up to his shoulders.

He shivered at the sound of his name spoken in her low, seductive voice.

'Lady P—'

'Cassandra,' she said.

'Cassandra.'

And she relaxed her inner muscles and rotated her hips about him.

'Stephen,' she said, 'you are very large.'

He laughed.

'And very, very hard,' she said, her eyes mocking him. 'You are very, very much a man.'

'And you, my lady,' he said, 'are very soft and very wet and very hot. Very, very much a woman.'

Her lips mocked too, though her breathing was not

quite steady, and he lowered both his head and his body and moved in her with deep, firm, rhythmic strokes, prolonging the intense, painful pleasure of their coupling for as long as he could before releasing into her and relaxing all his weight down onto her as the blood pounding through his temples gradually subsided and he wondered if he had waited long enough to give her too the ultimate pleasure.

He was ashamed of the fact that he was not sure.

'Cassandra,' he murmured as he withdrew from her and moved off her to lie beside her, his arm still beneath her head.

But there was nothing else to say. The exhaustion of sexual satiety overpowered him and he slid into a deep, satisfied sleep.

He was not sure how long he slept. But when he awoke he was alone – and still dressed in evening clothes that were going to be horribly rumpled. His valet would scold for a month and threaten to resign and find a gentleman who had greater respect for his skills.

The flap of his breeches had been neatly raised and buttoned, he realized with a flash of embarrassment.

The candles were no longer flickering. But the room was not quite dark. The light of early dawn was graying the window and the room itself. The curtains had been drawn back.

He turned his head and looked toward the dressing table. Lady Paget was sitting sideways before it, looking back at him. She was dressed, though not in last evening's gown. Her hair had been brushed smoothly back from her face and tied neatly with a ribbon at the nape of her neck. It fell in a thick column down her back. She had her legs crossed. One foot was swinging back and forth, a slipper half off it.

'Cassandra?' he said. 'I am so sorry. I must have—'

'We need to talk, Lord Merton,' she said.

Lord Merton? Not Stephen any longer?

'Do we?' he said. 'Would it not—'

'Business,' she said. 'We need to talk business.'

Cassandra had been awake for a long time. Indeed, she had done no more than doze a couple of times.

She stared for a long time at the ugly canopy above her head. She must remove it, she decided, or at least find a way to cover it with a fabric that was lighter and more cheerful. She must make the house into a home – if she was to remain here, that was. If she could afford to remain here.

And she turned her head and stared at the Earl of Merton for a long while in the flickering light of the candle. How very extravagant of her to let it burn! She had not extinguished the candles in the hall or on the landing either. As if she had *money* to burn.

He slept deeply and apparently dreamlessly. He looked as beautiful in sleep as he did when he was awake. His hair, short as it was, was rumpled and had freed itself of the combing that had tamed the waves and curls.

He looked younger.

He looked innocent.

He was *not* innocent – not sexually, anyway. There had not been a great deal of foreplay, either before they lay on the bed or after, and their actual coupling had lasted no longer than a few minutes. But he had known what he was doing. He was a passionate and accomplished lover even if a bit rushed on their first encounter.

Cassandra thought he was probably a very decent man from a decent family. For a moment she regretted choosing him. But it was too late now to choose again and to choose differently. She did not have the time to dally with several lovers before picking the one who best suited her.

Finally, when early dawn was beginning to gray the windows and make the candle's light unnecessary, she could lie in bed no longer. She edged away from him so as not to wake him, but he did not even stir. His arm was still stretched out along the bottom edge of her pillow, the fabric of his evening coat noticeably creased where her head had lain. She leaned over him and very carefully lifted and buttoned the flap of his breeches, darting looks up into his face as her fingers worked.

He must, she thought, look quite magnificent without his clothes.

Next time she would see him. She felt an unexpected eagerness for that moment.

She got up from the bed, extinguished the candle, noting ruefully how much it had burned down, and let herself quietly into the small, cramped dressing room beside the bedchamber. Without the benefit of any light, she chose a day dress from the wardrobe there and pulled it on, after first washing her hands and face in the cold water that remained in the pitcher from last evening. She felt for a hair ribbon on the upper shelf of the wardrobe and brushed back her hair and secured it at her neck.

All the time she could feel a slight soreness within, where he had been. It had been a long time . . .

Surprisingly, it was a rather pleasant feeling.

He was still not awake when she returned to the bedchamber. She drew back the curtains from the window and stood for a few moments looking down at the street, which was still quiet despite the fact that the darkness of night was fast lifting. Finally a laborer hurried past, head down.

And then she went to sit on the chair before her dressing table, turning it so that she could see the man on the bed and know when he awoke.

It amazed her that he had not woken long before now, eager to resume the pleasures of the night. Her lip curled with scorn that he had not done so. Had she played her part so poorly? Or supremely well?

She crossed her legs and swung one foot idly until he finally stirred. It took him a while to come fully awake and to turn his head and see her sitting there.

'Cassandra?' he said. 'I am so sorry. I must have—'

She cut him off. She did not want to know for what he was apologizing. For sleeping so long? The morning was still so early that even the tradesmen were not in the street yet, only that one laborer, who might have been on his way home from his night work. Or did he apologize for sleeping at all instead of availing himself of her willing body as many times as the night allowed?

He spoke her name as if it were a caress.

He had spoken it, she remembered, after he had finished with her body – as if she were not *simply* a woman's body made for his pleasure, but a person with a name.

She must be careful not to be seduced by this man. It was *she* who was the seducer.

'We need to talk, Lord Merton,' she said.

'Do we?' he said, raising himself on one elbow, a smile in his eyes. 'Would it not—'

– be better to tumble back into bed and talk later if at all?

'Business,' she said before he could finish. 'We need to talk business.'

This was the moment upon which the whole of her future hinged. She continued to swing one foot, careful not to increase the speed or otherwise show how tensely nervous she was. She half closed her eyes, half smiled.

'Business?' He sat up, swung his legs over the side of the bed, brushed his hands rather ineffectually over his clothes, and attempted to tidy the fall of his neckcloth. He still looked like a man who had slept fully clothed.

'I did not seduce you,' she said, 'for the pleasure of just one night in your company, Lord Merton. Especially when you slept through most of it.'

'I beg your—' he began.

She held up one hand.

'I take your sleeping so soundly as a tribute to the pleasure I gave you,' she said. 'I slept through most of the night too. You are a very . . . satisfactory lover.' She curved her lips upward at the corners.

He did not say anything.

'I want you tonight again and tomorrow night and every night into the foreseeable future,' she said. 'And I can see to it that you will want me equally as much and for at least as long, Lord Merton. Or do I not need to employ further seduction? Do you already want it?'

His answer gave her a slight jolt of alarm.

'I do not like the word *seduction*,' he said. 'It suggests weakness on the part of the seduced and cold calculation on the part of the seducer. It suggests an inequality of desire and need. It suggests a puppet and a puppeteer. I have never admired male seducers because they exploit women and make of them only playthings for their beds. I have never met a female seducer, though I am very familiar with the story of the sirens.'

'Did you not meet one last evening, Lord Merton?' she asked him.

He smiled at her.

'I met a lady,' he said, 'who *called* herself that. You, in fact. I would prefer to think that in your loneliness – pardon me, your *aloneness* – you looked for someone for whom you could feel the comfort of an attraction, and you found me. You did not seduce me, Cassandra. You were open and bold about the attraction you felt, something I have not encountered in any of the ladies of my acquaintance, who usually employ a whole arsenal of more subtle wiles if they are interested in capturing my attention. I appreciated your openness. I felt an equal attraction to you. I would have asked you to dance with me even if you had not collided with me just before the waltz began. I do not suppose I would have also invited you to share a bed with me quite so soon if you had not made it very clear that it was what *you* wanted, but our mutual attraction might have led us here eventually.'

He had misunderstood entirely. Which was just as well.

Our mutual attraction.

'Yes,' he said, 'I do want to sleep with you again and again into the future. But I must ask some questions first.'

She raised her eyebrows and regarded him haughtily.

'Indeed?' she said. She had somehow lost control over this business conference. She was supposed to be doing the talking, he the listening.

'Tell me about Lord Paget's death,' he said. He was leaning forward, his arms draped over his knees. His blue eyes were looking very intensely at her.

'He died,' she said, smiling scornfully. 'What more is to be said? You want me to tell you that his skull was cleaved in two with an axe, Lord Merton? It was not. It was a bullet that killed him – a bullet through the heart.'

He was still looking very directly at her.

'Did you kill him?' he asked.

She pursed her lips and looked back into his eyes.

'Yes,' she said.

She did not realize he had been holding his breath until he expelled it audibly.

'I might have found it difficult to wield an axe,' she said, 'but a pistol was a weapon I was quite capable of using. I used one. I shot him through the heart with it. And I have never regretted it. I have not for one moment mourned him.'

His head had dropped so that he was looking down at the floor and she was gazing at the top of his head. She thought his eyes might be closed. The fingers of both his hands curled into his palms. He did not speak for a long time.

'Why?' he asked at last.

'Because,' she said, and smiled though he was not looking at her. 'Perhaps because I felt like doing so.'

She ought to have said no to his original question. Was she trying to drive him away and sabotage her carefully laid plans? She could not have chosen a better way.

There was another loud silence. When he spoke again, his voice was scarcely audible.

'Did he abuse you?' he asked.

'Yes,' she said. 'He did.'

He lifted his head at last and looked intently at her again with troubled eyes, a frown between his brows.

'I am sorry,' he said.

'Why?' she asked him, her lip curling. 'Could you have done anything to prevent it but failed to do so, Lord Merton?'

'I am sorry,' he said, 'that so many men are brutes simply because they are physically stronger than women. Was it bad enough, then, that you had no alternative but to kill him?'

But he answered his own question before she could do so.

'It must have been. Why were you not arrested?'

'I shot him in the library,' she said, 'late in the evening. There were no witnesses, and by the time a number of people gathered there, drawn by the noise, there was no knowing who had done it. There was and is no proof that I did. Anyone could have. Anyone at all. The house was full of servants and other residents. The library window was open to the whole world beyond. No one can prove anything except that he died of a bullet wound.'

'And except,' he said, 'that you have confessed to me.'

'And to no one else besides you,' she said. 'You will fear from this moment on that when you are asleep one night I will kill you too in order to keep you silent.'

'I am not a tattler,' he said, 'and I am not afraid. You must not be either.'

'I do not fear you,' she said. 'A gentleman does not reveal a lady's secrets, and I believe you *are* a gentleman. And I do not fear you would ever abuse me. If you did, I would not kill you. Why would I when I can simply walk away from you as I could not from a husband? A widow has power, Lord Merton. She is free.'

Except that she was not. Her lack of money set her in thrall. And somehow this conversation was not proceeding at all as she had planned it in her mind. Then she had been able to control his answers as well as her questions. She was not sure there was a way of bringing it back under her control.

'I will be happy,' he said, 'to be your lover. I will treat you kindly. I promise you that. And when it is over, you will simply tell me and I will go.'

'But the trouble is, Lord Merton,' she said, 'that I cannot afford a liaison that is simply an affaire de coeur.'

It was not at all as she had intended to say it. But it was too late now. The words were out, and his gaze had sharpened further on her.

'Cannot *afford*?' he said.

'A man who succeeds to his father's title and property and fortune,' she said, 'is almost always going to consider his surviving stepmother an encumbrance. But most such men honor their obligations nonetheless. The present Lord Paget did not.'

'Your husband left no provision for you in his will?' he said, frowning. 'Or in your marriage contract?'

'Certainly he did,' she said. 'Do you think I would have killed him if I had known I would be left destitute, Lord

Merton? I was to have the dower house at Carmel for my use during my lifetime, and the house in town here. I was to have a money settlement, all my personal jewelry, and a comfortable pension for life.'

He was still frowning.

'Can Paget legally withhold any of those things from you?' he asked.

'He cannot,' she said. 'Neither can I legally kill a man. His father, in fact. It was a stalemate, Lord Merton, but he resolved it. He would not pursue prosecution against me if I just simply went away empty-handed.'

'And that is what you did?' he asked her. 'Simply went away? Even though there was no evidence against you?'

'Evidence, Lord Merton,' she said, 'can very easily be trumped up against someone one does not like.'

He stared at her for a few moments before closing his eyes and lowering his head again.

Seduction by a lady of questionable reputation followed by a business agreement by a courtesan – an *expensive* courtesan, an *irresistible* courtesan. And he would come to heel like a well-trained puppy because his appetite would have been aroused but not fully sated. He would be panting with lust for her.

That had been the plan. It had been clear in her head, and it had seemed perfectly reasonable. She had not expected it to be at all difficult to implement.

The plan had gone quite awry, however.

She began swinging her foot slowly again. She looked at his tousled golden blond curls with as much scorn as she could muster. She waited for him to get up and go away. She almost hastened him on his way by telling him to leave.

She did not fear what he would say to others after he had left. He *was* a gentleman, she believed. Besides, he would not wish openly to admit to anyone that he had been lured into the bed of a notorious murderer.

He lifted his head again, and it seemed to her as his eyes met hers in the growing light of day that he was paler than he had been, that his eyes were bluer. And very intense.

'You have nothing?' he asked her.

She raised her eyebrows.

'I have enough,' she lied. 'But if you are to be my lover, Lord Merton, you are also to be my protector. You will pay me for services rendered. You will pay me as you would the most celebrated of courtesans. Very well indeed, that is. And I will render services that will be ten times more satisfying than any courtesan would offer. Tonight was a mere pale sampling.'

It sounded like a foolish boast. She almost expected him to laugh at her.

'You were not attracted to me at all, were you?' he said. 'You came uninvited to Meg's ball in order to find a protector.'

She smiled at him – and her slipper finally fell off her foot and landed on the floor with a soft thump.

'A lady does, Lord Merton,' she said, her voice low, 'what a lady must.'

Go, she told him silently. *Please go. Go away and never let me have to see you again.*

There was rather a lengthy silence during which they continued to stare at each other. She would not look away, she decided. Neither would she say anything more before he did. She certainly would not jerk to her feet and rush inside her dressing room and slam the door and press her body back against it until he had gone.

'I will pay you weekly, Lady Paget,' he said at last, 'in advance. Beginning today. I will send a package as soon as I return home – or at the earliest respectable hour, anyway.'

And he named a weekly sum that had her heart thumping in amazement. Could courtesans possibly earn *that* much?

'That will be satisfactory,' she said coolly. He had stopped calling her *Cassandra,* she noticed. 'You will not be sorry, Lord Merton. I will service you very well indeed.'

A light flashed deep inside his eyes.

'I do not wish to be *serviced,* ma'am,' he said, getting to his feet, 'as if I were some sort of animal that functioned on blind lust alone. I doubt there *are* such animals, anyway, except those of the human variety. I will be your protector. Technically you will be my mistress. But I will bed you when our desire is mutual. I will bed you when you wish to be bedded and desist when you do not. We will be *lovers* or we will be nothing. Your weekly salary will not depend upon the number of times you make your body available to me upon that bed or any other. Is that clear to you?'

She gazed at him in some surprise. She found herself almost afraid of him. Not afraid in any physical sense. She was reasonably sure that he would never hurt her. But he was . . . She did not even know what he was, what it was about him that had made her suddenly afraid.

Was it the fear that she could not manipulate him as she had expected to do? He was young and good-natured and gentlemanly – and there was a definite air of innocence about him. She had expected him also to be rather weak, or meek anyway – to be easily controlled by the power of sex.

She might have misjudged him.

It was a ghastly possibility.

But he had agreed to be her protector for an indeterminate length of time. And he was paying her more than handsomely. She had been planning to demand a little more than half what he had offered.

'Oh, very clear,' she said, standing up after kicking off the other slipper, and stepping closer to him. She lifted her arms and busied herself with straightening his neckcloth and restoring some of its intricate folds. 'We have an agreement, then, Lord Merton.'

'We do,' he said, and he lifted his hands to take her by the wrists.

She raised her face to his and smiled.

He did not smile back. His eyes searched hers.

'You do not have to wear it with me,' he said softly.

'It?' She raised her eyebrows.

'Your mask of cold contempt for the world and all its human creatures,' he said. 'You do not need to wear it. I am not going to hurt you.'

She felt real fear then and would have turned and run after all if he had not been holding her wrists, though his grip was not a tight one. She smiled instead.

'How lowering,' she said, 'to smile at one's lover and protector and be told that it is an expression of cold contempt. Perhaps I ought to frown at you instead.'

He lowered his head and kissed her briefly but hard on the lips.

'You are going to Lady Carling's at-home this afternoon?' he asked.

'I believe I might,' she said. 'The lady did invite me, and I think it would be amusing to watch the reaction of her other guests.'

'My sisters will be three of them,' he said. 'They will treat you with courtesy, and Lady Carling herself will be kind. I will bring my curricle there and take you for a drive in the park afterward.'

'You will do no such thing,' she said, drawing back from him. 'You have nothing to gain and a great deal to lose by consorting with me publicly.'

'I will visit you here discreetly at night and with all due care to your reputation,' he said. 'But you are not a courtesan, Lady Paget. You are a lady, and one whose reputation with the *ton* is in need of restoration. I do not know what happened with your husband, though you have told me the bare bones. I believe there is more – much more – and we will speak of it as time goes on. But your reputation does need to be restored. It will be done at least partly in my company. And if you believe my reputation will suffer great harm from it, you do not understand the double standard with which the beau monde – and all of society for that matter – judges the behavior of men and women. Sherry, for example – Sheringford – is in the process of being forgiven, while the lady with whom he eloped would have had a far more difficult time of it if she had lived and chosen to return here. My reputation will remain virtually unsullied if I escort you about London. Yours will gain from association with me.'

'You do not need to be kind to me, Lord Merton,' she said.

'If the word *protector* means merely that I have exclusive

and unlimited access to your body,' he said, 'I do not really want the position. If I am your protector, then I will *protect* you as well as sleep with you.'

She sighed deeply and audibly.

'I believe,' she said, 'I found myself a monster last evening when I merely expected an angel – a *wealthy* angel. Your sisters, no matter how courteous they are to me this afternoon, will be quite appalled when you arrive at Lady Carling's to bear me off to the park with you.'

'My sisters,' he said, 'live their own lives, and I live mine. We do not control one another. We merely love one another.'

'It is their love for you,' she said, 'that will cause their horror.'

'Then they must be horrified,' he said. 'I will come for you at half past four.'

'You had better go home now,' she said, 'before Alice gets up and frowns at you. She will grow accustomed to you, but at first she will frown. You would not wish to face those black looks when you are at a disadvantage. Your coat and breeches are sadly wrinkled and your neckcloth is quite irredeemable. Your curls are breaking free and attempting to riot.'

He smiled – the first time he had done so in several long minutes.

'The bane of my life,' he said.

'Then you ought not to try taming them,' she said. 'Any red-blooded female would find her fingers itching to run through them and become entangled in them.'

He bowed to her and raised her right hand to his lips.

'I will see you this afternoon, then,' he said. He looked up into her eyes. 'And I will send that package this morning.'

She nodded.

And he was gone, closing the door quietly behind him.

She crossed to the window and stood looking down until he emerged from the front door. She did not hear it either opening or closing. She watched him walk with long, easy strides down the street until he disappeared around a corner. And even then she stood looking after him.

After a while she realized that she was crying. She went back into the dressing room and bent her face over the bowl.

She never cried. She never *ever* cried.

Alice must not see the trace of tears on her face.

7

Stephen had always been blessed with an even temper and a naturally cheerful outlook on life. Even as a boy he had very rarely lost his temper with any of his playmates or fought them with any degree of ferocity or lingering animosity. It was true that he had popped Clarence Forester such a good one a few years ago that the coward had fled with a bulbous nose and two black eyes rather than fight back like a man. It was true too that his fists had itched to do even worse to Randolph Turner a year or so after that, though he had been forced by circumstances, alas, to quell the urge.

But there had been perfectly good reasons for both those forays into violence – or potential violence. In both cases his sisters had been threatened, and he would probably kill if he had to in order to protect any of the three of them.

There *were* suitable occasions for anger and even violence.

He was angry today. *Furiously* angry. But this time it was on his own account.

The first person he took it out on was his valet, who had always served him well but who, in the nature of valets, liked to rule him with an iron thumb too whenever he could get away with doing so. He took one look at Stephen when the latter rang for him at a little past six in the morning, and began scolding and threatening as if he were dealing with a naughty boy.

Stephen let it go for a minute or two and then turned on him with cold eyes and colder voice.

'Pardon me if I have misunderstood the situation, Philbin,' he said. 'But are you not employed to serve my needs? Are you not employed to care for my clothes, among other duties? To have them clean and ironed and ready when I need them? I will expect these clothes to be all three when I next call for them. In the meantime you may have bathwater brought up for me and then set out my riding clothes while I bathe. You may then shave me and help me dress. If in your deepest fantasies you imagine that one of your duties is to talk to me while you work and offer your opinion on my behavior and the condition of my clothes when I return them to your care, then you must be forced to face reality – and forced to seek employment with someone who is foolish enough to allow such daydreams to flourish. Do I make myself clear?'

He listened in some surprise to his own tirade. Philbin had been with him since he was seventeen, and they had always had a perfectly amicable master/servant relationship. Philbin grumbled and scolded when he felt he had cause, and Stephen cheerfully mollified him or ignored him, whichever seemed appropriate to the circumstances.

But he would not apologize now. He was too angry, and Philbin was too convenient a target. Perhaps some other time he would make his peace with his man.

His valet stared at him with half-open mouth, and then he shut it with a clacking of teeth and turned to busy himself with hanging up Stephen's horribly creased evening coat. Stephen had a ghastly suspicion that Philbin was blinking back tears, and he felt horribly guilty – and even more irritated than he had before.

It was impossible for Philbin to button up his lips, though.

'Yes, m'lord,' he said, his voice wooden with injured righteousness. 'And I do not want to work for someone else, as you very well know. That was unkind, m'lord. Do you want the black riding coat or the brown? And the buff riding breeches or the gray? And the new boots or—'

'Philbin,' Stephen said testily, 'set out riding clothes for me, will you?'

'Yes, m'lord,' his valet said, having had some measure of revenge. He did not usually ask such petty questions.

And then Stephen carried his anger with him to Hyde Park, where he rode at a reckless gallop along Rotten Row until other riders started to arrive and it would have been dangerous to continue.

Soon he had been joined by a few male acquaintances, and the conversation and the fresh morning air soothed him until Morley Etheridge happened to mention last evening's ball and Clive Arnsworthy congratulated himself on having been able to secure a set with the delectable Lady Christobel Foley.

'Though everyone knows she has eyes for no one but you, Merton,' he said. 'You are going to find yourself with a leg shackle before the summer is out unless you are very careful. I could think of worse females to be shackled to, mind you. A dozen of them, in fact. A *hundred*.'

'Why stop at a hundred?' Etheridge asked dryly. 'Why not go for a thousand, Arnsworthy?'

'It is not a shackle on his leg Merton is risking, though,' Colin Cathcart said, blithely unaware of Stephen's black mood. 'It is an axe in his skull. It might be a glorious way to go, however, provided he is between the lady's thighs when it happens. Very shapely thighs they are too, as far as one could see through that green gown she was wearing, which did not leave a great deal to the imagination, by Jove. Did you take a good look, Arnsworthy? Did you, Etheridge?'

There was a general guffaw of bawdy laughter.

'I might have noticed her thighs,' Arnsworthy said, 'but my eyes started at her head and worked their way down. They almost did not get past all that red hair, but I did valiantly force my gaze downward to her bosom. There was no persuading it to go any lower after that, though. I have never been more thankful for the services of a quizzing glass.'

There was another burst of laughter.

'If the woman hoped—' Etheridge began.

'The *lady*,' Stephen said in the unfamiliar cold, clipped tone he recognized from his earlier confrontation with his valet, 'was a *guest* at my sister's ball, and as such was as deserving of respect and courtesy and gentlemanly restraint as any other lady present. She was not – and *is* not – a strumpet to be ogled and stripped of all dignity. You will not speak of her with disrespect in my hearing. Not unless you wish to answer to me on some quiet stretch of heath one morning.'

They all turned in the saddle as one, the three of them, and gawked at him with half-open mouths – just as Philbin had done earlier.

Stephen clamped his teeth together hard and stared straight ahead along the Row. He felt foolish – and furious. For two pins he really would slap a glove in each of their faces. And take them all on together too. For two pins—

'Worried for Lady Sheringford's reputation, are you, Merton?' Etheridge asked after an uncomfortable silence. 'There is no need to be. No one in his right mind believes the woman . . . the *lady* was invited. And your sister and Sherry handled the situation with admirable aplomb. Your sister talked with her and Sherry danced with her, and then they sent Moreland to dance with her and then you – or was it the other way around? Sherry's mother took her for a stroll all about the ballroom after supper. The verdict today is bound to be that the ball was a resounding success – and all the more so for the titillation of Lady Paget's appearance there. You need not fear, old chap. Most men of my acquaintance have always thought Sherry one devil of a fine fellow for being bold enough to do what he did all those years ago. He did what other men only dream of doing. And even the ladies are beginning to forgive him. It is all on account of your sister, who is the most respectable lady anyone could wish to meet.'

There were murmurings of assent from the other two before they all stopped to exchange pleasantries with another group of riders, and the embarrassing moment passed off.

But Stephen carried his anger with him for the rest of the morning. He sparred at Jackson's Boxing Saloon for half an hour before the old pugilist took him on himself for a bout when Stephen's first partner complained of the unnecessary ferocity of his punches.

He went to White's afterward and sat in the reading room with one of the morning papers held up before his face in such a way that it discouraged anyone from coming along to disturb him and carry him off elsewhere.

He was by nature gregarious and a favored companion of a large and varied number of gentlemen. But he sat morosely behind his paper and glared at the only one who dared smile and nod at him as he passed.

He did not read a single word.

He had been caught in a trap, and there was no decent way out.

He had woken up feeling embarrassed. He had made love to Cassandra rather swiftly and fully clothed, and then he had fallen asleep – and remained asleep for what must have been hours. It must have been a deep sleep too – good Lord, he had not even stirred when she buttoned him up and left the bed to get dressed. She had been sitting on the chair before the dressing table when he awoke, swinging her foot as if she had been there a long time waiting for him to return to the land of the conscious.

The only way he could have redeemed himself was to lure her back to bed, divest himself of his clothes and her of hers, and make love to her very slowly and very thoroughly.

But then she had sprung her trap and caught him in it – and there was nothing he could do about it. A leg shackle could not be more confining.

She had been abused during her marriage. It must have been very bad abuse – she had finally ended it by taking a pistol and shooting Paget through the heart.

Was it murder?

Or self-defense?

Was it unpardonable?

Or justifiable?

He did not know the answers and did not care. She had aroused his pity and sense of chivalry – as she had no doubt intended.

She had been cut off from all the benefits to which the widow of a man of property and fortune was entitled. Her stepson had tossed her out with the threat of prosecution if she should return or try to press her claim on the estate through some legal means.

She was poor. Stephen was not sure *how* poor. She had somehow got to London and rented that gloomy, rather shabby house. But he guessed she was very close to being destitute and that she already was desperate. She had gone to Meg's ball last evening, risking the degradation of being thrown out while half the *ton* looked on. She had done it in order to find a wealthy protector. She had done it so that she could live and avoid becoming a beggar with no home but the streets.

He did not believe he was exaggerating her poverty.

And he was the savior she had chosen.

The *victim*.

He had looked to her like an *angel* and she had discovered his identity and realized that he was a very wealthy man. She had thought he would be an easy touch.

And how right she had been!

Stephen turned a page of the paper so viciously that one corner of it tore off in his hand and the rest of that side fell down into his lap with a loud rustling sound. Several gentlemen looked pointedly and disapprovingly his way.

'Shhh!' Lord Partheter said, frowning over the top of his spectacles.

Stephen shook the half-mutilated paper into some sort of order, regardless of noise, and hid his face behind it again.

She was *right* because he felt both pity for her story – or the little of it he had heard, anyway – and concern for her poverty. He could no sooner have stalked out of that house a free man than he could have punched her until she was down and then kicked her in the ribs until they were all shattered.

He could have offered her a pension with no strings attached, and the thought had occurred to him even at the time. No one ought to be allowed to be as wealthy as he was. He would not even miss the amount that would enable her to live in modest luxury.

But it could not be done. He suspected that somewhere behind that facade of smilingly scornful, unfeeling siren there were probably the shreds of pride that her husband had tried to beat out of her. She would surely refuse the gift.

Besides, he could not go about offering a generous pension to everyone with a sorry story to tell.

And so her destitution would be on his mind and on his conscience.

He had felt forced to offer her a ridiculously high salary to grant him sexual favors that he was not at all sure he wanted. In fact, he was almost certain he did not.

He had paid for sexual favors in the past – and always more than the woman asked for. It had never seemed sordid before now. Perhaps it ought to have. Perhaps his moral conscience needed some honest self-examination.

Because perhaps all women who offered such services did so in order to ward off starvation. It was hardly something they would do for the mere pleasure of it, was it?

He frowned at the unwelcome thoughts, moved his hand to turn another page, and thought better of it.

Just this time yesterday he had had no more intention of employing a mistress than he had of flying off to the moon. Now he had employed one. Philbin, unusually subdued, had been dispatched to Portman Street with a fat package of money after helping Stephen on with his riding boots.

He had paid handsomely for last night's sexual encounter and for the exclusive rights to more of the same, at least for the next week.

He did not care about the money. He cared about the deception – he had thought she *wanted* him, that she had been *attracted* to him. He had thought it was mutual sexual pleasure they had sought. It was both embarrassing and humiliating to know the truth. And he cared about the trap and the leg shackle he wore just as surely as if she had lured him into marriage.

Why the devil should he also feel responsible for making her respectable? She was *not* respectable. She had killed her husband. She had sold her body to a stranger and trapped him into being her protector. She—

She had lived through a nomadic, insecure childhood and a nightmare of a marriage. Now she was doing what she needed to do to survive – to put food in her stomach and a roof over her head. There was no way on this earth she would be able to find any other employment but prostitution.

She was prostituting herself to him.

And he was allowing it.

He was *forced* to allow it on the assumption that she would not take his money unless it came for *services rendered*.

Hatred did not come naturally to Stephen. Even dislike did not. He liked people of all types. He enjoyed humanity.

But this morning he was consumed by hatred as well as by anger. The trouble was that he did not know whom he hated more or with whom he was more angry – Lady Paget or himself.

It did not matter. The simple fact was that he was going to make her respectable. And he was going to sleep with her enough times that she could preserve her pride and feel she was earning her salary.

His eyes focused upon a heading in the paper, and he read it and the accompanying article with great attention and without taking in a single word. It might have announced the end of the world and he would not have known it.

For of course he *did* care if she had killed her husband. It was at the crux of everything. Had she or had she not? She had said she had. Why say so if it was not true? He suspected, though, that much of what she had told him was not strictly true. And something about the way she had simply said *yes* to his question had not rung true.

Or was that wishful thinking on his part?

It was not a comfortable thing to know that the mistress he had just employed was a self-confessed murderer.

It was all very well to take into consideration the fact that she had probably been much abused. But actually to take up a pistol, which had probably not been simply lying around ready to be picked up and fired, and to point it at her husband's heart and pull the trigger, was . . .

Well, the very thought of it turned Stephen hot and cold.

It must have been unimaginable abuse if she had been driven to such desperate measures.

Unless she was evil.

Or unless she had not done it after all.

But why lie about such a thing?

And what sort of man was he to have been drawn into her net, even if he had imposed his own terms, when she had actually killed? Or said she had.

His brain felt very much as if it were whirling inside his skull just like a child's spinning top. At last he folded the paper neatly, set it aside, and rose to leave the club without speaking to anyone.

Alice, in a rare mood of open rebellion, refused to accompany Cassandra to Lady Carling's at-home. It was not that she did not approve of Cassie's attending such an event, especially when she had been invited by Lady Carling herself. Indeed, she thought it the very best thing that could possibly have come out of that risky business of last evening's ball. But she did *not* wish to meet Cassie's lover in any such public setting, where she would feel obliged to be civil to him.

'But it is to avoid going driving in the park with him that I want you with me, Alice,' Cassandra explained, watching her friend mending the seam of a pillowcase, a task that she ought to have been sharing. 'He mentioned a curricle. I would be very high off the ground and very much on public display. But there is room for only two on the seat of a curricle. I could refuse to abandon you if you were with me.'

But Alice would not go. She pressed her lips together and chose to be mulish. Her needle stabbed vengefully into the seam and back out again.

'You would be laughed to scorn, Cassie,' she said after a while. 'A widow of your age does not cling to a mere companion when a gentleman comes to take her on an outing.'

'You are not my *companion*,' Cassandra said. 'Not any longer. I have not been able to pay you for almost a year, and when I finally offered you some money this morning, you refused to take it.'

Alice wrapped the cotton thread about one finger and snapped it off rather than use the scissors, which were on a table at her elbow.

'I will not take one farthing of *his* money,' she said, 'or any other money you earn in such a way. It was not this I had in mind for you, Cassie, when you were a girl in my charge. Never this.'

For a moment her chin wobbled, but she brought it under control and pressed her lips together again.

'I think,' Cassandra said, 'he is perhaps a kind man, Alice. I think he is overpaying me, and I am sure he must know it. And he said that he would never − Well, he said that what is between us must always be mutual. That he would never − Well, *force* me.'

Alice turned the pillowcase the right way out, shook it furiously to rid it of some of the wrinkles, and rolled it ready to be ironed.

'Every piece of linen in this house is as close to being threadbare as makes no difference,' she grumbled irritably.

'After a week or two,' Cassandra said, 'we will be able to afford to buy new things to replace them.'

Alice glared.

'I am *not ever* going to set my head on any pillowcase bought with *his* money,' she said.

Cassandra sighed and lifted the hand that Roger was nudging with his cold nose. She set it down on his furry head, and he placed his chin on her lap, looked up at her with doleful eyes, and let out a sigh to match her own.

'His family seems genuinely genteel,' she said. 'They went out of their way to behave with kindness toward me last evening. They were at the same time, of course, saving themselves from embarrassment and perhaps even social disaster, but even so they all seemed like good people.'

'They will have an apoplexy apiece if they think he is courting you,' Alice said, 'or has taken you as his mistress.'

'Yes,' Cassandra agreed, pulling her fingers gently along Roger's silky ear. 'He is extremely handsome, Alice. He looks like an angel.'

'Some angel,' Alice said, setting her needle none too gently in the pincushion on the table. 'Coming home with you last night and then *paying* you this morning and offering more in future for more of the same. Some angel.'

Cassandra ran the fingers of her other hand along the stubby remains of Roger's other ear and held both ears up so that he looked sleepy and lopsided. She smiled at him and let go of his ears.

'Come with me this afternoon,' she said to Alice.

But Alice had her mind made up and was quite adamant.

'I am *not* going with you, Cassie,' she said, getting firmly to her feet. 'I have not been paid in almost a year, as you just pointed out, and that is as it should be. It also means

113

I am free. It means I am not your servant. And I can earn my own living and support the both of us as well as Mary and Belinda – and that dog – without your having to . . . Well. I know you think I am too old for anyone to employ, but I am only forty-two. I am not quite in my dotage. I am able-bodied enough to scrub floors if I have to or sew for twelve hours at a time in some seamstress's back room or do any number of other things. I am going to be busy on my own account this afternoon. I am going to call at some employment agencies. *Someone* must want me.'

'I do, Allie,' Cassandra said.

But Alice was not to be mollified. She went from the room, her back ramrod straight, her chin in the air, and left the door open behind her.

Soon a little face appeared about one side of it, and it broke into a delighted smile as the body followed the face into the doorway and then into the room.

'Doggie,' Belinda said, hurrying forward to catch him before he could flee.

But Roger, though an old, rather lethargic dog, was occasionally in the mood to play and was always willing to be petted. He met the child halfway across the room, his tail waving, his rear end wiggling, his tongue panting. She threw her arms about his neck, her gleeful laughter turning to high giggles and delighted screeches as he licked her face.

She had grown out of her dress about six months ago, but she was still wearing it. It was faded from many washings but spotlessly clean. All its worn places were carefully darned. Her cheeks were rosy from a recent washing – which would be repeated if Mary discovered that Roger had been kissing her. Her soft brown curls were held back from her face with a faded, half-frayed ribbon. She was barefoot, since she had outgrown her shoes and wore them only when she left the house.

She was three years old. Mary's love child.

And very, very precious.

'Hello, sweetheart,' Cassandra said.

Belinda turned a sunny smile on her and then giggled again as Roger rolled onto his back and waved his three paws in the air. She lay down on the floor beside him and patted his stomach and then wrapped one skinny little arm right about him.

'The doggie likes me,' she said.

'That is because you like him,' Cassandra said, smiling.

She would be able to pay Mary at last. She would even be able gradually to pay everything she owed her. Mary would be unwilling to take the back pay, but Cassandra would insist and Mary would not resist for long. She needed to buy new clothes for her daughter.

Cassandra would buy the child some little trinkets too. And Mary. Not Alice, though. Alice would not accept any gift in her present mood.

She had a protector, Cassandra thought, verbalizing the word very clearly in her mind. She was a mistress – paid for the sexual favors she would provide. There would, of course, be nothing mutual in the things that would happen between her and the Earl of Merton, despite his insistence that there would. For she would *never* want him despite his beauty and his undeniably appealing masculinity and virility. And despite what she suspected was a genuine kindness in his nature.

Nine years of marriage had killed any interest she could possibly have in what the Earl of Merton wanted her to enjoy with him. If he waited until she wanted what he wanted, he would wait forever and she would be taking money she had in no way earned.

She would earn her money. Every penny of it. She had *some* pride. He would never know that there was nothing mutual at all in their sexual relations.

She would give very good value for money.

It all seemed worthwhile as she watched the child play with the dog, both of them equally and blissfully happy – and trusting.

Two precious innocents.

Anything was worthwhile if it could push back by even one day the loss of such innocence.

8

Lady Carling's at-home was for ladies only. Stephen wondered as he lifted the door knocker and let it fall back against the door if a large number of them would still be in the drawing room or if by half past four most of them would have taken their leave. Perhaps Lady Paget would already have left in an attempt to avoid driving in the park with him.

Perhaps she had not even come, though that would be foolish of her if she hoped to be received ever again by at least some of her peers. She must surely have come to London with a longer-term plan than merely finding a protector to help pay her bills for a few months, until the end of the Season.

Carling's butler took Stephen's card up to the drawing room, and Stephen caught the buzz of feminine conversation as the door opened upstairs and then closed again. *Some* of the guests were still here.

'Lady Carling will be pleased to receive you, my lord,'

the butler said when he returned, and Stephen followed him back upstairs.

Many men would have been considerably disconcerted at the prospect of walking in on a company comprising exclusively ladies. Stephen was not among them. Most ladies, he found, were very willing to tease and laugh when they had one man at their mercy, and Stephen was always happy to oblige them and to tease and laugh right back at them. He was still somewhat out of humor today, it was true, but he had pushed most of his anger and irritability away while walking home from White's for luncheon. He could not remain angry for any protracted length of time. Or at least, he *would* not. No one would be granted that power over him.

He had apologized to Philbin, and his valet had made a stiff bow of acceptance and in so doing had spotted a virtually invisible film of dust over Stephen's boots, acquired when he had had the effrontery to *walk* home in them when those particular boots were meant to be worn only indoors or inside a carriage, as his lordship very well knew. Did his lordship know *nothing* of the damage such dust could do to the leather? And would his lordship remove them *right now* before the damage was irreparable and Philbin found it quite impossible to hold up his head before the other servants for the rest of his days?

Stephen had sat meekly down and allowed his boots to be pulled off, and the relationship had been restored to a happy normality.

Carling's butler opened the drawing room doors with a flourish and announced Stephen in deep, ringing tones that brought first silence to the room and then a burst of flutterings and twitterings from the ladies gathered there.

Lady Carling was on her feet and coming toward him, one hand outstretched.

'Lord Merton,' she said. 'How delightful.'

'Never tell me, ma'am,' he said, taking her hand in his and looking at her in mock horror, 'that your at-home is only for ladies. And all the way here I have been composing an abject apology for being so late arriving.'

'Well, in that case, Lord Merton,' she said, 'I will hear it anyway. We will *all* hear it.'

There was a chorus of assent from the ladies gathered there.

'Well, you see,' he said, 'I thought it would be mainly Carling's friends who would be here, and so I drove through the park on my way in the hope of brightening my afternoon by seeing some of my favorite ladies before I came. And when I found the park almost deserted, I drove over to Bond Street to see if any of them were *there*, lured by the shops. Then I tried Oxford Street, but all to no avail. And *now* I discover that every single one of the ladies I most wished to see has been here all the time.'

His outrageous flatteries were met with derision and laughter, and he looked about at them all, a grin on his face. All three of his sisters were there. So was Lady Paget, seated beside Nessie. She was smartly dressed in green again, though it was a sage green today instead of emerald. Her clothes must be one of the few assets she had been allowed to keep after her widowhood. She was wearing no jewelry, just as she had not been last evening.

She did not join in the laughter and teasing of the other ladies. But she did smile – that faint, slightly mocking smile she had worn at the ball last evening and in her bedchamber early this morning. It was a smile he had quickly realized was part of a mask she wore to cover any suggestion of vulnerability she might be feeling.

The sun shining through the window was on the side of her face and in her hair. She looked vividly, almost shockingly beautiful.

'Ladies,' Lady Carling said, linking an arm through his, 'shall we send him away again? Or shall we keep him?'

'Keep him,' a few ladies said, amid laughter.

'It would be a pity, Ethel,' the dowager Lady Sinden said, raising a lorgnette to her eyes and regarding Stephen through it, 'to doom our poor Lord Merton to wandering the streets and haunting the park for the next hour while he waits for his *favorite* ladies to leave your drawing room. It would be best to keep him here and thus keep him happy. Is it your curricle you have been driving half over London, Merton? Or a more sensible carriage?'

'My curricle, ma'am,' he said.

'Then you cannot take *me* riding in the park afterward,' she said, 'even though I am sure I must be your *very* favorite among the present company. I stopped riding in curricles when I turned seventy a number of years ago. I can get up into them, but I cannot get down out of them without two stout footmen having to lift me bodily down.'

'They must be weaklings of footmen even if they *are* stout, ma'am,' Stephen said, still grinning at her. 'I could lift you down with one arm. You can weigh no more than a feather.'

'Impudent puppy,' she said with a bark of laughter that set her three chins to swaying.

'But alas, ma'am,' he said, 'I cannot prove it to you today. I have come because I have already persuaded another lady to drive in the park with me, and she is here.'

'And who is the fortunate lady?' Lady Carling asked as she drew him down to sit beside her on a sofa. 'Did I promise such a thing last evening and have simply forgotten? But how could any lady *possibly* forget such a thing?'

She leaned forward to the tea tray in order to pour his tea.

'Alas, ma'am,' he said, 'Sir Graham was at your side and I dared not even ask. He might have throttled me. Lady Paget has agreed to drive with me.'

There was a small silence in the room.

'Stephen has a sporting curricle,' his sister Kate said, 'a quite terrifying-looking beast. But he is a notable whip, Lady Paget. You will be quite safe with him.'

'It had not occurred to me,' Lady Paget said in her low, velvet voice, 'that I might not be.'

Her eyes met Stephen's as he raised his cup to his lips, and for a moment he felt a return of this morning's anger. She was beautiful and she was desirable and she had him tangled in her web, like a spider with a fly. An ugly image. But an apt one.

'And it is a beautiful day for a drive,' Meg said. 'I thought it would rain this morning, but now, look, there is not a cloud in the sky. I do hope this weather bodes well for the summer.'

'It is more likely, Lady Sheringford,' Mrs. Craven said, shaking her head and looking mournful, 'that we will suffer for this fine spell all through July and August.'

The conversation fell into comfortably familiar channels until Stephen had finished his tea and got to his feet.

'Thank you for admitting me to your party, ma'am,' he said to Lady Carling. 'But if you will excuse Lady Paget and me, we will take our leave now. My horses will be getting frisky.'

He bowed to all the ladies and smiled at each of his sisters – and held out an arm to Lady Paget, who had also risen to her feet. She slipped one hand beneath his elbow as she thanked Lady Carling for her hospitality, and they left the room together.

There would be no great rush of conversation after the door closed behind them, Stephen realized – his sisters were there. But there would be a great deal of it over various dinner tables this evening and in other drawing rooms tomorrow.

And yet, if he was not completely mistaken, a few invitations would soon begin to trickle into Lady Paget's house. A few hostesses would realize the advantages of having her at their entertainments before the novelty of her notoriety had begun to wear off. And by that time invitations might be sent to her as a matter of course.

'It is a smart curricle,' she said as they stepped out of doors and the groom who had been walking his team back and forth in the street brought the vehicle up to the steps. 'I wish you would take me directly home, though, Lord Merton.'

'We will go through the park, as planned,' he said. 'It will be crowded at this hour.'

'My point exactly,' she said.

He took her hand in his, but she did not need any other assistance to ascend to the high seat. He went around the vehicle and climbed up beside her before taking the ribbons from the groom's hand.

'Are you so eager, then,' she said, 'to flaunt your new mistress before all your male friends, Lord Merton?'

He turned his head to look at her.

'You choose to insult me, Lady Paget,' he said. 'You will find me more circumspect, I hope. In private you are my *lover*. It is a relationship that concerns no one but you and me. In public you are Lady Paget, an acquaintance, perhaps even my friend, whom I choose to escort about town from time to time. And that description applies when you are with me and when you are not. Even when I am alone with my *male friends*.'

'You are angry,' she said.

'Yes,' he agreed. 'I am angry. Or, rather, I *was* angry. I daresay you did not mean to insult me. Are you ready to go?'

He smiled at her.

'I believe,' she said, 'we would both look remarkably foolish if we were to sit here from now until darkness falls, Lord Merton. I am ready.'

He gave his horses the signal to start.

Just two days ago, Cassandra thought as the curricle turned in to Hyde Park, she had walked here quite anonymously with Alice, and she had gone almost unnoticed beneath her heavy widow's veil. It had been a rare treat. She had *always* been noticed, even as a gawky, freckled child with hair that reminded people of carrots. She had been noticed as a growing girl, when her developing body had made her willowy and her freckles had begun to fade and people had stopped comparing her hair to carrots. And she had been noticed as a woman. She knew that her height and her figure and her hair drew men's eyes and held them wherever she went.

Her beauty – if that was what her appearance added up

to – had not always been an asset. Indeed, it rarely had been. Sometimes – most times, in fact – it was something to hide behind. Her smile – that half-scornful, half-arrogant expression that lifted the corners of her lips and went together with a raised chin and languidly observant eyes – was no new thing. It kept other people from encroaching too closely upon the person who lurked within.

This morning the Earl of Merton had called it a mask.

Last evening her beauty had been an asset. It had got her a wealthy protector when she quite desperately needed one. Though she wished now she had chosen someone else, someone who would be content with visiting her stealthily at night for one purpose only and paying her regularly for services rendered.

'Why did you come to fetch me from Lady Carling's,' she asked him, 'when doing so forced you into making a very public announcement that you were going to drive me in the park?'

'I believe,' he said, 'that every member of the beau monde would know by this evening whether I had come to Lady Carling's or waited for you to return home first.'

'And yet,' she said, 'you are angry with me. You were angry this morning, and you are angry again this afternoon. You do not really like me, do you?'

It was a very foolish question to ask. Did she want this liaison to end almost before it had begun? Was it necessary that he like her? Or that he pretend to? Was it not enough that he desired her? That he would pay to satisfy that desire?

'Lady Paget,' he asked her, 'do *you* like *me*?'

Everyone else did. He was, she suspected, society's darling. And it was not just his extraordinarily handsome, angelic looks. It was also his charm, his ease of manner, his sunny demeanor, his . . . Oh, that extra something that no words could adequately describe. Charisma? Vitality? Kindness? Genuineness? His beauty and popularity did not appear to have made him conceited.

He had taken his beauty and used it to make people his friends, to make them smile and feel good about themselves. She had taken her beauty and snared for herself first a husband and now a lover. He was a giver and she was a taker.

Was he?

Was *she*?

'I do not even know you,' she said, 'except in the biblical sense. How can I know if I like you or not?'

He turned his head to gaze very directly into her face – and she realized how very close they were, crammed together on the seat of his sporting curricle. She could smell his cologne.

'Exactly,' he said. 'I have no idea either if I will like you or not, Cassandra. But it seems strange to me that last evening you set out deliberately to seduce me while today you seem intent upon getting rid of me. Is that what you want?'

She wished his eyes were not so blue or his gaze so intense. There was no escaping blue eyes. Blue eyes made her uncomfortable. They drew her in deep and in so doing stripped her of everything she most wanted to keep in place – *not* her clothes, but . . . Well, they were fanciful thoughts, and she had never had them before. She had never noticed before now that she disliked blue eyes. Probably she did not. It was just *his* blue eyes.

He had called her Cassandra.

'What I want,' she said, smiling at him and lowering her voice, 'is *you*, Stephen. In my house, in my bedchamber, in my bed. All this is quite unnecessary.'

She swept her arm about to indicate the park and the afternoon crush of carriages and horses and pedestrians they were fast approaching.

'I have always thought,' he said, 'that a relationship between a man and a woman – even that between a man and his lover – ought to be about more than just what happens between them in bed. Otherwise it is not a relationship at all.'

She laughed at him, and something tugged at her heart and was instantly quelled.

'If you believe sex is not enough,' she said, 'then you have not yet spent enough time in *my* bed, Stephen. You will learn to change your thinking. Will you come tonight?'

She was not sure she had ever said the word *sex* aloud before now. It was extraordinarily difficult to say.

'Do you wish me to come?' he asked her.

'But of course,' she said. 'How else am I to earn my living?'

He turned his head to look at her again and she read in his eyes not the desire of a man who looked forward to bedding his mistress again tonight but something that looked almost like pain. Or perhaps it was merely reproach.

He did not truly believe, surely, that they could ever be *lovers*. He could not be *that* naive or unrealistic.

It was too late for further private conversation. It was partly a relief – she was wishing more than ever that she had chosen another man last evening, someone less innocent, less *decent*, someone more earthy, someone who would accept the connection between them simply for what it was – sex for money, regular sex for a regular salary. Someone who had not accused her of wearing a mask.

Even *thinking* the word *sex* was difficult.

Partly it was no relief at all to be among the crowd, to be on display as she had been last evening but even more so if that were possible. She was perched on a seat above most of the crowd. It was virtually impossible for anyone *not* to see her.

She wondered if it was deliberate on Lord Merton's part, and guessed that it was. He surely had other carriages that he might have used. And yet he had not brought her to flaunt before his male acquaintances. He had been angry when she had suggested it.

He smiled cheerfully at everyone, touching his hat to the ladies, calling greetings, stopping to exchange a few words whenever someone showed a willingness to talk to *him*. Cassandra guessed it was far fewer people than usual. But whenever someone did stop him, he introduced her, and she inclined her head and sometimes spoke.

As with most of the guests in Lady Carling's drawing room, some people were willing to speak with her, Cassandra found, even if only to ask her how she did. But of course, she had had Lady Carling to sponsor her there, and she had the Earl of Merton here. There had been the Earl and Countess of Sheringford last evening.

Perhaps there were always a few kind people. Perhaps her cynicism had become too extreme. Perhaps she need not be the total outcast she had expected to be. Or perhaps now she was a curiosity to whom some people could not resist drawing close. Once the novelty had worn off, so would her welcome.

It was hard *not* to be cynical.

It did not matter. In many ways she had always been an outcast.

Predictably, it was mostly gentlemen who stopped to speak with Lord Merton and therefore to be introduced to her. And Cassandra looked at them all and wondered if she might have chosen more wisely last evening. But how could one choose wisely when one knew absolutely nothing about the man concerned except perhaps his name and the fact that he was probably wealthy? Though how could one know even that when so many gentlemen lived beyond their means and were up to their eyebrows and beyond with debt?

She had thought she had chosen a husband wisely. She had been eighteen then. She was twenty-eight now. Perhaps the only wisdom she had gained in the intervening years was to know that when one chose a man to give security and stability to one's life, one ought to choose a protector rather than a husband.

Freedom was worth more than anything else of value life had to offer. Yet for a woman it was so very elusive.

Baron Montford came to exchange pleasantries with Cassandra and to chat with his brother-in-law for a few minutes. He had three other gentlemen with him, including Mr. Huxtable, who still looked somewhat satanic to Cassandra. He looked very directly at her with his dark eyes while the other gentlemen talked and laughed. At some time in his life his nose had been broken and not set quite straight, she could see. She was very glad she had not chosen *him* last night. She had the feeling that his eyes could see through her skull to the hair at the back of her head.

And then, just as those gentlemen were moving on in

the opposite direction from the one the curricle was taking and Cassandra looked around again, she saw a familiar face – that of an auburn-haired, good-looking young man, who was sitting in an open barouche beside a pretty young lady in pink. He was smiling at something she was saying to a couple of scarlet-clad officers on horseback.

The Earl of Merton's curricle was almost upon them. The officers rode on, the young lady smiled at the smiling young man, and they both turned their heads to look about at the crowd.

Their eyes alit upon Cassandra at almost the same moment. The two carriages were almost abreast of each other. Without thought Cassandra smiled warmly and half leaned forward.

'*Wesley!*' she cried.

The young lady put both hands up to her mouth and turned her head sharply away – as several others had done to a lesser degree during the past fifteen minutes or so. The young man's smile faded, and his eyes regarded Cassandra with dismay, wavered, and then looked away from her.

'Move on,' he said with some impatience to the coachman, who really had nowhere to go until all the carriages in front of him moved on too.

The Earl of Merton had a little more space in front of his curricle. Even so, it seemed to take an excruciatingly long time for the two vehicles to have completely passed each other.

'Someone you know?' Lord Merton asked quietly.

'Take me home,' she said. 'Please. I have had enough.'

It took him a little while to draw free of the crowd, but at last they were moving at a faster pace along a path that was blessedly free of much other traffic.

'Young, was it not?' he said. 'Sir Wesley Young? I have only a slight acquaintance with him.'

'I would not know,' she said foolishly, spreading her hands in her lap. 'I have never seen him before.'

'He just *looked* like a Wesley, then, did he?' He glanced across at her, smiling. 'Don't let him worry you. Giving the cut direct is something some members of the *ton* delight in doing. Many others have *not* given it. I believe you will find more and more people accepting you and treating you with open good manners as the days go on.'

'Yes,' she said. And she watched her hands begin to tremble and then shake. She curled one into a hard fist and gripped the handrail beside her with the other. She clamped her teeth hard together so that they would not chatter.

'Ah,' he said as they approached the park entrance at Marble Arch, and for a moment his gloved hand covered hers on her lap, 'you really *do* know him, then.'

'My brother,' she said, and clamped her teeth together again.

He had come to visit her a few times during her marriage. He had come to the funeral last year. And he had hugged her tightly afterward and assured her that he did not for a moment believe that she had had anything to do with the death. He had told her he loved her and always would. He had urged her to return to London with him, to live with him until she was over her mourning and grief and was healed enough to return home to live at the dower house.

And then, after she had said no and he had gone, he had written to her – twice. And then suddenly silence, even though she had continued to write to *him*. Until a

130

month ago, when she had written to tell him that her life had become so intolerable that she had to leave, that she would have to impose upon his good nature until she had her life in order and somehow found a way to move on. He had written back then to tell her that she must on no account come to London since her notoriety had preceded her. Besides, he would be unable to offer her any help in the immediate future as he had promised friends to travel to Scotland with them to explore the Highlands. He expected to be gone for at least a year. He was allowing the lease on his rooms to lapse.

He loved her, Wesley had assured her in that final letter. But it was impossible for him to change his plans – too many other people would be inconvenienced. And Cassie *must not* – he had underlined the words twice and so heavily that the ink had splattered into tiny blots above and below – come to London. He did not want her to be hurt.

'Your brother,' Lord Merton said. 'You were a Young, then?'

'Yes,' she said.

He turned his team out onto the street, slowing to avoid a crossing sweep, who jumped back out of the way and then reached out to pluck out of the air the coin Stephen threw.

'I am sorry,' he said.

That she was a Young? Or that her own brother had just given her the cut direct? Or both?

It was only after the funeral, of course, that things had got really nasty, that the accusations had started to fly, that *murder* had been spoken of rather than *accident*.

Cassandra wanted to be at home. She wanted to be in her own room, the door firmly shut behind her, the bedcovers over her body and her head. She wanted to sleep – deeply and dreamlessly.

'You need not apologize for something you did not do,' she said, raising her chin and speaking as haughtily as she was able. 'I was surprised to see him, that is all. I thought he was in Scotland. I daresay something happened to cause him to change his mind.'

Gentlemen did not go touring Scotland during the spring, when the whole of the fashionable world was in London for the Season. And gentlemen who were really not very wealthy at all did not go touring for a whole year. Gentlemen who were traveling in a group would not find it difficult to excuse one of their number who needed to change his plans because of a pressing family concern.

She surely had not believed him when she read his letter – so much shorter and terser than the letters he had used to write. She had chosen to believe because the alternative was too painful.

Now she could disbelieve no longer.

'Tell me about him,' Lord Merton said.

She laughed.

'I daresay, Lord Merton,' she said, 'you know him far better than I. Perhaps *you* ought to tell *me* about him.'

The streets seemed unusually crowded. Their progress was slow. Or perhaps it only seemed that way because she was so desperate to be home and alone.

He did not say anything.

'Our mother died giving birth to him,' she said. 'I was five years old, and I played mother to him from that day forward. I gave him something he would have lacked otherwise – undivided and total affection and attention. Hugs and kisses and endless monologues. And he gave

132

me something, someone, to love in place of my mother. We adored each other, which is unusual in a brother and sister, I believe. But though I had a governess from a very young age, and though Wesley was sent to school eventually, we clung to each other all through our growing years – or until my marriage when I was eighteen and he was thirteen, anyway. Our father was so often gone.'

He had been a compulsive and notorious gambler. Their fortunes had fluctuated from day to day. There was never any fixed home or security, even in the good times. There had always been the knowledge, understood even by young children, that desperate times were just the turn of a card away.

'I am sorry,' Lord Merton said again, and Cassandra realized that he was slowing before her house. She had not even noticed turning into Portman Street.

He secured the ribbons, jumped down from his seat, and came around the curricle to lift her down to the pavement.

'You have nothing to be sorry for,' she said again. 'No love is ever unconditional, Lord Merton. And no love is ever eternal. If you learn nothing else from me, learn that. It may save you from some pain and heartache in the future.'

He took her hand in his and raised it to his lips.

'May I expect you tonight?' she asked him.

'Yes,' he said. 'I have some commitments this evening, but I will come afterward if I may.'

If you may.' She smiled rather scornfully at him. 'I am yours whenever you choose, Lord Merton. You are paying well enough for me.'

She saw his lips tighten and understood what she was

133

doing to herself. She was showing him only darkness. Yet he was all light. And if light was stronger than darkness – though she was not at all convinced that it was – then it would not take him long to draw away from the aura of gloom she was no doubt casting over him.

She smiled a little differently, with facial muscles that were stiff with disuse.

'And if I may throw some of your own words from this morning back at you,' she said, 'you are mine whenever I choose. I choose tonight. I look forward to it with the greatest pleasure. I look forward to giving *you* pleasure. And I will. That is a promise. I cannot bear to take without giving in equal measure, you see.'

He stepped up to the door and rattled the knocker against it.

'I shall see you later, then,' he said. 'Think of those who have been kind to you today. Forget those who have not.'

She held on to her smile. She added a sparkle to her eyes.

'I shall be too busy thinking of just one person,' she said. 'I shall think of no one but you.'

The door opened and Mary looked out. Belinda was clinging to her skirt and peeping out from behind it. Roger came padding past them, bobbing down the steps on his three legs. He rubbed against her, his tongue lolling. He looked at the Earl of Merton and let out a token woof, which would not have scared a mouse within two feet of him.

Lord Merton looked from one to another of them, rubbed Roger's head briefly, touched the brim of his hat, and strode around his curricle to climb into the seat again. Cassandra watched him drive along the street.

'Is that *him*, my lady?' Mary asked rather stiffly.

Cassandra looked at her in some surprise. But there was no keeping anything from servants, even when there was a houseful of them.

'The Earl of Merton?' she said. 'Yes.'

Mary said no more and Cassandra swept past her into the house. It was a relief not to see Alice waiting there for her. She hurried upstairs to her room, Roger bobbing along beside her.

9

Alice arrived home soon after Cassandra.

She had trudged about London for four hours in the heat of the afternoon, going from one employment agency to another without any success. Her age was against her in almost any form of employment that was available. The fact that she had had only one employer and two forms of employment – as governess and lady's companion – in all her working life for the past twenty-two years was against her, despite her effort to explain that the very longevity of her employment proved that she must be both steady and trustworthy. She could not expect to be employed as a housekeeper, one of the few forms of employment for which her age might qualify her, since she had no experience in the tasks involved, and she could not expect to be anyone's chef for the very simple reason that she did not know how to cook anything more complex than a boiled egg.

The best she had been able to do was leave her name

and letters of introduction and recommendation at the two agencies that were willing to take them, in the faint hope that something would turn up.

Alice was well aware that it was a very faint hope.

The only really good thing that *had* happened to her during the afternoon was that she had encountered an old friend while she was sitting on a bench beneath the shade of a tree on the outer edges of a churchyard to rest her aching feet. She was amazed that she had recognized him after so many years. She was even more amazed that *he* had recognized *her*. But they both had, and he had stopped to talk with her and even sit beside her for a few minutes. Did Cassie remember Mr. Golding?

'Wesley's tutor?' Cassandra said after thinking for a moment.

'You *do* remember,' Alice said, beaming.

Cassandra remembered him. He had been a whole head shorter than her father, a thin, dark-haired, earnest young man with wire-framed spectacles. He had been hired when Wesley was eight and their father had just won one of his rare windfalls. Less than a month later the inevitable crash had come and Mr. Golding had been forced to leave, unable to stay when his employer could not pay him – though Alice had stayed, as always.

Cassandra remembered him only because she had been thirteen at the time, just the age when girls began to develop an awareness of men. She had fallen secretly and passionately in love with him after he had smiled at her one day and called her Miss Young and inclined his head to her with flattering deference as though she were an adult. She had mourned his departure for a whole week after he left,

137

convinced that she would never *ever* either forget him or love another.

'How is he?' she asked.

'Very well indeed,' Alice said. 'He is secretary to a *cabinet* minister, Cassie, and is looking very prosperous and very smart indeed. His hair has turned gray at the temples. He looks very distinguished.'

It struck Cassandra then that perhaps she had not been the only one in love with him fifteen years ago. He and Alice had probably been close in age, and for a whole month they had worked in near proximity to each other.

'He asked after you,' Alice said, 'and was surprised to hear that I am still with you. He called you *Miss Young*. Perhaps he did not hear of your marriage.'

And Alice did not tell him? Cassandra did not blame her.

'I told him you were now Lady Paget and a widow,' Alice said. 'He sent his regards.'

Ah.

And that was the last they would ever hear of Mr. Allan Golding, Cassandra thought, smiling at an unusually flushed Alice. She felt sorry for Alice's sake. She could not recall a time when Alice had had a close friend of her own.

They had dinner together and sat in the small sitting room afterward. Cassandra glanced wistfully more than once at the fireplace, in which kindling and coal had been set ready to be lit. But there was so very little coal left in the bin outside the kitchen door and, though she had some money now, there was not enough to allow for extravagances. She must save every penny she was able. Summer was coming, and all the *ton* would leave town then, including, no doubt, the Earl of Merton. She dared not think far enough ahead to decide what she would do then. But in preparation for the time when she must consider it, she must save as much as she could.

It was not a cold evening, only slightly chilly.

'He is coming tonight, I suppose,' Alice said abruptly at last, her head bent over some mending she was doing. She had not made any reference until now to the way Cassandra had spent the afternoon.

'Yes,' Cassandra said. 'He is.'

Alice stitched on, as if she had not heard.

'What I ought to do,' she said after five minutes or so had elapsed, 'is rob a stagecoach – with smoking pistols and a black mask.'

She raised her head when Cassandra said nothing, and they stared at each other until neither could control her facial muscles any longer and they bellowed with laughter, doubled over with it. They mopped their eyes, glanced at each other, and went off into whoops again – all far in excess of the humor of the joke.

And then they sat back in their chairs and looked at each other again.

'Allie,' Cassandra said fondly, 'he is a decent man. I did not choose him for that reason, or even for his looks. I chose him because I knew he must be as rich as Croesus and because I knew I could attract him. But some good fairy – or perhaps some good angel – was watching over me. He is kind and decent.'

And uncomfortable to be with. And the possessor of two blue eyes that could draw her in deep enough to drown.

'He is *not* decent,' Alice said, the laughter of a minute ago forgotten, 'if he is prepared to pay money for – No man is decent if he will do *that*, Cassie.'

'But he is a *man*,' Cassandra said. 'And I can be very alluring when I want to be. Last evening I wanted to be. He did not stand a chance, Allie. You must not blame him. Blame me if you must.'

Alice was not to be mollified, however, even though Cassandra smiled beguilingly at her.

'Besides,' Cassandra said, her smile fading as she sat back farther in her chair and gazed into the unlit coals, 'I think he has engaged my services as much out of kindness as out of lust. He is not stupid, Allie, and I am not much of a liar. He knows why I sought him out. I was really quite open about it this morning. There was no point in *not* being. He knows that my interest in him is strictly monetary, and I think he agreed to my terms because he felt sorry for me.'

It was a humiliating admission. If she had been the irresistible courtesan she had thought to be, he would have accepted her terms for no other reason than that they would give him unlimited access to her bed and body. It would have been so much better that way.

Alice was looking steadily at her, her needle suspended above her work.

'It is getting too late for you to be sewing,' Cassandra said. 'It is quite dark, yet I hate to light a candle before it is absolutely necessary.'

She had squandered candles last night. She must not continue to do that.

'You are tired,' she said. 'You have had a long, busy day. Why don't you go to the kitchen and make yourself a cup of tea and take it up to bed?'

'You do not want me here when he comes,' Alice said, threading her needle through the fabric, setting her work aside, and getting to her feet. 'And I do not want to be here either. I could not be civil to him. Good night, Cassie. I wish you did not have to do this for my sake, at least.'

'You have not been paid for almost a year,' Cassandra reminded her. 'You have done a great deal for my sake, Allie. You did not get paid through most of my childhood either, did you? But you stayed even though at that time you would have been able to find other employment without any trouble at all.'

'I loved you,' Alice said.

'I know.'

Cassandra went into the kitchen with her. Mary was cleaning the old grate on which she did the cooking. Roger was lying on the hearth. He thumped his tail in greeting without lifting his head.

'Mary,' Cassandra said, 'will you *never* stop working? That grate has probably not gleamed as brightly in all its long lifetime. Go to bed.'

'I'll never stop working for *you*, my lady,' Mary said fervently. 'Not after all of what you done for me, first coaxing his lordship to keep me on when Billy went away and I found out about Belinda being on the way, and then trying to protect me when his lordship would have—'

'Then do my bidding and go to bed,' Cassandra said, interrupting her. 'And if you hear a knock at the door, ignore it. I will answer it.'

'And then bringing me here with you when Billy was gone again and his present lordship dismissed me before he come back,' Mary added, refusing to be daunted. 'What you ought to do, my lady, is let *me* answer the door and do with that gentleman what you plan to do. It is only right and fitting. He can pay *me,* and I will give the money to *you.*'

'Oh, Mary.' Cassandra closed the distance between them and hugged her, heedless of her grubby apron and hands. 'That is the dearest offer anyone has made me in a long, long while. But you must not worry. The Earl of Merton is a kind and decent man and I like him. And it has been a long time . . . Well, never mind. But sometimes work can also be pleasure, you know.'

She felt her cheeks flushing and wished she had not tried to give any explanation at all.

Alice, having finished making her tea, banged the kettle down on the hob.

'He *is* a handsome gent,' Mary conceded. 'He looks like an angel, don't he, my lady?'

'I think maybe he is one,' Cassandra said. 'An angel sent to save us all. Go to bed now, both of you, so that I can get ready for him. And don't look at me, Alice, as if I were preparing myself for my own execution. He is *gorgeous.* There, I have said it. He is gorgeous and he is my lover and I am happy about it. It is *not* all about money. I like him and I am going to be happy with him. You will see. After a year of wearing black and being increasingly gloomy, I am going to be *happy.* With an *angel.* Be happy *for* me.'

He had called her *outrageous* last evening, and, oh, dear, she was.

They were both sniveling when they went off to bed.

Not, Cassandra guessed, with happiness.

And yet she had not completely lied, she realized in some surprise, even dismay. There *was* a part of her that almost looked forward to the coming night. She had been

142

lonely for a long, long time. She still was lonely. At least the night – and her bed – would not be empty. Not tonight, anyway, and not, if she was very fortunate, for most of the nights in the foreseeable future.

There had to be *some* silver lining to the cloud that had hung so persistently over her for so long. Surely there must be.

Perhaps being bedded by the Earl of Merton would push back the loneliness just a little bit.

Perhaps he was the silver lining.

She was so *weary* of the darkness.

Please, please, let there be some light.

Stephen dined at Cavendish Square with Vanessa and Elliott and a few other guests. Inevitably the latter included one unmarried young lady, who had come with her father.

His sisters were not persistent matchmakers. Indeed, they were all quite vocal in their hope that he would not marry too early in life and that when he *did* marry it would be for love. But they were not above drawing his attention to young ladies who were eligible and might just take his fancy. They knew his tastes too.

Miss Soames was to his taste. She was young and pretty and slender. She was sweet-natured and vivacious and had an infectious gurgle of a laugh. She had manners and conversation. She was modest but not overly shy.

Stephen sat beside her at dinner. He sat beside her in one of the carriages that conveyed them all to the theater afterward, and he sat next to her in Elliott's private box. He enjoyed her company and believed she enjoyed his.

It was an evening typical of many others.

And also different from many others.

For there was scarcely a moment all evening when his mind was free of thoughts about Cassandra.

And despite himself he looked forward with some impatience to seeing her again later.

He ought not. He ought to cling to the world that included Miss Soames and Lady Christobel Foley and their like, the world of his male friends and activities, the world of his family, the world of his parliamentary duties and all the other responsibilities that went with his title and his landholdings.

The world with which he had grown familiar in the past eight years. It was a world he liked.

Cassandra, Lady Paget, was of another world, and there was darkness there. And something undeniably enticing too.

It was not just the promise of frequent sex.

Surely there was more than just that to attract him.

But it was an unwilling, uneasy attraction, whatever it was.

Sir Wesley Young was at the theater too. He was seated in a box with seven other people, one of them the lady with whom he had been driving in the park this afternoon. There was a great deal of merriment in their box during the course of the evening.

His presence did not help Stephen concentrate his attention upon Miss Soames and the other members of his brother-in-law's party. He tried to imagine one of his own sisters in Lady Paget's situation – Nessie, for example. Would he have been able to ignore her in the park this afternoon, hopeful that the *ton* would not discover that she was his sister? Would he be able to make merry here tonight, knowing what he had done?

It was inconceivable! He would always stand by his sisters

no matter the consequences to himself. Some forms of love *were* unconditional and eternal, despite what Cassandra had said to the contrary.

While he ought to have been enjoying the play, one of his favorite activities, he entertained mental images of her five-year-old self hovering over her newborn brother, hugging and kissing him, crooning to him, talking to him, loving him because there was no one to love her except an often-absent father, and no one to love *him* unless she did it.

And Stephen's mind kept reverting to that scene at her door this afternoon.

The very domestic scene.

There had been the young, thin, wide-eyed maid who looked more like a waif than the sort of battle-axe of a servant he would have expected if he had thought about it. And a shy, mop-haired child with rosy cheeks. And an elderly dog who looked as if he had been through a war or two in his time but had lost none of his affection for his mistress.

Perhaps, he thought, Cassandra had had more than her own survival and well-being in mind when she had gone to Meg's ball in search of a protector.

Perhaps there was light in her life after all, even if it had been dimmed by circumstances.

This afternoon her house had looked rather . . .

Well, like a home.

As he left Merton House on foot after the theater party was at an end, Stephen's feelings were mixed. He wanted to see Cassandra again. He wanted to be inside her bedchamber again. He wanted to make love to her again, perhaps with a little more finesse this time and a little more attention to giving her full pleasure.

At the same time, he felt uneasy about conducting such business inside her home. Perhaps he ought to have rented a house in which to conduct their liaison. Perhaps he still ought.

He would think about it tomorrow.

10

Cassandra sat in the darkened drawing room as she waited. She had changed into a silk and lace nightgown that she very rarely wore. She wore a flowing robe over it. Both were white. She had brushed out her hair and tied it at the nape of her neck with a white ribbon.

Like a bride awaiting her bridegroom, she thought.

Some irony.

And it was not a comfortable outfit to wear in the chilly room.

He came late. But she had not been expecting that he would be early. She listened for the clopping of horses' hooves, the jingling of harness, the rumbling of wheels. But she was taken by surprise after all when the knocker rapped rather softly against the door.

He had come on foot.

He was wearing a long black opera cloak, she could see when she opened the door, and a tall silk hat, which he removed as soon as he saw her. She saw him smile in the light of a street lamp, and the cloak swirled around him as he stepped closer.

He was all darkness and light and virility.

Her breath quickened, half with dread, half with . . .

Well.

'Cassandra,' he said, 'I hope I am not very much later than you expected.'

He stepped into the hall and shut and bolted the door himself as the single candle in the wall sconce shivered from the outside air.

'It is only half past eleven,' she said. 'Did you have a pleasant evening?'

She turned to lead the way upstairs, extinguishing the candle as she passed it. Within a week or two, she supposed, this would all be very routine. Perhaps even tedious. There was much to be said for tedium. Tonight she could feel her heart thumping, robbing her of breath. She was as nervous as a bride, even though they had done this just last night and tonight should be easier.

That had been a little different, of course. She had not been his mistress then, employed to offer just this service. Paid in advance.

'Yes, thank you,' he said. 'I dined with Moreland and my sister and their other guests and then went to the theater with them.'

And now to the house of his mistress. A complete gentleman's night out.

She was glad Alice's room was on the upper floor with Mary's and Belinda's. She had wanted Alice to take the room next to hers when they moved in, but there was too much noise from the street outside, Alice had protested, sensitive to it after ten years of living in the country. The higher room was sure to be quieter.

Cassandra extinguished the candle outside her room and stepped inside. He followed her in and shut the door. There was enough light. She had angled the side mirrors of the dressing table, as she had done last night, so that the light from the single candle was many times reflected.

'May I pour you some wine?' She crossed the room to the tray she had set on a table beside the bed. It had been an extravagance, the wine, but today she had been able to afford it.

'Thank you,' he said.

She poured a glass for each of them and handed him one. He was standing not far inside the door. He had set his cloak over the back of a chair, his hat upon the seat. He was wearing black evening clothes with an ivory embroidered waistcoat, a white shirt with crisp collar points, and a neckcloth that had been knotted by an expert, though it was not ostentatious.

The Earl of Merton did not need ostentation. He had enough beauty and charisma of person to make further adornment quite unnecessary.

She clinked her glass against his.

'To pleasure,' she said, and smiled into his eyes.

'To *mutual* pleasure,' he agreed, and held her gaze as they both drank.

Even in the dim, flickering light of the candle his eyes were very blue.

He took her glass from her hand and carried it, with his own, to set back on the tray. Then he turned and opened his hands, palms out, toward her.

'Come,' he said.

He was standing right beside the bed. She half expected that he would tumble her to it without further ado and proceed to business. Instead, he set both arms loosely about her waist.

'And how was *your* evening?' he asked her.

'I sat in the drawing room watching Alice stitching at some mending,' she said, 'and did absolutely nothing myself. I was shamefully lazy.'

She had been horribly agitated, actually, though she had tried not to show it – or even admit it to herself.

Until last night she had only ever lain with Nigel. And that, God help her, had had the sanctity of marriage. It had not felt sinful.

Did this, then? They were consenting adults. They were harming no one by being together.

'Sometimes,' he said, 'laziness is a thoroughly enjoyable luxury.'

'Yes, it is.' She set her hands on either side of his slim waist. They were instantly warmed by his body heat.

He closed his arms about her, bringing her against him from bosom to knees, and kissed her.

It was somehow unexpected. And it was strangely alarming. She had expected to control this encounter as she had last night's. She had planned to undress him slowly tonight, exploring his body with her hands and mouth as she did so, driving him mad with need and desire. She *still* planned it, but . . .

But he was kissing her.

The alarming, unexpected thing was that it was neither a passionate nor a lascivious kiss. It was warm and comfortable and . . . Tender?

It was a kiss that tore at her defenses.

He kissed her lightly with parted lips, moving them over hers in unhurried exploration before touching them with the tip of his tongue and then moving on to kiss her closed eyelids, her temples, the soft, sensitive flesh beneath one earlobe, her throat.

And that throat felt suddenly raw within, as though with unshed tears.

Why?

She had expected passion. She had *wanted* passion. Passion could be held at a purely physical level. She had intended this to be only physical. She had wanted *sex* and nothing else. And that word was becoming easier to verbalize in her mind.

She had wanted *raw sex*.

Something mindless and carnal.

She had wanted to feel herself earning every penny of her living.

Her hands, she realized, were spread over his upper back, unmoving. She was being kissed. She was not kissing. She was receiving, not giving.

She was earning nothing.

He lifted his head a few inches from her own. He was not smiling, and yet something lurked in his eyes that seemed like a smile. She was leaning into him, she realized, all warm and relaxed, almost languorous.

'Cass,' he said softly.

No one had ever called her that before.

'Yes,' she said, a mere breath of sound.

And she realized at the same moment that it was not languor she felt at all, but . . . desire.

How could it be *desire*? He had done nothing to arouse it in her.

Had he?

'I want you,' he said. 'Not just your woman's body but the person inside it as well. Tell me you want me too.'

. . . but the person inside it . . .

She almost hated him. How could she fight *this*?

She did her best. She half closed her eyes and lowered the tone of her voice.

'But of course I want you,' she said. 'What woman could resist someone in whom man and angel collide in such erotic splendor?'

She smiled carefully at him.

But just when he ought to have resumed the kisses, passionate or not, he chose to look at her, his eyes searching her face.

She ought to have extinguished the candle.

'I am not here to hurt you,' he said softly. 'I am here to—'

'Love me?' She cocked one eyebrow.

By what rules did this man play the game of dalliance and seduction?

'Yes,' he said. 'In a manner of speaking. There are many kinds of love, Cass, and none of them are simple lust. I find simple lust well-nigh impossible. Especially for you, who are in some sort of relationship with me. Yes, I am here to love you.'

He did not know the *first thing* about love.

But did she?

. . . you, who are in some sort of relationship with me . . .

She drooped her eyelids over her eyes again and smiled.

'Take it off,' he said. 'Please.'

She raised her eyebrows.

'Your mask,' he said. 'You do not need it here with me. I promise you.'

She had the sudden feeling, the sudden fear, that she needed it with him more than with anyone else. He was a relentless ripper of masks, of carefully woven defenses.

He kissed her again, more deeply this time. His tongue traced the outline of her lips and then pressed into her mouth as he untied her hair ribbon and dropped it to the floor. Then his arms held her close, and after a minute or so he turned her and lowered her to the bed after pulling loose the tie that held her robe closed at the neck, and letting the garment slither to the floor.

He did not follow her down. He undressed beside the bed, dropping first his coat and then his waistcoat and shirt to the floor to join her robe and ribbon. He reached for the buttons at his waist and stepped out of his breeches and stockings and drawers. He took his time about it and made no attempt to turn away from her steadily watching eyes.

Dear God, he was beautiful. With most people clothes were a blessing in that they hid a multitude of imperfections. His clothes hid only perfection – well-muscled arms and shoulders and chest, which was lightly dusted with golden hair; a slender waist and hips; tight buttocks; long, tautly muscled legs.

Ancient Greek sculptors had doubtless idealized their models when sculpting the gods. They could have used the Earl of Merton just as he was.

He was as much god as angel.

He was blue and golden, like a summer sky – blue eyes, golden hair. All light. Blinding light.

'Blow out the candle,' she said.

She could not bear to look at him any longer, with the knowledge that she was in *some sort of relationship* with him – mistress and protector. That was all, as she had planned, as she had wanted. As she *still* wanted. She would hold that knowledge better without the sense of sight. She would hold images of Mary and Belinda and Alice in her mind's eye, and even Roger. Poor Roger, who had once tried to protect her . . .

She was Lord Merton's *mistress*, nothing else.

He came down beside her after putting out the candle, and she turned to him and reached for him, intent upon taking control of the encounter as she had planned it. But his hands were grasping the hem of her nightgown, and she lifted her arms while he peeled it off her and tossed it over his shoulder. Then, before she could lower her arms, he grasped both her wrists in one hand and held them above her head while he leaned over her, turning her onto her back again, and kissed her, first on the lips and then down over her chin to her throat, and on down to her breasts. He opened his mouth over the tip of one breast, breathed in, bringing a rush of cold air to the moistened nipple, and then closed his mouth about it and suckled her. Heat replaced cold, and a dart of pain that was not pain stabbed downward through her womb and out to her inner thighs, which suddenly ached with need.

His mouth left her breast and moved down to her stomach. She felt his tongue dart into her navel, and all her inner muscles contracted tightly.

His free hand was smoothing over her inner thighs, his fingers lightly circling. And then they were at the secret wet heat of her, light and feathering until one finger penetrated her to the first knuckle. He moved it in a hard circle.

She could have freed her hands. His grip on her wrists was not tight. She did not do so. She lay passive beneath his onslaught, though that was not at all an appropriate word to describe what he was doing. She had thought him an innocent. He was not. He was very skilled indeed. He knew how to use slow tenderness to build a passion that felt like a raging fire.

This was *not* as she imagined a man would use a mistress. She had expected all brute strength, orchestrated by her own seductive wiles. Though not with him once she had chosen him. With him she had expected an innocence that would be all at her mercy.

As though she were an experienced courtesan.

How foolish had been her expectations.

His fingers feathered her breast and closed lightly over her swollen nipple. She almost cried out with the pain of it – the pain that was not pain.

His body came over hers then, and his weight came down on her as he released her wrists and slid his hands beneath her buttocks. He lifted his head and she knew he was looking into her face, though she could scarcely see him in the darkness.

'There is a kind of love,' he said, his voice very low, 'that a man feels for his lover, Cass. It is more than lust.'

And he came into her even as his words undid her and made it impossible for her to brace herself against the invasion.

He was big and long and hard, as she remembered from last night. She clenched her muscles about him, as she had

155

done then, and slid her feet up the bed and hugged his strongly muscled legs with her own.

He smelled clean, she thought. His subtle, expensive cologne did not mask less pleasant odors. It merely enhanced cleanliness. His hair was soft and faintly fragrant. She slid the fingers of one hand into it as he rested his head on the pillow beside hers, his face turned away from her. She wrapped the other arm about his waist.

And he began the rhythmic thrust and withdrawal of intimacy, always the part that had required the greatest effort of endurance from her during most of her marriage.

He had more control over himself tonight. She soon knew that. It was not going to be over in a very few minutes. His movements were steady and measured. Deep and shallow, deep and shallow.

She could feel the wet slide of him inside her, hardness against softness, heat against heat. She could hear the suck and pull of their coupling.

It was a curiously enticing sound.

And a sort of yearning began there, where he worked toward his own pleasure, and spread to her bowels, her breasts, her throat. A yearning that was an ache, a pain that was not pain. She wanted to weep. She wanted to twine her legs tightly about his, raise them to his waist, wrap her arms tightly about him, press her face to his shoulder, cry out with the strange longing for she knew not what.

She wanted to abandon herself to that longing. To lose herself. For one blessed moment in her life to *give in*.

It was what she *ought* to do, she realized with an effort of conscious thought. She was his mistress. He was paying her handsomely to pleasure him, to flatter him by taking pleasure.

But if she feigned pleasure, she might be snared by her own game.

She felt helpless and frightened.

And aching with longing.

His hands slid beneath her again. His face was above hers once more.

'Cass,' he whispered. 'Cass.'

And as the rhythm ended and he pressed deep and held there while she felt the hot rush of his release, she knew that it was the very worst thing he could have said.

She wanted to be woman and mistress to him. She wanted to keep herself for herself. She wanted her two lives – her private life and her working life – to be kept strictly separate. But he had looked into her face in the darkness and called her by that name no one else had ever used, and told her with that one use of it that he knew who she was and that she was somehow precious to him.

Except that he did not, and she was not.

It was just *sex*.

She was suddenly alarmed by the realization that two hot tears were trickling diagonally across her cheeks and dripping through her hair to the pillow beneath. She hoped fervently that his eyes had not become accustomed enough to the darkness that he would notice.

All the aches and the yearnings subsided to be replaced by regret, though regret for *what* she did not know.

He drew out of her and moved to lie beside her. He turned her half away from him and snuggled in behind her before drawing her back to lean against his body, her head on his shoulder, his arm beneath her head and stretched along hers to the wrist, about which his fingers closed as her hand rested against her ribs.

She could hear his heart thudding steadily.

He smoothed back her hair with his free hand and set his lips against her forehead, just above the temple. The place one would kiss out of affection.

She could suddenly hear his words again.

There is a kind of love that a man feels for his lover.

She did not want his love, not any kind of love. She wanted his money in exchange for what she gave him here.

She repeated the thought over and over in her mind lest she forget what this was all about.

'Tell me about the child,' he murmured against her ear.

'The child?' she said, startled.

'At the door this afternoon,' he said. 'She was peeping about the skirts of your maid. Is she yours?'

'Oh,' she said. 'No. You mean Belinda. She is Mary's.'

'Mary is the maid?' he asked.

'Yes,' she said. 'I brought them with me to London. I could not leave them behind. They had nowhere else to go. Mary was dismissed when Bruce – the new Lord Paget – finally came to live at Carmel. Besides, she is my friend. And I love Belinda. We all need some touch of innocence in our lives, Lord – Stephen.'

'Mary has no husband?' he asked.

'No,' she said. 'But that does not make her a pariah.'

'Did you have no children?' he asked.

'No.' She closed her eyes. '*Yes.* I had a daughter who died at birth. She was perfect, but she was born two months too soon, and she would not breathe.'

'Oh, Cass,' he said.

'*Don't* say you are sorry,' she said. 'You had nothing to do with it, did you? And I miscarried twice before that.'

And probably once after, though the third time there

was only very heavy bleeding almost a month after she had missed her courses and she could never be sure there had been a child. Oh, but she knew there had been. Her woman's body had known it. So had her mother's heart.

'Don't deny me words,' he said. 'I *am* sorry. It must be the very worst thing any woman can be made to endure – the loss of a child. Even the loss of an unborn child. I am sorry, Cass.'

'I have always been glad of it,' she said harshly.

She had always told herself she was glad. But saying it now aloud to someone else, she knew that she had never been glad at all to have lost those four precious souls who might have become an inextricable part of her own soul.

Oh, how foolish to have said those words aloud.

'You have a voice,' he said, 'to match the mask you wear. I am more than relieved that you spoke in it just now or I might have believed you. I could not bear to believe you.'

She frowned and bit her lip.

'Lord Merton,' she said, 'when we are together in this room and this bed, we are employer and mistress, or if you prefer to coat reality in sugar, we are *lovers*. In the strictly physical sense that we share bodies for *mutual* pleasure. *Physical* pleasure. Man and woman. We are not *persons* to each other. We are bodies. You may use my body as you will – you are paying enough for it, God knows. But all the money in the world will not buy you *me*. I am off limits to you. I belong to myself. I am your paid servant. I am *not* and never will be your slave. You will ask me *no more* personal questions. You will intrude no further into my life. If you cannot accept this – that we are man and mistress – then I will give back the ridiculously large sum of money you sent me this morning and show you the door.'

She listened to herself, appalled. What was she *saying?* She did not have all his money left to give back. And she knew as surely as she was lying here in his arms that she would never find the courage to do this all over again with another man. If he took her at her word, she was destitute – and so were Mary and Belinda and Alice. And Roger.

He withdrew his arm from beneath her head and his body from against hers so that suddenly she found herself lying flat on her back. He swung his legs over the far side of the bed, got to his feet, and walked around to her side. He stooped and picked up his clothes, tossed them over the foot of the bed, and proceeded to get dressed.

Even in the darkness she knew he was angry.

She ought to say something before it was too late. But it was already too late. He was going to go away and never come back. She had lost him merely because he was glad she did not really think herself better off without her dead children.

She would not say anything. She *could* not. She was all done with seducing him, with playing the siren. It had been a desperate idea from the start. A foolish idea.

Except that there had seemed – there *still* seemed – to be no alternative.

She waited in silence for him to leave. After she had heard the front door shut behind him, she would put her nightgown and robe back on and go down to lock and bolt the door. And that would be the end of that.

She would make herself a cup of tea in the kitchen and dream up another plan. There had to be *something*. Perhaps Lady Carling would be willing to give her a letter of recommendation. Perhaps she could find an employer who had never heard of her.

He had finished dressing, except to pick up his cloak and hat from the chair just inside the door as he left. But instead of moving toward them, he was bending over the dressing table, and suddenly the room was lit up with a flare of light from the tinder box and he set the flame to the candle.

Cassandra blinked in the sudden light and wished she had pulled up the bedcovers while there was still darkness. She disdained to do it now. She gazed at him with all the scorn and hostility she could muster as he drew out the chair from the dressing table, turned it slightly, and sat down on it.

He had reversed the situation from earlier this morning, she realized – or yesterday morning, rather. He was seated on the chair, looking at her on the bed.

Well, let him look his fill. It was all that was left to him.

'Get dressed, Cassandra,' he said. 'Not in those things on the floor. Real clothes. Put them on. We are going to talk.'

Just as she had said yesterday.

There was no discernible anger in either his face or his voice, only a certain intensity in his eyes.

But it did not occur to her to defy or disobey him.

He had all the gentle power of angels, she realized as she crossed the room, naked, to her dressing room and began pulling on the clothes she had been wearing during the evening. It instilled fear. Not fear of bodily harm, but of . . .

She still did not know the answer. For some things there were no words.

But she *was* afraid of him. He was somehow in her life,

161

where she did not want him or anyone else to be. Not even Alice.

He was there.

. . . you, who are in some sort of relationship with me . . .

11

He ought simply to leave as soon as he was dressed, Stephen thought.

But he did not do so. He could not.

He knew nothing about the normal sort of relationship men enjoyed with their mistresses. But then, he could not think of her as his mistress despite that damnable exchange of money that her circumstances had made necessary.

. . . when we are together in this room and this bed, we are employer and mistress . . . man and woman. We are not persons to each other. We are bodies. You may use my body as you will . . . but all the money in the world will not buy you me.

He did not *want* to buy her. He wanted to . . . *know* the woman into whose bed he was buying his way. Was there something so wrong about that?

She did not want to be known.

I am off limits to you. I belong to myself. I am your paid servant. I am not and never will be your slave. You will ask me no more personal questions. You will intrude no further into my life.

Of course, she knew no more than he about the normal relationship between a man and his mistress. He doubted she had slept with any other man except her husband until last night. Despite the siren's act, which she tried so persistently to play, she was not a courtesan.

She was merely a desperate woman trying to make a living for herself and a few hangers-on. Though that was probably an unkind description of the people who lived with her. The former governess who had been walking in the park with her two days ago was probably past the age when she might find further employment with any ease. The maid was an unmarried mother and would be virtually unemployable as long as she chose to keep the child with her.

Stephen got to his feet and went to stand at the window while he waited for Cassandra to finish dressing. He opened the curtains and gazed out at the empty street. It was probably not a good idea to stand thus in the window, though, a candle burning behind him. The neighbors across the street might know that only women lived here.

He pulled the curtains across the window again and turned to lean back against the windowsill, his arms crossed over his chest.

Cassandra came out of the dressing room at the same moment. She looked at him and then took the chair. She arranged the skirts of her pale blue dress unhurriedly about her. A faint, mocking smile lifted the corners of her lips.

She had tied back her hair again but not put it up. Finally, when he said nothing, she looked up at him and raised her eyebrows.

'I beg your pardon,' he said, 'for prying into your life and causing you pain.'

Her eyebrows stayed arched upward.

'You did not cause me pain, Lord Merton,' she said. 'As I remember it, you caused me a great deal of pleasure. I hope I caused you at least an equal amount.'

'Where do your servants sleep?' he asked her. 'And the child.'

'On the floor above this,' she said. 'You need not fear that our pantings and moanings have been penetrating walls and keeping anyone from sleep. And they are not my servants. They are my friends.'

She was not a likable woman when her mask was in place, as it so often was. The very best thing in the world for him would be to leave. The money he had sent her yesterday morning would keep her and the others for a short while. After that . . . Well, she was not his responsibility. But the trouble was that the woman who wore the mask did not exist, and he did not *know* the woman behind it. He did not know if he would like her or not.

She did not want to be known.

She had killed her husband.

Good God, what was he *doing* here?

But she had brought with her to London an aging governess, a waif of a maid who had lost her job, the maid's very young child, and the damaged dog. She had determinedly sought him out as a protector so that they would not all starve – them, as well as herself.

'This is their home,' he said. 'I sully it when I come here to exercise my rights as your employer. I impinge upon the innocence of that child.'

That fact had bothered him since he saw her yesterday afternoon, rosy-cheeked and tousle-haired and wide-eyed. One of life's precious innocents. He had even thought at the time that perhaps she was Cassandra's. It made no real difference that she was not. This whole situation was . . . distasteful.

She had crossed her legs and was slowly swinging one leg. She gazed at him for a while without saying anything. Her smile still lingered.

'A gentleman with a conscience,' she said eventually. 'It seems a contradiction in terms. It must be very inconvenient to you, Lord Merton.'

'Often,' he agreed. 'It is what a conscience is intended to be if it has not become jaded. It is the guide by which I try to live my life and make my decisions about the course it will take.'

'Is it conscience that kept you here after you were dressed?' she asked him. 'Or a lingering lust for what you would lose if you left then? If it was the latter, you need not worry. You will never lack for bedfellows whenever you want them – and would not even if you were not titled and wealthy. If it is the former, it must be that you pity me and my pathetic little entourage. Do not. We will survive without you, Lord Merton. We are really none of your concern, are we?'

He answered her even though the question had been rhetorical.

'No,' he said. But he did not move.

'What is your purpose, then?' she asked. 'Do you wish

166

to set me up in some love nest? It is what other gentlemen do, especially the married ones. It would be very cozy, and you could visit me there whenever you wished without fear of sullying anyone's innocence. I would be like other women who take employment. I would have my home here and my place of employment there.'

Her foot swung a little faster. Her voice was low and mocking.

'It will not do, Cassandra,' he said.

She sighed audibly.

'Then this is the end, is it?' she said. 'I hope you will not mind not having *all* your money returned, Lord Merton. I have spent some of it, you see. I am very extravagant. But I have serviced you for two successive nights and ought to be paid something.'

She seemed to notice her swiftly swinging foot and stopped it abruptly.

It would be so easy simply to say yes, this *was* the end. It was what he surely wanted. He could go home to Merton House, sleep for what would be left of the night when he got there, and put this whole sorry episode behind him when he got up in the morning. He would be free of an entanglement he had not really wanted from the start.

He could resume the familiar life that he enjoyed.

He could not say yes.

'Cassandra,' he said, leaning forward slightly, 'we must start again. *May* we start again?'

She laughed at him.

'But certainly, Lord Merton,' she said. 'Shall I undress? Or would you prefer to do it for me? Or . . . would you like me to lie down as I am?'

She had not misunderstood him at all. But for reasons of her own, she had decided to needle him. Perhaps, he thought with a painful flash of insight, she hated herself for what she had chosen to do with him. Perhaps she hated herself for the killing she had somehow got away with – as far as legal proceedings went, anyway.

'Stay where you are,' he said. 'There will be no more sex tonight, Cassandra, and none for the foreseeable future. Perhaps never for the two of us.'

Her lip curled.

'And so,' she said, 'by suggesting that we start again you are inviting me to seduce you all over again, Lord Merton? It will be my pleasure. Never say never. I am better than that.'

He crossed the room to her in a few quick strides, went down on his knees in front of her chair, and possessed himself of both her hands. She gazed at him, startled, and the mask slipped.

'Stop it,' he said. 'Just stop it, Cassandra. That game is over. And game is all it ever was. That was not *you*. Or *me*. I am sorry for what I have done to you. Truly sorry.'

She opened her mouth to speak and closed it again, the words unspoken. She tried to look scornful and failed. He tightened his grip on her hands.

'Cassandra,' he said, 'if we are to go on, we must do it as friends. And I do not use that word as a euphemism for nothing at all. We must become friends. I need to continue helping you, and you need help. It is, perhaps, not quite an ideal basis for friendship, but it will have to do. I will support you for as long as you need support, and you will give me your confidence and trust and company in return. Not your body. I cannot pay for your body. I *cannot*.'

'Goodness me, Lord Merton,' she said, 'you *must* be desperate if you are prepared to pay for friendship. Is being an angel such a lonely business, then? Does no one want to be your friend?'

'Cass,' he said, 'call me Stephen.'

Why was he bothering? Why *was* he?

Her smile was back – and then was not.

'Stephen,' she said. It was almost a whisper.

'Let us be friends,' he said. 'Let me visit you openly here, with your former governess as your chaperone. Let me bring my sisters to visit you. Let me escort you about London as I did yesterday afternoon. Let us get to know each other.'

'Are you so desperate, then,' she said, 'to have access to my secrets, Lord Merton? Are you itching to know all the titillating details of the way I killed Nigel?'

He let go of her hands and got to his feet again. He turned away from her and ran the fingers of one hand through his hair. He looked at the rumpled bed, where they had made love just a short while ago.

'*Did* you kill him?' he asked.

Why had he not fully believed her the first time he asked? Why had he not recoiled in horror and put as much distance between himself and her as he could?

'Yes, I did,' she said without hesitation. 'You will not get me to deny it, Lord Merton – *Stephen*. You will not get me to invent a convenient stranger, a vagrant, who for no reason whatsoever but an inherent villainy climbed through the library window, shot my husband through the heart, and then took himself off again without even stealing anything of value. I did it because I hated him and wanted him dead and wanted to be free of him. Do you *really* want to be my friend?'

Why did he *still* not quite believe her? Because such a thing was unimaginable? But Lord Paget had died because a bullet had been shot into his heart. He tried to picture her with a pistol in her hand and closed his eyes briefly, appalled.

Was he mad? Was he besotted with her? Surely he was not. Of course he was not. He must simply be mad.

'Yes,' he said with a sigh. 'I do.'

'The whole *ton* would believe you were courting me,' she said. 'Your wings would soon be tinged black, Lord Merton. You would soon find yourself being shunned. Or becoming the laughingstock. Everyone would think you were my dupe. They would think you remarkably foolish. They would think you could not see beyond my beauty. I *am* beautiful. I say that without vanity. I know how other people look at me – women with envy, men with admiration and desire. Women would turn from you in disappointment and disdain. Men would look at you with envy and scorn.'

'I cannot live my life,' he said, 'according to what my peers expect of me. I must live it as I see fit. I suppose there was a reason why you noticed me in Hyde Park a few days ago, and why I noticed you. And it was not simply that you were looking for a protector and that I had an eye for beauty – especially as you were heavily veiled. You might have noticed a dozen others. So might I. But it was each other we saw. And there was a reason why we met again just the following day at Meg's ball. The reason was not just that we would tumble into bed together and then part bitterly a short while later. I believe in causes. And effects.'

'We were fated to meet, then?' she said. 'And to fall in love, perhaps, and marry and live happily ever after?'

'We make our own fate,' he said. 'But some things happen for a reason. I am convinced of it. We met for a reason, Cassandra. We can choose to explore that reason – or not. No effect is fated.'

'Only the cause,' she said.

'Yes,' he said. 'I think. I am no philosopher. Let us start again, Cassandra. Let us give ourselves a chance at least to be friends. Let me get to know you. Get to know me. Perhaps I am worth knowing.'

'And perhaps not,' she said.

'And perhaps not.'

She sighed, and when he looked back at her he could see that she had dropped all pretenses. She looked simply vulnerable – and lovely beyond belief.

A murderer? Surely not. But what did a murderer look like?

'I ought to have known,' she said, 'as soon as I saw you that you would be trouble. Instead, it was your friend I dismissed as potentially dangerous. It was he I thought I would not be able to control. The one who looks like the devil. Mr. Huxtable.'

'*Con?*' he said. 'He is my cousin. He is not evil.'

'I thought angels were safe,' she said, 'and so I chose you.'

'I am not an angel, Cassandra,' he said.

'Oh, believe me, you *are*,' she said. 'That is the whole trouble.'

He smiled at her suddenly, and for a moment there

was a gleam in her eye, and he thought she was going to smile back at him. She did not do so.

'Let me call on you tomorrow afternoon,' he said. 'Or this afternoon, I suppose I mean. A formal call. On you and your former governess. Pardon me, remind me of her name.'

'Alice Haytor,' she said.

'Let me call on you and Miss Haytor,' he said.

She was swinging her foot again.

'She *knows*,' she said.

'And doubtless believes I am the devil incarnate,' he said. 'Shall we see if I can charm her out of her strong disapproval of me?'

'She also knows,' she said, 'that it is all my fault, that I seduced you.'

'She can know no such thing,' he said, 'because it is not true, Cassandra. You signaled strong interest in me. I was not seduced. I chose to be interested in return. You *are* beautiful. And desirable. I deserve Miss Haytor's disapproval. I made the wrong decisions concerning you and my attraction to you. Allow me to try to win her respect.'

She sighed again.

'You will not just go away, will you?' she said.

They looked at each other.

'I will,' he said. 'If you tell me to go away and stay away, I will do it. If the *real* Lady Paget tells me, that is. Do you want me to leave, Cassandra? Do you want me out of your life for now and always?'

She stared at him and then closed her eyes.

'I do,' she said after a few moments, 'but I cannot say it with my eyes open. Stephen, *why* did I meet you?'

'I do not know,' he said. 'Shall we discover the answer together?'

'You will regret it,' she said.

'Perhaps,' he agreed.

'I already regret it,' she said.

'Tomorrow afternoon?' he said.

'Oh, very well.' She opened her eyes and gazed at him again. 'Come if you must.'

He raised his eyebrows.

'Come,' she said. 'And I shall tell Mary not to put a spider in your teacup.'

He smiled.

'And now go,' she said. 'I need some sleep even if you do not.'

He crossed the room to put on his cloak and take up his hat. He turned toward her. She was standing in front of the chair.

'Good night, Cassandra,' he said.

'Good night, Stephen.'

He walked home wondering what on earth he had got himself into now. His life seemed to have been turned upside down in the past two days.

Had they *really* been fated to meet? For what possible reason – except that he help keep her and her friends from starvation?

But the reason was for them to discover. Some events, some moments, were dropped deliberately into one's life, he believed, by an unseen hand. But that hand had no power to dictate one's response. It was up to the individual concerned to make something out of those events and moments.

Or not.

*   *   *

It rained all morning, but by early afternoon the rain had stopped, the clouds had moved on, the sun was shining, and the roads and pavements had dried off.

'It is a *perfect* afternoon for a walk,' Alice said stubbornly, having crossed to the sitting room window to prove with her own eyes that she was quite right. 'We have been promising ourselves a walk in Green Park, Cassie. It will be less crowded than Hyde Park.'

'When you arrived home for luncheon,' Cassandra reminded her, 'you declared that your feet would surely drop off if you had to walk one more step today.'

Alice had spent the morning trying to discover agencies she had missed yesterday and revisiting those at which she had left her name, in the hope that something had turned up overnight.

She had said that about her feet before Cassandra had finally plucked up the courage to mention very casually that the Earl of Merton was to call this afternoon – a formal social visit to take tea with them, not official business.

'It is amazing what a little luncheon and a cup of tea and an hour's sit-down can do to restore one's energy,' Alice said brightly. 'I am ready to go again – and this afternoon I will not even get wet.'

'I agreed that I would be here when he came, Alice,' Cassandra said. 'It would be ill-mannered to be from home after all, and you taught me never to be bad-mannered. Besides . . .'

'Besides *what*?' Alice was cross. She had turned from the window, a frown on her face.

Cassandra had no work on her lap – she could not seem to settle to anything these days. She had no excuse to look anywhere else but back at her old governess.

174

'I think our . . . *liaison* is at an end, Allie,' she said. 'In fact, it is. He found it distasteful – mainly, I believe, because Belinda lives here. He said something about sullying innocence. Though it was not only that. I think he really must be an angel. I led an angel astray. He feels guilty. He wants to make amends. He wants to start again, and he wants us to be *friends*. Have you ever heard anything so absurd in your life? But he wants to keep on paying me too, and I do not know how I am going to make myself say no, though of course I ought. I cannot accept a handsome salary just for being someone's friend, can I?'

'Come for a walk,' Alice said firmly, 'before it is too late. Just get your bonnet, Cassie, and never mind about changing your dress.'

Cassandra shook her head and looked down at her hands in her lap. She examined her fingernails. They needed cutting. She was wearing her sprigged muslin dress for the occasion. Pretty clothes were something she *did* have left. Nigel had always insisted that she dress well.

'I do not want even to set eyes on him,' Alice said, 'let alone sit and take tea with him. I don't *like* him, Cassie, and I do not need to meet him to know that. He hurt you.'

'No, he did not.' Cassandra looked up with troubled eyes. 'If any hurting was done, it was the other way around. He has not hurt *me*. He is . . . lovely, Allie.'

Lovely and terribly troubling.

All morning – and all last night after he had left – she had thought about his lovemaking and the aches and yearnings it had aroused in her. And that pain that was not pain. It was sexual desire she had been feeling. She had admitted that eventually. She had never before felt sexual desire. She had not even known there was such a thing for women.

And all morning she had been thinking about their conversation afterward.

I suppose there was a reason why you noticed me in Hyde Park a few days ago, and why I noticed you . . . And there was a reason why we met again just the following day at Meg's ball. I believe in causes. And effects.

If there was a reason for everything, why had she met Nigel?

Some things happen for a reason. I am sure of it. We met for a reason, Cassandra. We can choose to explore that reason – or not. No effect is fated.

He had found a way for fate and free will to exist side by side. How clever of him.

Let us start again, Cassandra. Let us give ourselves a chance at least to be friends. Let me get to know you. Get to know me. Perhaps I am worth knowing.

Did he not feel he knew enough about her? She had told him – twice – that she had killed Nigel. What was there more to know about someone who had admitted to doing that?

Perhaps I am worth knowing.

'Perhaps,' she said to Alice, 'he is worth knowing.'

'After what he has done to you?' Alice came back to her place and sat down with a thump. 'And don't talk to me about your having seduced him, Cassie. You had *reason* to do it, though heaven knows I opposed it quite vigorously from the start. He had no such excuse for allowing himself to be seduced, except that he is a *man*.

176

If he needs a woman that badly, why does he not marry? That is what wives are for!'

Cassandra looked at her and, for the first time all day, smiled with genuine amusement.

'Well.' Alice's cheeks turned pink. 'It is *one* thing they are for. Don't you go misunderstanding me, Cassie. Women are worth a great deal more than *that*, as I have tried to instill in you from childhood on. I *still* think we ought to go to Green Park. It may be raining again tomorrow. And it is I who ought to be finding some source of income. And I *will*. I bought a paper this morning. It was a dreadful extravagance, but there is notice there of several positions for which I intend to apply. Some of them are unsuitable, it is true, but there are several distinct possibilities. A woman's usefulness cannot possibly be over at the age of forty-two. I refuse to believe it.'

Cassandra smiled at her and noticed that her former governess's eyes were swimming in tears.

'Cassie,' she said again, 'it is *I* who must look after us. You know it as well as I do.'

'It is you who have always looked after me, Allie,' Cassandra said. *'Always.'*

Alice dabbed at her eyes with a handkerchief.

'It is important to you that we receive the Earl of Merton, then, is it?' she asked.

'Yes.' Cassandra nodded. 'And he asked particularly that you be with me, you know – as a chaperone.'

Alice made a rather ugly sound, like a snort.

'I *must* have told you that story sometime during your growing years,' she said, 'about the stable doors being shut after the horse had bolted.'

It was too late for them to go walking now even if they wanted to. A carriage that was passing along the street outside drew to a halt outside the door. Cassandra could hear it clearly from where she was sitting.

Their visitor had arrived.

12

Stephen called upon Katherine, Lady Montford, late in the morning after leaving the House of Lords. He went with the intention of asking her to accompany him when he called upon Cassandra. But Meg was with her, having brought Toby and Sally to play with Hal in the nursery, and he was able to ask both of them to go with him.

'I ought to have asked about yesterday afternoon and your ride in the park as soon as I saw you, Stephen,' Meg said. 'You have taken it upon yourself to bring Lady Paget into fashion, then, have you? It is very kind of you. She is not particularly easy to like, is she? There is a habitual look on her face that suggests – well, a certain contempt for everyone she beholds, as though she held herself superior. I know it is probably just her way of protecting herself against what really is a very difficult situation, but even so her manner does not invite intimacy.'

'I told her I would call this afternoon,' Stephen said, 'but it would not be quite the thing to go alone, would it?'

'She certainly does not need even the whisper of more gossip,' Kate agreed. 'You are quite right about her manner, of course, Meg, but I daresay that if I were all alone in London and everyone believed I had murdered my husband – with an axe – I would behave in much the same way. *If* I had the courage to appear in public at all, that is. One must admire her. I will be pleased to come with you this afternoon, Stephen. Hal will be ready for a rest after a busy morning, and Jasper is going to the races.'

'So is Duncan,' Meg added. 'They are going together, in fact. I will come too.'

It had been easier than Stephen had feared. There had been no awkward questions. It was obviously not clear to his sisters that he was nursing a guilty conscience.

When he arrived outside Cassandra's door on Portman Street during the afternoon, then, it was in a manner that was above reproach. He arrived openly, for every neighbor on the street to see if they wished, and he handed down two eminently respectable ladies to the pavement while the footman who had accompanied his coachman rapped the knocker against the door.

A few minutes later, they were seated in the sitting room, making polite conversation with Cassandra, who was pouring the tea, and with Miss Haytor, whom Stephen recognized from Hyde Park a few afternoons ago. She was sitting straight-backed in her chair, a prunish look on her face, but she was not an unhandsome woman.

And the prunish look was understandable. He just hoped he would not lose this gamble he had taken. He hoped she would not say anything that would reveal to his sisters the truth of his relationship to Cassandra. He doubted she would, though. She was clearly a lady.

In the meanwhile he set out to charm her, concentrating much of his conversation on her while the other ladies talked among themselves.

But all the while he was aware of Cassandra, who was playing the part of hostess with some ease of manner, though her face had that slightly scornful look that Meg had mentioned earlier. He wished she would relax and be herself. He wanted his sisters to like her, almost as if he really were paying her court.

She was wearing a mushroom-colored muslin dress that would have looked dowdy on most women, he thought. On her it looked simply stunning. It accentuated her figure and drew attention to the bright glow of her hair. She looked elegant.

She looked like a lady. She looked like someone to whom nothing sordid could possibly ever have occurred.

And then something happened to relax them all, though it caused Cassandra some initial dismay.

The sitting room door, which had seemed to be shut, clicked open and the shaggy, disreputable-looking dog came padding in with a bobbing gait and a lolling tongue.

'Oh, dear,' Cassandra said, standing as he approached, 'the latch did not catch on the door again. I am so sorry. I will take him out of here.'

'I'll do it, Cassie,' Miss Haytor said, getting to her feet too.

'Oh, but he is adorable,' Kate said. 'Please let him stay – if he is allowed in the sitting room at all, that is.'

'Roger tends to be Cassandra's shadow whenever he is given the opportunity,' Miss Haytor said, sitting down again. 'He believes the whole house is his and that he is lord and master here. And usually he is.'

181

For the first time she smiled. She even chuckled when Kate smiled back.

Cassandra took her seat again and half smiled too. Stephen, watching her, saw a look of pure affection on her face and felt something catch at his heart, something so elusive that it was quite impossible to grasp on to it or understand quite what it was.

'Roger,' he said as the dog padded past and he reached out a hand to scratch his good ear. 'You have a distinguished name, sir.'

The dog stopped, set his chin on Stephen's lap, and gazed up at him with one mournful eye. The other eye was glazed over and blind.

'You are either one very unfortunate dog,' Stephen continued, 'who keeps running into trouble and coming out of it the worse for wear, or you are one very *fortunate* dog who survived a terrible disaster.'

'The latter,' Cassandra said.

'Oh, how very dreadful, Lady Paget,' Meg said. 'It is only in very recent years that I have had pets in the house – my eldest son brought a whole litter of puppies inside when he could no longer stand having to go out to the stables every time he wanted to see them, and of course their mother had to come too, though she was not at all house-broken at the time. But I know how quickly pets become family, as precious in their own way as the human members.'

'I believe,' Cassandra said, her gaze still on Roger, 'a part of me would have died with him had he not recovered from his injuries, Lady Sheringford, but he did. I refused to let him die.'

Her gaze moved up the short distance from the dog's head to Stephen's face before she looked away.

No one asked what the accident had been, and she did not volunteer the information.

'You are going to be covered with hairs, Lord Merton,' Miss Haytor said.

He smiled at her.

'My valet will doubtless scold, ma'am,' he said, 'but he will brush off every last one of them. And a valet must be provided with something to scold about from time to time, you know, if he is to feel wanted and enjoy his work.'

She almost smiled back at him. But she had not forgiven him quite yet – if she ever would.

No one had thought to cross the room to close the sitting room door and make sure it was shut fast this time. As a result, a little curly haired, rosy-cheeked head appeared about it, as it had about the maid's skirts the day before, and the child, seeing the dog, stepped inside the room. She was wearing a pink dress that was faded, though it was spotlessly clean and had been crisply ironed.

'Doggie,' she said, laughing as she came.

But Roger seemed quite happy where he was, having his ear smoothed out and his head scratched, though he did humph a lazy welcome and opened his eye when she buried her fingers in the hair on his back and bent her head to kiss him.

'Oh, dear,' Cassandra said, sounding embarrassed again. 'I am so sorry. I will take—'

But the child appeared suddenly to have noticed that there were people in the room as well as the dog, and that one of them was a lady wearing a flower-trimmed straw bonnet. She stepped away from Roger and Stephen and pointed at Meg's bonnet.

'Pretty,' she said.

'Why, thank you,' Meg said. 'And your curls are pretty too. Perhaps you can spare one. I'll cut it off with the scissors I have in my reticule and take it home with me and paste it onto my own head, shall I? Do you think it would look pretty on me?'

The child was giggling with glee.

'No-o!' she cried. 'It would look s-silly.'

'I suppose you are right,' Meg said with a sigh. 'I will have to leave it on your head, then, where it looks quite lovely.'

The child lifted one foot and held her leg behind the knee.

'I got new shoes,' she said.

Meg looked at them.

'They are very fine indeed,' she said.

'My others was too small,' the child said, 'because I am a big girl now.'

'I can certainly see that,' Meg said. 'I daresay the old shoes were very much too small. Would you like to sit on my knee?'

Cassandra sat down again, exchanging glances with Miss Haytor as she did so. But they need not have worried. It might not be perfect etiquette to allow a shaggy, decrepit dog and a servant's child to wander into the sitting room while one was entertaining noble guests, but those noble guests were charmed. Stephen knew both Meg and Kate were. And he certainly was. This was a house, he realized, where children and pets were allowed to roam virtually at will. It was a home. He had felt it yesterday from without the door. Today he was sure of it.

Cassandra did not live in perpetual gloom. Even now she was looking at the child with exasperated affection.

'I have a little boy,' Meg said when the child was on her lap, 'but he is older than you. And I have a little girl who is younger. And another boy who is a tiny baby.'

'What are their names?' the child asked.

'Tobias,' Meg said, 'though we call him Toby. And Sarah, whom we call Sally. And Alexander, who is Alex. What is your name?'

'Belinda,' the child said. 'What else could you call *me*?'

'Hmm, let me see,' Meg said, making a show of thinking. 'Belle? I have a niece who is Belle, short for Isabelle. Lindy? Linda? Lin? None of them sound as pretty as *Belinda*, though, do they? I think maybe your name is perfect as it is.'

Roger had settled on the floor across Stephen's boots. Kate had turned her attention to Miss Haytor. Stephen was smiling at Cassandra, who was biting her lip and looking back, an answering smile surely lurking in her eyes.

He was glad he had come. He was glad Meg and Kate had come with him. And he was glad about that faulty catch on the drawing room door. This was so much better than last night despite the sensual pleasures the night had brought him. This was a new beginning and a good one. Cassandra was seeing the best of his family, and he was seeing the best of hers.

A new beginning . . .

Did he really want one?

A beginning of what?

But before he could either ponder the question or enter the conversation again, there was a tap on the drawing room door and the horrified face of the thin maid appeared around it.

'Oh, my lady,' she said with a gasp, 'I am so sorry. I was

getting the clothes in off the line and Belinda and Roger went inside. I thought they was in the kitchen, and then I couldn't find them *anywhere*. Belinda!' she said in loud, urgent whisper. 'Come out of here! And bring the dog with you. I *am* sorry, my lady.'

'I believe both of them have been entertaining our visitors, Mary,' Cassandra said, finally looking fully amused. 'And Belinda has been able to show off her new shoes.'

'Belinda and I are becoming friends, Mary,' Meg said. 'I do hope you will not scold her for coming in search of the dog. She is a delight, and I have been happy to meet her.'

'Roger has been keeping my feet warm,' Stephen added, smiling at the maid.

'You must be very proud of your daughter,' Kate said.

Belinda slid off Meg's lap and wrapped her arms about Roger's neck. He lumbered to his feet and bobbed out of the room ahead of her. The maid closed the door, and Stephen heard her give it an extra tug until it clicked shut.

'That was all very embarrassing,' Miss Haytor said with a little laugh. 'You will not be accustomed to mingling with the children of servants and with household dogs, Lady Montford, Lady Sheringford.'

Meg laughed.

'Oh, you are quite wrong,' she said, and she proceeded to describe their upbringing in Throckbridge. 'When you spend all your days in a small village, Miss Haytor, you become quite accustomed to mingling with people of all stations in life. It is a healthy way to grow up.'

'I still miss that life on occasion,' Kate added. 'I used to teach the very young children at the village school. We used to dance at assemblies that were for everyone, not just for the gentry. Meg is very right. It was a healthy way to grow up. *Not* that either of us is complaining about the good fortune that befell us when Stephen inherited the Merton title, of course.'

'I am certainly not complaining,' Stephen said. 'There is much privilege in the position. There is also much responsibility and much opportunity to do good.'

He looked at Miss Haytor as he spoke. Perhaps it was not a wise thing to say, as she might well be thinking that his position also gave him much opportunity to do ill, but he smiled at her, and it seemed to him that she had lost much of her prunish look in the half hour they had been there.

And Rome, to use the old cliché, had not been built in a day.

It was time to leave. He could see Meg preparing to stand up. But before she could do so, there was a knock on the front door, and they all turned their heads to look at the sitting room door, as though it offered a window through which they might see who the new caller was. After a few moments the door opened and the maid appeared again.

'Mr. Golding, my lady,' she said, 'to call on Miss Haytor.'

Miss Haytor jumped to her feet, her cheeks suffused with color.

'Oh, Mary,' she cried, 'you really ought to have called me out. I will come—'

But it was too late. A gentleman came past Mary into the room, and then looked acutely embarrassed to find it occupied. He stopped abruptly and bowed.

Cassandra got to her feet and hurried toward him, both hands outstretched, her face glowing.

'Mr. Golding,' she said. 'It has been a long time, but I do believe I would have known you anywhere.'

He was a small, thin, wiry man of middle years and unprepossessing appearance. His dark hair had receded from his forehead and thinned to an almost bald patch on the crown of his head and silvered at the temples. He wore wire-rimmed spectacles halfway down his nose.

'Little Cassie?' he said, setting his hands in hers and looking as delighted as she. 'I would *not* have known *you* except maybe for your hair. But you are Lady Paget now, are you not? Miss Haytor told me that when I met her yesterday. I am sorry about your husband's passing.'

'Thank you,' she said, and she turned to present him to her other guests, her face still bright and happy and quite incredibly beautiful. She explained that he had been her brother's tutor for a short while when they were children, though now he was secretary to a cabinet minister.

'I came to pay my respects to Miss Haytor,' Golding said after he had made his bows. 'I did not intend to walk in on you and your visitors, Lady Paget.'

'Do have a seat anyway,' Cassandra said, 'and a cup of tea.'

But he would not sit down, clearly intimidated by the company.

'I merely came,' he said, 'to see if Miss Haytor would care to join me for a drive out to Richmond Park tomorrow. I thought we might take a picnic tea.'

He looked at Miss Haytor, clearly uncomfortable.

'Just the two of us?' she asked, the color still high in her cheeks, her eyes bright. She looked really quite handsome, Stephen thought. She must have been a pretty girl in her day.

'I suppose it is not quite the thing, is it?' he said, turning his hat in his hands and looking as though he would be glad of a hole opening at his feet to swallow him up. 'I just do not know who else I could ask to accompany us. I suppose I could—'

Beginnings needed middles before they could find endings, Stephen thought, whether in this potentially budding romance between two middle-aged people who had been a governess and a tutor together in a long-ago past, or in his new relationship with Cassandra, his new *friendship* with her that might lead anywhere as far as either of them knew now. But he wanted to discover where that anywhere was.

'If you have no great objection,' he said to Golding, 'and if Lady Paget has no plans for tomorrow afternoon, perhaps she and I could join the two of you on your picnic. The ladies could be each other's chaperone.'

'That would be very decent of you, my lord,' Mr. Golding said, 'though I do not wish to impose.'

'It is no imposition at all,' Stephen said. 'I only wish I had thought of it for myself. Now all we need, Golding, is to have two ladies agree to accompany us.' He looked inquiringly from Miss Haytor to Cassandra and back again. 'I ought to have asked you first, Miss Haytor, if you mind my being one of the party. Do you?'

He shamelessly smiled his most charming smile at her.

But he could see from her eyes that she very badly wanted to go.

'You are quite correct, Lord Merton,' she said sternly. 'If Cassie is with me, I will be able to chaperone her and see that she comes to no harm. Mr. Golding, I would be delighted to come.'

They all looked questioningly at Cassandra.

'It seems,' she said without looking at Stephen, 'that I am going on a picnic tomorrow.'

'Splendid,' Golding said again, rubbing his hands together, though he still looked horribly embarrassed. 'I will have a hired carriage outside the door at two o' clock, then.'

'Perhaps,' Stephen said, 'since you are presumably supplying the tea, Golding, you will allow me to supply the carriage?'

'That is decent of you, my lord,' Golding said, and he bowed himself out of the room without further ado.

'It is time we all took our leave,' Meg said, getting to her feet. 'Thank you for tea and your kind hospitality, Lady Paget. And it has been very pleasant to meet you, Miss Haytor.'

'It has indeed,' Kate said. 'I wanted us to share some teaching stories, Miss Haytor, but we have not had a chance, have we? Perhaps next time.'

'I will look forward to tomorrow, ma'am,' Stephen said, making her a bow before following the others out of the room. Cassandra was with his sisters.

He let Meg and Kate go out to the waiting carriage while he lingered in the hall to take his leave.

'I have always had a weakness for picnics,' he said. 'Fresh air. Food and drink. Grass and trees and flowers. Congenial company. They are a powerful combination.'

'The company may not be very congenial,' she warned him.

He laughed.

'I am sure,' he said, 'I will like Golding very well indeed.'

She half smiled at his deliberate misunderstanding of her meaning.

'I meant myself,' she said. 'You must know that I do not want to go, that this new . . . relationship you spoke of last night is doomed to failure. We cannot be friends, Stephen, having once been protector and mistress.'

'Lovers cannot be friends, then?' he asked her.

She did not reply.

'I have a need to make amends,' he told her. 'Instead of bringing some joy back into your life, I did the opposite, Cass. Let me make amends.'

'I do not want—'

'We all want joy,' he said. 'We all *need* it. And there is such a thing, Cass. I promise you.'

She merely stared at him, her green eyes almost luminous.

'Tell me you will look forward to the picnic,' he said.

'Oh, very well,' she said. 'If my doing so will make you feel better, I will say it. I will not sleep tonight for eager excitement to have the picnic begin. I shall say my prayers for good weather every hour on the hour.'

He smiled at her and flicked her chin with one finger before hurrying outside and climbing into the carriage to take his place opposite his sisters, his back to the horses.

'Oh, Stephen,' Kate said when the door had been closed and the carriage rocked into motion, 'I did not understand this morning. Or perhaps I *chose* not to understand. Are none of us to have a smooth road to matrimony and happiness, then?'

'But it was a rough road that led three of us to happiness, Kate,' Meg said quietly. 'Perhaps a smooth road does not do it. Perhaps we should *wish* this rough road on Stephen.'

But she did not smile or look particularly happy. Neither

did Kate. Stephen did not ask them what they meant – it was all too obvious.

They were wrong, though.

He was merely attempting to set right a wrong.

He was merely trying to bring some joy to Cassandra's life so that his conscience could rest in peace.

They rode on in silence.

13

Cassandra spent the following morning on Oxford Street. She was not shopping for herself, however. She had asked Mary if she might take Belinda with her in order to buy her a sunbonnet for the summer to replace the quaint hat that had once belonged to a stable boy. She did not offer to buy more clothes for the child. One had to be careful with Mary. She was very proud. She was also very protective of her daughter, whom she adored.

The task was accomplished at the very first shop they entered, and Belinda came out wearing a pretty blue cotton bonnet with a slightly stiffened brim and a frill to shield her neck and shoulders from the rays of the sun. It was tied beneath the chin with sunshine yellow ribbons, which were attached to the bonnet with clusters of tiny artificial buttercups and cornflowers.

Belinda was wide-eyed with the splendor of it and turned when they left the shop to admire her image in the glass.

They strolled along the street, hand in hand, until they

stopped outside a toy shop. Soon Belinda's nose was pressed to the glass as she stared silently through it. She showed no visible excitement, no expectation that anything in the window or the shop would ever be hers. She demanded nothing. But she was obviously lost to the world around her.

Cassandra watched her fondly. Just having the chance to stand and gaze was probably enough to make this the high point of Belinda's day. She was a remarkably contented child.

She was gazing, Cassandra realized, not at everything in the window, but at one particular toy – a doll. It was not the largest or fanciest. Indeed, it was just the opposite. It was a baby doll, made of china and wearing only a simple cotton nightgown as it lay on a white woolen shawl. After gazing and gazing, Belinda lifted one hand and waved her fingers slowly.

Cassandra blinked back tears. As far as she knew, Belinda had no toys.

'I think,' she said, 'that baby needs a mama.'

'Baby.' Belinda pressed her hand against the glass.

'Would you like to hold him?' Cassandra asked.

The child's head turned and she gazed up at Cassandra with big, solemn eyes. Slowly she nodded.

'Come, then,' Cassandra said, and took the child's hand again and led her inside the shop.

It was a foolish extravagance. She was no longer Lord Merton's mistress, was she? And she had already bought the bonnet. But food and clothing and shelter were not the only necessities of life. Love was too. And if love must cost her some money this morning, then so be it.

It all seemed worthwhile when the shop assistant leaned

into the window and lifted out the doll and placed it in Belinda's arms.

Cassandra would not have been surprised to see the child's eyes pop right out of her head. Belinda gazed at the china baby with slightly open mouth and held it stiffly for a few moments before cradling it in her arms and rocking it gently.

'Would you like to take him home and be his mama?' Cassandra asked gently.

Again Belinda's eyes turned upward, and she nodded.

Behind them a smartly dressed little girl was petulantly demanding the doll with the long blond ringlets, *not* the stupid one with the velvet dress and pelisse. *And* she needed the baby carriage because the wheels had come off hers. *And* the skipping rope because the handles on the one she had had for her birthday last week were an ugly green.

The baby doll came without clothes, Cassandra discovered. She bought the nightdress to go with it and then, because Belinda kissed the baby's forehead and promised in a whisper to keep him warm, she bought the blanket too.

She had had no idea children's toys were so expensive.

But as they walked out of the shop she did not regret the extravagance. Belinda was still virtually speechless. But she did remember something of the persistent teachings of Mary. She looked up at Cassandra, her baby held close in her arms.

'Thank you, my lady,' she said.

There was nothing careless about her gratitude. It was heartfelt.

'Well,' Cassandra said, 'we could not just leave him there without a mama, could we?'

'She is a girl,' Belinda said.

'Oh.' Cassandra smiled, and looked up into the smiling faces of Lady Carling and the Countess of Sheringford.

'I *thought* that was you, Lady Paget,' Lady Carling said. 'I told Margaret it was, and we crossed the road to make sure. What a charming child. Is she yours?'

'Oh, no,' Cassandra said. 'Her mother is my housekeeper, cook, maid – my everything.'

'She is Belinda,' the countess said, 'and I see that she is wearing her smart new shoes. How do you do, Lady Paget? It looks as if you have a new baby, Belinda. May I see her? *Is* she a girl?'

Belinda nodded and moved the blanket back from the doll's face.

'Oh, she is lovely,' the countess said. 'And she looks warm and contented. Does she have a name?'

'Beth,' Belinda said.

'That is pretty,' the countess said. 'Beth is usually short for Elizabeth. Did you know that? But Elizabeth is far too big a name for such a tiny baby. You are wise to call her Beth.'

'Margaret and I are on our way to the bakery for a cup of tea,' Lady Carling said. 'Will you join us, Lady Paget? I am sure there will be at least one cake there to take Belinda's fancy. And surely they serve lemonade.'

Cassandra's first instinct was to say no. But it could do her no harm to be seen in public with such ladies. If she could become gradually more and more accepted in society, perhaps eventually she would be able to find some elderly or sickly lady who needed a companion and would trust her enough to employ her. It was not a happy prospect, and she did not know what would happen to Alice and Mary when the time came, but . . .

Well, it did no harm to accept any olive branch that was freely extended to her.

'Thank you,' she said. 'Belinda, would you like a cake?'

Belinda, saucer-eyed again, nodded and then remembered her manners.

'Yes, please, my lady,' she said.

The ladies sat talking for almost an hour while Belinda sat quietly at the table, first eating the white cake with the pink icing that she had chosen with meticulous care, then holding her cup with both hands to drink the lemonade, and finally wiping her mouth and hands carefully with her linen napkin so that she could rock her doll again. She murmured to it and kissed it as the ladies talked.

'It is a lovely day for your picnic in Richmond,' the countess said.

'A picnic?' Lady Carling looked at Cassandra with interest. 'How lovely for you. There is no better way to spend a summer afternoon, is there?'

'My former governess, who lives with me, is only forty-two years old,' Cassandra said. 'Far too young to go as far as Richmond for a picnic alone with a gentleman of the same age – or so she believes. When Mr. Golding came calling yesterday afternoon to ask her to go, she hesitated, though she clearly wanted to say yes. And so Lord Merton offered his services and mine as chaperones.'

They all laughed – at the very moment when the Earl of Merton himself and Mr. Huxtable, angel and devil, walked past the bakery window. Cassandra's heart or stomach – or *something* – turned over. There was a very young lady on Lord Merton's arm, the one with whom he had danced the opening set at his sister's ball, and his head was bent to listen to what she said. He was smiling down at her.

A young woman who must be her maid was walking a few steps behind them.

It was not jealousy Cassandra felt. It was . . . Oh, it was the knowledge that she was nominally his mistress, that she had spent two nights with him in her bed, that she had enjoyed the experience far more than she cared to admit, that she had both seen and felt his gorgeous body against hers.

They were thoughts that had no business leaping to mind like this.

He wanted to be her friend.

It was with someone like that very young lady that he belonged. She was laughing at something he said, and he was laughing back at her.

It was with her he belonged. Not with Cassandra. He was youthful and carefree and charming and filled with light.

She ought not to have allowed him to try to turn their failed affair into friendship.

Ah, but he was so . . .

He was so *lovely*.

'Oh, there are Stephen and Constantine,' Lady Sheringford said, and at the same moment Mr. Huxtable saw them and said something to the other two, and they all looked through the window and smiled. Lord Merton raised one hand to wave.

He said something to the young lady, but she shook her head and after another moment or two took her leave and continued on her way, her maid closing the distance to walk beside her. The two gentlemen came into the bakery and approached the table.

'Is *this* how ladies stay so slender?' Mr. Huxtable asked, one eyebrow cocked in irony.

'No, of course not,' Lady Carling said. 'It is walking about shopping that does that, Mr. Huxtable. Besides, it is only Belinda who has had a cake. The rest of us have been very good and very self-denying. Lady Paget, I noticed, did not even put sugar in her tea and only the merest splash of milk. Do pull up two chairs and join us.'

But Cassandra was feeling inexplicably breathless. She did not belong in this family group. Besides, it was time to take Belinda home. Mary would be worrying.

'You may have our chairs,' she said, standing. 'Belinda and I must be going.'

Belinda got obediently to her feet, looking up at the Earl of Merton as she did so.

'I got a new doll,' she said.

'Is it a doll?' he said, looking astonished. He went down on his haunches beside her. 'I thought it was a baby. May I see it?'

'It is a her,' she said, drawing the blanket away from the doll's face. 'She is Beth. Elizabeth really, but that is too big a name.'

'Beth suits her better,' he agreed, touching the side of one finger to the doll's cheek. 'She must be very cozy in that blanket with you to rock her. She is fast asleep.'

'Yes,' she said as he smiled at her.

Cassandra swallowed awkwardly and was convinced that everyone must have heard. There was a look of open tenderness on his face, yet he was an aristocrat looking at a servant's child. Her illegitimate child. It would be *very* easy indeed to come to care for him, to come to trust him when experience had taught her to trust no man, especially the gentle ones.

Nigel had been gentle . . .

Lord Merton got to his feet.

'Allow me to walk the two of you home,' he said, looking at Cassandra.

How could she say no without causing something of a scene before the interested gaze of Lady Carling and his relatives?

'That is not necessary,' she said. 'But thank you.'

'Do enjoy the picnic this afternoon,' the countess said.

'Picnic?' Mr. Huxtable said, his dark gaze locking on Cassandra's. 'Am I missing something?'

'Lady Paget's companion is going on a picnic to Richmond with a gentleman friend, Constantine,' the countess explained, 'and Stephen and Lady Paget are going with them as chaperones.'

'Fascinating,' he said, his eyes still on Cassandra, his eyebrows raised. *'Chaperones?'*

Cassandra bent to help Belinda wrap the doll more tightly in the blanket. She kissed the child on the cheek and took her free hand in hers. But when they were outside, Belinda stopped, handed the doll to Lord Merton without a by-your-leave, and took his free hand so that she walked between them, attached to each.

He carried the doll in the crook of his arm, meeting the glances of several passersby with a look of sheepish amusement.

It all seemed horribly domestic to Cassandra, almost as if the doll was real and both it and Belinda were her children – or theirs.

Was he genuine after all?

Ah, but how could one possibly know?

Were there such pure beings as angels?

And what was she doing consorting with one if there were?

Alice was excited about this afternoon, though she would not have admitted it even if she were stretched on the rack. Alice had always been a mother figure to Cassandra, more than just a governess and companion. She had always been an emotional rock of stability. During the past ten years she had perhaps kept Cassandra from losing her sanity. But now Cassandra felt guilty over the fact that she had never really thought of Alice as a woman. Alice had been very young – not even twenty – when she first came to live with them. Even when Cassandra married, Alice was only in her early thirties. And yet all these years she had never had a beau, never had a chance for marriage or personal happiness.

Had she loved Mr. Golding all those years ago? Had she had hopes then? Had she thought of him at all, dreamed of him, perhaps, in the intervening years? Had meeting him again two days ago been a momentous occasion in her life? Was hope now being reborn? Perhaps painfully?

Cassandra felt deeply ashamed that she did not know the answers to any of the questions. But she would do all in her power to see to it that a relationship had a chance to develop now if both parties wanted it and if there was anything she could do to facilitate it short of shamelessly matchmaking.

She looked forward to the picnic for Alice's sake.

Oh, and for her own sake too, she admitted reluctantly as Belinda told Lord Merton that she had a new bonnet and he declared that he had not seen anything more fetching for a long, long time. She ought *not* to be looking forward to it. She ought not to allow him to befriend her when it was with young ladies like the one he had been with earlier that he belonged. Young ladies without the emotional baggage she dragged along with her.

But since she was committed now to spending the afternoon in his company, she was simply going to enjoy herself.

It seemed an age since she had last done that.

Had she *ever* done it? Simply enjoyed herself?

He had promised her joy. He had promised her that there was such a thing as joy.

It sounded altogether more precious than happiness.

And more impossible.

But she was going to enjoy herself.

Oh, she *was*.

When they arrived at the house on Portman Street, Belinda stood quietly on the doorstep while Cassandra took the key from beneath the flowerpot beside the steps rather than use the door knocker. She opened the door, and Belinda took her doll carefully from Lord Merton's arm and went streaking off in the direction of the kitchen, shrieking loudly and talking so fast that her words tripped all over one another. But amid the excited jumble, Cassandra did distinguish a few words – pink icing and Beth and buttercups and bonnets and two grand ladies and a white wool blanket and a frill to stop her neck from getting sunburned and a gentleman who had carried Beth without waking her.

Poor Mary must be deafened, Cassandra thought, smiling as she withdrew the key and put it back in its hiding place.

And suddenly a terrible pain smote her, as it did occasionally, always crashing in on her without any prior warning.

She had no living children of her own.

Only four dead babies.

No one to come running to deafen *her*.

She drew a deep breath through her nose and let it out slowly through her mouth before turning to offer her hand to Lord Merton.

'Thank you,' she said. 'But do you see how extravagant I am, Stephen? Do you see how I have spent your money today?'

'To make a child happy?' he said, raising her hand to his lips. 'I cannot for the life of me think of a better use for it, Cass. I will see you this afternoon?'

'Yes,' she said, and she stepped inside the house as he went striding off down the street. A man who was charming and amiable and physically perfect. And very, very attractive.

Ah, yes, it would be very easy indeed to care for him as well as to lust after him. And perhaps he was genuine.

Or perhaps not.

She was going to enjoy this afternoon anyway. She had been extravagant with money this morning. She was going to be extravagant with feelings this afternoon.

She had hoarded feelings for so very long.

She was not even sure there were any left inside her to squander.

She would find out later today.

It amused Stephen later in the afternoon to hand Miss Haytor into his open barouche and watch her scurry to seat herself beside Cassandra rather than take the empty seat opposite. Now Stephen had to sit there with Golding. Miss Haytor, he could tell from her rather flustered manner, was very nervous.

Perhaps, he thought, this was the closest she had come to being courted. It was a sad thought. But – better late than never.

Golding too seemed even more agitated than he had yesterday as he supervised the stowing of his large, very new picnic basket onto the back of the carriage. If the basket was full of food, it would surely feed an army.

Golding, dressed formally and smartly, was almost tongue-tied as the journey began. Miss Haytor, dressed immaculately in a dark blue walking dress and pelisse, was stiff and silent.

Cassandra, looking ravishing in pale spring green with a straw bonnet, seemed as amused as Stephen felt, though he guessed there was no malice in the smile she exchanged with him – as there was none in his.

The burden of conversation, Stephen decided, was going to be his for the time being, anyway. But making conversation had never been difficult for him. Often it was simply a matter of asking pertinent questions.

'You were once a teacher, Golding?' he asked as his barouche picked up speed. 'And you and Miss Haytor once taught together?'

'We did, indeed,' Golding said. 'Miss Haytor was Miss Young's governess, and I was Master Young's tutor. But his need of me lasted all too short a time, and I was forced to move on. I regretted leaving. Miss Haytor was an excellent teacher. I admired her dedication and her well-educated mind.'

'I was no more dedicated than you, Mr. Golding,' Miss Haytor said, finding her tongue at last. 'I once found you in Sir Henry Young's study at midnight, trying to devise a method of teaching Wesley long division that he would understand. And my own education was far inferior to your own.'

'Only in the sort of formal education that attendance at university can provide,' he said. 'At the time you were far more widely read than I, Miss Haytor. You were able to recommend several books that have since become my favorites. I always remember you when I reread them.'

'That is kind of you, I am sure,' she said. 'But you would have discovered them for yourself eventually, I daresay.'

'I doubt that,' he said. 'With so many books waiting to be read, I often do not know where to start and so do not start at all. I would like to hear what you have been reading in the last few years. Perhaps I will be inspired to try something new again that is not merely concerned with politics.'

Stephen met Cassandra's eyes. They did not smile openly at each other. They might have been caught doing so and might have made the other two self-conscious again. But they smiled anyway. He knew she was smiling though her face was in repose. And he knew he was smiling back.

And even if he misinterpreted her expression, at least she was not wearing her habitual mask this afternoon. She had not been wearing it this morning either. Indeed, this morning he had been unwary enough to feel that he could fall in love with her if he allowed himself to do something so foolish. When Con had drawn his attention to the bakery, it was Cassandra he had seen. He had not even noticed Meg and Lady Carling for a few moments. And when he had walked home with her and the child, he had felt . . .

Well, never mind. They had been foolish feelings.

Stephen had brought only a coachman with him, and Golding had brought no servants of his own, having had a hackney cab drop him and his basket in Portman Street. When they arrived at Richmond Park after a longish drive, then, the gentlemen carried the basket between them while the ladies walked ahead to choose a decent spot for a picnic.

They found one on a grassy slope some distance into the park beneath some of the ancient oaks for which the park was famous, looking down upon lawns and across at rhododendron bushes with more oaks behind them. In the distance they could see the Pen Ponds, which were always kept well stocked with fish.

A few other people were out strolling, though not very many, and no one else appeared to be picnicking. No one else was up on their slope. As Stephen had hoped, they were to enjoy a quiet, secluded afternoon.

After the two men had set down the basket, Golding opened it and drew out a large blanket – one explanation for the fact that the basket had not been as heavy as Stephen had expected it would be. Golding shook it out and would have spread it on the grass himself, but Miss Haytor hurried to help him, grasping two corners while he held the others. Together they set it down flat, without a wrinkle.

'It is too early for tea,' Golding said. 'Shall we go for a walk?'

'But someone may make off with the basket and the blanket while we are gone, Mr. Golding,' Miss Haytor pointed out.

'Quite right,' he said, frowning. 'We will not be able to walk far. We will have to keep them in our sight.'

'I am quite content to sit here,' Cassandra said, 'and bask in the sunshine and breathe in the fresh air and drink in the sight of so much green countryside. Why do you not walk with Mr. Golding, Alice, and Lord Merton and I will stay here.'

Miss Haytor looked suspiciously at Stephen. He smiled his best smile at her.

'I will protect Lady Paget from harm, ma'am,' he said. 'The public setting of the park and the other people strolling here will be effective chaperones for both you and her.'

She was still not quite convinced, he could see. But her desire to walk – *alone* – with Golding was being weighed against caution.

'Allie,' Cassandra said, 'if we have driven all this way merely to stroll together in a tight circle about the picnic basket, we might as well have stayed at home and eaten in the back garden beneath Mary's clothesline.'

Miss Haytor was convinced. She went down the slope with Golding and then took his offered arm as they turned in the direction of the distant ponds.

'I believe,' Cassandra said, seating herself on the blanket and removing first her gloves and then her bonnet and setting them down beside her, 'I have been incredibly selfish.'

'In sending them off walking while we remain here?' he asked.

'In keeping Alice with me all these years,' she said. 'She started to look for other employment when I accepted Nigel's marriage offer. She even went to one interview and was impressed with both the children and their parents. But I begged her to come with me into the country, at least for a year. I had never lived in the country and was somewhat apprehensive. She came because I was so insistent, and then she stayed, year after year. I thought only of *my* needs and told her more times than I can count that I did not know how I would live without her.'

'It is basic human need to be needed,' he said. 'She very obviously loves you. I daresay she was quite content to stay with you.'

She turned her face toward him. She was sitting with her knees bent, her arms clasped around them.

'You are too kind, Stephen,' she said. 'She might have met someone to marry years ago, though. She might have been happy.'

'And she might not,' he said. 'Not many governesses are in a position to meet prospective husbands, are they? And her new employers might not have needed her for anything more than imparting a certain body of knowledge to their children. The children might have resented her. She might have been dismissed soon after acquiring the position. Her next one might have been worse. *Anything* might have happened, in other words.'

She was laughing, her face still turned toward him.

'You are quite right,' she said. 'Perhaps after all I have been saving her for this happy reunion with the love of her life. I think Mr. Golding may well *be* that. Today is not for gloom and guilt, is it? Today is for a picnic. I have always associated that word with pure enjoyment. But there were never any picnics during my marriage. It is strange, that. I did not even realize it until today. I came here to enjoy myself, Stephen.'

He sat with one knee raised, the sole of his Hessian boot flat on the blanket, one arm draped over his knee, the other slightly behind him, bracing his weight. They were sitting in the dappled shade offered by the spreading branches of one of the oaks. His hat was on the blanket beside him.

He watched, fascinated, as she lifted her arms, drew the

pins from her hair, and shook it free over her shoulders and along her back. She set the pins down on the brim of her bonnet and drew the fingers of both hands through her hair to release any tangles.

'If you have a brush in your reticule,' he said, 'I will do that for you.'

'Will you?' She looked back at him. 'But I removed the pins so that I can lie back on the blanket and look at the sky. Perhaps you will brush it later, before I put it back up.'

The strange thing was that she was not flirting with him. Neither was she using her siren's voice or eyes. Yet he felt the tension between them like a palpable thing – and doubted she did. She was as he had never seen her before, relaxed and smiling and without artifice.

He was dazzled.

She was far more attractive to him than when she was trying to attract.

She stretched out on the blanket, adjusting her clothes to make sure her dress decently covered her ankles. And she laced her hands behind her head and gazed upward. She sighed with obvious contentment.

'If only we could keep our connection with the earth,' she said, 'all would be well with our lives. Do you think?'

'Sometimes,' he said, 'we become so intoxicated by the strange notion that we are lords of all we survey that we forget we are creatures of the earth.'

'Just like butterflies,' she said, 'and robins and kittens.'

'And lions and ravens,' he said.

'Why is the sky blue?' she asked.

'I have no idea.' He grinned down at her, and her eyes turned toward him. 'But I am very glad it is. If the sun merely beamed down its light from a black sky, the world would be a gloomier place.'

'Just like before a thunderstorm,' she said.

'Worse.'

'Or like nighttime with a brighter moon. Come down here and look,' she said.

He deliberately misunderstood her. He lowered his head over hers and slowly searched her face, his eyes coming to rest finally on her green eyes. They were smiling.

'Very nice indeed,' he said. He meant it too.

'Likewise.' Her eyes were roaming over his face as well. 'Stephen, you are going to have wrinkles at the outer corners of your eyes when you are older, and they are going to make you impossibly attractive.'

'When the time comes,' he said, 'I'll remember that you warned me.'

'Will you?' She lifted her hands and set two fingertips lightly over the spots where the wrinkles would be. 'Will you remember me?'

'Oh, always,' he said.

'And I will remember you,' she said. 'I will remember that once in my life I met a man who is perfect in every way.'

'I am not perfect,' he said.

'Allow me to dream,' she said. 'To me you are perfect. *Today* you are perfect. I will not know you long enough or intimately enough to learn of your weaknesses and vices, which are doubtless legion. In memory you will always be my perfect angel. Perhaps I will have a medallion made and wear it about my neck.'

She smiled.

He did not.

'We will not know each other for long?' he asked her.

She shook her head.

'No, of course not,' she said. 'But that does not matter, Stephen. There is today, and today is all that matters.'

'Yes,' he said.

As far as he knew, there were no people walking in sight of them. If there were, they must already be scandalized enough. What difference would it make if he—

He kissed her.

And she kissed him back, first cupping his face gently with her palms and then sliding her arms about his neck.

It was a warm, unhurried, quite chaste kiss that did not even involve their tongues. It was the most dangerous kiss Stephen had ever shared. He knew that as soon as it ended and he lifted his head to look down into her face again.

Because it had been a kiss of shared affection bordering on love. Not lust. *Love.*

'And now,' she said, 'will you do as I suggested a few minutes ago and come down here and look? Upward? At the sky?'

She spoke softly, without smiling, despite the teasing nature of her words.

He stretched out beside her and looked upward – and knew what she had meant when she spoke of connection to the earth. He could feel it, firm and eternal beneath him despite the thickness of the blanket. And above him he could see the blue, cloudless sky and – connecting the two – the leafy branches of the oak tree.

And he was a part of that connection, that gloriously spinning place, as was Cassandra.

He reached over and took her hand in his. He laced his fingers with hers.

'If you could just step off into the sky,' she said, 'and be a new person, *would* you?'

He gave the question some consideration.

'And so lose myself as I know me, and everything and everyone that have helped shape me into the person I am?' he said. 'No. But temporary escape would be good now and then. I am greedy and want the best of both worlds, you see. Would you?'

'I can lie here,' she said, 'and dream of letting go and floating off into blueness and light. But I would have to take myself with me or the whole exercise would be pointless. And so nothing would really be changed, would it? If I had to leave myself behind in order to escape . . . Well, I might as well be dead. And I think I would hate that. I want to live.'

'I am glad to hear it,' he said, chuckling.

'Oh, but you do not understand,' she said. 'It surprises me. For a long time I have thought that if given the choice without actually having to take my own life, I would choose death.'

He felt a sudden chill.

'But you no longer feel that way?' he asked her.

'No,' she said. She laughed softly. 'No! I want to *live*.'

He squeezed her hand more tightly, and they lay together in silence while he pondered what she had just said. What must her life have been like if she would have preferred death to life – and if the preference was so habitual that it actually surprised her now to discover that she preferred life?

Sometimes he forgot – or chose to forget – that her life had been so intolerable that she had killed.

But he would not think of that today.

He turned his head to look at her after a few minutes, and she returned the look. They both smiled.

'Happy?' he asked.

'Mmm.'

He sighed and set his free arm over his eyes. He had not stepped out into space, but he had stepped into something new after all. This was not seduction. This was not even simply friendship. This was . . . He did not know what it was. But he had the feeling his life would never be the same again.

And he was not sure if the thought alarmed him or exhilarated him.

After a few minutes he drifted off into that pleasant state of being asleep and yet half aware too of everything around him.

14

Stephen was asleep. He was not exactly snoring, but he was breathing deeply in such a way that there was no doubt he was sleeping.

Cassandra closed her eyes and smiled – and felt a desperate sort of tenderness for him and for the stolen, carefree pleasure of the afternoon. She had decided to enjoy herself, and that was what she was doing. All her defenses, all her anxieties, all her mistrust of anyone outside her own tiny circle of friends, had been left at home, to be taken up again after the picnic was over.

Perhaps.

Or perhaps not.

She allowed herself the cautious belief that perhaps after all there was one good man in the world, and he was lying beside her, his fingers relaxed about her own. She knew he was not perfect. As he kept reminding her, no one was. But he seemed as close to being perfect as anyone could be.

And if he did have character flaws or even vices, she would never know. For, of course, she would not know him for long. Not beyond the end of the Season, at the latest. And if she was very fortunate, she would never hear any unsavory stories about him in the future.

She was going to live in the country again. She had decided that just now, while lying here. It was as if this little piece of the country, the earth beneath her, the sky above, the tree branches between, had cleared her mind of a dense, dark fog that had befuddled it for a long, long time. She was going to find a little cottage in a small village somewhere in England, well off the beaten track, and she was going to live there and grow flowers and embroider bright tablecloths and handkerchiefs and go to church every Sunday and help serve teas at parish functions and dance at local assemblies and . . .

Well.

She swallowed against a lump in her throat. Perhaps she had stepped off into the sky, after all. But it was not an impractical dream. Or an impossible one.

For something else had just struck her with over-whelming force.

She had been a victim for ten long years. She had not been able to help the vicious beatings. Nigel had been stronger than she, and he had been her husband and had had the legal right to discipline her as he saw fit. But she had developed a victim's mind, a cowering, abject thing intent more than anything else upon remaining hidden in every conceivable way, upon figuratively holding her breath lest someone notice her and come at her, fists flying. And her victim's mentality she *could* help. If her mind was not under her control, then life was really not worth living.

Life had not felt worth living for almost ten years.

Today, suddenly, it did. She turned her head toward Stephen, tears in her eyes, but he was still sleeping. *Fortunately*, he was still sleeping.

Ah, how terribly beautiful he was. How achingly attractive. How she longed . . .

But he had no part in her new dream. How could he? She had seduced him and made him feel obligated to her. It was all quite unfair. He should be back firmly in his own world with young ladies like the one who had walked with him this morning.

But this new dream did have something to do with him. She had him to thank for it. By being kind to her when he had absolutely no reason to be, he had reminded her of her own worth. Of her power over her own life.

Could she make such an extravagant claim for him when her acquaintance with him was so slight, when it had begun in such an ugly manner, with seduction and then ensnarement?

Was he *really* an angel?

She smiled through her tears at the fanciful thought. She would be seeing wings and a halo soon.

She was no longer going to be penniless and dependent and abject and frightened and defensive and all the horrid, cringing things she had been since Bruce had tossed her out of her home and washed his hands of her.

She was going to fight boldly back.

Tomorrow she was going to find a lawyer who would be willing to take on her case despite her near-poverty. With Stephen's money she was going to pay him a small retainer, with a promise of the rest of his fee when he had got justice for her. According to both her marriage contract and Nigel's will, she was entitled to have received a lump sum payment from his personal fortune and a monthly pension from the estate. She was also supposed to have retained all the jewelry that had been given her since her marriage. It was her *personal property*. She was to have had use of the dower house too and the town house here in London for the rest of her natural life, unless she married again. She had no interest in the dower house, but the London house would have been worth having this spring.

Bruce had told her she might have her freedom but nothing else. The implication had been that if she did not accept his ultimatum, everything would be lost to her, even her freedom. Even, perhaps, her life.

And she had believed him.

It was absurd!

If he had believed that her guilt in his father's death could be proved, he would have had her arrested without further ado. He would not have suggested making any deal with her.

He could prove no such thing because there *was* no proof.

She had known all this before. Why, then, did it seem like a blazing revelation today?

She was going to go after her money and her jewelry and even the town house. Any decent lawyer would surely be able to get all three for her with very little trouble. Both a marriage contract and a will were legally binding documents. He would not be risking much by taking her small retainer and waiting for the rest of his fee.

She closed her eyes and could feel the world spinning – with her on it. She was *alive*. And Stephen's warm, relaxed hand was in her own, their fingers loosely laced.

If only the world could be made to slow on its axis. If only this moment could be prolonged. If she wanted, she was well aware – if she *chose* – she could fall in love with him. Deeply. Head over ears. Irrevocably.

She did not so choose. She was taking joy out of this single afternoon. She was borrowing some of his light. The light that was within herself was so very dim. Just a short while ago, if asked, she would have said that it had been extinguished altogether. But it had not. He had rekindled it in her. He was all light. Or so it seemed.

She had nothing nearly as powerful or precious to offer in return and so she would not cling to him. She would let him go as soon as she was able.

She had spoken the truth a little while ago, though. She *would* remember him. Always. She would not literally have a medallion made to wear about her neck, of course. But she would not need one. She believed she would always be able to close her eyes and see him – and hear him and feel the warm clasp of his hand. She would remember the subtle musk of his cologne.

As soon as she had her money and jewels, she would return all of *his* money – with thanks. And all ties between them would be severed, all debts paid, all dependence on one side and obligation on the other at an end.

Their relationship – if that was an appropriate word for what was between them – would be somehow healed. And it would end.

He would remember her – *if* he remembered – with respect and perhaps a little fond nostalgia.

She lifted her head slightly and looked down the slope to the left. In the far distance she could see two figures, and she was almost sure they were coming this way. She was almost certain too that they were Alice and Mr. Golding. And, goodness, Alice would go for Stephen's head with her reticule if she saw them stretched out on the blanket like this, hand in hand, her hair all loose about her shoulders.

It would be grossly unfair.

Cassandra chuckled, nevertheless, at the mental image she had conjured, and she turned her head toward Stephen and squeezed his hand.

'I think,' she said, 'it is time to sit up and make ourselves respectable again. Not that *you* are looking disreputable, but I need to put my hair up. Will you give it a quick brush for me?'

He smiled sleepily at her.

'I believe I almost nodded off,' he said.

She laughed. 'I believe you almost did.'

She sat up, found the brush in her reticule, handed it to him, and turned half away from him, pulling her hairpins closer as she did so.

He drew the brush with a firm stroke through the full length of her hair on the left side. He moved the brush a little farther to the right and did it again. Within a minute the whole mass of her hair was smooth and crackling, and her scalp was tingling.

'You do that awfully well,' she said, gathering her hair at the neck and twisting it into a knot before stabbing pins into it to stop it from falling down again. She drew on her bonnet.

'Cassandra,' he said, 'was your husband Belinda's father?'

Her hands paused on the ribbons.

'No,' she said.

'The present Paget, then?' he asked. 'The son?'

'No,' she said again, tying a bow to one side of her chin.

'I am sorry,' he said. 'I have wondered.'

'It was not rape,' she said. 'I believe Mary really loved . . . the father.'

She waited for him to ask more questions, but he did not do so.

She sighed.

'Nigel had three sons,' she said. 'Bruce is the eldest, and then there are Oscar and William. Oscar has been in the army for years. I have met him only two or three times, none recently. He did not come home for his father's funeral. William has always been a wanderer. He was in America for several years. Then, four years ago, he came home for a few months before going to Canada with a fur trader. Belinda was born seven months after he left. Mary claims that he did not know about her when he went away. I like to believe her. I have always been fond of him, though he certainly *does* have his faults.'

'Paget did not dismiss her?' he asked.

'Nigel?' she said. 'No. He left the management of the household to me. I did not tell him that Mary's child was his granddaughter. Indeed, I believe he was unaware that there *was* a child in the servants' quarters.'

Until the end.

'Bruce dismissed her, though, when he came to live at Carmel,' she said. 'She had nowhere to go, no family members who were willing to take her in. She was in a desperate case. It was no particular kindness to bring her and Belinda to town with me, but at least we all had one another. Alice too. And Roger.'

Alice and Mr. Golding were quite distinguishable now. Cassandra raised an arm to wave.

'William Belmont is still in Canada?' Stephen asked.

'I do not know,' she said. 'I ought not even to have told you all this. It was not my secret to tell, was it? But I will add that Mary is not loose of morals. I believe she really loved William. No, I am sure she *loves* him. And waits for him.'

He rested a hand on her shoulder and squeezed.

'I stand in judgment on no one, Cass,' he said. 'Me of all people.'

He lowered his hand and turned his head to smile at the approaching couple.

Alice and Mr. Golding strolled all the way to the Pen Ponds and about them before making their way back to the picnic site at the same leisurely pace. They talked for a long time about books, and then they reminisced a bit about shared experiences when they had both taught the Young children, even though that span of time had been all too short. He surprised Alice then by talking of his wife of eight years, who had died three years ago.

It had not occurred to her that perhaps he had been married – that perhaps he still was.

It saddened and then rather amused her to realize that he had not carried a torch for her all these years. For, of course, she had not carried one for him either. She had known him briefly, had fallen violently in love with him because she had been a lonely girl with almost no chance to meet young men, had mourned him for perhaps a year after he left, and had then more or less forgotten him – until she met him again two days ago.

He was still a good-looking man in a thin, bookish sort of way. He was still good company. And oh, it felt very good indeed to have a man conversing exclusively with *her* for all of an hour. And to be walking with her arm drawn through his. If she was not very careful indeed, she would fall in love with him all over again – and how foolish *that* would be at her age.

Then he asked about Cassie, and she realized that he did not *know*.

'It must have been distressing,' he said, 'for Lady Paget to lose her husband at so young an age. Was she very fond of him?'

Alice hesitated. It was not for *her* to answer that question either way. Though if what he assumed had been true, of course, she would quite readily agree with him without feeling that she was breaking some confidence. She could answer noncommittally, but it was possible, even probable, that he *would* hear the rumors one of these days, and then he would think that she had not trusted him.

'He was an abuser of the worst order,' she said. 'Any fondness she felt for him when she married him quickly died.'

'Oh, goodness me,' he said. 'Miss Haytor, how dreadful! There is no man more despicable, I believe, than a wifebeater. He is the worst kind of bully.'

She could have left it at that.

'He died violently,' she said. 'Some say that Cassie did it. Indeed, I believe she is notorious here in town, where the story is that she is an axe murderer.'

'Miss Haytor!' He stopped abruptly and dropped her arm in order to turn to look at her with shocked, dismayed eyes. 'It cannot possibly be true!'

'He was shot,' she said, 'with his own pistol.'

'By . . . ?' he asked, his dark eyebrows arced up into his forehead. 'By Lady Paget?'

'No,' she said. And when he continued to stare at her, not moving, 'It could have been me.'

'Could have?' he said.

'I hated him enough,' she said. 'I never thought it possible that I could hate anyone with any degree of intensity, but I hated him. A thousand times I thought of leaving to seek employment elsewhere, but a thousand times I remembered that my dear Cassie did not have the same freedom to leave and that I was almost all she had to comfort her. I could have done it, Mr. Golding. I could have killed him. He had beaten her terribly any number of times, and he was at it again that night. Yes, I could have done it. I could have taken that gun in my own hands and . . . shot him.'

'But you did not?' He was almost whispering.

'I might have done it,' she said stubbornly. 'Perhaps I did. But I would be a fool to confess because there is no proof of who did it. *Anyone* would be a fool to confess. He deserved to die.'

And so much for a possibly rekindled romance, she thought as he took off his spectacles, withdrew a handkerchief from his coat pocket, and proceeded to polish them without looking at them at all. It was just a shame that there was still quite a distance to go to the picnic site. The poor man must wonder what he had walked into. He must be desperate to get away. She looked steadily and defiantly into his eyes as he put his spectacles back on and looked back at her, a frown creasing his brow.

'Lady Paget might have been forced to endure many, many more years of such violence,' he said, 'if someone had not stopped Lord Paget by killing him. I cannot condone killing, Miss Haytor, but neither can I condone violence against women. Especially against a wife, who has been given into a man's keeping so that he might love and cherish her and protect her from all harm. This is one of those situations in which rules, whether legal or moral, cannot satisfactorily decide an issue. I cannot congratulate Lord Paget's killer, but neither can I condemn him – or her. If you did it out of love for Lady Paget, then I honor you, Miss Haytor. But I do not think you did it at all.'

And without further ado, he offered his arm again, she took it, and they resumed their walk back to the picnic site.

They must have been gone forever, Alice thought, peering ahead and being quite unable at first to see two seated figures where she expected to see them on the slope. But the next time she looked, there they were, seated side by side, the picnic basket off to one side of them.

She was feeling surprisingly hungry.

She was also feeling oddly elated. He would not condemn her if she had done it. But he did not believe she had.

And he believed women – wives – were to be loved and cherished and protected.

During tea Stephen amused himself with thoughts of what his friends would think if they knew he was sitting here now in Richmond Park, sharing a picnic tea with the infamous Lady Paget and her companion and a politician's secretary. It was *not* what anyone would expect of the Earl of Merton. Indeed, there would be a number of people looking for him at Lady Castleford's garden party this afternoon.

Yet he was enjoying himself enormously. The tea Golding had brought with him, presumably prepared by a caterer, was delicious. But picnic fare was always more appetizing than any other, he had found.

It struck him too, and also with some amusement, that if he had not inherited his title so unexpectedly, *he* would quite possibly be someone's secretary by now and proud of the fact.

Everyone seemed to be sharing his enjoyment. The conversation was lively, and they all did their share of laughing. Even Miss Haytor, whose cheeks were flushed and whose eyes were bright. She looked decidedly handsome, and had seemed to have shed a year of age for every hour of the afternoon.

Cassandra herself seemed to have lost years along with her companion. She usually looked all of her twenty-eight years. Today she looked several years younger.

It was still early when they finished eating.

'I suppose,' Golding said, 'I ought not to have suggested such an early hour for leaving Lady Paget's. There is still much remaining of the warmest part of the day. It seems a shame to leave so soon.'

It was a concern they all seemed to share. They did not want the afternoon to end.

'Perhaps,' Miss Haytor suggested, 'Cassie and Lord Merton would care to go for a stroll while you and I guard the blanket and the picnic basket, Mr. Golding.'

'Oh, that *would* be pleasant,' Cassandra said, getting to her feet before Stephen could offer either his assistance or his opinion. 'After eating all that food, I am in dire need of some exercise.'

'There are some trees to climb,' Stephen said with a grin as he got up to join her. 'But perhaps it would be more sedate to walk instead. Ma'am?'

He offered his arm, and Cassandra took it. Miss Haytor was regarding him with some severity as they turned away. Perhaps he ought not to have made that remark about climbing trees in her hearing.

'I believe,' he said when they were out of earshot, 'the picnic must be deemed a success.'

'Alice,' she said, 'has been positively glowing, has she not? I have never seen her quite like this. Oh, Stephen, do you think—'

But she did not complete the thought.

'I do indeed,' he said. 'I think they are very pleased with each other. Whether anything more develops from the connection remains to be seen and is up to them.'

'The voice of caution,' she said with a sigh. 'I hope she does not get hurt.'

'People do not always get hurt,' he said. 'Sometimes they find love, Cass. And peace.'

'Oh.' She smiled. 'Do they? Do they really? I will wish those things for Alice, then – love and peace. And partly for a selfish reason. I will feel less guilty for having clung to her all these years.'

Instead of going down the slope and walking along the grassy valley as the other two had done, he led them along the crest of the rise, winding their way among the ancient oaks, dipping their heads to avoid branches. He liked the view from up here, the seclusion, the shade from the brightness of the sun. He liked the proximity of trees.

They walked in a silence that was companionable while he counted days. There had been the day in the park when Con had pointed out the black-clad widow and remarked that it must be as hot as Hades beneath her black clothes and veil. There had been Meg's ball the evening of the

226

following day and their first night together. There had been the drive in the park and the second night. There had been the formal visit yesterday with Meg and Kate to take tea with Cassandra and Miss Haytor. And . . . there was today. No matter how he counted, back from today or forward from that ride in the park, the total was the same.

Four days.

That was as long as he had known Cassandra. Not even a week. Not even close.

It felt as if he had known her for weeks or months.

And yet he did not know her very well at all, did he? He knew almost nothing about her.

'Tell me,' he said, 'about your marriage.'

She turned her head sharply to look at him.

'My marriage?' she said. 'What is there to say that you do not already know?'

'How did you meet him?' he asked her. 'Why did you marry him?'

Their steps had slowed and now stopped altogether. She slipped her hand from his arm and took a few steps to the side so that she could lean back against a giant trunk. He followed her, though he did not stand too close. He rested one arm on a low, sturdy branch. The trunk itself would have hidden them from the picnic blanket. But a glance over the top of the branch assured him that they were out of sight anyway. They had walked farther than he thought.

'We never had a fixed home,' she said. 'And there was never stability or security in our house. There was no lack of affection, but it was carelessly given. My father was very sociable, and he often invited gentlemen back to wherever we were living at the time. Always gentlemen, never ladies. It was of no concern to me until I was fifteen or so. Indeed,

227

I always enjoyed the company and the occasional notice the gentlemen took of me. I enjoyed having my father sometimes set me on his knee while he talked to them all. But after I started to grow up, I had to endure leers and risqué remarks – and a few surreptitious touches and pinches. Once a kiss. My father would not have allowed any of it had he known, of course. He had illusions about sometime giving me a Season and seeing to it that I met all the right people. He was a baronet, after all. But he did not know what was happening under his own nose, and I never told him. It was never bad enough to be dangerous, though it got worse as I grew older.'

'You *ought* to have told him,' he said.

'Perhaps.' She shrugged. 'But I had nothing to which to compare my life. I took it as normal. And Alice was always there to offer some protection. Then one day Baron Paget came home with my father, and he kept coming. He and my father were friends – they were about the same age. He was different from the others. He was kind and invariably courtly and gentle in manner, and he started to tell me about his home in the country, where he spent most of his time, and about the park surrounding the house, and the village and neighborhood. As far as I knew he did not gamble. Then, one day, when we were alone together – my father had left the room for some reason – he told me it could all be mine if I would do him the great honor of marrying him. He knew I could bring no dowry to the marriage, he told me. It did not matter. All he wanted was me. He would make a generous marriage settlement on me, and he would love and cherish me for the rest of his life. At first I was dismayed – but only for a short while. You cannot understand, perhaps, the great temptation his offer was to me – for a life of security and stability in a rural heaven. He seemed to be a man like my father but with all the flaws stripped away. I suppose I married him more as a father than as a husband.'

'What went wrong?' he asked after a longish silence.

She spread her palms against the trunk on either side of her.

'Nothing at all for six months,' she said. 'I will not say I was blissfully happy. He was an older man and I was not at all in love with him. But he seemed a *good* man, and he was kind and attentive to me, and I loved the country and the neighborhood. I was with child, and I was over the moon with happiness about that. I was very contented, perhaps even happy. And then one day he went to visit a distant neighbor and did not come back for three days. I was frantic with worry and made the mistake of going to look for him. He was sweet and kind when I got there and called upon his friends gathered there – all men – to witness how much his new wife loved him. He laughed heartily with them and came home with me. He was quiet in the carriage. He even smiled at me a number of times, but I was frightened. I realized he must have been drinking, and I did not recognize his eyes. After we arrived home . . .'

She swallowed and paused for a while. When she resumed, she sounded breathless.

'After we arrived home, he took me into the library and told me very quietly that I had shamed him in such a way that he did not know how he would be able to hold up his head with his friends ever again. I apologized – more than once. But then he started to hit me, first with the flat of his hand, and then with his fists and even his boots.

I cannot talk more about it. But two days later I miscarried. I lost my child.'

Her head was back against the trunk, her eyes closed. Her face was barred with light and shade. It looked to have not a vestige of color.

'And that was not the only time,' he said softly.

'No,' she said. 'Not for either the beatings or the miscarriage. He was two men, Stephen. No one could ask for a kinder, gentler, more generous man when he was sober – and sometimes he was sober for months at a time. In fact, *usually* he was. When he was drunk, there were no signs except for his eyes – and his violence. One of the neighbors, who once saw me when my eye still had the violet remains of a beating, told me that she had always suspected he had killed his first wife. She died – officially – after a terrible fall from horseback when she was trying to jump a high fence.'

He did not know what to say, though he *wanted* to tell her that it was a good thing she had killed Paget before he could kill her. Good God, the man had killed three of her babies.

'I used to think it was my fault,' she said, 'that he was so angry with me. I used to try to please him. I used to do all in my power not to do anything I thought might *displease* him. And when I knew he was drinking, I used to try to hide, to stay out of his way or . . . Well. None of it worked, of course.'

There was a lengthy silence.

'There,' she said eventually, turning her head to look at him, a wan smile on her lips. 'You *did* ask.'

'And no one ever helped you?' he asked her.

'Who?' she said. 'My father died within a year of my marriage. He would have had no right to intervene anyway.

230

Wesley did not visit often, and he never saw Nigel's bad side. I never told him about the beatings. He was just a boy. The only time Alice tried to intervene, he cuffed her and shut her out of the room and locked the door and then redoubled his efforts on *me* because I was not wife enough to face up to my shortcomings and the punishment I deserved.'

'His sons?' he asked.

'They were almost never there,' she said. 'I daresay they knew him of old. Though I suppose the first Lady Paget was tougher than I to have borne the three of them. Or perhaps in those days Nigel's sober spells lasted longer.'

He would not ask about Paget's death. He had upset her too much as it was. He supposed he ought not to have asked at all. This had been a carefree afternoon until he had asked his question.

But his need to know her better and to get her to open up to him – or to *someone* – had outweighed his desire to keep the atmosphere of the afternoon light.

'And talking of climbing trees,' he said softly after a short while, as though nothing had been spoken of between them since they left the picnic site. 'Have you ever done it?'

She tipped back her head to look upward into the great spreading branches of the oak above them.

'I used to do it all the time as a girl,' she said. 'I think I must have been born dreaming of escaping into a blue heaven or falling into it. This tree is a climber's paradise, is it not?'

She pulled free the ribbons of her bonnet and tossed it to the ground. She eyed the lowest branch, clearly considering the best way up onto it. He cupped his hands as if to help her mount a horse, and almost without hesitation, she set her foot in them and he hoisted her upward. He scrambled up after her.

It was easy after that. The branches were wide and sturdy and more or less parallel to the ground. They climbed without talking until, looking down, Stephen realized they had come quite a way.

She sat sideways on one branch, her back against the massive trunk, and then drew up her legs and hugged them with both arms. He stood on the branch below and held a branch above while wrapping his other arm about her waist, beneath her own arms.

She turned her face to him, smiling and then laughing.

'Oh, to be a child again,' she said.

'One can always be a child,' he said. 'It is just an attitude of mind. I wish I had known you when you were younger – before you armored yourself in cynicism and scorn to hide all the pain and anger. I wish you had not had to live through all that, Cass. I wish I could will it away or kiss it away, but I can't. I can only assure you that you will harm only yourself if you remain closed against all the possible goodness the world and life have to offer you.'

'What is the guarantee,' she said, 'that life will not punch me in the eye again?'

'Alas,' he said, 'there is none. But it is my belief that the world is far fuller of goodness than it is of evil. And if that seems rather naive, let me put in another way. I believe goodness and love are far stronger than evil and hatred.'

'Angels are stronger than devils?' she asked, smiling.

'Yes,' he said. 'Always.'

She lifted her arms and set her hands gently against the sides of his face.

'Thank you, Stephen,' she said, and kissed him lightly on the mouth.

'Besides,' he said, 'you know more about love than you realize. You became my mistress not just because of your own poverty, or even primarily because of it. You have a companion who is perhaps too old to find satisfactory employment, and you have a maid who is probably unemployable if she tries to keep her illegitimate child with her. You have the child herself. And the dog. He is a member of your family too. You did it all for them, Cass. You sacrificed yourself for love.'

'With such a beautiful man,' she said, 'it was hardly a sacrifice, was it?'

She was using her velvet voice.

'Oh, yes,' he said. 'It was.'

She set her hands flat on the branch to either side of her and tipped her head sideways to rest against his chest.

'It is strange,' she said, 'how speaking of the unspeakable has released something. I feel very . . . happy. Is that why you did it? Is that why you asked?'

He dipped his head to set his lips against her warm hair.

'Are *you* happy?' she asked him.

'Yes,' he said.

'But it is not quite the right word,' she said. 'You promised me joy today, Stephen, and you have delivered. They are not quite the same, are they – happiness and joy?'

'Happiness is more fleeting,' he said, 'joy more enduring.'

They stayed as they were for a while, and he found himself wishing that time would stand still, at least for a while. There was something about her that drew him. It was not just her beauty. It was certainly not her seductive ways. It was . . . He could not put words to what it was. He had never been in love, but he did not imagine that this was what being in love felt like. How puzzling human emotions could be at times – though he had not noticed it much before meeting Cassandra.

She sighed and raised her head.

'But then comes disaster,' she said. 'Someone goes off to drink for three days, and . . . And there goes happiness. Does joy remain? How can it?'

'One day,' he said, 'you will learn that love does not always betray you, Cass.'

She smiled at him.

'You are the only person who has ever called me that,' she said. 'I like it. I will remember it – that private name spoken in your voice.'

She kissed him briefly on the lips again and swung her legs over the side of the branch and joined him on his.

'This is the point,' she said, 'at which one realizes that climbing a tree was not such a wise idea after all. One has to go back down, and descending is always ten times harder than ascending.'

But she laughed when he would have offered assistance and swung her way down to the ground as if she had been climbing trees every day since she was a girl. She was smiling up at him when he jumped down onto the ground to join her, and he thought he had never in his life seen anyone lovelier.

Cass joyful.

It was a picture he would carry with him for the rest of his life.

Very close to his heart.

Dangerously close.

For despite everything, she had killed her husband, and there was no denying that as a dark, heavy burden she must carry with her through life.

And there was no denying that it would be a heavy burden for him to consider shouldering if he were ever to consider falling in love with her.

If?

Was it already too late?

What the devil did falling in love *feel* like?

15

Stephen spent the morning of the following day at the House of Lords, participating in a debate on an issue that particularly interested him. He went to White's afterward, as he often did, for a late luncheon with some of his friends and would probably have proceeded to the races with them if his mind had not been distracted by something – or someone – he had seen from a distance just before arriving at the club.

Wesley Young.

And of course his mind had been on Cassandra ever since yesterday. She had even inhabited his dreams. He had been standing on that tree branch again, kissing her, and they had floated off into the sky, happy enough until they tried to find their way back while she fretted over the fact that the dog needed to be fed and he tried to see where they were going through her windswept red hair.

Such an absurd dream.

He could not remember dreaming about a woman ever before.

'Does anyone know where Sir Wesley Young lives?' he asked now of no one in particular.

All of them shook their heads except Talbot, who seemed to recall that Young had bachelor rooms on St. James's Street, not far from the club. The house with the bilious yellow door and the semicircular fanlight above it.

'I remember standing in front of that door after having a few drinks, while Young fumbled with his key,' Talbot said. 'And it did nothing to settle my stomach, I can tell you, Merton. It quite put me off drinking more than half a dozen glasses more once I was inside.'

The fact that he had seen Young not far from here might mean, Stephen thought, that he had been going home for luncheon – or leaving to take it elsewhere.

He disappointed himself and a few of his friends by deciding against going to the races. He went instead in search of the bilious yellow door, which turned out to be not quite so bilious after all when viewed in sunlight and with a sober stomach.

Stephen knocked upon it.

This was really quite irrational, he realized. And purely impulsive. He was not even sure why he was doing it except that he had somehow got himself – and his emotions – entangled with Cassandra and could not resist the reprehensible urge to interfere in her life.

He ought not to be doing it. She had not asked it of him.

He had not even made any arrangement to see her again after yesterday's picnic. He had felt the need of a cooling-off period. Within four days he had got himself embroiled in madness. It was quite unlike him. He led a normally tranquil, rather predictable life, and he liked it.

His dream had not cooperated with his very sensible decision, of course.

Neither had his waking spells when, if he was honest with himself, he had lain in his bed wanting her, desire like a raging fever in his blood.

It simply would not do. He needed to *do* something for her and then resume the normal, perfectly happy course of his life.

Young's valet opened the door and took Stephen's card. He asked him to wait in a downstairs visitors' room – typically dark and gloomy – while he saw if Sir Wesley was at home, a sure sign that he was. If he had not been, Stephen would have been turned away at the door.

Young came in person within a few minutes, looking both surprised and mystified. He was dressed as though he had been about to step out.

'Merton?' he said. 'This is an unexpected honor.'

'Young?' Stephen inclined his head.

He was auburn-haired and good-looking, though he had none of the vivid beauty of his sister. The family resemblance was unmistakable, though. He had a pleasant, good-humored face, a fact that irritated Stephen.

There was an awkward silence.

'Would you care to step up to my rooms?' Young asked, breaking it.

'No, thank you,' Stephen said. He had no wish to engage in small talk either. 'I have given the matter much thought during the past few days, and I have come to the conclusion that there are absolutely no circumstances under which I can imagine myself riding past one of my sisters in Hyde Park and giving her the cut direct.'

Young seated himself in an old leather chair without

inviting his guest to sit too. Stephen sat anyway in a lumpy chair opposite him.

'Especially,' he said, 'if she were friendless and destitute.'

Young flushed and looked annoyed – not without reason, perhaps.

'You must understand, Merton,' he said, 'that I am not a wealthy man – or perhaps you *cannot* understand that. It is important to me that I make an advantageous marriage, and this year I am – *was* – close to doing just that. It was selfish of Cassie to come to London now of all times, especially when I had specifically warned her not to.'

'Selfish,' Stephen repeated as Young got restlessly back onto his feet and crossed the room to gaze into the empty fireplace. 'Where else was she to go?'

'She might at least,' Young said bitterly, 'have lived quietly here so that no one would have noticed her. But I have heard since that afternoon in the park that she had already appeared at Lady Sheringford's ball and at Lady Carling's at-home. And somehow she persuaded you to take her driving in the park at the very busiest hour. She has to understand that after what she did she is fortunate to be alive and free. She certainly cannot expect decent people to receive her. She cannot expect me to – But why am I explaining all this to you? I scarcely know you, Merton. And it is none of your business how I choose to treat my own sister.'

Stephen ignored the rebuke, though Young was quite right, of course.

'You believe what you have heard about her, then?' he asked. 'Did you know Paget well?'

Young frowned down at the grate.

'He was the most amiable fellow you could hope to meet,' he said. 'And generous to a fault. He must have spent a king's ransom on jewels for her. You ought to have seen them all. I went to Carmel a few times to visit. I was disappointed in Cassie. She had changed. She had lost the warmth and sparkle of humor she had always had when we were growing up. She scarcely spoke. She clearly regretted having married a man who was no younger than our father, and I thought that very unfair to Paget, who doted on her. She knew his age when she married him, after all. Did she kill him? Well, *someone* did, Merton, and I cannot think anyone would have had any motive except her. She wanted to be *free*. She wanted to come back here and behave just as she is behaving. She obviously has you besotted, and everyone knows you are as rich as Croesus.'

'Would the sister you remember actually *kill* a man,' Stephen asked him, 'in order to be free to enjoy life again?'

Young crossed back to the leather chair and dropped heavily into it.

'She was mother, sister, and friend to me when we were growing up,' he said. 'But people change, Merton. *She* changed. I saw it with my own eyes.'

'Perhaps,' Stephen said, 'she was *made* to change. Perhaps all was not as it seemed in that marriage. Your visits, I take it, were infrequent and not lengthy?'

Young frowned at his own boots and said nothing.

He knew, Stephen thought. He had probably always known – or strongly suspected, anyway. Sometimes it was easier not to know, though, to shut one's mind to the truth.

'I was very young,' Sir Wesley said, as if reaching for an excuse.

'You are past your majority now, though,' Stephen said.

'She needs a friend, Young. She needs someone of her own who will love her unconditionally.'

'Miss Haytor—' Young began. He had the decency not to complete the thought.

'Yes,' Stephen said. 'Miss Haytor is her friend. She is not family, though. Neither is she a man.'

Young moved restlessly in his seat, but he would not look at Stephen opposite him.

'The young lady who was with you in the park,' Stephen said. 'I do not have an acquaintance with her, I'm afraid.'

'Miss Norwood,' Young said.

'Do you still have hopes of marrying her?' Stephen asked.

'She was indisposed when I arrived to escort her to a garden party yesterday afternoon,' Young said with a twisted smile. 'She was expected to be indisposed for some days to come. I saw her at Vauxhall last evening, though, looking in perfect health. She was with her parents and Viscount Brigham.'

'Then I would say,' Stephen said, 'that you had a fortunate escape. There will be those members of the *ton* who will respect you far more if you stand staunchly by your sister than if you pretend you do not even know her. And of course there will be those who will not. Which group would you rather impress?'

He got to his feet to leave.

'What is your interest in Cassie?' Young asked him, keeping his seat. 'Is she your mistress?'

'Lady Paget,' Stephen said, 'is in dire need of a friend. I am her friend. And although I know from her own lips that she had motive more than sufficient to kill the bastard who was her husband, something tells me she did not do it. I know nothing about the circumstances of his death beyond the fact that he was shot with a pistol, *not* hacked to pieces with an axe. But I will tell you this, Young. Even if at some time I discover beyond all doubt that it *is* true, that she *did* shoot him, I will still be Lady Paget's friend. He *was* a bastard. Did you know that she had two miscarriages and one stillbirth, none of them necessary?'

Young looked directly at him then, the color draining from his face. Stephen did not wait for him to say anything. He took up his hat and cane from just inside the door and let himself out of the dingy parlor and out of the rooming house.

Well, how was *that* for interfering in lives that were really none of his business?

He found his steps leading him toward Portman Street and Cassandra's house. He had no idea why. Perhaps he needed to confess what he had just done. She would, he suspected, be furious with him, and she had every right to be. But was he sorry? He was not. He would do it again given the chance.

And did he *really* believe Cassandra was innocent of murder? And even of the lesser crime of killing in self-defense? Was it just wishful thinking on his part?

She was not at home. It was almost a relief.

'She has gone out with Miss Haytor, my lord,' the maid told him.

'Ah,' he said. 'Some time ago?'

'No, my lord,' she said. 'Just this minute.'

But there was no sign of her in either direction along the street. She would not be back soon, then.

'Mary,' he said, 'may I have a word with you?'

Now what the devil was he up to?

'With me?' Her eyes grew saucer-wide, and she touched a hand to her bosom.

'Can you spare me a few minutes?' he asked her. 'I will not keep you long.'

She stood back from the door to admit him, and he gestured toward the kitchen. She scurried ahead of him.

He noticed in passing that there was a distinctive gilt-edged card propped against a vase on the hall table, with Lady Paget's name written on it in an elegant hand. It was an invitation to Lady Compton-Haig's ball the following evening. He had a duplicate addressed to him on the desk in his study.

It was beginning to happen for her, then? She was beginning to be accepted into society?

The child was sitting on the floor beneath the kitchen table, the dog stretched out at her feet. He raised his eye to Stephen and thumped his tail lazily on the floor but did not otherwise move. The child was singing softly to her doll, which was wrapped in its white blanket. She was rocking it.

Mary turned to face Stephen, and it occurred to him that she really was rather pretty in a thin, pale sort of way. She had fine eyes, and the color his presence had put in her cheeks became her.

'Mary,' he said, and realized he could not ask what he most wanted to know. She probably did not have the answer, anyway. He felt suddenly foolish. 'What happened to the dog?'

She looked down and twisted her apron.

'Someone,' she said, 'a-a *stranger*, was trying to beat Lady Paget out in the stables, and Roger tried to defend her. He did too – she was not near so badly beat up as she usually – As might have been expected. But Lord – But the strange man caught hold of a whip and whipped the dog so vicious that he lost the sight of his eye and lost the tip of his ear, and his leg was crushed so bad that part of it had to be cut off.'

'Crushed with a whip?' Stephen asked.

'With a – a shovel, I think,' Mary said.

'And did this stranger – or Lord Paget – get hurt too?' Stephen asked.

She darted him a glance before returning her attention to her apron.

'He got bit something fierce, my lord,' she said. 'In his arms and legs and on the side of his face. He took to his bed for a whole week before he could get up and go about his business. Lord Paget, I mean. When he went rushing to her rescue, that was. I don't know what happened to the strange man. He must of escaped.'

Stephen wondered if she would think back and wince at the gaping holes in her story.

'The head groom wanted to put Roger down,' Mary said. 'He said it was the kindest thing to do. But Lady Paget had the crushed part of his leg took off and then carried him to her own room, and she kept him there until he was better, though none of us but her thought it would happen. Lord Paget never said he was to be put down though we was all expecting it. Roger must not of recognized him when he came to the rescue and attacked him too.'

Stephen set a hand on her shoulder and squeezed.

'It is all right, Mary,' he said. 'I know. Lady Paget told me herself. Not about Roger, but about the rest of it. She did *not* tell me about Lord Paget's death, but I will not try to squeeze that story out of you.'

Yet it was what he had come inside to ask, he realized.

'I am sorry if I have caused you distress,' he added.

'She didn't do it,' she whispered, her eyes like saucers again, her cheeks suddenly pale.

He squeezed a little harder before releasing her.

'I know,' he said.

'I worship her,' she said stoutly. 'Did I do wrong coming here with her? I cook and clean for her and do everything I can, but did I bring shame on her by coming? And did I add a burden on her because she has to feed me and Belinda? I know she feels obliged to pay me. I know she don't have no money – or didn't until—' She stopped abruptly and bit her lip.

'You did right, Mary,' he said. 'Lady Paget needs someone to look after her, and it appears to me as if you do that very well indeed. And she needs friends. She needs love.'

'*I* love her,' she said. 'But I am the one who caused her all the trouble in the end. It was all my fault.'

She threw her apron over her face, and Belinda stopped rocking her doll and looked up.

'No, this has been my fault,' he said. 'I ought not to have come in to pester you with questions. How is Beth today, Belinda? Is she sleeping?'

'She is being naughty,' she said. 'She wants to play.'

'Does she?' he said. 'Perhaps you ought to play with her for a little while, then, or tell her a story. Stories often put babies to sleep.'

'I'll tell her one, then,' she said. 'I know one. She has just eaten, and if I play with her she may be sick.'

'I can see,' he said, 'that you are a very good and wise mother. She is fortunate.'

He turned his attention back to Mary, who was smoothing her apron down over her skirt again.

'I have kept you long enough from your work – or perhaps from your leisure hour,' he said. 'And I am sorry about the questions I asked. I am not usually so inquisitive about other people's business.'

'Do you care for her?' she asked.

'Yes.' He raised his eyebrows. 'I am afraid I do.'

'Then I forgive you,' she said, and blushed hotly.

'Will you be offended,' he asked her, 'if I leave you money to take Belinda to Gunter's for an ice when you have free time one afternoon? No child should go through life without that experience. No adult either.'

'I got money,' she said.

'I know.' He smiled. 'But it would give me pleasure to treat Belinda – and you.'

'Very well, then,' she said. 'Thank you, my lord.'

He took his leave after setting down some coins on the table – just enough for two ices – and hurried from the house. He made his way homeward even though there was still plenty of the afternoon left. He was in no mood for any of his usual pursuits. He did not even consider going to the races after all, though he would not have missed very much.

He tried to think of all the young ladies with whom he usually liked to dance and converse, even flirt in a mild sort of way.

He could scarcely bring one face to mind.

If memory served him correctly, he had not yet reserved even one set with anyone for tomorrow's ball.

She had been to blame for what had happened at the end, Mary had just said. For Paget's death, he had taken her to mean. And she had been quite adamant that Cassandra had not done it.

Immediately after saying so, of course, she had said she worshipped Cassandra. It was easy to lie for a loved one.

The dog had been maimed while taking a whipping intended for his mistress. His leg had been crushed with a shovel – also intended for Cassandra? Would she be dead now instead of her husband if Roger had not intervened on that occasion? And would the official story have been that she was another victim of a fall from horseback?

He had a headache, Stephen discovered when he arrived home.

He *never* suffered from headaches.

'Go away, Philbin,' he told his man when he found him in his dressing room, putting away some freshly ironed shirts. 'I'll just be barking at you if you open your mouth, and I'll be damned before I'll be apologizing to you every second day of my life.'

'The new boots pinching, are they, m'lord?' Philbin asked cheerfully. 'I told you when you got them that—'

'Philbin,' Stephen said, grasping his temples with the thumb and middle finger of one hand, 'go. Now.'

Philbin went.

Cassandra had looked through the paper Alice had bought a few days ago and had written down the names and addresses of three lawyers she hoped might be able to help her. Alice, when she knew what Cassandra was going to do, advised that she talk with Mr. Golding or even the Earl of Merton. Both would surely know the best lawyers for such a case.

But Cassandra was tired of leaning upon men. They were rarely reliable, and even if that was probably an unfair judgment of Mr. Golding and undoubtedly of Stephen, then she was tired of having no real control over her own life. Less than a week ago she had thought to get that control by acquiring a wealthy protector. Now she was going to do what she ought to have done at the start.

It was not easy, though, as she discovered when she called upon the three lawyers one by one, Alice at her side. Alice had insisted upon accompanying her. Nobody would take a lady seriously, she explained, if she was alone.

Nobody took her seriously anyway.

The first lawyer was not taking new clients, as he was far too busy with the ones he already had – even though he had advertised his services in the paper. The next lawyer was far more blatant about recognizing her name, and sent out the message that he was not a criminal lawyer and would not represent ruthless murderers even if he were.

Alice wanted to go home after that. She was very upset. So was Cassandra, but the effect of the man's rudeness to her – which, by the way, he had not had the courage to deliver in person – was to make her lift her chin and square her shoulders and march onward with an almost militant stride.

The third lawyer admitted them to his inner sanctum, bowed low to Lady Paget and smiled obsequiously, listened to her story with attention and sympathy, and assured her that she had a perfectly legitimate case and that he would get her money and her jewels and the dower house and town house too in the mere snap of two fingers. He named his fee, which sounded exorbitant to Cassandra, though he claimed that he was giving her a considerably reduced rate on account of the fact that her case would give him no trouble at all and she was a *lady* for whom he felt considerable respect and sympathy. And he would take only half of the fee in advance – not one penny more.

Cassandra offered what she had. If her claim was an easy one and if he could get her money with little delay, then she would be able to pay him in full very soon. But while her money was being withheld from her, she explained, she really had quite limited means.

It seemed that it had not occurred to him that someone with the title *Lady* Paget might also be virtually penniless – despite the story she had told. His manner changed. It became brisk and cold and irritated.

He could not possibly proceed on so small a retainer.

He had a wife and six children . . .

He regretted having wasted his precious time . . .

There was, of course, his consultation fee . . .

And there would be a great deal of work involved in . . .

Lady Paget could not possibly expect him . . .

Cassandra did not even listen. She got to her feet and swept from the office and the building, Alice scurrying along behind her.

'Perhaps,' Alice said when they were outside and striding along the pavement, 'the Earl of Merton would—'

Cassandra rounded on her, her eyes blazing.

'Just a few days ago,' she said, 'the Earl of Merton was the devil incarnate in your eyes because he was paying me a generous salary for the use of my body. And yet now, Alice, you think it perfectly unexceptionable to beg a small fortune from him though he is no longer making use of my body?'

'Oh, shush, Cassie,' Alice said, looking around in an agony of embarrassment.

Fortunately there were not many pedestrians on the street, and none were within earshot.

'I was merely thinking of a *loan*,' Alice said. 'If that man is right, you would soon be able to pay it back.'

'I would not pay that man a *farthing*,' Cassandra said, 'if he could get me my money with the crown jewels thrown in *tomorrow*.'

And then her shoulders slumped.

'I am sorry, Allie,' she said. 'I had no right to snap at you of all people. But tell me I am right. Tell me all men are rotten to the core.'

'Not *all* men are,' Alice said, tapping her on the arm, and they resumed walking. 'But *that* one was rotten right *through* the core. I pity his poor wife and six children. He thought because you are a woman he could make a great deal of money from you. And he could have. You would not have argued with his fee, would you, though it was outrageous. Unfortunately for him, he was too greedy to wait.'

Cassandra sighed deeply. So much for taking charge of her life. So much for firmness of purpose and planned action. But she would try again. She was not going to give in.

No more today, though. All she wanted to do now was creep home to lick her wounds. As if in sympathy with her mood, heavy clouds had gathered overhead and a wind was beginning to whip up the dust in the gutters. There was a sudden chill in the air.

'It is going to rain,' Alice said, looking up.

They hurried home and arrived just as the first large, round drops were beginning to fall. Cassandra heaved another sigh as the key she had retrieved from under the flowerpot turned in the lock and she and Alice stepped inside. This place was beginning to feel like home. Like sanctuary.

Mary came hurrying from the kitchen, wiping her hands on her apron.

'There is a gentleman in the sitting room, my lady,' she said.

'Mr. Golding?' Alice said, brightening.

Stephen? Cassandra did not say it aloud. He had not said anything after the picnic yesterday about seeing her today. It had been a relief – she was seeing too much of him. And yet there had been something dreary about today without him – alarming thought.

She opened the door to the sitting room to find a young man pacing inside.

She turned cold as he stopped to look at her.

'Cassie,' he said. He looked miserable.

'Wesley.' She stepped inside and closed the door behind her. Alice had already disappeared.

'Cassie, I—' he began. He stopped, and she heard him swallow. He ran the fingers of one hand through his auburn hair, a gesture that looked very familiar. 'I was *going* to say that I did not recognize you the other day, but that would be stupid, would it not?'

'Yes,' she agreed, 'that would be stupid.'

'I don't know what to say,' he said.

She had not seen much of him in the last ten years, yet she had always adored him. He was someone of her very own. Foolish her.

'Perhaps you could begin,' she said, 'by telling me what happened to the walking tour in the Highlands.'

'Oh,' he said. 'A few of the fellows could not – Dash it all, Cassie, there was no such tour.'

She took off her bonnet and set it, with her reticule, on a chair close to the door. She went and sat in her usual place beside the fireplace.

'You must understand,' he said, 'that Papa did not leave

much money behind – or much of anything at all, in fact. I decided this year that I must look seriously about me for a bride who could bring a decent portion to the marriage. I did not want you to come here and spoil everything for me. Not *this* year.'

Wesley was doing something not very different from what she had done, she thought – he was looking for someone who could provide for his financial needs.

'I suppose,' she said, 'having an axe murderer for a sister *does* rather interfere with your matrimonial chances, does it not? I am sorry.'

'Nobody believes that,' he said. 'Not the axe part, anyway.'

She smiled, and he resumed his pacing.

'Cassie,' he said, 'that time I visited when I was seventeen. Do you remember? You had the yellow remains of a black eye.'

Had she? She could not remember his being there close to the time of any of her beatings.

'I had walked into the door of my bedchamber, had I?' she said. 'I seem to recall that happening once.'

'The stable door,' he said. 'Cassie, did – Did Paget ever *hit* you?'

'A man has a right to discipline his wife when she is disobedient, Wesley,' she said.

He looked at her, frowning and troubled.

'I wish,' he said, 'you would talk in your real voice, Cassie, not in that . . . sarcastic one. *Did* he?'

She stared at him for a long time.

'He was an infrequent drinker,' she said. 'When he *did* drink, he did so for two or three days without stopping. And then he would – turn violent.'

'Why did you never let me know?' he asked her. 'I would have—' He did not complete the thought.

'I was his lawful wife, Wes,' she said. 'And you were a boy. There was nothing you could have done.'

'And you killed him?' he said. 'Not with an axe, but you *did* kill him? Was it self-defense – when he was beating you?'

'It does not matter,' she said. 'There were no witnesses who will ever talk, and so there will never be proof. He deserved to die, and he died. No one deserves to be punished for killing him. Leave it.'

'It *does* matter,' he said. 'It matters to me. Just to know. It makes no difference to anything, though. I am thoroughly ashamed of myself. I hope you will believe that and forgive me. I have been thinking only of myself, but you are my sister, and I love you. You were my mother too when I was a child. I never felt alone and unloved even when Papa was out gambling for days on end. Let me – Let me at least *be* here for you, Cassie. Late enough, admittedly, but not *too* late, I hope.'

She rested her head against the back of the chair.

'There is nothing really to forgive,' she said. 'We all do selfish, despicable things from time to time, Wes, but they do not have to define us if we have a conscience strong enough to stop us from *becoming* selfish and despicable. I did *not* kill Nigel. But I am not saying who did, not to you or to anyone else. Ever. And so I will always be the prime suspect even though his death was ruled an accident. Most people will always believe I killed him. I can live with that.'

He nodded.

'The lady in the park,' she said. 'Are you still courting her?'

'She was a shrew,' he said, and pulled a face.

'Oh.' She smiled at him. 'You had a fortunate escape, then.'

'Yes,' he said.

'Come and sit down,' she said. 'It is giving me a stiff neck to keep looking up at you.'

He sat in the chair beside hers, and she held out her hand to him. He took it in his own and squeezed tightly. Heavy rain was beating against the window. It sounded almost cozy.

'Wes,' she said, 'do you know any good lawyers?'

16

Stephen had suffered another night of disturbed sleep. He really ought not to have interfered in business that was absolutely none of his concern. He ought not to have called upon Wesley Young, and he certainly ought not to have questioned the maid even so far as to ask what had happened to the dog.

It was not in his nature to interfere in other people's business.

He half hoped he would not see Cassandra again. He wanted his old, placid life back.

Had it really been *placid*?

Was he that dull a dog – at the grand age of twenty-five?

He only half hoped never to see her again, though. The other half of himself leapt with what felt very like gladness when he did.

He was walking down Oxford Street with his sister Vanessa, since when he had called on her earlier she had complained of being in the mopes because the children were still sleeping and Elliott was out of town for a couple of days and would probably be home only just in time to dress for the evening's ball, for which she desperately needed a length of lace to replace a torn frill on the gown she wanted to wear.

The errand had already been accomplished when Vanessa exclaimed with pleasure and Stephen, following her gaze, saw Cassandra approaching on the arm of her brother.

That was when half of some part of his being – his heart? – leapt with gladness. She was looking elegant and lovely in a pale pink walking dress and the straw bonnet she had worn to the picnic. She appeared flushed and rather happy.

Stephen swept off his hat and bowed to her.

'Ma'am?' he said. 'Young? A lovely afternoon, is it not?'

Young, seeing him, looked suddenly embarrassed.

'Indeed it is,' Cassandra said. 'How do you do, your grace, my lord?'

'I am extremely well,' Vanessa said. 'Sir Wesley Young, is it not? I believe we have met before.'

'We have, your grace,' he said, inclining his head to her. 'Lady Paget is my sister.'

'Oh, how wonderful,' Vanessa said, smiling warmly. 'I did not realize you had relatives in town, Lady Paget. I am so glad you do. Are you planning to attend Lady Compton-Haig's ball this evening?'

'I believe I will,' Cassandra said. 'I have had an invitation.'

She had accepted it, then. Stephen had not known if he hoped she had or if he would have preferred it if she had not. Now he knew. He was glad she was to be there.

Was the happy glow on her face a result of her brother's being with her? If it was, then Stephen no longer regretted having interfered.

'Perhaps, Lady Paget,' he said, 'you would be so good as to reserve the opening set for me?'

She opened her mouth to reply.

'I am afraid, Merton,' Young said stiffly, 'that is *my* set.'

'Then another later in the evening,' Stephen said.

A smile played about her lips. Perhaps she was thinking that she had come a long way in a week.

'Thank you, my lord,' she said in her velvet voice. 'It would be a pleasure.'

Sir Wesley Young clearly had no wish to prolong the encounter. With another half-bow he bade them both a good afternoon and continued on his way along the street with Cassandra on his arm.

'I do believe,' Vanessa said as they resumed their own course in the opposite direction, 'that Lady Paget could wear a sack and still look more beautiful than anyone else in London. It is most provoking, Stephen.'

'You are quite lovely enough to turn heads, Nessie,' he said, grinning at her.

She had always been the plainest of his sisters – and the most vivacious. She had always seemed beautiful to him.

'Oh, dear,' she said. 'It *did* seem as though I was fishing for a compliment, did it not? And I got it. How very gallant of you. It is time I went home, Stephen, if you do not mind terribly. What if Elliott has come home and I am not there?'

'Would he have a fit of the vapors?' he asked.

She laughed and twirled her parasol.

'Probably not,' she said. 'But *I* might if I discovered I had missed ten minutes or more of his company.'

He maneuvered her about a noisy group of people coming in the opposite direction without looking where they were going.

'*How* long have you been married?' he asked her.

She merely laughed.

'Stephen,' she said a little later, 'do you like her?'

'Lady Paget?' he said. 'Yes, I do.'

'No, but I mean,' she said, 'do you *like* her?'

'Yes,' he said again. 'I do, Nessie.'

'Oh,' she said.

There was no interpreting that single syllable and he did not ask for an explanation. Neither did he ponder the answer he had given to her questions. All he had admitted to, after all, was liking Cassandra. Or *liking* her, rather. Was there a difference in the meaning of the word, depending upon whether one spoke it with emphasis or not?

He shook his head with exasperation.

Enough of this.

Enough!

Sir Wesley Young had been inclined to scold his sister when he learned that she had put up no fight whatsoever to retain her valuables or to claim what was rightfully hers when the present Paget turned her out of his home. With a little effort she could have been a wealthy woman now instead of being destitute.

He did *not* scold, however. He had been almost twenty-two years old when Paget died, and he had gone down to Carmel for the funeral. He had felt the rumblings of unpleasantness brewing while he was still there, but he had left before any open accusations had started to fly, assuring Cassie before he went that he loved her and always would, that she could come to him at any time for support and protection.

And then, as rumors of just how nasty the situation had become reached him in London, he had developed very cold feet. He had feared being caught up in his sister's ruin. He had stopped writing to her.

He could not make the excuse that he had been only a boy, for the love of God. He had been a *man*.

And then, the final act of cruelty and cowardice, which would give him sleepless nights and troubled days for a long time to come, he believed, he had tried to prevent her from coming to London. He had lied about that walking tour of the Scottish Highlands. And when she had come anyway, and when he had come face-to-face with her in the park, he had *turned his head away and ordered the hired coachman to drive on*.

Oh, yes, there would be well-deserved nightmares over that one.

All he could do now, though, since the past could not be changed, was make amends as best he could and hope that at some time within the next fifty years or so he would be able to forgive himself. So he had asked around yesterday and this morning to discover the very best lawyer for Cassie's type of case, and he had made an appointment and taken her there this afternoon.

It all seemed very promising. Indeed, the lawyer was astonished that Lady Paget had even thought it might be difficult to recover her jewels, which were her own personal property, and to be granted what was her due according to her marriage contract and her husband's will. He was quite happy to take a modest retainer – which Wesley insisted upon paying – in the firm conviction that the matter would be settled within a couple of weeks or a month at the longest.

They had been walking home along Oxford Street when they had come face-to-face with Merton. Wesley was not pleased about it. Merton had been his conscience yesterday, or at least the prompter of his conscience, and Wesley did not feel particularly kindly disposed toward him. His conscience ought not to have needed prompting from any outside source.

However, the meeting did not last long, and Wesley returned his sister to the house on Portman Street, where Miss Haytor was eager to talk to her about the visit to some museum she had made with an old friend of hers – Mr. Golding, actually, who had been the only private tutor Wesley had ever had, though he had not stayed long and Wesley scarcely remembered him.

He went home to relax for a while before dining and getting ready for the evening's ball. But his man informed him that yet again there was someone downstairs in the visitors' parlor, wanting a word with him.

Wesley did not recognize the visitor, though the man got to his feet when he entered the room and came toward him, one hand extended. He was a strong, athletic-looking man with light brown hair and a deeply bronzed face.

'Young?' he said. 'William Belmont.'

Ah, yes, of course. He was the present Paget's brother, one of Cassie's stepsons. Wesley had met him at Cassie's wedding and again during one of his visits to Carmel a number of years ago. He had gone to America after that, had he not?

'I am pleased to see you again,' Wesley said, shaking his hand.

'My ship from Canada docked a couple of weeks ago,' Belmont told him, 'and I went immediately to Carmel to find everything much changed. Where is your sister, Young? She is here in London somewhere, is she not?'

Wesley was instantly wary.

'It would be best to leave her alone,' he said. 'She did *not* kill your father. No conclusive evidence could ever be found against her and she was never charged with anything because there was nothing to charge her *with*. She is trying to make a new life, and I am here to see to it that she has a chance to do just that and that no one bothers her.'

It ought to have been true too, from the moment of her arrival in town. It was true now, however. Anyone who wanted to get to Cassie was going to have to go through *him*. And even though he was not particularly happy at the breadth of Belmont's shoulders, he was not going to be deterred.

But Belmont merely made a dismissive gesture with one hand.

'Of course she did not kill my father,' he said. 'I was *there*, for the love of God. I have not come to stir up any trouble for her, Young. I have come to find Mary. Is she still with Cassandra?'

'Mary?' Wesley looked blankly at him.

'She left Carmel with Cassandra,' Belmont said. 'I assume she is still with her. And Belinda. I *hope* they are.'

Wesley still looked blank. Miss Haytor's name was Alice, not Mary.

'Mary,' Belmont said impatiently. 'My *wife*.'

* * *

261

Cassandra felt very different dressing for this evening's ball than she had felt last week dressing for Lady Sheringford's. She had received an invitation to this one, and she had an escort – in addition to an engagement to dance the opening set and one other.

She looked forward to dancing with Stephen tonight with far more eagerness than she ought to be feeling.

She checked her hair in the mirror to make sure it was firmly enough pinned up that it would not fall down as soon as she started to dance. *That* would be something of a disaster! She had become far too dependent during the past ten years upon the services of a lady's maid.

She drew on her long gloves and smoothed them out until they were no longer even slightly twisted.

The lawyer had thought she had an excellent case. He thought he could get her all that was owed her in a fort-night, though Cassandra would be perfectly happy with a month. She would be able to pay Stephen back and forget that she had ever done anything as sordid as offer herself to him as a mistress.

Though she did not regret the two nights she had spent with him. Or the picnic.

The picnic, she knew, would always be one of her most treasured memories.

He was going to be hard to forget.

But he had restored some of her faith in men. Not all were unreliable and untrustworthy and downright nasty.

She would remember him as her golden angel.

She took up her ivory fan and opened it to make sure it was in perfect working condition.

During his outing with Alice this afternoon, Mr. Golding had invited her to join him in Kent for a couple of days at the end of the week to celebrate his father's seventieth birthday with the rest of his family. It was surely a significant invitation.

Alice had not said yes – or no. She had waited to see if Cassandra could spare her. But she had been almost vibrating with suppressed excitement and anxiety. Ten minutes after Cassandra had arrived home, five after Wesley had left, she had been seated at the escritoire in the sitting room, writing Mr. Golding a letter of acceptance.

She was in her own room upstairs now, trying to decide what clothes she would take with her.

Cassandra slipped her feet into her dancing slippers and went downstairs to wait for Wesley. Her timing was perfect. He rapped on the door as she was descending the stairs, and she was able to wave Mary back to the kitchen and open the door herself.

'Oh, Cassie,' he said, looking her over admiringly. 'You will cast every other lady into the shade.'

'Thank you, sir.' She laughed and twirled before him, suddenly lighthearted. 'You look very handsome yourself. I am ready to leave. We do not need to keep the carriage waiting.'

But he stepped inside anyway and closed the door behind him.

'I am still outraged about your jewels,' he said. 'A lady ought not to be seen at a ball without any. I have brought you this to wear.'

She recognized the slightly scuffed brown leather box as soon as she saw it. One of her favorite activities when she was a girl had been to lift it out of her father's trunk and open it carefully to gaze inside and sometimes to touch the contents with a light fingertip. Once or twice she had

263

even clasped it about her neck and admired herself in a glass, feeling horribly wicked all the time.

She took the box from Wesley's hand and opened it. And there was the silver chain as she remembered it, though it had been polished now to a bright sheen, with the pendant heart made of small diamonds. Their father had given it to their mother as a wedding gift, and it was the one possession of any value that had not been sold during any of the lean times, or even pawned.

It was not an ostentatious piece and was probably not of any great value. Indeed, the diamonds might even be paste for all Cassandra knew. Perhaps that was why it had never been sold or pawned. But its sentimental value was immense.

Wesley took it out of the box and clasped it about her neck.

'Oh, Wes,' she said, fingering it, 'how wonderful you are. I will wear it just for tonight. And then you must put it away and keep it for your bride.'

'She would not appreciate it,' he said. 'No one would except us, Cassie. I would rather you kept it as a sort of gift from me. Though as far as that goes, I daresay it belongs to you as much as it does to me. Devil take it, you are not *weeping,* are you?'

'I think I am,' she said, dabbing at her eyes with two fingers and laughing at the same time. And she threw her arms about his neck and hugged him tightly.

He patted her back awkwardly.

'Is your maid *Mary?*' he asked.

'Yes.' She stood back from him, still fingering the necklace as she looked down at it. 'Why?'

'No reason,' he said.

A minute or so later he was handing her into the carriage he had hired for the evening, and they were making their ponderous way through the streets to the Compton-Haig mansion.

How different her arrival was this time. This time she was handed down to the red carpet by a liveried footman and made her way inside the house on her brother's arm. This time she felt free to look around and appreciate the marble hallway and the bright chandelier overhead and the liveried servants and the guests all decked out in their evening finery.

This time a few people caught her eye and nodded to her. One or two even smiled. She could happily ignore those who did neither.

Wesley led her along the receiving line, and this time she could meet the eye of everyone in it because she had been invited and because her name could no longer inspire the shock it had created last week.

And this time, as soon as they had stepped inside the ballroom and she was looking about her, admiring the banks of purple and white flowers and green ferns, Sir Graham and Lady Carling came to speak with her and to be introduced to Wesley, with whom they did not have an acquaintance. And then Lord and Lady Sheringford came to bid them a good evening, and Mr. Huxtable came to ask Cassandra for the second set. A couple of Wesley's friends came to speak with him, and one of them – a Mr. Bonnard – reserved a set later in the evening with her.

'Damn me, Wes,' he said, lifting a quizzing glass halfway to his eye, his head held firmly in place by the height and stiffness of his starched shirt points, 'I did not know

Lady Paget was your sister. She certainly got all the looks in the family. There were precious few left for you, were there?'

He and the other friend, whose name Cassandra had already forgotten, brayed with identical merriment at the witty joke.

And then Stephen was there, bowing and smiling and asking, a twinkle in his eyes, if Lady Paget had been kind enough to remember to reserve a set for him.

She fanned her cheeks.

'The first and second sets are spoken for,' she said, 'and the set after supper.'

'I sincerely hope,' he said, 'none of those dances are the waltz. I shall be severely out of sorts if they are. May I dance the first waltz with you, ma'am, and the supper dance too if they are not one and the same? And one other set if they are?'

He was openly distinguishing her. It was not poor etiquette to dance twice in an evening with the same lady, but it was something everyone present always noticed. It usually meant that the gentleman concerned was seriously courting the lady.

She ought to say yes to only one dance. But his blue eyes were smiling, and the lawyer had said two weeks, even though he had admitted that it might be one month, and after that she would be leaving London forever to find herself a pretty little cottage in an obscure English village, and she would never see him again. Or have to face the *ton* again.

'Thank you,' she said, her hand falling still as she smiled back at him.

And she remembered how, only a week ago, she had

stood alone in just such a ballroom as this, looking consideringly at all the gentlemen before picking him out as her prey.

Now there was a little corner of her heart that might always belong to him.

The more fool she.

'Shall we?' Wesley said, and she could see that couples were beginning to gather on the dance floor for the opening set.

The evening was not, after all, to pass without some unpleasantness.

Mr. Huxtable came to claim the second set very early and led Cassandra onto the floor long before most other couples came to join them. It was clear to her that he wished to talk with her – but that he did not want to do so in anyone else's hearing.

He was an extraordinarily handsome man, she thought as they came to a stop in the middle of the floor and turned to face each other. He was handsome despite, or perhaps because of, his slightly crooked nose. Many women must find him impossibly attractive. She was not one of them. She did not like dark, brooding men who carried an aura of danger about with them. She was very glad indeed she had not chosen *him* last week. Would she have succeeded? Could she have seduced him – and trapped him into paying her a large salary to be his mistress?

'I do not need to sidle by slow degrees into what I wish to say to you, do I?' he said now.

Oh, he was very dangerous indeed.

She was startled but would not show it. She waved her fan slowly before her face.

'Absolutely not,' she said. 'I would prefer plain speaking. You wish to warn me away from your cousin, I daresay. He needs someone big and dark and strong like you to protect him and frighten away dangerous women like me, does he? Though I have always thought the devil's function was to destroy innocence, not protect it.'

'Plain speaking indeed,' he said – and smiled at her with what looked like genuine amusement. 'Merton is *not* a weakling, Lady Paget, though many people may think so. Unlike many men, he does not seem to feel the need always to be flexing his muscles in order to demonstrate how tough and manly he is. Did you choose him because you thought he *was* weak?'

'*I* chose *him*?' she asked haughtily.

'I saw you collide with him in Margaret's ballroom,' he said.

'An accident,' she said.

'Deliberate.'

She raised her eyebrows and fanned her face.

'It is really none of your business, is it?' she asked him.

'When outdone in an argument,' he said, 'it is always good strategy – or perhaps the *only* strategy – to fall back upon a cliché.'

Would the musicians *never* be finished tuning their instruments? Would the dancers never be finished with their conversations on the sidelines? How many people were watching the two of them? Cassandra smiled.

'How do you fit into Lord Merton's family, Mr. Huxtable?' she asked him.

'He has not told you?' he said. 'I am the ultimate bad, dangerous cousin, Lady Paget, the one who is bound to hate all the others with a passion and be ever ready to do them harm. My father was the Earl of Merton, and I was his eldest son. Unfortunately for me, my mother fled to Greece when she knew she was expecting me, and by the time her father – my grandfather – hauled her back to England, breathing fire and brimstone every step of the way, and demanded that my father do right by her or take the consequences, I had run out of patience and decided to put in an appearance two days before the happy couple wed. I was therefore quite indisputably illegitimate. Unfortunately for my father, a whole string of my younger brothers and sisters died either at birth or soon after, the only survivor being the youngest, who was also – in the words of my father himself – a blithering idiot. Jonathan became earl after my father's death, but he died on the night of his sixteenth birthday, and the title passed to Stephen.'

Cassandra read a whole world of pain and bitterness in the brief, rather flippantly related story, but it had not been told in order to arouse her sympathy, and she allowed herself to feel none.

'I am surprised, then,' she said, 'that you really do not hate him. He has what ought to have been yours. He has your title, your home, your fortune.'

Other couples were beginning to drift onto the floor.

'Yes,' he said, 'it *is* surprising.'

'Why do you *not* hate him?' she asked.

'For one very simple reason,' he said. 'I know someone who would have loved him, and I love that someone.'

He did not explain, though she waited.

'Are you hoping that Stephen will marry you?' he asked.

She laughed softly.

'You may rest easy on that score,' she said. 'I have no

designs upon Lord Merton's freedom. I have known the kind of servitude marriage brings to a woman, and once was quite enough.'

They were very soon going to be within earshot of couples in every direction. The musicians had fallen silent and were ready to strike up the tune of the first country dance in the set.

'Shall we talk about the weather?' she suggested.

He chuckled deep in his throat.

'Thunderstorms and earthquakes and hurricanes?' he said. 'They sound safe.'

17

Stephen could not make up his mind whether Cassandra's gown was pure red or a bright burnt orange. It was somewhere between the two, he supposed. It shimmered in the light of the candles and was really quite magnificent. It dipped low in front to accentuate her bosom. Its soft folds, falling from a high waist, hugged her curves and outlined her long, shapely legs. Her bright hair was swept high on her head while wispy ringlets curled along her neck.

She always carried herself proudly. But tonight she looked almost happy. How very different she looked from the mysterious lady with the scandalous reputation who had boldly forced her way into Meg and Sherry's ball last week and then looked about her as if she held everyone else gathered there in contempt.

She danced every set before the waltz – which was also the supper dance. She even danced once with Con and smiled at him and conversed with him whenever the figures of the dance brought them together.

Stephen danced every set before the waltz too. He danced with young ladies who were making their come-out this year and had been signaling their interest in him from the start. It was not a fact that made him in any way conceited. He was, after all, one of England's most eligible bachelors. He conversed easily with them all and smiled at each partner in turn and focused his attention upon each.

But he was always aware of Cassandra.

He was beginning to wonder if his life would ever return to normal – whatever that was.

He looked forward to the supper dance and thought the time would never come.

He must be careful, though. He must not do anything impulsive that he might regret for the rest of his life.

He was not ready for matrimony. He was only twenty-five. He had told himself that he would not even give marriage serious thought until he was thirty. And even then he would take his time, choosing someone who could look beyond his title and wealth to like *him*. Perhaps even to love him. And someone he could genuinely like and admire and love.

The supper dance came at last, and he approached Cassandra to claim it. She was standing with her brother and a group of guests with whom Stephen did not have a close acquaintance. She turned to watch him approach.

'Lady Paget, ma'am,' he said, bowing, 'this is my set, I believe.'

'And so it is, Lord Merton,' she agreed, using her velvet voice. And she reached out her hand to set on his sleeve.

Such formality. The picnic seemed like a dream. Strange that he should remember the picnic far more than he did the two nights he had spent in her bed.

'The supper dance is also the waltz,' he said as he led her away. 'May I dance the last set of the evening with you too?'

'You may,' she said.

They faced each other on the floor as other couples assembled about them.

'Is there anything new to report in Miss Haytor's budding romance?' he asked, grinning at her.

'Oh, yes, indeed,' she said, and told him about this afternoon's outing and the upcoming birthday party in the country.

'With Golding's *family*?' he said. 'Can a marriage offer be far behind?'

'I think it very likely there will be one soon,' she said. 'Perhaps even while they are still in Kent. And I believe she will be happy. She must have given up all hope of marrying years ago, must she not? Concern for me kept her incarcerated in the country all those years.'

'Don't blame yourself,' he told her, not for the first time.

'You are quite right.' She laughed. 'You will not let me feel guilty for all the world's woes, will you?'

'Absolutely not,' he said.

He noticed the necklace she wore. It was the first time he had seen her wearing jewelry.

'Pretty,' he said, his eyes focused on it. The point at the bottom of the jeweled heart reached almost to her décolletage.

'It was my mother's,' she said, fingering it with her

gloved hand. 'My father gave it to her when they married, and it was the one thing of value in our household that was never sold. Wesley gave it to me this evening.'

Her eyes became suspiciously bright.

'You are fully reconciled with your brother, then?' he asked.

'I think,' she said, 'the memory of that incident in the park when he drove past pretending not to see me or know me must have gnawed at his conscience. Perhaps it disturbed his dreams. He came to see me yesterday.'

'And you do not bear a grudge?' he asked.

'Why would I?' she said. 'He is my brother and I love him. He was sincerely sorry for being a coward and trying to ignore my existence. If I had refused to forgive him, who would suffer the more? And perhaps there is no simple answer to that question. Perhaps we would have suffered equally. And for what? To satisfy wounded pride or outraged righteousness? The thing is that he *did* feel remorse and he *did* come to set matters right with me. And now he is risking his own reputation by being seen in public with me and openly presenting me to his acquaintances as his sister.'

Young had not, then, mentioned Stephen's visit to him in his rooms. Stephen was thankful for that. Even given the happy outcome he had had no right to interfere in her life, and she might well resent his having done so.

Not that he was sorry. Family quarrels were the saddest things.

The orchestra played a chord, and Stephen bowed while Cassandra curtsied. He smiled as he set his right arm about her waist and took her right hand in his. She smiled as she set her free hand on his shoulder.

'I think,' she said, 'the waltz is the loveliest of dances. I have been looking forward to this one all evening. You lead so well. And your shoulder and hand are firm and strong, and you smell divine.'

He did not remove his eyes from hers. She laughed.

'And here I am,' she said, 'being as outrageous as I was at your sister's ball last week. I should be behaving with a fashionable ennui instead. I should make it appear as if it is as much as I can do to drag myself about the ball-room floor with you.'

He laughed.

But their eyes held and hers were sparkling with merriment and sheer enjoyment. He swung her in a circle and continued to do so as they danced so that everything about them became a swirl of color and light with her as the vivid center of it all.

Cassandra.

Cass.

She was still smiling, her cheeks flushed, her lips slightly parted, her spine arched so that she kept the correct distance between them. It did not matter. He could feel her body heat anyway. He could smell it and her – a mingling of soft perfume and woman.

A smell of pure enticement.

They paused for a moment between tunes, neither speaking nor looking away from each other, and then continued to waltz to a slower, hauntingly lovely melody.

He *liked* her, he had told Vanessa.

Ah, it was a euphemism indeed.

Her flush deepened and he began to feel uncomfortably warm. The heavy smell of the flowers began to seem oppressive. Even the music suddenly seemed overloud.

He waltzed her past one set of French windows, which were thrown back to admit the cool air of the night. There was another set just ahead. When they reached them, Stephen twirled Cassandra through them, out onto a wide balcony, which was blessedly deserted.

And even more blessedly cool.

They continued to dance, but without the twirls. Their steps gradually slowed, and he turned her hand in his to set it palm-in against his coat, over his heart. Her other hand slid off his shoulder to twine about his neck, and then he drew her closer so that her bosom was against his chest and her cheek against his.

He did not spare a thought to reality or decorum or any of the social graces that usually came as second nature to him.

When the music ended, they stopped dancing but did not move away from each other. They stood close for several silent moments, their eyes closed – at least, *his* were.

And then he drew his head back from hers, and she drew hers back from his, and they gazed deeply into each other's eyes in the light of a lamp flickering at one corner of the balcony.

They kissed each other.

It was not a deeply passionate kiss, but it was several degrees warmer than the ones they had shared at the picnic. It was a kiss that spoke volumes without any necessity for words.

He was in no hurry to end it. Once it was ended, words *would* be necessary, and he really did not know what he would say. Or what she would say.

He drew back his head eventually and smiled down at her. She smiled back.

And they both became aware – at the same moment, it seemed – that they had an audience. A few people must have decided to make their escape into the fresh air after the dance ended. A few others must have looked toward the French windows and seen what was framed in one of them, backlit by the balcony lamp. Others had probably been drawn by curiosity to see what was taking the attention of the first two groups.

However it was, the audience was an embarrassingly large one, and it was perfectly clear that they had all witnessed that kiss. It had not been a thoroughly improper kiss, it was true, except that *any* public embrace was improper, especially between two people who had no business kissing each other under any circumstances.

They were not married.

They were not betrothed.

Stephen became aware of three things – four if he counted Cassandra's sharp intake of breath. He became aware of Elliott somewhere inside the ballroom, his eyes fixed upon Stephen, his eyebrows raised, his expression grim. He became aware of Con, one eyebrow lofted, his expression inscrutable. And he became aware of Wesley Young elbowing his way through the crowd, his look murderous.

And he realized in a flash that he had ruined everything for Cassandra after working hard for the past several days to restore her to respectability, to see to it that she was accepted back into the *ton*, where she belonged.

'Oh, goodness,' he said, taking her hand in his and lacing their fingers while raking the fingers of his free hand through his hair. 'This was not quite the way we planned to make the announcement, but it seems our hand has been forced by my own impulsive behavior. Ladies and gentlemen, may I present Lady Paget to you as my betrothed? She has just agreed to honor me with her hand, and I am afraid I allowed my enthusiasm to overcome good breeding.'

He squeezed her hand slowly.

And he shamelessly smiled his most charming smile.

Cassandra could feel only a frozen sort of dismay.

She had been about to raise her eyebrows, don her most haughty expression, and sweep past everyone on her way to the dining room for supper. She had brazened out worse than that kiss. She could do it again.

Except that there *were* such things as last straws, and this might very well be it.

Before she could make any move, however, Stephen had taken matters into his own hands and made his announcement.

And *now* what?

He released his grip on her fingers only to draw her hand through his arm and hold it close to his side.

When all else failed, Cassandra thought, one smiled.

She smiled.

And then Wesley was out on the balcony, having pushed his way past everyone else, and he stood in front of them, fury turning to an almost comic bewilderment.

'Cassie,' he said, 'is this *true*?'

What else could she do but lie?

'It is true, Wes,' she said, and realized as she spoke that she could not after all have simply walked away from that very public kiss and so have averted disaster. Wesley had just rediscovered her. He had just atoned for his own cowardice in ignoring her when she needed him most, and now he had taken on the role of her self-appointed protector. There would have been a nasty and very public scene if Stephen had not spoken up as he had. Wesley would probably have punched him in the nose or slapped a glove in his face – or both.

It hardly bore thinking about.

Wesley smiled abruptly. Perhaps he too had realized the necessity of acting out this charade. He drew her into a hug.

'I misunderstood at first, Merton, I must confess,' he said. 'But I am delighted by the truth even if it seems to me you might have consulted me first. Dash it all, though, Cassie is of age.'

He stretched out his right hand, and Stephen shook it.

The audience did not disperse quickly despite the fact that supper awaited everyone. There was a buzz of conversation, most of it sounding pleased, even congratulatory – or so it seemed to Cassandra, though she did not doubt there were plenty among the spectators who would be horrified to learn that the very eligible and beautiful Earl of Merton had allied himself with an axe murderer.

Many young ladies would be inconsolable tonight, she did not doubt.

Stephen's sisters all converged on him from various directions, and all hugged first him and then Cassandra with apparently warm delight. Their husbands shook his hand and bowed over hers. So did Mr. Huxtable, though it seemed to Cassandra that his very dark eyes penetrated through to the back of her skull as he did so.

It was hard to know how pleased his family really was.

They could not *be* pleased, surely, but they were polite and gracious people – and they were being forced to deal with the shock of such an announcement under the interested gaze of half the beau monde.

They really had little choice but to appear delighted.

'My love,' Stephen said, smiling down at her and drawing her hand through his arm again, 'we must speak with Lord and Lady Compton-Haig.'

'Of course.' She smiled back at him.

Must they? *Why?* For the moment she could not even remember who those people were.

Most of the other guests had either lost interest at last or, more likely, chose to discuss the whole salacious incident over supper. The crowd had thinned. Lady Compton-Haig was standing with her husband at the ballroom doors, and Cassandra recalled that – of course! – they were the hosts of this ball.

'Yes, of course,' she said again.

They had been kind enough to send her an invitation – her first apart from the verbal invitation to attend Lady Carling's at-home last week.

'Ma'am.' Stephen took the lady's hand in his after they had crossed the room, bowed over it, and raised it to his lips. 'I do beg your pardon for using your ball as the forum for my announcement without even consulting you first. I did not intend it to be tonight, though the beauty of your ballroom and the loveliness of the music did prompt me into making my offer this evening. Then, when Lady Paget accepted, I – well, I lost my head, I am afraid, and then had no choice but to explain to everyone exactly *why* I was kissing her out on your balcony.'

Viscount Compton-Haig pursed his lips. His wife smiled warmly.

'But you must not apologize, Lord Merton,' she said, 'for making the announcement tonight. I am vastly pleased and honored that you *did*. We have no children of our own, you know, though Alastair does have two sons from his first marriage, of course. I never expected to have such an announcement made in my own home. I intend to make the most of it. Come, Lady Paget.'

And she linked her arm through Cassandra's and led her off in the direction of the dining room, nodding and smiling about her as she went. She seated Cassandra at the head table, next to herself. Stephen, who had come along behind with the viscount, sat beside her on the other side.

Most of the guests seemed intent upon their supper and their own conversations, Cassandra noted in some relief. It did seem, though, that the buzz of conversation had a higher, more animated tone than usual. And there were a number of people who looked their way and smiled or nodded or simply stared. On the whole, the atmosphere did not seem unduly hostile, though the mood of the *ton* might well grow more ugly tomorrow when everyone had had time to digest the news and realize that a widow who was still something of a pariah – she had received only this one invitation, after all – was about to walk off with one of the most eligible, most coveted matrimonial prizes in all England.

The funny thing was that since that kiss, she and Stephen had scarcely glanced at each other. They had not exchanged one private word. Although they were sitting next to each other at supper, they were each kept busy talking with other people. And smiling – eternally smiling.

He was going to have to suffer some acute embarrassment for a while when no notice of their betrothal appeared in the papers and when it became clear to everyone that they were not in fact engaged at all.

But men recovered easily from such embarrassments. And the female half of the human race would rejoice and quickly forgive him.

Oh, she wished she had not come tonight. Or agreed to dance the waltz with him. Or allowed him to twirl her out onto the balcony. Or allowed him to kiss her there.

Though that was unfair. She had not *allowed* anything. She had been a full and willing participant.

But not in the announcement he had then felt obliged to make.

Though honesty forced her to admit that he had had very little choice but to do exactly what he had done.

She hoped the lawyer had not exaggerated when he had said *two weeks*.

Lord Compton-Haig, at the prompting of his wife, rose to propose a toast to the newly betrothed couple, and everyone rose and clinked glasses and drank before heading back to the ballroom and a resumption of the dancing. Stephen led out the Duchess of Moreland, his sister, and Cassandra danced with the duke. Fortunately it was a rather intricate country dance and did not allow for much private conversation. From the sober look on Moreland's face, Cassandra guessed that he would have had a great deal to say to her if he had had the opportunity.

He had, once upon a time, she remembered, been Stephen's official guardian.

He said only one thing of a personal nature, and it somehow sent shivers along Cassandra's spine.

'You must come to dinner one evening soon, Lady Paget,' he said. 'I shall have the duchess arrange it. And you may tell us at your leisure how you plan to make Merton happy.'

She smiled back at him.

'You must not concern yourself about that, your grace,' she said, noticing his very blue eyes, the one distinguishing feature between him and the dark-eyed Mr. Huxtable. 'My hopes and dreams for the Earl of Merton must be very similar to your own.'

He inclined his head and moved off to dance the next figure with another lady.

After that set, Cassandra really wanted nothing else than to beg Wesley to take her home. It could not be done, however. She could not so publicly abandon the man whose marriage offer she had supposedly accepted just this evening.

But that thought gave her another, better idea. The duke had returned her to Wesley's side, but her brother was busy conversing with a group of friends and did no more than flash a smile in her direction. She opened her fan and looked about the room. It was easy to spot Stephen – he was striding toward her, a warm smile lighting his face.

Oh, how he must resent her!

And how she resented him. There *must* have been another way to deal with that crisis. Heaven alone knew what it was, though.

'The final set is about to begin,' he said, 'and it is mine, I believe.'

'Stephen,' she said, 'take me home.'

His eyes searched hers, his smile arrested. He nodded.

'A good idea,' he said. 'We will avoid the crush after the set is ended. You came with your brother?'

She nodded.

'I will tell him I am going home with you instead,' she said. 'He is just here.'

Wesley turned away from his group even as she spoke.

'Wesley,' she said, 'Stephen is going to take me home in his carriage. Do you mind?'

'No,' he said. He held out a hand to Stephen. 'I will expect you to treat her kindly, Merton. You will have me to answer to if you do not.'

Oh, men! They were such ridiculous, possessive creatures. Sometimes it seemed they believed women could not breathe without their assistance.

But there was some comfort in knowing that Wesley was now a man. *You will have me to answer to if you do not.* There had been no one to say those words to Nigel before she married him, except her father, who had been too genial and too trusting for his own good.

She kissed his cheek.

'I do not expect, Young,' Stephen said, 'ever to have the need to answer to you. Your sister will be in good hands.'

They found the Compton-Haigs and asked to be excused from participating in the last dance. Lady Compton-Haig appeared charmed more than offended, and she and her husband accompanied them downstairs and waved them on their way after Stephen's carriage had been brought up to the door.

Cassandra set her head back against the soft upholstery

of the carriage seat as the vehicle rocked into motion and closed her eyes.

Stephen's hand found hers in the darkness, and his fingers curled about it. She was too weary to withdraw it.

'Cassandra, my dear,' he said, 'I am so very sorry. I ought to have wooed you more privately and far less recklessly. I certainly ought to have made you a marriage proposal before announcing our betrothal to all the world. But disaster loomed for you, and it was all I could think of to do.'

'I know that,' she said. 'I was furious with you for only a very short while. We were incredibly indiscreet – *both* of us. I do not blame you, and I do assure you that I was not involved in any deliberate seduction. It was just – indiscreet. Unfortunately, your response will make tomorrow and the days following it uncomfortable for you as people look for the official announcement in the papers and do not find it. But they will recover. People always do. They even started sending out invitations to an axe murderer after a scant week.'

'Cass.' He squeezed her hand. 'There *will be* an announcement. Not in tomorrow's paper, it is true. It is too late for that. But it will appear in the morning after's. And we will have to decide when the nuptials will be and where – either here at St. George's with half the *ton* in attendance, or somewhere more private. Warren Hall, perhaps. People will want to know either way. They will shower us both with questions.'

Ah. She might have guessed that he would take gallantry to the extreme.

'But Stephen,' she said without opening her eyes or turning her head, 'you did not make me an offer, did you?

And I did not accept. And *would not* accept even if you were to make one now. Not tonight, not ever. Not you or anyone else. One thing I will never do again in this life is marry.'

She heard him draw breath to reply, but he said nothing.

They rode the rest of the way to her door in silence.

He vaulted out of the carriage as soon as it had rocked to a halt, set down the steps, and assisted her to alight. Then he put the steps back up, closed the door, and looked up to instruct the coachman to drive home.

'Stephen,' she said sharply, 'you are not coming inside with me. You are not invited.'

The carriage rumbled off down the street.

'I am coming anyway,' he said.

And she realized, as she had done last week after she had chosen him, that there was a thread of steel in Stephen Huxtable, Earl of Merton, and that in certain matters he could be quite inflexible. This was one of those matters. She might remain out here arguing for an hour, but he was coming inside at the end of it. She might as well let him in now. A few spots of rain were falling, and there was not a star in sight overhead. There was probably going to be a downpour in a short while.

'Oh, very well,' she said irritably, and bent to find the house key beneath the flowerpot beside the steps.

He took it from her hand, unlocked the door, allowed her to step inside before him, and closed and locked the door behind him.

Alice, Mary, and Belinda would have gone to bed hours ago. They would be no help whatsoever. Not that they would even if they were present. A glance at Stephen's face in the dim light of the hall candle confirmed her in her suspicion that he was angry and mulish and was going to be very difficult to deal with.

He strode into the sitting room, came back with a long candle, lit it from the hall candle, extinguished the latter, and led the way back into the sitting room.

Just as if he owned the house.

Of course, he *was* paying the rent on it.

_18_

It was a devilishly ticklish situation.

She _had_ to marry him. Surely she could see that. Her tenure with the _ton_ was precarious, to say the least. If she withdrew from this betrothal now, she would never recover her position.

'Cass,' he said as he fixed the candle in its holder on the mantel, 'I love you, you know.'

He felt a little weak at the knees, saying the words aloud. He wondered if he meant them. He had told Nessie this afternoon that he _liked_ her as opposed to simply liking her without the emphasis, but did that mean he loved her with a forever-after kind of love?

He thought it might mean that. But everything had happened too quickly. He had not had sufficient time to _fall_ in love.

None of which mattered now.

Good Lord, he had _never_ before kissed a woman in

public – or even *nearly* in public. It was unpardonable of him to have done so tonight. Especially with Cassandra.

'No, you do not,' she said, seating herself in her usual chair, crossing her legs, and swinging her foot, her dancing slipper dangling from her toes. She stretched her arms along the arms of the chair and looked perfectly relaxed – and rather contemptuous. The old mask. 'I believe you like me well enough, Stephen, and for reasons of your own you have decided to befriend me and bring me into fashion – and support me financially until I can stand on my own feet. There is doubtless some lust mingled in with the liking because you have been in my bed twice and enjoyed both experiences sufficiently to think you would not mind trying it again. You do not *love* me.'

'You presume to know me, then,' he asked her, irritated, 'better than I know myself?'

There was truth in what she said, though. He wanted her even now. Her orange-red dress gleamed in the light of the single candle, her hair glowed just as brightly, and her face was beautiful, even with its scornful expression. He was in her house late at night again, and he could not help thinking of what a pleasure it would be to go upstairs with her and make love to her again.

'Yes, I do,' she said, and her expression softened slightly as she looked fully at him. 'I believe you were born compassionate and gallant, Stephen. Acquiring your title and properties and fortune have not made you less so, as they would with ninety-nine men out of one hundred, but more so because you believe you must prove yourself worthy of such good fortune. You gallantly offered me marriage tonight – or announced our betrothal, rather.

And now you are gallantly convincing yourself that you really *wish* to marry me. In your mind, that means that you must *love* me, and so you believe that you do. You do not.'

Irritation had blossomed into anger. Yet he did wonder if she was right. How could he be in love so suddenly like this? And with someone so different from his ideal of a prospective wife? How could he be contemplating this marriage he had trapped himself into with anything less than dismay?

And yet . . .

'You are wrong,' he said, 'as you will see in time. But it does not matter, Cass. Whether you are right or I am, the situation is the same. We have been seen together enough times in the past week to have aroused interest and specu-lation, and tonight we were caught alone out on the balcony, in each other's arms, kissing each other. There is only one thing we *can* do. We must marry.'

'And so,' she said, her fingers drumming slowly on the arms of her chair, 'for one small and thoughtless indiscretion we must both sacrifice the rest of our lives? Of course it is what the *ton* now expects. It is what it *demands*. Do you not see how ridiculous that is, though, Stephen?'

It *was* ridiculous and would be something worth defying if they actively disliked each other.

'One small and thoughtless indiscretion,' he said. 'Is that what that kiss was, Cass? Did it mean nothing else?'

She raised her eyebrows and was silent for a while.

'We spent two nights in bed together, Stephen,' she said, 'but have since reverted to celibacy. You are an extraordinarily attractive man, and I do not believe I am without some charms. We were waltzing together and had become heated in the ballroom. We sought coolness out on the balcony and discovered solitude there as well. What happened was almost inevitable – and indiscreet, of course. *And* thoughtless.'

'It was nothing more than lust, then?' he said.

'No, it was not.' She smiled at him.

'I believe you know,' he said, holding her eyes with his own, 'that it was. If anyone is practicing self-deception here, Cass, it is you, not me.'

'You are very sweet,' she said in her velvet voice.

He was annoyed again. And frustrated. He stood with his back to the fireplace, his hands clasped behind him.

'If you fail to honor this engagement,' he said, 'there will be a horrible scandal.'

She shrugged.

'People will recover,' she said. 'They always do. And we will have supplied them with what they most enjoy – a salacious topic of gossip.'

He leaned a little toward her.

'Yes,' he agreed. 'Under more normal circumstances we could perhaps hope to suffer nothing worse than a few weeks of severe discomfort. But – forgive me, Cass – these are not normal circumstances. Not for you, anyway.'

She pursed her lips and regarded him with an amused smile.

'The beau monde will rejoice over *you*, Stephen,' she said. 'The lost sheep returning to the fold. All the ladies will weep tears of joy. Eventually you will choose one of them and live happily ever after with her. I promise you.'

He stared at her until she raised her eyebrows again and looked downward rather jerkily. She drew her slipper back onto her foot by clenching her toes, uncrossed her legs, and smoothed her gown over her knees.

'Sometimes,' she said, 'your eyes are uncomfortably intense, Stephen, and speak more eloquently than words. It is very unfair of you. One cannot argue with eyes.'

'You will be ruined,' he said.

She laughed. 'And I am not already?'

'You are recovering,' he said. 'People are beginning to accept you. You are beginning to receive invitations. My family has accepted you. Your brother has reconciled with you. And now you could be betrothed to me. What is so very bad about that? Do you believe I will beat you after we are married? That I will cause you to miscarry our children? *Do* you? Will you look me in the eye and tell me you fear I may be capable of such dastardly behavior?'

She shook her head quickly and closed her eyes.

'I have nothing to bring to any marriage, Stephen,' she said. 'No hopes, no dreams, no light, no youth. Only chains that I drag about with me like wraiths. And the prospect of more chains that the nuptial service would hang on me as soon as I vowed away my freedom. No, I do *not* believe you would mistreat me. But I cannot do it, Stephen. I simply cannot. For your sake as well as mine. We would be miserable – both of us. Believe me, we would.'

He felt a chill about the heart. There was no mask now. Her voice was shaking with the passion of sincerity.

Marrying was something she could not do again.

Once had been enough.

Too much.

There was no further argument that might convince her.

And so he too was free, with a freedom he no longer wanted.

Perhaps tomorrow he would think differently. Maybe by then he would have returned to sanity.

There was a lengthy silence, during which he sat down in the chair opposite hers. He slumped slightly in it, propped one elbow on the arm, and rested his head in his hand.

He could not feel any relief yet because there were other, much stronger feelings.

Disappointment.

Grief.

Bewilderment.

Desperation.

Then he had an idea.

'Cass,' he said, 'are you willing to compromise with me?'

'*Half* marry you?' she asked, her smile slightly twisted, her eyes – what? Wistful?

'Let me send the announcement of our betrothal to the papers,' he said. 'No, wait before you shake your head. Listen to what I have to say. Let me arrange a proper celebration of our engagement at Merton House. Let us stay betrothed for what remains of the Season. And then you can break it off quietly during the summer, when the *ton* will be dispersed all over England. We will decide together then how best you can be supported for the rest of your life. But at least we—'

'I will not need your support, Stephen,' she said. 'And I will even be able to pay back what you have given me. I called on a lawyer with Wesley this morning, and he is quite confident that he can recover my jewels and get the money that was settled on me in my marriage contract and in Nigel's will. And use of the town house here too, and even of the dower house, which of course I do not want. Bruce frightened me into believing I had to make a choice between my freedom and my widow's settlement, but he would not have given me the choice if he had believed I could be convicted of murder, would he? I have realized that during the past few days, and I have decided to fight rather than cower. I am going to be comfortably well off after all. I am going to be independent.'

He felt a rush of gladness for her. He wished he had thought of it for himself, for of course she was quite right. The present Paget had relied upon his ability to browbeat the woman who had been terrorized for nine years by his father.

It was as well he had not thought of it first, though. It was good that *she* had, that quite unassisted she had found a way to set her life and her future to rights and also, more important, a way to heal herself.

'And what will you do with your independence?' he asked her.

'I'll buy a cottage somewhere in the country and live obscurely and happily ever after there,' she said. She smiled at him, a genuine smile this time. 'Wish me well, Stephen?'

'And that will be preferable to marriage with me,' he said. It was not really a question. The answer was obvious, and it both saddened and gladdened him.

'Yes,' she said softly. 'But I *will* accept your compromise, Stephen. You must be allowed to be chivalrous. I will not humiliate you before the whole *ton* when you have been so kind to me. Announce our betrothal, then, and I will celebrate it with you and with whomever you choose to invite to Merton House. I will play the part of happy, enamored fiancée for the rest of the Season. And then I will set you free.'

Perhaps.

He did not say it aloud. He just looked at her and nodded. And she looked back and smiled.

'Now that it seems I will be able to pay back everything you have paid me,' she said, 'may I count myself already free of the obligation of being your mistress?'

'Of course,' he said, inexplicably hurt. 'But I never did demand much of you in that capacity, Cass. If I have pressed my company on you, it has not been because you are my mistress but because I have wanted to help you.'

'I know that,' she said, 'and I am grateful. I am also free – or will be as soon as my money and property have been safely restored to me. Since I *am* essentially free, then, let me issue a free invitation. Stay with me tonight?'

He felt an instant stabbing of desire and longing. But he considered his answer. Was this wise? Did she know how to prevent conception? Should he endanger her for a third time? And it was a fine time to think of *that* now, when there had been those two previous encounters.

'How humiliating,' she said, smiling, 'if you say no.'

Her companion was in the house, sleeping upstairs. So were Mary and young Belinda. He wished—

'It ought to be the easiest thing in the world,' she said, 'instead of the most difficult.'

'What should?' he asked, getting to his feet and closing the short distance between them in order to set his hands on the arms of her chair and lean over her.

'Seducing an angel,' she said.

He kissed her.

It would not be sordid. He was going to marry her. He did not know how it was going to be done, but it would be.

She was going to be his wife.

He drew her to her feet, and they wrapped their arms about each other and kissed more deeply and with growing desire.

'I think,' she said at last, drawing back her head, 'this ought to be continued upstairs, Stephen.'

'Because we might be interrupted here?' he asked, grinning at her.

'As we were on the ballroom balcony earlier?' she said. 'No, but—'

At which interesting juncture there was a soft knock on the sitting room door.

What on earth?

It must be at least midnight.

Someone must be ill, Cassandra thought, breaking away from Stephen and hurrying across the room to open the door. Alice? *Belinda?*

Mary was standing just beyond the door, and beside her –

'William!' Cassandra cried, stepping forward to catch up her stepson in her arms – though he was only a little more than a year younger than she. 'You have come back. And you have found us.'

'And not before time,' he said when they stepped apart. He set one arm loosely about Mary's shoulders. 'I dashed off without pausing to think, and I discovered a ship about to sail for Canada and was on it and surrounded by nothing but ocean before it struck me that I had done entirely the wrong thing. My first thought, though, was that if I disappeared for a while, everything would simmer down. I just went too far, that was all – literally. It takes an infernally long time to go to Canada and come back. Especially since I took nothing with me and had to work to pay my passage out and then earn enough to pay my passage home. I was fortunate not to have to wait until next year.'

'Come inside the room, where there is more light,' Cassandra said. 'And yes, Mary, you must come too. Of course you must.'

Good heavens, William was Belinda's *father*.

'You cannot *imagine* how I felt, Cassie,' William said, stepping inside the room, 'when I got to Carmel a week ago to find Mary and Belinda gone, and to hear that *you* had been—'

He broke off abruptly when he saw there was someone else in the room.

'Stephen,' she said, 'this is William Belmont, Nigel's second son. The Earl of Merton, William.'

The two men bowed to each other.

'I have not had the pleasure before now,' Stephen said.

'That is because I have rarely been in London,' William explained. 'I have always hated the place. I spent several years in America, and then a couple in Canada. I have just returned from a second stay there. The wide open spaces have always called to me, though I must confess that for the past year there has been a far more insistent call.'

He looked behind him to where Mary was still lurking in the doorway, and he reached out one arm toward her.

'Have you met my wife, Merton?' he asked. 'Did you know Mary was my wife, Cassie? She says not, but I find it hard to believe. That was what the whole infernal row was all about.'

The row? *That night?*

Cassandra looked from William to Mary in wonder.

'You are William's *wife*, Mary?' she said.

'I am sorry, my lady,' Mary said, staying where she was in the doorway. 'When Billy come home from across the sea and learned about Belinda, he went off and got a special

297

license, and we was married twenty miles away from Carmel the day before . . . The day before he went off again. He told me he would come back when he could, and he did.'

She gazed at William with wide eyes and desperate tenderness.

'Come closer, love,' he said, beckoning with his fingers until she came near enough that he could take her hand in his. She remained several steps behind him, though. 'Mary would make a sturdy frontierswoman, would she not, Cassie? She only looks frail. I will not be putting the matter to the test, though. I am going to settle down here in this country instead, heaven help me, and look after her and Belinda. *After* I have set everything right for you, that is. Though how Bruce could be such a knuckle-head as to believe—'

He stopped again and eyed Stephen, who was standing before the fireplace as before, his hands clasped behind him.

'I had better come back tomorrow and talk to you,' William said. 'Not that I am leaving tonight, if you have no objection. I am staying with my wife and daughter.'

Cassandra looked consideringly at Stephen. She was not really betrothed to him. She would never marry him. But he had been extraordinarily kind to her. She owed him something – honesty. Although he had asked her about her life and her marriage, and although he had asked her if she had killed Nigel – to which she had said yes – he had not asked for any details. He must wonder, though. And, of course, she had lied to him.

'Talk now,' she said. 'The Earl of Merton is my betrothed, William. He made the announcement just this evening.'

Mary spread one hand over her bosom and then the

other when William went striding across the room to shake Stephen by the hand.

'And glad I am to hear it,' he said, 'if you are a decent man, Merton. Cassie deserves some happiness. *You* do not believe all that claptrap about her, then? Axe murderer, indeed! Even on the frontier there are not many women who can heft an axe. Not enough to do serious damage with, anyway.'

'I do not believe it,' Stephen said quietly, and he looked at Cassandra with serious eyes. 'And even if it were true, I would guess it to have been self-defense rather than murder.'

'My father could be a brute,' William said. 'It was the old demon bottle, not him. Though the contents of the old demon bottle could not have got inside him to make him a brute if he had not lifted a hand to drink it, could they? It was him, then. When he drank, which was not often, though it was too often even at that, he became someone else. It sounds as if Cassie must have given you some details.'

'Yes,' Stephen said.

'She did not tell you, did she,' William said, his eyes narrowing, 'that she shot him during one of those times? You did not tell him that, did you, Cassie?'

She shrugged.

'I think we should all sit down,' she said, and instead of taking her usual chair, she sat on an old, lumpy love seat, and Stephen sat beside her, his sleeve brushing her bare arm.

William motioned to Alice's usual chair, and Mary sat down on the edge of it, looking decidedly uncomfortable. He perched on the arm and took one of her hands in his.

'The trouble with my father,' he said, looking at Stephen, 'was that he never looked drunk, did he, Cassie? Unless you looked at his eyes, that was. And he very rarely drank at home, and almost never alone. When I told him about my marriage during the morning, though, he was probably sober. He must have started drinking after I had left. He did not like what I had told him above half. And once he started drinking, he could not stop. By the evening . . . Well. I heard him yelling and went to see what was happening.'

'I had been sent with another bottle,' Mary said, her voice almost a whisper as she gazed at William with unhappy eyes. 'It was not my job. I *never* got sent. But Mr. Quigley had just scalded his hand on the kettle, and Mrs. Rice was tending it, and it was late and there was not many servants still in the kitchen, and someone told *me* to take it. I ought not to have gone. I knew you had told him, Billy, and you said you was coming for me before night, and . . . And Mrs. Rice said to be careful because his lordship was drinking again.'

'It was not your fault, love,' he said. 'None of it was. I ought not to have gone off to secure a room at the inn for us because he had said we could not sleep together beneath his roof. It was left to Cassie to hear you screaming and go to your aid. But she only got cuffed for her pains. And then Miss Haytor went to try and help. All I heard when I came in was him shouting. I did not hear any screams. But by the time I opened the library door he had his pistol in his hand. It would not have been wise for anyone to scream.'

'I think,' Cassandra said, and she realized suddenly that her hand was clasped firmly in Stephen's, 'it would be best to say no more, William. The death was officially ruled an accident. Your father was cleaning his pistol and it discharged. No one will ever prove otherwise. I do not want—'

'Who knows what he would have done with the gun if I had not come in,' William said. 'Maybe he would have shot one of you. But when I went to wrest it out of his grasp, he struggled for only a moment. And then he turned it quite deliberately and shot himself with it. Through the heart.'

There were a few moments of total silence in the room. Cassandra saw that Alice was standing in the doorway.

'It is what I told you at the time, Cassie,' she said. 'I *saw*. You did not. Mr. Belmont was between you and Lord Paget. And Mary had her hands spread over her face. But I saw. Lord Paget shot himself.'

'I suppose,' William said, 'there was a great deal of self-loathing in his condition. Perhaps he suddenly realized that he had a gun in his hands. Perhaps he realized he was about to commit murder with it. Perhaps a small window of sobriety opened in his mind. However it was, Cassie, it was neither murder nor an accident that happened. He shot himself.'

Stephen had the back of her hand pressed against his lips. His eyes were closed.

'I fled,' William said, 'because when it became known that I had married Mary, it would have been assumed that I had quarreled with my father and shot him. I might have been charged with murder. *Mary* might have been charged as my accomplice. I fled because I was muddle-headed and thought it would be best to let everything calm down for a while. I thought that without me there and without anyone knowing about my marriage, his death would be ruled an accident – as it was, officially. I told Mary not to tell anyone about our marrying. I told her I would be back for her within a year. I am a bit late on that promise, sorry, love. But I assumed *you* knew about the marriage, Cassie. I assumed he had told you or that Mary had. I had *no idea* anyone would blame you for his death and think you did it. *With an axe,* no less. Has the world gone mad?'

'You thought I was trying to make you feel better, Cassie,' Alice said from the doorway. 'You did not want to believe that Mr. Belmont had killed his father, even though you thought he had done it to defend you and to defend Mary. You thought I lied to make you feel better.'

'I did,' Cassandra admitted.

But if it was true, what Alice had told her and what William now confirmed, then Nigel had committed suicide. He would have been denied a proper burial if the truth had been known.

Would she have minded?

Would she mind?

He might have killed someone that night. Instead, he had killed himself.

She was too numb to analyze her thoughts and feelings.

'It was a damn fool thing to run the way I did,' William said. 'Pardon my language.'

'It was,' Stephen agreed. 'But we all do foolish things, Belmont. I would advise you not to compound the error now, though, by dashing out to tell the world the truth. The truth is ugly and might not be believed anyway. I would suggest that everyone retire for the night and that

I go home. Let decisions be made tomorrow or the next day.'

'That is very wise advice,' Alice said, looking at him with approval.

'You were not here, Alice,' Cassandra said, 'when I told William that Lord Merton and I are betrothed.'

Alice looked from one to the other of them.

'Yes' was all she said. She nodded her head. 'Yes.'

And she withdrew and presumably went back upstairs to her room. William stood and drew Mary to her feet and led her out of the room, his arm about her shoulders.

They were *husband and wife*, Cassandra thought. They had been for longer than a year. Since the day before Nigel died.

By his own hand.

Alice had not been lying all this time.

'Why did you tell me,' Stephen asked, standing and waiting for her to get to her feet too, 'that you had killed your husband?'

She felt almost too weary to stand.

'Everyone believed it anyway,' she said. 'And part of me wished it had been me.'

'And you wanted to protect that miserable apology for a man?' he asked her.

'Don't judge William too harshly,' she said. 'He is not a bad man. Mary loves him, and he is Belinda's father. Besides, he *married* her, a mere maid in his father's house, because she had borne his child. And he came back for her even though he must have still feared that he might be accused of murdering Nigel. I believe he must be fond of her. I did not want him charged with murder, Stephen. He is *Belinda's father.*'

303

He framed her face with his hands and smiled at her. And what a *ghastly* moment, she thought, in which to realize that she was bone deep in love with him.

'If there is an angel in this room,' he said, 'it is certainly not me.'

He bent his head and kissed her softly on the lips.

'Will you stay the night?' she asked him.

He shook his head.

'No,' he said. 'I *will* make love to you again, Cass. But it will be on our wedding night and in our marriage bed. And it will be a loving to end all lovings.'

'Boaster,' she said.

It would be never, then, she thought with some regret. She would never make love with him again.

'I will ask you on the morning after our wedding night,' he said, 'if it was a boast.'

And his smile caused his eyes to twinkle.

He set one arm about her waist and led her toward the front door.

'Good night, Cass,' he said, kissing her again before opening the door. 'You are going to have to marry me, you know. You are going to be horribly lonely otherwise. You are about to lose all your family to matrimony.'

'Except Wesley,' she said.

He nodded.

'And except Roger,' she said.

'And except Roger,' he agreed, grinning as he stepped outside and pulled the door closed behind him.

Cassandra set her forehead against the door and closed her eyes. She tried to remember why she could not marry him.

19

'I am going out for a walk,' Cassandra said, though she made no move to put words into action. She was standing at the sitting room window, looking out on a day that had not quite made up its mind whether to rain or to shine, though it seemed more inclined to decide upon the former.

She had not slept well – hardly surprisingly.

Now this morning everyone had become insubordinate.

Mary had refused to stop working in the kitchen or to stop addressing Cassandra as *my lady*.

'You are my stepdaughter-in-law, Mary,' Cassandra had tried to explain, but to no avail.

'*Someone* has to cook our breakfast and make our tea and wash the dishes and all the rest of it, my lady,' Mary had said, 'and it had better be me since I daresay neither you nor Miss Haytor nor Billy knows one end of a frying pan from the other. And I am no different today than what I was yesterday and last week and last month, am I?'

William had been working on the sitting room door

when Cassandra came downstairs, and now the door shut tight without having to be given an extra yank. Since then he had mended the clothesline outside so that it was no longer in danger of falling to the ground, taking a load of clean washing with it. And he was in the process of cleaning every window in the house, inside and out.

William always had been energetic and restless, of course, and far happier being busy with some manual labor than idling away his time at more gentlemanly pursuits. Nigel had intended him for the church, but William had openly rebelled after finishing his studies at Cambridge.

Alice was the worst of all this morning. She was attacking the sheets with her needle, and she was downright prunish. She had an annoying I-told-you-so look on her face, an expression to which she was entitled as she had indeed told Cassandra that William had not shot his father but that Nigel had shot himself.

And Alice had given Cassandra an ultimatum, or what amounted to one.

Either Cassandra agreed to honor the betrothal that had been announced verbally last night at Lady Compton-Haig's ball and would be announced in writing in tomorrow's papers, or Alice would have nothing more to do with Mr. Golding.

It was ridiculous and it was a non sequitur. But Alice was adamant.

'I daresay,' she had said a few minutes ago, 'Mr. Golding means no more than friendship by inviting me to accompany him to his family's home to celebrate his father's birthday. I daresay that after we return I will not see him again except by chance. But I will not even *think* of seeing him again, Cassie, if you are going to insist on continuing

306

with this silly and wholly unrealistic plan of settling in a small country cottage somewhere in the country.'

'It is my idea of heaven,' Cassandra had protested.

'Nonsense,' Alice had told her. 'You would be bored and miserable within a fortnight, Cassie. You would be far better off marrying the Earl of Merton, since despite everything the two of you seem fond of each other and I believe that after all he is a harmless, even decent, young man. Besides which, there will be a new scandal if you break off the engagement now, and you really do not need another. You ought to have thought of all this before allowing him to kiss you in the middle of a ball. If you insist upon going to live in the country, I am going with you. And there is no point whatsoever in giving me that look. Looks do not kill. Mary will not be going with you, after all, will she? And though you will doubtless soon be able to hire half a dozen servants to take her place, you will not *know* any of them. Or any of your neighbors. And what will they think if a strange widow comes to take up residence in their village without even as much as a companion to lend her respectability? No, Cassie, if you go, I go too.'

She had seemed to know the main power point of her argument.

'And I will never see Mr. Golding again,' she had added once more for good measure, snapping off her thread with her fingers.

And so Cassandra had threatened to go out for a walk.

'I'll take Roger with me,' she said now, drumming her fingers on the windowsill.

Though Roger, the traitor, had been shadowing William about the house all morning. So had Belinda, her doll clutched to her bosom, her eyes as wide as saucers.

'You do that, Cassie,' Alice said without looking up from her work. 'And take an umbrella.'

But it was too late. A carriage was approaching along the street, and it looked far too grand a conveyance to be on Portman Street even before Cassandra saw that there was a ducal coat of arms emblazoned on the door.

It drew to a halt outside her house, and she felt curiously resigned when the liveried coachman opened the door and set down the steps and handed the Duchess of Moreland down onto the pavement. She was not even surprised when he then proceeded to hand out the Countess of Sheringford and Lady Montford.

But of course. The whole triumvirate.

Their brother had announced his betrothal to her last evening.

'We have visitors, Alice,' Cassandra said.

Alice set aside her work.

'I will leave you to them,' she said. 'I still have some packing to do.'

And off she went before Mary could tap on the door and announce the three ladies.

And so it began, Cassandra thought. The grand charade.

'Lady Paget,' the Duchess of Moreland said, sweeping toward her across the room and drawing her into a hug. 'But you are going to be our sister. I am going to exercise a sister's right and call you Cassandra. May I? And you must call me Vanessa. We simply refused to wait until a more decent hour to call upon you, and so you must forgive us. Or not, I suppose. Anyway, here we are.'

She smiled sunnily.

The Countess of Sheringford hugged Cassandra too.

'Last evening,' she said, 'we were inhibited by a rather

308

large audience and so could not greet you quite as we wished. It was wretched of Stephen to kiss you like that out on the balcony when I certainly brought him up to know better, but we were delighted nevertheless to discover that he was so deeply in love that he had grown reckless. Stephen is almost never reckless. And we are very pleased that it has happened with *you*. Our only wish for him has always been that he find love and happiness, Cassandra. I am Margaret.'

'And I am Katherine, Cassandra,' Baroness Montford said, third in line to hug her. 'Stephen engaged and planning a wedding! My mind has still not fully comprehended the reality of it. But there is so much to do we scarcely know where to begin. We know that you have no mother and no sisters, though it was a pleasant surprise to discover that Sir Wesley Young is your brother and that you are not all alone in the world. Meg, Nessie, and I are going to be your sisters after you marry Stephen, but we have no intention of waiting until that happens. We are going to help you celebrate your betrothal and plan your wedding.'

'It is really quite wicked of us to be almost glad that you have no female relatives of your own,' Vanessa said. 'But we *are* glad, nevertheless. We are going to have *enormous* fun for the rest of the Season – unless you plan to marry before it ends, of course. Where do you—'

'Nessie!' Margaret laughed and linked an arm through Cassandra's. 'Poor Cassandra's head will be spinning on her shoulders if we do not soon curb our enthusiasm and stop jabbering. We have come to take you out for coffee and cakes, Cassandra – provided you do not have other plans for the rest of the morning, that is. And when we are sitting down and are relaxing, we are going to discuss your betrothal ball at Merton House. We are going to see to it that it is the grandest squeeze of the Season.'

Cassandra looked from one to the other of them – beautiful, fashionable, elegant ladies, all well married – and wondered if they could possibly be as delighted by her betrothal to their brother as they claimed to be. It did not take much power of observation to understand that they adored him.

Of course they were not delighted. They must be dismayed, alarmed, worried . . . They were, she guessed, making the best of a bad situation, of what they thought was a fait accompli.

She made an impulsive decision. Putting on an act for the *ton* during what remained of the Season was one thing. Deceiving Stephen's sisters was another.

'Thank you,' she said. 'I would be delighted to go out for coffee in your company. And I will be pleased to help with the ball. There will be no wedding to plan, though.'

They all looked inquiringly at her.

'There will be no *wedding*,' she said.

None of them spoke. The duchess clasped her hands to her bosom.

'I like your brother,' Cassandra said. 'He is probably the kindest, most decent man I have ever known. He is undoubtedly the most handsome. He is also very . . . well, *attractive*. I believe he finds me attractive too. Indeed, I know he does. That kiss resulted from our mutual attraction, nothing else. It was unpardonably indiscreet – on both our parts. The Earl of Merton behaved with great presence of mind and gallantry when he saw we had an audience. He announced our betrothal. But it is something neither of us wants, and we cannot allow the whole of the rest of our lives to be dictated by one foolishly impulsive kiss, though he, of course, feels obliged to protect my reputation. I cannot humiliate him by refusing to have the betrothal announced and celebrated, and so I have agreed to remain betrothed until the Season ends. Then I will put a quiet end to it. Your brother's reputation will suffer scarcely a dent, I do assure you. Indeed, everyone is sure to be very relieved for him. Yourselves included.'

His sisters exchanged glances.

'Bravo, Cassandra,' Vanessa said.

'It is so *good* of you,' Katherine said, 'to be frank with us.'

'Now,' Margaret said briskly, 'we have to decide whether to let Stephen know that we know. Will he be annoyed with you for telling us, Cassandra?'

'Probably,' Cassandra said. 'I am sure he considers our betrothal real, and I believe he hopes to make me change my mind. He does not, of course, really *want* to be married to me. But he is unfailingly gallant.'

'And also,' Vanessa said dryly, 'incurably in love. That has been very obvious to us for a few days. And he openly admitted to me just a day or two ago that he really *likes* you, Cassandra. That, when there is emphasis upon the word, is an enormously significant admission for a *man* to make. I do believe that the male lips and tongue were formed in such a way that it is virtually impossible for them to utter the word *love,* especially in combination with those other two words on either side of it – *I* and *you.*'

'And so,' Margaret said, 'we must disagree with you, Cassandra. It would seem altogether probable to us that Stephen really does wish to marry you.'

Cassandra could think of no answer to make.

'We will say nothing to Stephen of what you have told us, then,' Katherine said, looking from one to the other of her sisters for confirmation. 'And perhaps we will never need to. We must warn you, Cassandra, that his happiness is very dear to our hearts, and if his happiness can be achieved only through having you for a bride, then we will do all in our power to see that there is a wedding for us to plan.'

'But you cannot *possibly* want me for him,' Cassandra said, spreading one hand over her bosom. 'I am twenty-eight years old, I was married for nine years, my husband died under sufficiently mysterious circumstances that I stand accused of his murder in public opinion, and Lord Merton and I have known each other for little longer than a week.'

She counted the points off on the fingers of her free hand.

'You need to know something about us, Cassandra,' Margaret said with a sigh. 'Perhaps it is due to the fact that we were not born and bred as aristocrats and have therefore found it impossible to *think* like aristocrats even if we have almost perfected the behavior most of the time. However it is, we all contracted marriages that were potentially disastrous, and we have all somehow made them work. More than that, we have all made them into love matches. Why should Stephen be any different from us? Why should we warn him against the potential disasters of allying himself with you when the potential for happiness is there too?'

'We have learned to trust love,' Katherine said with a smile. 'We are eternal optimists. I will tell you *my* story one of these days. It will raise the hair on the nape of your neck.'

'If we do not leave here soon,' Vanessa said, 'we will be having coffee and cakes for *luncheon* instead of for midmorning refreshments.'

'I will go and fetch my hat,' Cassandra said.

She was not sure, as she climbed the stairs, whether her decision to tell Stephen's sisters the truth had freed her of complications or merely entangled her in more.

He had told Vanessa, even before last evening, that he *liked* her.

She smiled – and felt the ache of tears in the back of her throat.

William was on his hands and knees in the upstairs hallway, mending a loose floorboard that had been squeaking ever since she moved in.

After leaving the House of Lords, Stephen made his way homeward rather than toward White's Club as he usually did. He had much on his mind.

White's would be an uncomfortable place for him anyway today, after last evening. He would be the victim of some merciless teasing if he went there. The House had been bad enough, though no one there had made any open remarks. He had intercepted several knowing smirks, though.

Every gentleman's worst nightmare was that he would somehow be trapped by a small, inadvertent indiscretion at a public entertainment into an unwanted leg shackle.

His own indiscretion had hardly been a small one. And hardly inadvertent.

Good Lord!

But was his leg shackle unwanted?

He had fallen in love with Cassandra. He had lain awake

last night trying to force his mind into total honesty, trying to strip away the layers of guilt and gentlemanly honor and wishful thinking that clouded it so that he might know the truth of his feelings. Not that the truth mattered one iota now. Cassandra must be persuaded into agreeing to marry him.

But the truth had stared him unwaveringly in the eye no matter how much artifice he had stripped away.

He *was* in love with her.

But did it naturally follow that he also wanted to marry her? Did he want to marry *anyone* this early in his life?

Those questions, of course, did not need to be agonized over. He had been caught in a rather deep embrace with her, and marry her he must. Especially given the precarious nature of her reputation.

He was going to have a quick luncheon, he decided as he approached Merton House. Then he was going back out. He needed to talk to William Belmont. The truth of *that* debacle had been wonderful to hear last night, but Stephen was not at all sure that blurting out the truth for the whole world to hear was the right thing to do.

Paget had committed suicide while in a drunken rage.

His body would quite possibly be exhumed from the churchyard and reburied in unconsecrated ground.

And Cassandra was his widow.

She would be embroiled in a newly unsavory sensation.

If Belmont's story was believed, that was. The chances were that most people would still believe the old axe murderer story. It was more salacious. The new story would merely revive a scandal that was becoming old news. Most people probably did not *really* believe it and were growing bored with thinking it.

Perhaps Belmont could be persuaded merely to reinforce the official verdict on the death, which was that it had been accidental. He could claim quite truthfully that he had been there and had seen what happened. His word would carry some weight – except among those who were determined to believe the worst. He was the late Paget's son, after all.

And there was Cassandra to see after luncheon. He would take her out somewhere if the sun made up its mind to shine. He would begin his campaign of persuasion. He would use all the charm he could muster to persuade her to fall in love with him.

Actually, he could hardly wait to see her again.

He bounded up the steps to the front door and knocked lightly rather than produce his own key. He tossed his hat to the footman who opened it and grinned at his butler, who was just emerging from the nether regions of the house.

'There is no need to fall into a panic, Paulson,' he said. 'A luncheon of cold meats and bread and butter will be more than sufficient. Can it be on the table within the next half hour?'

But Paulson had something to tell him.

'Lady Sheringford and the Duchess of Moreland and Baroness Montford are here, my lord,' he said. 'They are in the ballroom, I believe. They *did* say that they would not stay for luncheon, but they have been here longer than an hour and have doubtless forgotten how late it is. I have taken it upon myself to have a cold repast set out for them. I will add a place for you, my lord. All will be ready in ten minutes.'

His sisters? In the *ballroom*?

It did not take any great intellectual effort to guess the reason why. They were taking charge before he could even ask them to. They were planning his betrothal ball.

'Thank you, Paulson,' he said as he turned to the staircase. He took the stairs two at a time.

Should he *tell* them? he wondered. About the betrothal being a mock one, as far as Cass was concerned, that was? He would not, he decided before he reached the top of the stairs. It was an irrelevant point. By the end of the Season the betrothal was going to be real on both their parts. They were going to marry during the summer. At Warren Hall, he hoped, though he would be quite agreeable to St. George's here in town if that was what she wanted when the time came.

He found his sisters standing in the middle of the ball-room, their heads tipped back to regard the chandeliers overhead. There were three of the latter, it being a large and magnificent room, though it had not been much used in his time. A single gentleman did not have a great deal of opportunity to host lavish entertainments in his own home.

His betrothal ball would be an exception. He looked forward to it with some enthusiasm.

Stephen stood in the doorway, his hands clasped behind his back.

'I have counted seventy candle holders in this chandelier. There will be an equal number in the one at the other end. The middle one is larger. It must hold a hundred candles or more. That is at least two hundred and fifty candles in all, not counting the wall sconces. It will be an *impossible* extravagance. The candles alone will cost a fortune.'

The voice was coming from the orchestra dais at the far end of the room. Stephen had not noticed her before she spoke up.

Cassandra.

Her head was tipped back too.

As if Paulson and the housekeeper would not know how many candles would be needed to light the ballroom – without having to count holders and give themselves a crick in the neck into the bargain.

'I was about to send for the reserves when I heard my house had been invaded,' Stephen said, raising his voice. 'But it would be a pointless exercise, I can see. You have taken possession until after the betrothal ball, I suppose?'

'Unless *you* want to plan it all on your own, Stephen,' Margaret said as he walked farther into the room.

He grinned as he kissed her on the cheek and turned to do likewise for his other two sisters.

'Perhaps,' he said, 'I ought to call out the reserves after all to make sure none of you escape before the day.'

Cassandra was approaching along the ballroom floor, looking slightly pink in the cheeks.

He went to meet her and twined an arm about her waist before dipping his head to kiss her briefly on the lips. It was a heady sensation, seeing her like this in his own home.

'My love,' he said.

'Stephen,' she said as he turned her so that they were facing his sisters.

They all wore identical smug expressions.

'We went out for coffee and cakes,' Cassandra said. 'I was congratulated by at least a score of people, Stephen, though the notice has not even appeared in the papers yet.

It was all quite dizzying. And gratifying,' she added as if as an afterthought.

'It is a good thing, then,' he said, 'that we meant what we said when we announced our betrothal at the ball last night.'

Her eyes smiled at him. There were identical smiles on his sisters' faces. He wondered how they really felt about his betrothal.

'A very good thing,' Cassandra agreed. 'Though it was *you* who made the announcement.'

'As was only right and proper,' Meg said. 'One shudders to imagine what would have been the reaction if *you* had made it, Cassandra.'

It was a comment that sent all the ladies into paroxysms of merriment.

'And the very *idea*,' Nessie said, 'that you might *not* have meant it, Stephen. Or that Cassandra might have contradicted you. It makes me feel quite vaporish just to *think* of it.'

'And we would not have had this lavish ball to plan,' Kate added. 'Or the even more lavish wedding this summer.'

They all chose to be hugely amused again as if they were in some sort of conspiracy against him.

Stephen hugged Cassandra closer to his side and smiled down at her.

'I see that you and my sisters are getting along famously,' he said. 'I might have warned you that they would not wait until after the wedding to take you under their wing.'

'We were discussing the colors of the floral arrangements before we turned our attention to the chandeliers,' she said. 'We all agree that the effect has to be bright and sunny, like a garden, though we have not yet decided exactly *what* colors there will be or how many.'

'Yellow and white,' he suggested, 'with lots of greenery?'

'Perfect.' She smiled into his eyes.

'Inspired,' Nessie said. 'Cassandra is going to wear a sunshine yellow gown, Stephen. It will look quite stunning with her coloring, though of course she would look quite stunning even in mud brown. I am *mortally* jealous of that hair.'

'Paulson will scold me for a month,' he said, 'if I do not spirit you all to the dining room within the next five minutes. He has had a cold luncheon set out for us all.'

'Oh,' Cassandra said, 'I really must not—'

' – say no,' he said hastily. 'I agree. You really must not. You would not enjoy being on the wrong side of Paulson for the rest of your life, Cass.'

'I am rather hungry,' Kate said, sounding surprised. 'Of course, I resisted having a cake with my coffee. Paulson is a dear, and I shall tell him so.'

Stephen's sisters made their way out of the room without further ado. He kept Cassandra where she was for a few moments longer, until they had the ballroom to themselves.

'I was coming to call on you later,' he said. 'I could scarcely wait. I have been thinking of you all morning instead of concentrating upon the business of the House. You look lovely in that particular shade of pink. It ought to clash horribly with your hair. How clever of you to know that it would not.'

'Oh, Stephen,' she said with a sigh. 'I *wish* last evening had not happened. You and your sisters are so dreadfully . . . *decent.*'

He grinned at her.

'If you are still bent upon making this a temporary

betrothal,' he said, 'you will discover how horribly *in*-decent I can be, Cass. I will fight for you quite mercilessly and with every dirty tactic I can muster.'

She laughed and cupped his cheek with one palm.

He kissed her, prolonging the embrace just long enough to leave her slightly breathless.

'An angel with grubby wings,' she said. 'It is a contra-diction in terms.'

He took her hand in his, laced their fingers together, and led her in the direction of the dining room. Bless his sisters for bringing her here.

To his own home.

20

It was almost fortunate, Cassandra thought during the following week, that her temporary betrothal and preparations for the ball kept her so very busy. For it was difficult to be patient. Her lawyer had warned her that though he expected a speedy and successful resolution to her claim, nevertheless they could not reasonably expect to hear anything for two weeks, perhaps longer. In the meantime, she must not worry.

They did not, of course, hear anything. And she did, of course, worry.

But life had become impossibly busy. There was a dinner party to attend at Wesley's one evening. Cassandra had not taken him into her confidence, as she had Stephen's sisters. He would not approve. And he would surely blame Stephen, which would be grossly unfair. He was delighted by the engagement. He saw it as a solution to all her problems.

'For even if you recover your money and jewels, Cassie,'

he said, 'you will still be alone, and there will still be people who will think the worst of you. Merton will be able to protect you from all that.'

She *had* told her brother what William had said about Nigel's death. She had also told him that William had been persuaded to say nothing to anyone else at least until her claim had been settled. Wesley reluctantly agreed that it was probably a good idea not to stir up the old scandal again just when people were beginning to lose interest.

There was another dinner party and small soiree to attend at Sir Graham Carling's, and a private concert to which Cassandra had received an invitation the very day notice of her betrothal appeared in the papers. There was a garden party the day after that, and again she had received a personal invitation.

Every day Stephen took her driving or walking in the park. On the day of the garden party, he took her for a morning ride on Rotten Row instead, having hired a horse for her for the occasion. It seemed to be years since she had last ridden and probably was. She had almost forgotten how exhilarating it was to be seated sidesaddle on a horse's back, feeling its power and energy beneath her and controlling it all with the skill in her own hands.

But it was the preparations for the ball that consumed so much of her time that she even suggested on one occasion that perhaps she ought to give up sleeping until she had time to indulge in it again.

There were lists – endless lists – to be drawn up and acted upon. There were invitations to send and flowers to order and an orchestra to engage and a menu to be planned and a program of dances to be drawn up and . . . Well, the tasks were never-ending, it seemed. Stephen's sisters could have done it all very well without her, Cassandra knew. Indeed, even *one* of them could. They might have grown up in a country vicarage, but they were now perfectly competent ladies of the *ton*. They insisted, however, that they work together and that Cassandra make one of their number.

'It is going to be such *fun*,' Vanessa said, having chosen to ignore Cassandra's claim that she would never actually marry Stephen, 'to have another sister. I have two sisters-in-law from my first marriage and three from my marriage to Elliott, but there is always room for more. There is *nothing* as wonderful as family, is there?'

Cassandra began rather wistfully to believe that indeed there was not. Stephen's sisters did not live in one another's pockets. They had their own separate lives, and they lived in different parts of the country except during the spring, when they met in London for the parliamentary session and the Season. But there was a closeness among them that made her heart ache with envy and longing.

She met Viscountess Burden and the Countess of Lanting, sisters-in-law of Vanessa and Katherine, during the week and even they claimed to be eager to welcome Cassandra into their larger family.

Yes, family – and sisterhood – were precious commodities indeed.

And life was busy.

Even at home it was not tranquil.

William was a wealthy man. Even apart from his portion as Nigel's son, he was rich, having amassed something like a fortune in the fur trade during his years in America and Canada. Now he was ready to settle down. He wanted to buy land, to become a gentleman farmer with Mary at his side and his family already begun.

But Mary had dug in her heels. She would have been out wandering the roads of England as a vagabond, or in jail somewhere as a vagrant, if it were not for the kindness of Lady Paget, who had little enough of her own, the good Lord knew, when she was sent away from Carmel but who had taken Mary and Belinda – not to mention Roger – with her when she went. Mary was *not* going to abandon her ladyship now just because Billy had come home, not, at any rate, until she was married right and tight to the Earl of Merton, who was a proper gentleman no matter what he did when he first met her ladyship – though *that*, no doubt, was on account of the fact that he fell in love with her, as what man would not when she was so beautiful? He had more than made up for his sins since. And if Lady Paget chose *not* to marry his lordship, though it would be remarkably foolish of her not to – *not* that Mary had any right to judge her betters, especially to call them *foolish* – then Mary would stay with her until she got her money and settled somewhere with proper servants. Though Mary wanted to see those servants with her very own eyes first, because there was no knowing what riffraff there might be in London who thought they could cook and clean for a lady. Mary was staying, at least for now, and if Billy did not like it and wanted to go off looking for land before she was good and ready to go with him, then so be it.

Every time Mary delivered this lengthy speech or some variation on it, she ended up in tears, her apron up over her face, and William had to offer a shoulder for her to cry on while he patted her back and grinned and assured her that he had no intention of going anywhere before Cassie was settled. And Mary must be a goose if she thought he would go.

Alice was no better. She returned from her three days in Kent looking ten years younger. Her eyes glowed. So did her cheeks. So did her whole person.

'Cassie,' she said before she had been back in the house ten minutes, 'they are wonderful people, Allan's family. They are a close-knit group and yet they opened the arms of friendship to me. More than friendship, actually. They treated me like one of themselves.'

Allan now, was he?

'I am so glad,' Cassandra said. 'You are to see more of Mr. Golding, then?'

'The silly man wants me to marry him,' Alice said.

'Silly indeed,' Cassandra agreed. 'Did you say yes?'

'No,' Alice said, setting her cup in the saucer with a slight clatter. The cup never had made the full distance to her mouth.

'No?'

'No,' Alice said firmly. 'I asked him to give me time to think about it.'

Cassandra set her own cup and saucer down on the table beside her.

'Because of me, I suppose,' she said.

Alice pursed her lips but would not deny it.

'Alice,' Cassandra said with a severity that was not feigned, 'if you and Mary between you force me into marrying Stephen, I will have the greatest difficulty forgiving either of you.'

Alice merely looked mulish.

'Of course,' Cassandra said, 'both of you would deny

that you had done any such thing. You are both postponing your futures or even denying them altogether just in case I do *not* marry him. I will not allow such tyranny. I will give both of you notice – very *short* notice. I will terminate both your employments.'

'What employment?' Alice asked. 'I have not been paid in almost a year. I think that means I am no longer your servant, Cassie. I am only your friend. You cannot give your friends the sack. And if you try to get rid of Mary, she will only give you the length of her tongue and burst into tears and make you feel like a worm. And then she will stay and refuse to let you pay her, and you will feel like a giant worm. And Mr. Belmont will stay with her because, to his credit, he is besotted with her – and with Belinda. And you will be forever tripping over him as he mends everything in this house that needs mending – a never-ending task if ever I saw one. You will end up feeling like a *dragon*.'

Cassandra shook her head and picked up her cup and saucer again.

'I am going to buy a cottage with *one bedchamber*,' she said, 'and there will be no room in it for anyone but me.'

Having had the last word, she drank her tea to the dregs with some satisfaction.

And why were Alice and Mary suddenly on Stephen's side when less than two weeks ago they had both thought him the devil incarnate? But that, of course, had been before they met him. How could *any* woman resist those angelic looks once she had set eyes upon him? And how could any woman resist his warm charm when it was directed her way? He did not play fair. For every time he came to the house – and he came every day – he had a word and a smile for Mary and a word and a smile for Alice.

Oh, he did *not* play fair. For of course, *she* had to look upon all that beauty every day too, and *she* had to expose herself to all that charm. And *she* had memories of more than just good looks and charm.

And always at the back of her mind was one needling question: Why could she *not* marry him when there was not a bone or muscle or blood cell in her body that was not giddy with love for him?

She had not killed Nigel, and Stephen knew it. She was not so foolish that she still believed every man in the world to be rotten to the core. She had been unfortunate to marry a man with a sad illness that was destructive both of others and of himself. It had not been her fault that he could not be cured of that illness. Neither had all the beatings she had suffered been her fault, though for all the years of her marriage she had blamed herself.

There was no real reason why she should not marry Stephen and reach for a little happiness after all the years of pain. Except that she felt used and sullied and world-weary, and Stephen seemed the opposite. She could not convince herself that she would not somehow be harming him by marrying him. That she would not be stealing some of his light.

And did he really love her? If that kiss had not happened to force him into offering her marriage and to make him gallantly claim to be in love with her, would he ever have freely wanted to do either?

Perhaps eventually, Cassandra thought, she would regain her confidence and self-esteem to such a degree that she would consider marrying again. But not now. Not yet. And not Stephen.

But how could there ever be anyone else *but* Stephen?

One thing she no longer doubted – in the privacy of her own heart. She loved him with all her being.

Stephen had not been as busy as Cassandra, or at least no busier than he usually was. He had offered his assistance with the planning of the ball, which was to be held at *his* house to celebrate *his* betrothal, but his sisters had looked at him collectively with the sort of fond impatience they had sometimes shown him when at the age of ten or so he had arrived home with torn breeches or muddy boots just when they were preparing for a church bazaar.

Men were not needed for *ton* balls, it seemed, in any capacity but to dance with the ladies and make sure that none of them were wallflowers.

He concentrated most of his energies that week upon persuading Cassandra to marry him during the summer – without actually saying a word on the subject. He concentrated upon making her fall in love with him.

It was no longer a matter of gallantry.

It was a matter of his own lifelong happiness.

He did not tell her that, though. The very last thing he wanted to do was trap her into marrying him by engaging her pity. He had told her once that he loved her, but now actions must convince her that he had spoken the truth.

The ballroom looked quite stunningly gorgeous. It looked like a summer garden, complete with sunshine. Not that there *was* sunshine, but the yellow and white flowers and the banks of green ferns gave the illusion of light, and the candelabra overhead had been washed and polished and rubbed into such brightness that the three hundred candles seemed almost superfluous.

The ballroom *smelled* like a garden too. And it seemed filled with fresh air. It would not seem so for much longer, of course. In about an hour's time the guests would begin arriving and even all the open windows would not keep the air cool. Meg had predicted that this ball would be a squeeze to end squeezes, and Stephen tended to agree. Not only were balls at Merton House rare, but this one was to celebrate his betrothal to an axe murderer. That term was still bandied about in clubs and drawing rooms, he gathered, though he doubted anyone believed any longer in the literal truth of it. He wished the truth could be told, but on the whole he thought it might be wiser to allow the whole subject to drop.

He had just hosted a family dinner to precede the ball – something *he* had arranged. His sisters and their husbands and Con and Wesley Young had attended. Now they were all strolling about the ballroom, relaxing, before the room filled with ball guests.

The musicians had set up their instruments on the dais, Stephen could see, but they had gone belowstairs for their dinner.

'Is it as lovely as you imagined it?' he asked Cassandra, coming up behind her and wrapping an arm about her waist.

'Oh, lovelier,' she said, smiling at him.

She was wearing a sunshine yellow gown, as promised. It shimmered when she moved. It was fresher than gold, brighter than lemon. Its short puffed sleeves and deep neckline were scalloped and trimmed with tiny white flowers. So was the deep flounced hem. She wore the heart-shaped necklace her brother had given her, and the almost-matching bracelet of tiny diamonds arranged in the shape of hearts that he had given her as a betrothal gift.

She would return it when she ended the engagement, she had told him when he gave it to her earlier this evening – the only reference either of them had made all week to that potential event in the future.

'It is going to be a perfect evening,' he said. 'I am going to be the envy of every man present.'

'I think it altogether likely,' she said, 'that all the unmarried young ladies will be wearing deepest mourning. You will be a dreadful loss to all but one of them when you do eventually marry, Stephen.'

'This summer?' he said, and grinned at her.

He turned his head toward the doorway. He could hear Paulson's voice, unusually loud, unusually agitated.

'The receiving line has not yet been formed, sir,' he was saying. 'No one is expected for another hour. Allow me to show you into the visitors' parlor for a while and bring you refreshments there.'

Stephen raised his eyebrows. If the early guest had been persistent enough to get this far into the house despite Paulson's vigilance, it was probably futile still to be suggesting the visitors' parlor. He strode toward the doors, and Cassandra followed.

'Receiving lines be damned and balls and expected arrival times and visitors' parlors, you fool,' a harsh, impatient voice replied, presumably addressing Paulson. 'Where *is* she? I am determined to see her even if I have to ransack the house. Ah, the ballroom. Is she in *there*?'

Stephen was aware of all his family turning in some surprise to the ballroom doors as a gentleman appeared there, a black cloak swirling about his legs, a tall hat upon his head, a thunderous frown upon his face.

'Bruce,' Cassandra said.

The man's eyes alit upon her at the same moment, and with a slight movement of his head Stephen dismissed Paulson.

'Paget?' Stephen said, stepping forward and extending his right hand.

Lord Paget ignored it – and him.

'You!' he said, addressing Cassandra harshly and pointing an accusing finger at her. 'What the *devil* do you think you are up to?'

'Bruce,' Cassandra said, her voice low and cool, though Stephen could hear a slight tremor in it, 'we had better talk in private. I am sure the Earl of Merton will allow us the use of the visitors' parlor or the library.'

'I will not, *by thunder,* talk in private,' he said, striding a few paces into the room. 'The whole world needs to know what you are, woman, and the whole world will hear it from me, starting with these people. What the devil—'

Stephen had taken one step closer. Paget was not a small man. He was of slightly above-average height, in fact, and he was not puny of build. But Stephen took hold of his cloak at the neck and of his shirt beneath it and lifted the man onto his toes with one hand. He moved his head forward until there was a scant three inches of space between his nose and Paget's.

He did not raise his voice.

'You will not talk at all in my home, Paget,' he said, 'except with my permission. And you will not use language that is offensive to the ears of ladies even when that permission is granted.'

His knuckles were pressing lightly but deliberately against the man's windpipe so that his face turned slightly purple.

'*Ladies?*' Paget said. 'The only female I see before me, Merton, is no lady.'

Stephen's frayed temper snapped. He slammed Paget back against the wall two feet behind him, his hand still at the man's throat. His free hand, closed into a fist, was poised at shoulder height.

Paget's hat tipped to an impossible angle and tumbled to the floor.

'Perhaps,' Stephen said, 'my ears have deceived me, Paget. But assuming they have not, I will hear your apology.'

'Apology be damned,' Wesley Young's voice said from just behind Stephen's shoulder, quaking with fury. 'Let me at him, Merton. No one talks to my sister that way and gets away with it.'

'You had better apologize, Paget,' Elliott's cool voice said from the other side, 'and then do as Lady Paget has suggested. There are guests expected here soon, and no one wants them to find you with a bloodied nose. Least of all you, I would imagine. Take your discussion to a private room. Lady Paget's brother and her betrothed will be happy to accompany you, I am sure.'

'I do apologize for my language to the *ladies* in the room,' Paget said from between his teeth, and Stephen was obliged to lower his fist and release his hold on the man's clothing though his meaning had been insolently clear. The apology did not include Cassandra.

Paget straightened his cloak and turned his glare on her.

'In a different time and place,' he said, 'you would have been burned at the stake as a witch long ago, woman, before you could do any real harm. I would have enjoyed watching and stoking the fire.'

Stephen's fist bounced his head off the wall, and blood spurted from his nose.

'Bravo, Stephen,' Vanessa said.

Paget drew a handkerchief from a pocket somewhere inside his cloak and dabbed at his nose before glancing at the scarlet blood.

'I suppose, Merton,' he said, 'she has persuaded you and every other man in London – and even some of the ladies – that she did *not* murder my father in cold blood. And I suppose she has you convinced that the same thing will not happen to you when she has tired of you and wants to be free to find herself a new victim. And I suppose you fully support her outrageous claim to my father's money and all the jewels he lavished upon her before she shot him through the heart? She is the very devil, but she is clever.'

'No, don't, Stephen,' Margaret said. 'Don't hit him again. Violence brings a moment's satisfaction but no real solution to any problem.'

A woman's logic.

'No, don't, Wes,' Cassandra said.

Stephen did not take his eyes off Paget's face.

'And I suppose,' he said, his voice soft, 'you have persuaded yourself through a lifetime of self-deception that your father was not an intermittent drinker and a vicious abuser when he had been drinking? I suppose you think that violence perpetrated against women is not strictly speaking violence if it is against a wife. Wives must be disciplined and husbands have a legal right to administer that discipline. Even when that violence causes a woman to lose the child she is carrying.'

333

'Oh, Stephen,' Katherine said, her voice high-pitched and half strangled.

'My father very rarely drank,' Paget said, looking about him with fury and contempt. 'He drank far less often than most men. I will not have his memory besmirched by the lies this woman has told you, Merton. When he did drink, he could be rough, it is true, but only when the person concerned deserved punishment. This woman had every man in the neighborhood fawning over her. There is no knowing what she—'

'And your mother too?' Stephen asked softly. 'Was your mother as deserving of punishment? Even the last one?'

He was overreaching himself. He was angry and had not given himself time to consider his words.

But Paget had blanched. He mopped up a few more trickles of blood from his reddened nose.

'What has she told you of my mother?' he asked.

'Even if Cassie killed Paget,' Wesley Young said, 'I would support her. I would *applaud* her. That bastard deserved to die. And I will apologize to the ladies, but I will not withdraw the word. However, she did *not* kill him.'

'What has she told you of my mother?' Paget asked again, just as if Young had not spoken.

'Only what rumor whispered,' Stephen said with a sigh. 'We all know how unreliable rumor can be. But what my betrothed suffered for nine years at the hands of her husband, your father, is not rumor. And what is more, Paget, you know it. And you know that *if* she killed him, she did so to save her own life or the life of someone else endangered by his violence. You probably even know that she did *not* kill him. But it has been convenient to you to pretend that you *do* believe it and that at any time you can

334

have her arrested and punished for the crime. You have been enriched by the belief and by the way you have bullied her into believing in your power.'

'My mother died when she fell from her horse,' Paget said. 'She tried to jump a fence that was too high for her.'

Stephen nodded. Time was marching onward. What time *was* it?

'Bruce,' Cassandra said, and Stephen turned his head to look at her. 'If you have anything else to say to me, you must come and talk to me tomorrow. I live on Portman Street.'

'I know,' Paget said. 'I just came from there.'

'I did not kill your father,' she said. 'I cannot prove that I did not, and you cannot prove that I did. His death was ruled a tragic accident, and so it was. I have no wish to intrude further upon your life. I have no wish at all to live at the dower house or even in the town house. I want merely what is mine so that I can live my own life and never see you or trouble you ever again. You might as well give in to my lawyer's very reasonable demands. You can have no defense against them.'

His temper was up again. He pointed a finger at her and drew breath to speak. But someone else had appeared in the doorway. For one horrible moment Stephen thought it was an early guest, though not so very early at that. But it was William Belmont.

'Lord,' he said, his eyes passing over the people gathered just inside the doors. 'I got home half an hour ago and Mary told me you had called, Bruce – and that she had told you that Cassie was here. Mary usually has a bit more sense than to give away information like that, especially when you are the one who gave her the boot a month ago. You have a bloody nose, I see. Courtesy of Merton, I suppose? Or of Young?'

'I have nothing to say to *you*,' Paget said, his brows snapping together.

'Well, I have something to say to *you*,' Belmont said, looking about again. 'And since it looks as if you did not do the sensible thing and ask to speak privately to Cassie when you got here, then I have something to say to everyone present.'

'No, don't, William,' Cassandra said.

'But I will,' he said. 'He was my father, Cassie, as well as your husband. He was Bruce's father too, and he ought to know the truth. So ought everyone who is preparing to welcome you into their family as Merton's bride. Cassie did not shoot our father, Bruce. Neither did I, though I *was* there, you know, and got my hand on his wrist to wrestle the gun from him. He had started to cuff Mary around because I had told him earlier in the day, before he started drinking, that I had married her and that Belinda was mine. Cassie and then Miss Haytor had been drawn by Mary's screams, and then I came into the house and was drawn by his raised voice coming from the library. He had his pistol pointed at Cassie. But when I went for him and tried to take the gun, he turned it quite deliberately and pointed it at his own heart and pulled the trigger.'

'Liar!' Paget cried. 'That is a filthy lie.'

'Miss Haytor had already told the same story before I came here a few days ago and gave my identical version,' Belmont said. 'And if you think I would be prepared to tell that story against my own father, Bruce, in order to protect my stepmother, then you know nothing about family loyalties. Or about nightmares. He killed himself while in

336

a drunken rage. And if we are wise, we will acquiesce in the official verdict of accidental death and treat Cassie with the proper respect due our father's widow.'

Paget's head had dropped, and his eyes had closed.

'We are perilously close to the beginning of the ball,' Stephen said quietly. 'The earliest guests will be here within a quarter of an hour, I daresay. Paget, let one of my brothers-in-law show you to a guest room, where you may bathe your nose and straighten your clothes. It does not matter if you are not dressed quite as you would if you had planned to attend a ball. Stay and attend this one anyway. And smile and look glad for Cassandra. Tell anyone who looks willing to listen that the accidental death of your father was tragic but that you are happy to see your stepmother moving on with her life. Tell them it is what your father would have wanted.'

'Are you *insane?*' Paget asked viciously.

But Con had moved up on one side of him and Monty on the other, and both were smiling.

'You chose a good moment to arrive in London,' Monty said.

'I daresay,' Con said, clasping a hand on his shoulder, 'Lady Paget wrote to you to announce her betrothal and beg for your blessing, did she, Paget, and you did even better than she asked and came in person. You even rode nonstop, did you, in order to arrive in time for the ball?'

'And got here just in time,' Monty said with a grin, 'though you did not have a moment to spare to change into your ball clothes. It is an affecting story. The ladies will all be in tears if they get wind of it.'

'We had better think of an explanation for the nose, though,' Con said as they led him from the room between the two of them. 'It ought not to be hard. A man meets with all sorts of accidents when he is in a hurry to wish his stepmother well in her new marriage.'

Stephen reached out and took Cassandra's hand in his. She was looking very pale, and her hand was cold. He smiled at her and looked at William Belmont.

'You will stay too?' he asked. He had asked before, but Belmont had refused, since Mary was quite adamant in *her* refusal to attend such a grand affair, even if she *was* Mrs. William Belmont and sister-in-law of Lord Paget.

'Not me,' Belmont said. 'I am going home for my dinner, which was ready half an hour ago. Bruce adored our mother, you know, but he would never see the truth. He was afraid of it, I expect. He spent most of his adult years as far away from Carmel as he could get. As I did too, of course. I ought to have done more for you than I ever did, Cassie. I am sorry for it now, though apologies are cheap, aren't they?'

And he turned and was gone.

Stephen lowered his head to look into Cassandra's face. 'All right?' he said.

She nodded. Her hand was beginning to warm in his.

'Such melodrama,' she said. 'Oh, Stephen, I am so sorry. You must be cursing the day your eyes first alit on me in the park.'

He smiled slowly at her and kissed her briefly on the lips, though he was aware of his family close by, all buzzing in reaction to what had just happened.

'I bless the day,' he said.

She merely sighed.

'Stephen,' Meg said briskly, 'it is time the receiving line was formed. Your guests are going to start arriving *at any moment.*'

338

Stephen grinned about him.

'And a man gets to celebrate his betrothal only once,' he said.

His sisters proceeded to hug both him and Cassandra.

'You will have children with *Stephen*,' he heard Vanessa whisper to Cassandra while they were in each other's arms. 'They will never make up for the ones you lost, but they will warm your heart. I promise you they will. Oh, I *do* promise.'

21

How could she possibly stand in a receiving line, all things considered, Cassandra wondered over the next hour, smiling and greeting large numbers of guests and thanking them for their good wishes on her engagement?

But she did it.

How could she possibly dance all the rest of the evening, smiling all the while, and how could she possibly converse and laugh between sets just as if this really were the happiest evening of her life and she had not a care in the world?

But she did it.

She even almost enjoyed herself.

She *did* enjoy herself apart from the needling twinge of guilt over the fact that she was deceiving everyone. Except Stephen, of course. And his sisters. And she guessed that they had told their husbands.

It felt like a wonderfully celebratory occasion, and the ballroom was the loveliest she had ever seen, and Stephen looked happy and more handsome than ever. He looked as he *ought* to look at his betrothal ball, she thought rather wistfully.

Perhaps she did too.

They danced the opening set together.

'He stayed,' Stephen said while they waited for the music to begin. 'Are you surprised?'

Bruce had indeed come to the ball. He was even dressed appropriately. He really had just arrived in London, it seemed. His bags had still been outside Merton House in his traveling carriage. He had gone to Portman Street and then here without first stopping at a hotel.

'Appearances were always important to Bruce,' she said. 'He stayed away from home for years, I believe in the hope of distancing his reputation from Nigel's if scandal should ever break – as it did not until after his death. He probably sent me away at least partly in the hope of distancing himself from the rumors beginning to circulate about me. Perhaps tonight he has realized his mistake. Perhaps he has understood that his best hope for lasting respectability is to stick staunchly by the official verdict on his father's death. And he can do that best by standing by me and making it appear as if he came to London to give his blessing on my betrothal to you. Poor Bruce.'

He smiled at her, and then smiled about at his guests. It was the opening set of their betrothal ball, and of course most eyes were upon them.

Oh, it *almost* seemed real, Cassandra thought as the music began and they moved off into an energetic and intricate country dance. Within moments they were both laughing.

During the evening Cassandra danced with all three of Stephen's brothers-in-law as well as with her own brother.

She danced with Mr. Golding, who had come with Alice, and with Mr. Huxtable.

'It would seem, Lady Paget,' that last gentleman said as they danced, 'that everyone has misjudged you. And I believe everyone is beginning to realize it, especially with Paget smiling benignly on you with every step you take. A pity about his nose, but one really ought to be careful to move it out of the path of a carriage door when a sudden gust of wind is slamming it shut.'

'Anyone who believes *that*,' she said, laughing, 'is probably *still* expecting to see me swing an axe about my head before this is all over.'

He raised one eyebrow.

'Before *what* is all over?' he asked. 'The ball? One hopes it is not something else to which you refer, Lady Paget. My young cousin is cheerful by nature, but I do not believe I have seen him this happy before now.'

'And you believe,' she said, 'that I can make him happy?'

'It would seem rather obvious that you can,' he said.

'I am forgiven, then,' she asked him, 'for colliding with him at Margaret's ball?'

'I will forgive you,' he said, 'on your wedding day. *After* the wedding.'

'I shall look forward with renewed eagerness, then,' she said, laughing again, 'to my wedding, Mr. Huxtable.'

'You may also call me Con,' he said, 'after your wedding.'

He was a man difficult to decipher. Did he like her or did he not? Did he like Stephen, or did he not?

She danced the supper dance with Bruce. He asked her and she could hardly say no. But it was hard not to feel bitter over all the dreadful things he had said to her before banishing her from Carmel, over the terror she had felt while traveling here with her small entourage of refugees with no idea how she was going to care for them or herself, over the ghastly rumors he had done nothing to quell and perhaps much to spread, over the way he had come here this evening, heedless of who might hear his righteous tirade. It was pure good fortune that he had arrived when he had and not an hour later.

The one satisfaction for her was his reddened, slightly swollen nose.

How splendid Stephen had looked . . .

But she ought not to find satisfaction in any form of violence. She *had*, though, and she still did. For once in her life someone had actually fought *for* her rather than against her. She knew just what a fist to the nose felt like.

'You must know, Cassandra,' Bruce said stiffly as he led her onto the floor, 'that I have never liked you. You were an opportunist fortune hunter when you married my father. You had not a feather to fly with after growing up with that worthless father of yours. You thought to live in the lap of luxury for the rest of your life, and you almost did. The jewels my father bought you are worth a fortune, as I am sure you know. But you paid for your scheming ways. You got what you deserved. I doubt you will with Merton. He is altogether a weakling and a milksop. You have chosen more wisely this time. However, if William is to be believed – and I daresay he is – you did not *kill* my father, and so I am doing my utmost tonight to dispel the rumors that followed you here apparently with a vengeance. I will be happy to dispel them. I will be happy to see you marry Merton. I will be happy to have you off my back, to be able to forget about you, and perhaps – if I am very fortunate – never to see you again.'

He smiled warmly at her all the time he spoke.

The dance was about to begin.

'You are not considering marriage on your own account, Bruce?' she asked him, smiling back.

'I am not,' he said.

'I am very glad,' she told him. 'Very glad, that is, for the lady who might have been your wife.'

'I will see my lawyer tomorrow morning,' he said. 'I will take him to see *your* lawyer. You may wish to meet us there at noon, Cassandra. You will get everything to which you are entitled provided you are prepared to swear *in writing* that you will make no further claim on my estate. Ever.'

He smiled. She smiled back.

'I will be there with Wesley,' she said. 'My lawyer will advise me on what I ought to agree to, in writing or otherwise.'

They danced in silence, smiling at the air to the side of each other's face. And they were watched, Cassandra guessed, by guests curious to interpret what Lord Paget's appearance here tonight meant. But it could surely mean only one thing to them. Would he have come if he truly believed she had murdered his father? Would he have come if he did not wish her well, if he did not wish to convey the blessing of his family on this second marriage of hers?

Cassandra could almost hear what was being thought, even said – and what would be said in the coming days.

Perhaps they had all been wrong about her, they would surely say. The rumors had been rather extreme, after all. What woman was capable of hefting an axe high enough and firmly enough to cleave a man's skull in two? Not that they had really *believed* those stories, of course, but even so . . . And she had denied nothing, had she? And one could believe a woman with hair *that* color capable of anything. They *must* have been wrong about her, though. Not only was Lord Paget here, he was also dancing with her, conversing with her, smiling with her. They were clearly on the best of terms with each other.

Paget had behaved well, Stephen thought as the evening neared its end and he could, at last, claim Cassandra again for one more set.

He could not say he was happy Paget had come or happy that he had felt obliged to invite the man to the ball instead of pounding him to a bloody pulp, which would have been far more satisfying.

But, all things considered, matters had perhaps worked out for the best. Although there would always be people who would think the worst of Cassandra – that was human nature, after all – nevertheless most people would now conclude that they must have been duped by gossip. And most would convince themselves that they never listened seriously to gossip anyway and had not believed this particular item for a moment. Cassandra's reputation would be restored.

And after coming here and smiling his way through the evening and even dancing with Cassandra, Paget could hardly now claim that she had no right to her personal property or to the monetary provisions made for her in her husband's will and the marriage contract.

Stephen did not know how wealthy she would be, but he guessed that she would at worst be very comfortably well off. She would be independent. She would be able to do with her life whatever she chose to do.

It was not a realization that depressed him. Quite the contrary. She would have fought him to the bitter end, he knew, if it had seemed that she *needed* to marry him. And he would have hated to feel obliged to persuade her into matrimony only because she had no real alternative. He would have spent the rest of his life wondering whether she had really *wanted* to marry him. And wondering if pity had somehow warped his judgment.

Now he could fight for her without any qualms at all. She *would* say yes. But she would say it because she *wanted* to, because she had the freedom to decide whichever way she wanted. And he would fight because he wanted her. There would be no other reason.

He smiled at her as he took her in his arms. He had been smiling all evening, of course, but this time he saw only her, and he felt only the love that almost overwhelmed him. He could still scarcely believe it had happened to him – long before he had started to look for it, and in a totally different direction than he would have turned if he had been deliberately looking.

'I suppose,' he said, 'you are still determined to break off our engagement once the summer comes?'

'Of course,' she said. 'And only I can honorably do it. I will not fail you, Stephen, or trap you. This is all very temporary.'

Did she feel anything for him? It was impossible to know. He was as certain as he could be that she felt a fondness for him. He knew she was physically attracted to him. But did she feel anything approximating to love? To romantic love? And to that deeper love that would endure through a lifetime?

She was free now to love.

Or not to.

But she was not free to tell him that she loved him, was she? She had promised to break off their engagement when the Season was over.

I will not fail you, Stephen, or trap you.

This was going to be a difficult courtship. They were trapped in an engagement that she was honor-bound to break and he was honor-bound to convert into marriage.

Love seemed a minor consideration.

Except that it was everything.

They waltzed in silence. And they waltzed in a space that seemed to contain only the two of them. He could smell the flowers she had helped choose, and the scent of her hair and of *her*. He could feel her body heat and hear her breath. And he could see the proud arch of her neck, the beauty of her face, the bright glory of her hair, the sunshine of her gown.

And it seemed to him that the darkness that had been in her had gone, to be replaced by light. Had he had some small hand in that? If he had, and if she was lost to him at the end of the Season, then perhaps there would be some consolation in the lonely years he would face before he could begin to forget her.

Not that he *would* lose her.

And not that there would be any consolation.

Most things in life had come easily to him. Even when he was a boy he had known that Meg had carefully saved enough of the portion their mother had brought to her marriage so that he might go to Oxford and receive enough of an education that he could find steady, gainful employment for the rest of his life. Since he had inherited his title and all that went with it, life had been very easy indeed for him. And very happy too. He had never had to fight hard for what he wanted.

He would fight now.

He wanted Cass.

'You look almost fierce,' she said.

'Fiercely determined,' he said.

'To do what?' she asked him. 'Stay off my toes for the last few minutes of the waltz?'

'That too,' he said. 'But not just that. Determined to enjoy what remains of the Season. Determined to see to it that you enjoy it too.'

'How could I *not* enjoy a little piece of eternity in company with an angel?' she said.

But she laughed as she said it, her eyes dancing with merriment, and he did not know if it was a flippant, essentially meaningless answer or something that came so deeply from the heart that it had come out sounding unbearably sentimental.

The waltz was at an end, and so was the evening.

Within twenty minutes everyone had left except for a few stragglers, mostly family, and Wesley Young's hired carriage had pulled up outside Merton House and Young was waiting to hand his sister in. Miss Haytor and Golding were already inside the carriage.

Stephen stood on the pavement at the bottom of the steps, both Cassandra's hands in his own. He raised them one at a time to his lips.

'Good night, Stephen,' she said.

'Good night, my love.'

And she was. His love, that was.

How could he convince her of that without burdening her with the truth?

Courtship was not an easy business at all.

Perhaps it was as well. There was that saying about anything worth having being worth fighting for.

Old sayings had a tendency to be filled with truth and wisdom.

She raised a hand from inside the carriage a few moments later, and then she was gone.

The next month went by for Cassandra too slowly and far too quickly.

She wanted it over with so that she could begin the rest of her life. Everything had been settled with great ease between her and Bruce with the aid of their lawyers and Wesley. Not only was she to be granted what she was owed by the marriage contract, but also she was to be paid the pension to which she was entitled by Nigel's will, including all the back payments. Her jewelry had already been sent from Carmel.

She was a comparatively wealthy woman. She could live more than comfortably for the rest of her life, especially when she intended to live that life somewhere in the country with only the expenses of a small cottage and a few servants to consider.

Mary was going with William, of course. He was already in the process of purchasing land in Dorsetshire and the small manor that stood upon it. They hoped to move there in the autumn. In the meanwhile they stayed with Cassandra, and Mary insisted upon continuing as house-keeper, maid, and cook.

Belinda was excited at the prospect of moving to a big house far away with her mama and papa.

Alice was going to marry Mr. Golding, and she was

going to do it within the month. Cassandra had shame-lessly promised that she was going to marry Stephen, and Alice had believed her and decided to follow her heart. She was bubbling over with happiness, and Cassandra felt not the smallest pang of guilt for her lie. She was just going to have to convince Alice when the time came that she had had a sudden change of heart and could not marry Stephen after all.

It would be too late for Alice to confront her with the deception by then.

Cassandra *needed* for Alice to be happy. Only so could she forgive herself for her selfishness in keeping Alice with her all these years.

But time moved too slowly even though there was much to make Cassandra contented, even happy. And there was much to look forward to. The agent who had helped William find his land and manor was now looking for a suitable cottage for her.

Time moved slowly because every day brought her closer to Stephen and deepened her regard for him. She saw him every day, sometimes more than once. She might go riding with him in the morning, perhaps, and join a party to Vauxhall with him in the evening.

She *liked* him. Oh, she did indeed. It was almost worse than the love. She could be *friends* with this man in a friendship that would last a lifetime. She was sure it must be so. Apart from Alice, who had been her governess and surrogate mother for many years, she had never had friends. No one, anyway, with whom she could relax and talk – and laugh – on any subject on earth without having to make an effort to keep the conversation going. And no one with whom she could be comfortably silent for minutes at a time without her mind racing for some subject – any subject – with which to fill the silence.

She loved him too, of course. She yearned for him physically, a desire made even worse by the fact that she had had him twice and knew how close to her grasp a physical heaven was. But it was more than just physical. She *cared* for him in a way that was far too deep and complex for any words. Or if there *were* words, she certainly did not know them. The word *love,* she thought, was like a tiny doorway into a vast mansion that filled the universe and beyond.

Sometimes she wondered why she could not simply marry him and be happy for the rest of her life. He had said he loved her, after all – *once.* And he always seemed happy when they were together.

But how could he *not* appear thus when he was a man of honor?

And how could she possibly force him into marriage?

Whenever she began to wonder why not, she forced herself to list the reasons. She had deliberately singled him out for seduction. She had trapped him into becoming her protector. She had taken money from him – *which she had since repaid in full.* She had not stopped him from kissing her out on that balcony at Lady Compton-Haig's ball. She had allowed him to announce their betrothal immediately afterward. She had not put a firm stop to the farce the day after. She had . . . Well, she usually stopped there. Why go further? The list was shudderingly long as it was.

Of course she could never marry him.

Sometimes the list kept growing longer in her head even when she tried to stop thinking. She was three years older than he and had been married before. Her father had been a gambler, her husband a drinker. Such a woman was not a suitable bride for the young and charismatic Earl of Merton.

But, though the last month of the Season crawled along far too slowly, it also galloped along at an alarming pace. For once it was over, Stephen would be returning alone to Warren Hall for the summer and she would be going to an as yet unknown destination – her new home.

And they would never see each other again.

Ever.

It was July. People had already started to trickle out of London to return to their estates or to seek out cooler, fresher air close to the sea or at one of the spas. The parliamentary session was almost at an end. The frantic pace of social activities was beginning to wind down for another year.

And Cassandra had left town. Oh, it was for only a few days, it was true. She had gone into Kent for Miss Haytor's marriage to Golding and would be back. But Stephen was starting to feel nervous – or continuing to feel nervous, to be more accurate. He had courted her quite relentlessly for a whole month, but he was still not sure if she felt anything more for him than a fondness and a friendship.

Neither was enough for him.

Now that it was too late, he wondered if he ought to have told her every day that he loved her. But if he had done that and it had not worked, he would probably *now* be wondering if he ought to have kept quiet about his feelings.

There were no rules of courtship, it seemed. And there were no guarantees that even the most persistent of efforts would bear fruit.

But he could not wait much longer to press the issue. He had been delaying doing so, he realized, because he feared her answer. Once the question was definitely asked and her answer definitely given, there would be no room left even for hope.

Assuming, that was, that her answer would be no.

When had he become such a pessimist?

Cassandra had expected to be back in town on the Tuesday after the wedding. But Stephen ran into William Belmont by chance on Monday and discovered that she had returned just before he left the house.

Stephen lost no time in going to call on her.

She really was not expecting him. And Mary had become careless, having seen him almost every day for the past month and a half. She did not go to the sitting room first to see if Cassandra would receive him. She merely greeted him with a smile – she was outside polishing the brass knocker on the door – and then went ahead of him to tap on the sitting room door, open it without waiting for an answer, and let him in.

Cassandra was standing before the empty fireplace, one wrist propped on the mantel, the other hand pressed to her mouth. She was weeping quite audibly.

She turned her head toward him, red-eyed and aghast, before turning it sharply away again.

'Oh,' she said, making an attempt at bright normality, 'you took me by surprise. I look a mess. I arrived home only an hour ago and changed into something comfortable but not very elegant.'

She was plumping a lone cushion on the chair beside the fireplace, her back to him.

'Cass.' He had hurried across the room to set both hands on her shoulders, making her jump. 'What is the matter?'

'With me?' she asked brightly, straightening up and deftly evading his grasp as she went to move a vase a tenth of an inch from its original place on a table behind the chair. 'Oh, nothing. Something in my eye.'

'Yes,' he said. 'Tears. What has happened?'

He followed her and handed her a handkerchief. She took it and dabbed at her eyes before turning toward him, though she did not look at him. She smiled.

'Nothing,' she said, 'except that Alice has got married and is going to live happily ever after with Mr. Golding, and Mary and Belinda are going away with William, *also* to live happily ever after, and I was indulging in a little self-pity. But they were partly tears of happiness too. I *am* happy for all of them.'

'I am sure you are,' he said. 'Will *you* live happily ever after too, Cass? Will you marry me? I love you, you know, and they are not just words spoken to make you feel better about the situation. I *do* love you. I cannot imagine life without you. Sometimes I think you are the very air I breathe. Can I hope that you love me too? That you will forget about ending our betrothal and marry me instead? This summer? At Warren Hall?'

There. It was all blurted out. He had had a month to prepare a decent speech, but when it had come to the point he had not been prepared at all. And he had not chosen a good moment. She was in deep distress, and his words had not helped. Almost before he had stopped speaking she was across the room and looking out the window.

But she did not say no. He waited with bated breath, but she did not say anything at all.

She was not silent, though, he realized after a few moments. She was sobbing again and doing a damnably poor job of stifling the sounds.

'Cass.' He went to stand behind her again, though he did not touch her this time. He heard a world of misery in the one word he had uttered. 'It is not just self-pity, is it? Are you trying to find a way to let me down gently? Can't you marry me?'

It took her a few moments to bring herself sufficiently under control to answer him.

'I think I probably have to,' she said then. 'I think I am with child, Stephen. No, I don't *think*. I *am*. I have been trying to tell myself otherwise for a few weeks, but I have . . . *missed* for a second time now. I am with child.'

And she wailed so uncontrollably that all he could do was grasp her by the shoulders, turn her, and hold her against him while she wept into his shoulder.

He felt weak at the knees. His heart felt as if it were somewhere near the soles of his boots.

'And that is so dreadful, is it?' he asked when her sobs had subsided somewhat. 'That you are with child by me? That you must marry me?'

Not like this, he thought dully. *Not like this. Please not like this.*

But he had slept with her on two successive nights when he ought not to have done so, and now he must bear the consequences. They both must.

She had tipped back her head and was looking up at him with red, frowning face.

'Oh, I did not mean it that way,' she said. 'I did not mean

it that way at all. But how can I do it again, Stephen? I thought I was barren after the last time. It was more than two years before Nigel died. How can I do it again? I *cannot*.'

Tears ran unheeded down her cheeks again, and he understood.

'I cannot offer guarantees, Cass,' he whispered, cupping her face with his hands and drying her cheeks with his thumbs. 'I wish I could but I can't. What I *can* promise, however, is that you will be loved and cherished – and given the very best medical care – throughout what remains of the nine months. We will have this baby if love and wanting can accomplish it.'

He blinked away tears from his own eyes.

Cass was expecting a *baby*.

His baby.

And she was terrified of losing it.

So was he.

'I can do it alone, Stephen,' she said. 'You don't need—'

He kissed her. Hard.

'I do,' he said, 'because it is my child and you are my woman. And because I *love* you. It does not matter now if you love me or not, but I will keep on wooing you in the hope that one day you will. And I will make you happy. I promise I will.'

'I have loved you almost from the first moment,' she said. 'But, Stephen, it seems so unfair—'

He kissed her hard again and then smiled at her.

She smiled a little tremulously back at him.

'Have you seen a physician?' he asked her.

'No.'

'Tomorrow you will,' he said. 'I'll have Meg go with you.'

'She will be scandalized,' she said.

'You do not know my sisters very well yet, do you?' he said.

She rested her forehead against his chin.

'Cass.' Terror caught at him again. 'I will keep you safe. I swear I will.'

Foolish words when she was going to have to go through a pregnancy and, he hoped, childbirth essentially alone.

It was no wonder many women were of the opinion that men were helpless, rather useless creatures.

'I know you will,' she said, wrapping her arms about his neck. 'Oh, Stephen, I did not want things to happen this way, but I do love you. I do. And I will see to it that you never regret any of all this.'

He kissed her again.

He was feeling rather dizzy. It was done. Not at all as he had planned it. Not in any way as a result of all his careful wooing. But because one evening more than a month ago he had allowed her to seduce him and had then agreed to be her protector because she was destitute and he was angry.

An inauspicious beginning.

A beginning that had begun a child's existence.

A somewhat sordid beginning that had somehow kindled a mutual love and passion.

Life was strange.

Love was stranger.

Cass was going to be his wife. Because she was with child. And because she loved him.

They were going to be *married*.

Stephen laughed and grasped her about the waist and swung her around in a complete circle until she laughed too.

22

Cassandra arrived at Warren Hall, Stephen's principal seat in Hampshire, on a sunny, breezy day in July. She was going to stay at Finchley Park, one of the Duke of Moreland's properties a few miles away, until her wedding, but it was here Stephen was bringing her first. He wanted to show her what was to be her home.

As soon as the carriage turned between the high stone gateposts that marked the entrance to the park, Cassandra fell in love with it. The driveway wove its way through a dense forest of trees, and there was an instant impression of seclusion and peace and – strangely – of belonging. Perhaps it was because Stephen's hand was in her own and he was so obviously happy to be here.

'It has been my home for only eight years,' he said, watching the passing scenery and her with equal attention. 'I did not grow up to it. But it felt immediately . . . *right* when I first saw it. As if it had been waiting for me all my life.'

'Yes.' She turned her face from the window to smile at him. 'I think – I hope – it has been waiting for me too, Stephen. It seems I have always been waiting for my life to begin, and now at the grand age of twenty-eight I have the odd feeling that it is happening. Not *about* to happen, but happening. The present, not the future. Have you noticed how so much of our living is done in the future, Stephen, and so is not really living at all?'

It was only with Stephen she could talk in such a way and be sure to be understood. The future had almost always been the only part of her life that had seemed bearable. At times even the future had crashed to a halt, and she had been left without hope. Mired in despair. But no longer. For once in her life she was living the present and enjoying every moment of it.

He squeezed her hand.

'It seems that good things often have to happen at someone else's expense, though,' he said. 'Jonathan Huxtable had to die at the age of sixteen for me to inherit, and Con had to be illegitimate.'

'Jonathan was his brother?' she said.

'He had some sort of . . . illness,' he told her. 'Con once told me that his father always called the boy an imbecile. But Con also told me that Jonathan was pure love. Not loving, Cass, but love itself. I wish I had known him.'

'So do I,' Cassandra said, returning the pressure of his hand. 'How did he die?'

'In his sleep,' Stephen said. 'On the night after his sixteenth birthday. Apparently he had already outlived the span predicted for him by the physicians. Con says Jonathan would have loved me – the one who would take his place when he died. Is it not strange?'

'I think I am beginning to understand,' she said, 'that love is *always* strange.'

But they had no further chance to explore that idea. The carriage had drawn clear of the trees and Cassandra, moving the side of her head closer to the window, could see the house, a large, square mansion of light gray stone with a dome and a pillared portico and marble steps leading up to the main floor. There was a stone balustrade surrounding what seemed to be a wide terrace before the house, though there was an opening in front for steps leading down to a large parterre garden of flowers and paths and low shrubs.

'Oh,' she said, 'it is beautiful.'

Was it possible that this was to be her home? Her mind touched briefly upon the imposing splendor of Carmel, which she had always found somehow gloomy and oppressive – even during the first six months of her marriage. But she pushed the memories away. They were of no significance to her any longer. They were the past. This was the present.

'It is, is it not?' Stephen said, sounding both pleased and excited. 'And it is going to have a new countess in two weeks' time.'

He had purchased a special license rather than deal with all the bother of banns. Even so he had suggested that they wait two weeks instead of marrying immediately. Perhaps they *ought* to marry without delay, he had said, given the circumstances, but he wanted them to have a wedding to remember, surrounded by their closest family and friends. And he wanted, if she did not mind terribly much, to marry in the small chapel on the grounds of Warren Hall, rather than in London or even at the village church.

Cassandra had not minded the wait, though she had felt her own lack of family and friends. Not a *total* lack, though. Wesley was coming – he had gone straight to Finchley Park with the duke and Vanessa and would meet her there this evening. And Alice and Mr. Golding, and Mary and William and Belinda, were going to come the day before the wedding.

All of Stephen's family members were coming. So were the duke's mother and his youngest sister and her husband, and Sir Graham and Lady Carling, and Lord Montford's sister with her husband. And Mr. Huxtable, of course. And Sir Humphrey and Lady Dew were coming from Rundle Park near Throckbridge in Shropshire, with their daughters and their husbands, and the vicar of Throckbridge, who had been Stephen's main teacher until he was seventeen.

The Dews, Cassandra learned, had been like a part of the Huxtables' family while they had lived in Throckbridge. They had allowed Stephen to ride the horses from their stables. Vanessa had been married to their younger son for the year before his death from consumption. They considered Vanessa's children to be their grandchildren.

'A new countess,' Cassandra said. 'The Countess of Merton. I will be very glad to shed my Lady Paget persona, Stephen. It is the only reason I am marrying you, of course.'

She looked into his eyes and laughed.

His lips were curved into a smile.

'That is such a lovely sound,' he said.

She raised her eyebrows in inquiry.

'Your laughter,' he said. 'And what it does to your mouth and your eyes and to the whole of your face. I think there has been precious little laughter in your life, Cass. If I have given you that, it is of far more precious value than a name or a title.'

And she found herself blinking and then laughing again as two tears spilled over onto her cheeks.

'Perhaps,' she said as the carriage began to make its turn onto the terrace and she could see that there was a stone fountain on the part of it that jutted out toward the garden, 'it was your young cousin who gave this place its aura of peace and love, Stephen. And perhaps it was you who gave it its air of happiness. And perhaps some kind fate, or angel, has kept me waiting all these years so that I would be ready to come here and be healed. And to heal anyone who ever shares this home with us. I will pass on the peace and the love and happiness to everyone who comes here, Stephen. And to our children.'

She almost wished she had not spoken those last words aloud. Terror came rushing at her again – it was never far away.

He wrapped one arm about her, drew her close, and kissed her.

She was daring to trust happiness.

She was daring to trust.

Roger, stretched out on the seat opposite, snuffled in his sleep as the carriage slowed, and then stirred and lifted his head.

Then the carriage drew up before the house, and Stephen helped her alight, and the carriages bringing Margaret and the Earl of Sheringford and their children and Katherine and Lord Montford with their son were coming along behind.

She was home, Cassandra thought. Soon to be surrounded by family.

And with Stephen at her side.

Her golden angel.

It all seemed too much to believe.

Except that she was learning to trust.

Roger padded down from the carriage and lifted his head to pant at her and invite a tickle beneath the chin.

The chapel in the park at Warren Hall was small. It was rarely used now as there was a sizable, comfortable, and picturesque church in the village, and it was only a little more than a mile away from the house.

But the chapel had been traditionally used for family christenings and weddings and funerals, and tradition was important to Stephen, who had come to it late in life. He had spent many hours over the last eight years wandering about the churchyard outside the chapel, reading the headstones of his ancestors buried there, feeling a family affinity with them. There was a time when he had not felt particularly kindly disposed to his great-grandfather, who had cast out his son, Stephen's grandfather, for marrying a woman who was his social inferior, Stephen's grandmother. The estrangement had lasted through two ensuing generations until the senior branch of the family came to an end with Jonathan's death and a search of the junior branch had had to be made to find Stephen.

But family quarrels were sad things. Why perpetuate this one, even with a dead man? The head gardener had been instructed to tend all the family graves regularly.

And Stephen had always dreamed that he would marry at the chapel when the time came, though he had always known that his bride, whoever she turned out to be, might well have other ideas.

Vanessa had married Elliott here.

And he would marry Cassandra here.

The chapel had been decked with purple and white flowers. Candles burned on the altar. All the pews were occupied. There were hushed whispers from the family and friends gathered there. Someone spoke aloud – Nessie and Elliott's Sam – and was shushed to silence. Someone giggled – Meg and Sherry's Sally – and got sharply whispered at for her pains.

Stephen, seated in the front pew, his eyes on the wavering flame of a candle, drew a few steadying breaths. He was nervous, a fact that had taken him completely by surprise this morning since the last two weeks had dragged by and he had thought today would never come. His nose was itching, but he resisted scratching it when he remembered that he had done so a minute or two ago, and perhaps a minute or two before *that*. Someone was sure to have noticed – Sherry or Monty, most like – and would tease him about it afterward.

He cracked his knuckles instead and then winced when it seemed to him that the sound had filled the chapel. Elliott beside him gave him a sidelong look, in which Stephen read a certain amusement.

It was all very well for old married men to be amused.

And then there was the sound of a carriage approaching outside the chapel, and since all the guests were here, most of them having come on foot, it could only be Cassandra arriving from Finchley Park. Soon there were sounds from the churchyard path outside, someone telling someone else to hang on a minute while he straightened the train of her dress.

And then she was in the doorway and Stephen was on

364

his feet without any memory of actually standing up. But everyone else was standing too, and he heard the echo of the vicar instructing them to do so.

She was wearing a high-waisted, short-sleeved dress of purple satin with an extravagantly flounced train. Daringly, she wore no hat but only purple flowers woven into her red curls.

Stephen's mind searched for a more effective word than *beautiful* and failed utterly.

For a moment he forgot to breathe. And then it occurred to him to smile, but he discovered that he was already doing so.

Lord, why had no one warned him about wedding days?

Though, come to think of it, both Sherry and Monty had done nothing else all through a breakfast at which Stephen had not eaten a single mouthful. Meg had grown quite cross with Sherry, had she not? She had asked him if he could not see that poor Stephen was already slightly green and did Duncan actually want to make him *vomit*?

He could see Cassandra looking back at him as her brother stepped up beside her, presumably having finished adjusting her train. Her eyes, those enticingly slanted green eyes, looked larger than usual. Her teeth bit down on her lower lip, and Stephen knew she was as nervous as he.

And then she released her lip and smiled.

And he felt so happy that he stopped himself only just in time from laughing out loud.

How odd *that* would have been.

He had flashing images of seeing her in Hyde Park, so heavily shrouded in black mourning clothes that it was impossible to see her face. And of seeing her at Meg's ball a day later, a vivid siren with her emerald green gown and startling red hair and mask of proud scorn.

And yet surely he had known even then. Surely he had.

He would *surely* have recognized her anywhere in the whole universe in the whole of eternity.

His love.

Except that *love* – that mysterious, vast, all-encompassing power – could not possibly be contained in a single word.

She was at his side and they were turning to face the vicar, and Young was giving her hand into the keeping of the man who would cherish it and her through a lifetime and beyond if it proved possible. And the vicar was addressing his dearly beloved in a voice that might have filled a cathedral, and Stephen was vowing to love, honor, and keep her, and she was vowing to love, honor, and obey him, and he was holding his breath as he took the ring from Elliott's damnably steady hand in the hope that he could put it on her finger without dropping it. And then he was smiling at her when he did *not* drop it, and the vicar was pronouncing them man and wife.

And it occurred to him that he had missed his own wedding service, that it was over, and Cass was his wife, and if he did not lead her to the altar for communion without further delay he might well make an utter ass of himself and whoop for joy or something equally ghastly.

Cass was his *wife*.

He was *married*.

And then, before he knew it, the communion service was over, the register had been signed, they had left the church, smiling to left and right as they went, and everyone was out on the churchyard path, hugging and kissing both Stephen and Cass.

The blue sky was raining rose petals.

And at last Stephen laughed.

The world was a wonderful place, and if it was true that there was no such thing as happily ever after, then at least sometimes there was happiness pure and unalloyed, and one ought to grasp it with both hands and carry it forward to make the hard times more bearable.

Today he was happy, and from the look on her face, so was Cass.

The wedding breakfast, for which several neighbors had joined the wedding guests, had stretched well into the evening. But finally everyone had left Warren Hall. Even those people who had been staying here had now moved to Finchley Park so that the bride and groom might be left alone.

Her bedchamber was square and spacious, Cassandra had discovered. It had a large adjoining dressing room and a cozy sitting room beyond that. A door at the opposite side of the sitting room presumably led to Stephen's dressing room and bedchamber.

They shared a large suite of rooms overlooking the fountain and the flower gardens before the house.

Cassandra, brushing her hair even though her new maid had already brushed it to a bright sheen, looked out on darkness and listened to the soothing sound of the fountain through the open window and waited for Stephen to come.

He was not long. She turned to smile at him as he tapped on her dressing room door and let himself in.

'Cass,' he said, coming toward her, his hands reaching out for hers, 'alone at last. I love them all, but I thought they would never leave.'

She laughed.

'Your staff would have smirked for a month,' she said, 'if everyone had left early and we had retired to bed even before it was dark.'

He chuckled.

'I daresay you are right,' he said. 'They will smirk for a month anyway when we do not go down for breakfast before noon.'

'Ah,' she said, 'you plan to sleep that late, do you?'

'Who said anything about sleeping?' he asked.

'Ah,' she said.

And she released her hands from his and loosened the sash of his dressing gown. He was naked beneath it. She opened it back and moved against him, feeling his warm, strong nakedness against the fine silk of her nightgown.

'Stephen,' she said, her mouth against his throat, 'you have no regrets?'

He slid his fingers through her hair until his hands cupped her face and lifted it toward his.

'Do you?' he asked.

'Unfair,' she said. 'I asked first.'

'I believe,' he said, 'that life is made up of constant occurrences of decisions to be made. Where do I go now? What shall I eat now? What shall I do now? And every decision, small or large, leads us inexorably in the direction we choose to take our lives, even if unconsciously. When we saw each other in Hyde Park and again at Meg's ball, we faced choices. We had no idea where they would lead us eventually, did we? We thought they were leading in one direction, but in reality they were leading here, via numerous other choices and decisions we have made since. I do not regret a single one of them, Cass.'

'Fate has led us here, then?' she said.

'No,' he said. 'Fate can only present the choices. *We* make the decisions. You might have chosen someone else at Meg's ball. I might have refused to dance with you.'

'Oh, no, you could not have done that,' she said. 'I was too good.'

'You were,' he admitted, grinning.

'I might have let you go,' she said, 'when I understood that you would carry on with our liaison only on your own terms.'

'Oh, no,' he said, 'you could not have done that, Cass. I was too good.'

'But what are you good for *now*?' she asked him, lowering both her voice and her eyelids. 'Only to talk through your wedding night?'

'Well,' he said, 'since words do not appear to be satisfying you, I had better try action.'

They smiled at each other until their smiles faded and he kissed her.

She knew his body. She knew his lovemaking. She knew how he felt inside her. She knew the sight of him and the smell of him and the feel of him.

But she knew nothing, she discovered over the next half hour – and through the night that followed. For she had known him in lust and in guilt, and she had felt his pleasure and her own almost-pleasure.

She had not known him in love.

Not before tonight, their wedding night.

Tonight she recognized his body and his lovemaking, but tonight there was so much more. Tonight there was *him*. And there was *her*. And four separate times there was *them*. Or, since even that word suggested a plurality and therefore

369

a duality, there was the entity they became when they soared over the precipice of climaxing passion together to that place beyond that was not a place and was not any state that could be described in words or even remembered quite clearly afterward – until it happened again.

'Cass,' he said sleepily when daylight was already showing its face at the window and a single early bird was already practicing its choral skills from somewhere nearby, 'I wish there were a thousand ways to say *I love you*. Or a million.'

'Why?' she asked him. 'Would you now proceed to say them all? I would be asleep long before you had finished.'

He chuckled softly.

'Besides,' she said, 'I cannot imagine ever growing tired of hearing just those three words.'

'I love you,' he said, rubbing his nose across hers after propping himself on one elbow.

'I know,' she told him before he rolled onto her and showed her again without words.

'I love you,' she said afterward.

But he only grunted sleepily and was asleep.

Another bird, or perhaps the same one, was singing to someone else too, someone who was already up in that early dawn. He had not spent the night at Warren Hall. Nor had he gone to Finchley Park with the rest of the family. How could he when he and Elliott had scarcely spoken to each other for many years?

Elliott had accused him of stealing from Jonathan, who was easy prey. And Elliott had accused him of debauchery, of having fathered the bastard children of a number of women in the neighborhood.

Elliott, who had once been his closest friend and partner in crime.

Constantine had never denied the accusations.

He never would.

He had spent the night at the home of Phillip Grainger, an old friend of his in the neighborhood.

He stood now in the churchyard outside the little chapel where Stephen had married Lady Paget the day before. There were still rose petals dotted about on the path and grass, hurled at the bride and groom by the children.

He stood at the foot of one of the graves, looking down broodingly at it. His long black cloak and tall hat, worn against the chill of the early morning, gave him an almost sinister appearance.

'Jon,' he said softly, 'it seems that the family will go on into another generation. Nobody has admitted anything yet, but I would wager a bundle that Lady Merton is already with child. I think she is decent after all. I know *he* is, though I used to wish he weren't. You would like them both.'

A few rose petals, browning around the edges, littered the grave. Con stooped down to remove them, and he brushed one petal off the headstone.

'No,' he said, 'you would *love* them, Jon. You always did love extravagantly and indiscriminately. You even loved me.'

He did not come often to Warren Hall these days. It was a little painful, if the truth were known. But sometimes he yearned for Jon. Even for this, all that was left of his brother – the slight mound of a grave and a headstone that had already darkened and mossed slightly with age.

Jon would have been twenty-four now.

'I'll be on my way,' Con said. 'Until next time, then, Jon. Rest in peace.'

And he turned and strode away without looking back.

Epilogue

The world had been reduced to a cocoon of pain and a few blessed moments of respite in which her breath might be caught but no real rest could be grabbed.

It had been a long and hard labor, but Margaret had not stopped assuring her for hours on end that this was the very reason the birthing of a baby was called *labor*.

'Men know *nothing*,' she had said after Stephen had come for one of his frequent visits but had put up no great resistance to being shooed out again. 'They cannot even bear to *watch* pain.'

Perhaps, Cassandra had thought from deep within her cocoon, pain was difficult to watch when one had caused it but could do nothing either to stop it or to share it. But she did not spare many thoughts to such sympathies. She spared more to the conviction that she would not allow Stephen near her *ever again*.

Please, please, please, please, please, she thought as she drew breath against another onslaught of pain that tightened her abdomen unbearably and ripped through her womb.

Please *what?*

Stop the pain?

Let this baby be born?

Let it be born alive?

And healthy?

Please, please.

The seven months of her marriage had been almost unbelievably happy ones.

They had also been filled with terror.

Her terror.

And Stephen's, always masked with a brisk cheerfulness.

'She is doing well.' The calm voice of the physician, who was a man and knew *nothing.*

'She is at the point of exhaustion.' Margaret's voice.

'She is almost there.' The physician.

And then a deep breath and a –

Please, please.

An unbearable urge to push. And a pushing and a pushing until a voice urged her to stop, to conserve her energy until there was another contraction. And then –

Oh, please, please.

A frantic, unending pushing until all the breath was gone from her body and the world was pain and pushing –

And a gushing that suddenly released all the unbearable pressure and gave her a moment to breathe and –

A baby's cry.

Oh.

'Oh,' she said. 'Oh.'

'You have a son, my lady,' the physician said. 'And he

appears to have ten toes and ten fingers and a nose and two eyes and a mouth that is going to give you notice for some time to come whenever he is hungry.'

And Margaret was dashing from the room to tell Stephen, who nevertheless was not allowed inside the room until she had returned to wash the baby and bundle him inside a warm blanket and set him in his mother's arms while she cleaned both Cassandra and the bed and then stood back to smile at mother and child with flushed satisfaction.

Margaret and the physician left the room while Cassandra gazed in wonder at the red, ugly, beautiful face of her son.

Her *son*.

Where was Stephen?

And then he was there, white-faced, with dark circles beneath his eyes as if *he* had been in hard labor for many hours. As in a way he probably had, poor thing. He was approaching the bed as though he was afraid to come closer, his eyes on hers. As though he was also afraid to look at the blanket-bound bundle.

'Cass,' he said. 'Are you all right?'

'I am tired enough to sleep for a month.' She smiled at him. 'Meet our son.'

And he leaned closer, his eyes wide with wonder, and gazed downward.

'Could anyone be more beautiful?' he asked after a few awed moments.

He was looking with a father's eyes – as she was with a mother's. Both Margaret and the physician had assured her before they left that the slight distortion of the baby's head would right itself within a few hours, a day or two at most.

'No,' she said. 'No one could.'

'He is crying,' he said. 'Ought you to do something, Cass?'

'I think,' she said, 'he wants his papa to hold him.'

Or his mother to offer a breast.

'Dare I?' He looked terrified.

But she lifted the bundle, which seemed to weigh nothing at all, and Stephen took their son from her, and he stopped crying immediately.

'Well,' she said, 'so much for what he owes his mama.'

But Stephen was laughing softly, and Cassandra, relaxed and exhausted against her pillows, gazed up at him. At them.

Her two men.

Her two loves.

And perhaps, after a good long rest – a good *long* rest – she would allow Stephen to touch her again after all.

Perhaps she would.

Well, *of course* she would.

He was looking down at her, his eyes so full of love that they almost glowed.

'Thank you,' he said. 'Thank you, my love.'

She had a *child*, she thought as she gazed back at him, too exhausted to do anything more than allow her lips to curve upward at the corners.

She had a living child.

And a life filled with love.

And hope.

She had Stephen.

What more could she possibly ask for?

She had her own private angel, after all.

Against the scandal and seduction of Regency England, New York Times *bestselling author Mary Balogh introduces an extraordinary family – the fiery and sensual Huxtables.*

Turn the page for more titles in this series, Available now from Piatkus.

FIRST COMES MARRIAGE

The arrival of Elliot Wallace, the irresistibly eligible Viscount Lyngate, has thrown the sleepy village of Throckbridge into a tizzy. It soon becomes clear that Elliot seeks a convenient marriage to a suitable bride, and desperate to rescue her eldest sister Margaret from a loveless union, Vanessa Huxtable – a proud and daring, a young widow – offers herself up instead.

In need of a wife, Elliott takes the audacious widow up on her unconventional proposal while he pursues an urgent mission of his own. But then a strange thing happens: as the wedding night approaches they become inexplicably drawn to one another. And, as intrigue swirls around a past secret – one with a striking connection to the Huxtables – Elliott and Vanessa are uncovering the glorious pleasures of the marriage bed and discovering that when it comes to wedded bliss, love can't be far behind.

978-0-7499-4281-6

THEN COMES SEDUCTION

In a night of drunken revelry, Jasper Finley, Baron Montford, gambles his reputation as London's most notorious lover on one woman. His challenge? To seduce the exquisite, virtuous Katherine Huxtable within a fortnight. But when his best-laid plans go awry, Jasper devises a wager of his own.

For Katherine, already wildly attracted to him, Jasper's offer is irresistible: to make London's most dangerous rake fall in love with her. Then Jasper suddenly ups the ante. Katherine knows she should refuse. But with scandal brewing and her reputation in jeopardy, she reluctantly agrees to become his wife. Now, as passion ignites, the seduction really begins. And this time the prize is nothing less than both their hearts . . .

978-0-7499-4286-1

AT LAST COMES LOVE

Only desperation could bring Duncan Pennethorne,
the infamous Earl of Sheringford, back home after the
spectacular scandal that had shocked even the jaded ton.
Forced to wed in fifteen days or be cut off without a
penny, Duncan chooses the one woman in London in
frantic need of a husband: Margaret Huxtable.

A lie to an old flame forces Margaret to accept the
irresistible stranger's offer. But once she discovers who
he really is, it's too late – she's already betrothed to
the wickedly sensual rakehell. Quickly she issues an
ultimatum: if Duncan wants her, he must woo her.
And as passion slowly ignites, two people marrying
for all the wrong reasons are discovering the joys
of seduction – and awaiting the exquisite pleasure
of what comes after . . .

978-0-7499-4291-5